Don't Touch My Hair!!!

TALL TALES OF A BLACK AMERICAN PRINCESS
BOOK TWO

K.D. BLADE

ISBN: 979-8-9870470-4-0

Cover designed by K.D. Blade

Illustrations by K.D. Blade

Published by Ink Blade Books, LLC

Music Playlist

Listen to these Playlists while you read!
  Spotify: *Night Skins:* https://spotify.link/w3zZ555KEXb
  Youtube: Don't Touch My Hair! https://youtube.com/
playlist?list=PLo3wDwWygL05hAWw25WeKqFLmp
s3X6jWG&si=WW7DrkrtTf0G5yFg

Examples of the songs:
  - Affirmations - Memethegoat
  - Na$ty - Kirby
  - This is America- Childish Gambino
  - What's Goin' On - Marvin Gaye
  - About Damn Time - Lizzo
  - Destroy Everything You Touch - Ladytron
  - I Don't Know Anything- Mad Season
  - Found Love - Rihanna
  - The Rain - Missy Elliot
  - Bullet - Nova Twins
  - White Horses - Wolf Alice
  - What's Up - 4 Nonblondes
  - Where Is My Husband! - RAYE
  - Break My Soul - Beyoncé

- I Only Have Eyes For You - The Flamingos
- It Feels So Good- Sonique
- Big Dawgs - Hanumankind, Kalmi
- Rain On Me - Lady Gaga, Ariana Grande
- Little Wing - Jimi Hendrix
- Step By Step - Whitney Houston
- Bag Lady - Erykah Badu
- Golden - Jill Scott
- Everything Is Everything - Lauren Hill
- Life Has Its Trials - Dorothy Ashby
- Goodbye Horses - Urban Heat
- Mount Everest- Labyrinth
- Waterfalls - TLC
- Don't Go Yet- Camila Cable, Major Lazer
- Toxic Love - Tim Curry
- Fame - David Bowie
- My Life - Mary J. Blige
- Can You Get To That - Funkadelic
- Papa Was A Rollin' Stone - The Temptations
- Man Funk - Guts, Leron Thomas
- Black Hole Sun - Soundgarden
- Rooster - Alice In Chains
- Kunst - KMFDM
- Everyday People - Sly & The Family Stone
- Pick Up the Pieces - Average White Band
- Voodoo Cadillac - Souther Culture on the Skids
- Manhattan (First We Take Manhattan) - Enrique Morente
- The Choice Is Yours - Black Sheep
- Electric Relaxation - A Tribe Called Quest
- Soul Bossa Nova - Quincy Jones
- I'm A Woman -Koko Taylor
- Little Red Rooster - Willie Dixon
- Flood - Muddy Waters
- Spoonful - Howlin' Wolf
- And much much more...

Trigger Warnings

Warning: this is a book about werewolves. They eat people and you'll hear them chew.

This is a book of horror. There will be blood. There will be situations that will frighten, unnerve, and unsettle. You might get queasy.

This is a book about women and race. There are familiar scenarios with frightening extremes.

Let's do some box breathing:

Inhale for the count of 4

Hold for the count of 4

Exhale for the count of 8

Hold for the count 4

Repeat 3x

Whenever something you read upsets you, take a moment, box breathe, and set your knee-jerk reaction aside.

Okay, ready? *Read...*

The Walnut Creek Werewolves

Jaharia knew that Montaveous was cheating. She put a tracking app on the underside of his Toyota Tundra and his smartphone.

It wasn't love. She hadn't told her friends about her suspicions because they tended to sleep with any guy she liked. Snooping and suspicion were a natural part of her dating experience. His arguments and evasions had to be cheating. What else could it be?

She followed him to Walnut Creek Park in her Nissan Juke. She watched him change into ugly muddy sneakers across the parking lot. She glared with disgust at the Tundra's bloated contours and lofted wheels. She hated that Tundra. Just like she hated him. The oversized tires were too reinforced to slash.

It was sunset. The cypress, live oak, and mesquite trees were a rough fringe below the vibrant pink to purple sunset. The horned moon was a torn fingernail in the sky.

Montaveous was an ugly runner. His elbows were tucked against his sides like a Tyrannosaurus Rex. His chin jutted out like a turkey. His feet kicked behind him. She wished that she were in front to see what else bounced to the rhythm of his stride.

He left the cement walkway onto a winding stone path

between juniper trees. She checked her phone, but yes, he was on a dirt bike trail.

Jaharia wasn't a runner. Her body's abundant curves were encased in capris, a waist trainer, a sports bra, and a black cutoff Metallica hoodie. She was not supposed to sweat or scuff her sneakers during her recon mission. She patted her hair, braided down under a black baseball cap. She tucked her sunglasses into her cleavage.

The juniper trees on either side of the trail wove a tunnel with their branches that looked like the ridges inside an open mouth. She hesitated only a moment before she stepped off the cement walkway. Then she hurried to keep up. The limestone path was easy to see under the scrim of gray dirt.

She followed the orange dot through one switchback trail after the next. She paused at another tunnel of trees. They were so close together that she could not see beyond the first few trunks.

Jaharia gave up. This was dumb.

Then the orange dot on the tracking app abruptly stopped and came back.

She scrambled over to a fallen cypress tree. She crouched low moments before Montaveous sprinted out of the trees. His face was a mask of terror. He made the mistake of looking behind him. Just in time for a blur of fur to pounce on his back.

It was dark in the gloom of the trees, but the furred attacker was not a dog or a human. It was wrong, with huge yellow teeth and horrifying long limbs. A thick fan of a tail. A ridge of bristled fur down the muscular back.

The werewolf's weight knocked Montaveous to the ground. He screamed as teeth and claws sank into his torso and thighs. It was a horrible sound, like a rabbit trapped in a cat's mouth. Only worse because it was Montaveous. He dug at the dirt, desperately crawling away while the werewolf ripped out his shoulder blades and down his sides with fast slashes and bites to stop his squirming.

The werewolf snarled as she ate. Jaharia could see the lack of a scrotum between the furry haunches. The werewolf dragged Montaveous back into the tunnel. He woke enough to feebly whimper. His blood smeared across the limestone trail.

Jaharia stayed crouched in the bushes, squeezing her phone. She listened to the werewolf eat her boyfriend. The wet snap of bone. The gulp of meat. The charnel scent broke through the cypress and greenery of the bush. She wished that his terrible breathy whimpers would stop.

She was too afraid to run. She was terrified that if she covered her ears then she might make the wrong sound.

Full dark settled on the trees. The forest was awake and active now that the humans had stopped running, jogging, walking their dogs, and riding their bikes. In the distance, there was the sounds of cars. Sirens and airplanes and police helicopters.

Jaharia had to get back to the parking lot. But how? She had no idea where she was. She was lost in the park. How many acres did Walnut Creek Park span? Everything was bigger in Texas, including an urban park in Austin.

"Girl, what are you doing?" a woman asked with a deep voice.

Jaharia yelped, flailing. Her phone flew out of her hand. She landed on her back, screeched, and floundered to her feet.

Several werewolves watched her with predatory patience, illuminated by the smartphone landing face side up. The animal shine in their eyes had her quivering with fear.

One had transformed into a regal Black woman. Her brown skin was as dark as the shadows she stood in. She was naked. She carried her heavy curves lightly. Her afro was perfectly coifed. There was no hint of monstrousness besides the animal shine in her pupils when she offered Jaharia her phone. The werewolf tapped on the screen with a long nail.

"Sister stalker? You're too grown for this foolishness."

"Yes, ma'am," Jaharia whimpered. She deleted the app and showed the werewolves the empty screen.

"We're keeping the Tundra. Montevous had it coming."

"He cheated on me." Jaharia brushed the leaves off her clothes. She tried and failed to act calm. "I won't say nothing."

"We know. We have your scent."

Jaharia squeaked with terror.

The werewolf pursed her lips towards the trail. "It's time for you to go."

Jaharia walked straight and tall like Beyoncé into the shadowy gloom of the forest. She waited for the killing bite, but nothing stopped her retreat. She turned on the phone's flashlight. The werewolves were gone. The tunnel was empty except for the bloody smears.

Every rocky path looked the same, but she eventually found cement again. She drove to her apartment to get her passport. Screw her job and her lease. She had always wanted to visit Tokyo.

~

THE WEREWOLVES FOLLOWED JAHARIA TO HER apartment and then to the airport. They watched her endure getting her duffle bag, shoes and hair inspected by TSA.

Professor Onyx fluffed her afro with her long fingernails, irritated by the TSA agent pawing her blue gloved fingers through Jaharia's hair under the pretense of security. Sixty years had passed since Professor Onyx was Turned into a werewolf and yet she never stopped feeling a kinship to the struggle of being a Black woman in America.

"How do you want to take care of her?" A werewolf said. "That arm candy is dumber than a bag of hair. I wouldn't trust her farther than I could throw her."

Professor Onyx gave the werewolf a long look. "What's your name, Youngblood?"

"I'm Velma." Velma the werewolf adjusted her fake glasses and wig, unnerved by the pack leader's hard stare.

"That girl is smart enough to go when the getting is good, Velma. She doesn't need telling twice. Let's go."

"Are you sure? She could come back."

"She carried her bag on. She's not coming back." Professor Onyx walked towards the short term parking lot. Velma followed her through the sliding doors with one last glance back at Jaharia.

Meanwhile, TSA let Jaharia out of the secondary inspection. She stuffed her hair into a maroon silk sleeping bonnet, shoved her feet back in her sneakers, and hefted her purse. She rolled her suitcase through the flow of people to the distant gate. The TSA agent's gross touch dissolved the last reservations of leaving the United States of America for good.

Dominque

The werewolves stole Dominque's sneaker collection. She was more upset about that than the cruel fun they had at her expense. She dragged herself through the shredded remains of shoeboxes and tissue paper. They had yanked her display cabinets off the wall and dropped them on her while hunting for a hidden vault of money and shoes. Her nice upscale apartment was trashed.

Her homemade cleaning kit was also stolen. That was one indignity too many. The rage and despair of knowing that the werewolves planned to wear her sneakers brought the first Turn. This wasn't a random attack. They knew that she was a Sneakerhead.

A Sneakerhead didn't just love sneakers. It was a lifestyle. A personality. She was proud of it.

Dominque screamed as her body split open and turned inside-out like a pair of wet socks. She gripped a hunk of Nike shoebox cardboard. She glared through the burst blood vessels in her eyes to concentrate on the swoosh logo.

Just do it.

The twisted bones became a hand then a paw then back into a hand. Self-discipline was how Dominque got her sneaker collection in the first place. She worked hard, scrimped, saved, and stalked Sneakerhead websites to pounce on flash sales. She even navigated the dangerous trade in the back of box trucks.

A bunch of hairy assholes didn't get to steal her treasures. If they were smart, they would've made sure that she was dead.

Dominque crawled out from under the bookshelf, dragging pieces of broken glass out of her skin. She showered off, watching blood swirl down the drain. For once, she didn't care about the water bill. She washed her hair three times to get the stink of the Turn out. Then did a full deep condition. She self-soothed by finger-combing oil through her dense 4c curls.

She sniffed the shrapnel of her apartment. Slowly she learned to use her nose and parse out individual scents.

The werewolves had stolen every electronic besides an ancient purple iPod that she hadn't used in a decade but amazingly still worked. An Aux cable connected to speakers tangled under her bed that they had missed. It felt like a victory.

The iPod contained albums by Erykah Badu, Lauren Hill, and Jill Scott. A bunch of songs like 'Call Tyrone' and 'Golden' that she genuinely liked but hadn't listened to in ages.

She practiced Turning, timing the transformation like a gunslinger practiced their quick draw. She cobbled together an outfit that wouldn't hamper the Turn. It wasn't much. Just a pair of old black basketball shorts and an oversized bleach-stained University of Texas t-shirt from college.

She only had a busted pair of Crocs left to wear. The werewolves had taken everything else. Work heels, party pumps, and sandals. Dominque spent real money on footwear. The Crocs were just for cleaning the house. At least it hid her funky long toenails. They grew back every time she tried to cut them short.

She didn't remember the werewolves' faces but she remembered that they had worn socks with their FILA slides. No doubt to hide their own raggedy toenails and ashy feet.

Her courage failed when she stared at herself in the broken mirror. She was dressed, as ready as she could get. She looked like a scared girl. Nothing more. She needed something else to make them pay attention.

She drove her 2008 gold Toyota Corolla to the old lady who lived by the Mexican panderia. Everybody in the neighborhood called her Aunt Jemima because she made the best pancakes and looked just like that lady on the maple syrup bottle. Dominque figured that old Black ladies didn't get old around here if they didn't know what was what.

She parked in front of the one story A-framed house with its neatly manicured lawn and huge flowering bushes of Brides of Barbados. She knocked respectfully on the back door under the covered carport and waited on the stoop. The screened-in door opened. The second metal reinforced door creaked wide. Aunt Jemima seemed to fill the whole doorway.

"Come on in, chile." Aunt Jemima had a funny way of talking. Cartoonishly Southern like a caricature of Mammy from the *Gone With the Wind* movie. It made Dominque's skin crawl but she stepped into the warm yellowy-green kitchen.

The walls were dingy yellowy-white, like plastic that had been in the microwave too many times. A brown stained glass lamp hung above a round table by a booth seat corner. Heavy green curtains with gold tassels limited the light filtering through the glass brick windows.

Every wall, counter, and table was crowded with shelves of creepy old-timey Black figurines. Red licorice rubber lips. Big staring eyes. Wrapped hair or jutting braids with little red bows. Gingham and polkadots painted on the ceramic dolls. Black memorabilia was the salt and pepper shaker, the napkin holder, the table cloth, and the cookie jar. There were framed advertisements for Crackling Bread and Ho' Cakes with dancing black-face minstrels cake-walking with canes and worn top hats.

Those tiny beady eyes stared at her from every direction. The manic smiles were too big and hungry. The worst was the Felix the Cat clock that looked from side to side while the long crooked tail swayed.

Dominque didn't like the grotesquely racist decor *at all* but she kept her opinions to herself. She was a guest.

She obediently sat at the kitchen table on a wooden chair with a small cushion on the seat.

Aunt Jemima set a large brown plastic cup of sweet tea in front of her. "Let me fix you a plate."

Aunt Jemima piled a plate high with a stack of buttermilk pancakes, eggs, bacon, and cheese grits. She loaded them from cast-iron skillets on the crowded stove.

The smell and sight of food failed to entice. Dominque was too angry. Too nervous. She didn't want comfort food weighing her down like a bowling ball in her gut. Even the tea smelled too sweet. She shook her head and mumbled at the orange plastic placemat. "No, thank you, ma'am. I need a gun."

Aunt Jemima didn't ask why Dominque needed to borrow her gun. Instead she gave her a box of bullets. "You gonna need your strength. Those 'uns are a bunch 'a mean ol' boys who don't know nothin' about nothin'."

Dominque kept her eyes firmly on her fists which bunched the pilled fabric of her shorts on her thighs. Lord, she *loathed* the way Aunt Jemima talked. It was like she was talking Black but getting crucial things wrong. Playacting a role that she clearly was.

"Thank you, ma'am, but I'm not hungry."

Aunt Jemima tapped on the box of bullets so it rattled. "You put them down like the low down dirty dogs they are and make sure they stay down. Then you give me a call. Don't you worry none about cleaning up."

"Yes, ma'am."

Aunt Jemima didn't press her further. Dominque had gone inside of herself, needing to gather that anger up into a tight fist of vengeance. She followed Aunt Jemima into a bedroom.

She had a whole steamer trunk full of guns in her sewing room. She lifted the lid, showing Dominque the haphazard pile filling the huge trunk to the brim. Dominque picked one at random.

The Glock felt heavy in her hands, final, and also dangerous. Ready to bite her. Ready to kill. Not caring who it killed. Dominque hated guns. She hated that it made her feel a little braver. "I'll give it back. Thank you, ma'am."

Aunt Jemima waved dismissively at the gun as they walked back into the kitchen. "That gun ain't nothin' special. I found it dropped in my trash can the other day. You're bulletproof now." She tapped on the box again still on the table by the pancakes. "Well, not against these 'uns. Watch yourself now."

"Yes, ma'am." Dominque looked down at her horrible scuffed green Crocs that weren't supposed to see the light of day. She got angry all over again.

She carefully filled the magazine with bullets. Her fear of guns warred with her need for vengeance. There was no time to practice. Just point, shoot, and pray that it hit its target.

Aunt Jemima put a machete on the table and told her where to find them. Dominque took the weapons and left her plate uneaten. She wasn't hungry. Not for pancakes. She put the gun in the glove compartment of her Corolla. The machete lay on the floor behind the passenger seat.

The assholes hadn't gone far. A handful of miles from her apartment on the other side of a cemetery by I-35 in one of the militant pockets of Rundberg that still resisted gentrification. She drove past stray chicken coops and half-built cars instead of ultra-modern houses.

The werewolves were in a rundown split-level duplex at a dead-end road that fed into Walnut Creek Park's creek. Cars roared overhead on North Lamar Boulevard The radio fuzzed, unable to settle on a station in this dead zone.

Dominque slipped into the house, her heart pounding in her ears. She held the machete in one hand and the gun in the other. The werewolves were too busy trying on their new shoes with a bunch of stolen clothes to notice. They were so sure of their own power that they hadn't even locked the front door.

She Turned quick, forgetting about the gun, the machete,

and everything but the need to kill. The weapons clattered onto the scratched up laminate floor as she charged.

One of the werewolves had his own gun. She felt the explosive pain in her shoulder. The pain and the sound was so big, like a thunderclap. It felt like being punched in her sensitized eardrums.

She fell, rolled, and leapt up to rip his throat out, trachea to spine. He fell, trying to Turn and shoot at the same time.

Dominque was a whirlwind of teeth and claws, fury and vengeance. She bit, tore, and threw their bloody corpses around the room. She kicked their bodies a few times.

"Fuck you!" She spat, panting. She swayed, looking around but the werewolves were dead.

The bullet hole foamed green around the wound. She used the machete to pick it out. The bullet plinked against the stained carpet and scattered clothing.

She gathered her shoes into a trash bag. The werewolves had a lot of stuff. She took it all, putting it in the trunk of her Corolla. She drove to Aunt Jemima's house.

The old lady clicked her teeth as Dominque limped up the steps. "That's why I told you to eat. There was an antidote in the dressing! Sit! Eat!"

This time Dominque sat and ate. Aunt Jemima bustled out. She was gone a while.

The pancakes were gritty and half-cooked. The grits weren't spiced at all. The eggs were chalky with bits of shell mixed in. The bacon was gummy. She ate them anyway. Her arm healed. She rubbed the smooth skin, shaking her head with chagrin. It was damn miraculous.

She fell asleep on the couch while cleaning her sneakers.

She jerked awake when Aunt Jemima came in. The door shrieked as the hinges stretched and wooden edge slapped the frame.

Dominque quickly stood, holding her trash bag of recovered treasures. Her brown skin was dark with an embarrassed blush. She couldn't believe that she had fallen asleep!

"Um, thank you, ma'am. I'll just be going."

Aunt Jemima smelled funny. The air around her hummed like angry bees. There was a rotten sweetness to her scent, like rancid peaches.

Dominque had been too preoccupied to notice before but now, as the old woman came in with that too-big smile, the stench choked. Those bulging staring eyes didn't blink as often as they should. The flared nostrils. The rolling jerky walk as if her knees had rubber springs in them, pitching drunkenly from side-to-side.

Her hips bumped into the furniture as she entered the living room. A few of the ugly tchotchkes wobbled and fell. She didn't even glance at them as they broke.

Dominque stared at the broken figurines. A black head had rolled to the edge of the couch. The wide staring gaze. The rubbery red smile. The wrapped hair.

Then she looked back up at Aunt Jemima. And knew it wasn't Aunt Jemima. It was someone else, wearing her skin like an ill-fitting suit. Pretending to be Aunt Jemima like the figurines were a rough facsimile of a real Black woman.

The dingy stained glass light had been kind to wrinkled flesh. But now Dominque saw that the skin was pinched in some areas, like leather stapled across a mask. It was folded where it should be smooth. And Aunt Jemima was bigger than before. Not just her belly but everywhere. Even her head was swollen like the Pillsbury Doughboy filled with rotten cottage cheese.

"You forgot to kill the werewolves."

"No, I killed them." Dominque protested, valiantly pretending that things were fine fine fine.

The voice was different now. Dropping the act. Now Aunt Jemima sounded White, like the Karens and Beckys at the coffee shop who demanded to see the manager and never ever tipped. Young and a little muffled. As if speaking from *inside* the skin like a person wearing a mascot costume.

Aunt Jemima lifted the Glock out of a fold of skin in her hip like it was a deep pocket in an apron. "You did your best but you didn't kill those Youngbloods. You forgot to shoot them. I even gave you the right bullets."

Dominque held her trash bag but the sneakers weren't going to save her. By the menacing way this person wearing Aunt Jemima's face looked at Dominque's boobs, she wasn't after her shoes.

The Not-Aunt Jemima massaged her breasts. "Oooh, these are so heavy."

She began to smushed and smooth her body, shaping it like the skin was playdough to reduce her breasts. Her butt inflated like a balloon. Then she pushed them back.

Dominque was sorry that she'd eaten anything. She wanted to throw up. "What are you?"

"I'm a boo hag."

"What's that?"

"I'm a skin witch."

"What do you want from me?"

"Nothing. You already gave me what I wanted. Those Youngbloods were more than enough."

"What's a Youngblood?"

"It's a pack werewolves. One of the biggest. Usually Brother Ruffin doesn't let his pups wander but these boys don't listen. They think that they're too big and strong to be ingredients."

Ingredients.

Dominque already knew that she was in trouble but this was much much worse. The witch was scary in a way that the werewolves weren't. "Are you going to eat me too?"

The boo hag patted her bloated breasts. They jiggled grotesquely. "I'll let you keep your skin. You're more useful to me whole. I reward good behavior."

Dominque couldn't stop staring at that stretched skin. She *knew* that Aunt Jemima hadn't willingly given this witch anything. The house was stolen, just like her skin. "Is Aunt Jemima still alive?"

The hungry smile stretched wider, digging too deep into the cheeks. "She wouldn't be of any use to me if she were dead."

"But you're wearing her skin."

"I'm not a necromancer. I need living flesh."

"But how?" Maybe it was sheer morbid curiosity or raw fear but Dominque couldn't shut up. "How does it work?"

"Think of a jawbreaker. There are many, many layers. Each layer is a person. I prefer werewolves because their power lies inside of transformation. This old woman has been around."

"So Aunt Jemima is a witch too?"

"No, she's just a decrepit human female. Her skin is so fragile that I had to turn her into a werewolf to make sure that she didn't tear when I put her on."

Dominque licked her lips. She held out her trash bag. "You can have my sneakers if you give Aunt Jemima back her life, her skin, and her house."

"After everything you've done to get your treasures back?"

Dominque nodded, too scared to think about the consequences of making a deal with a witch. "She's special."

"What's so special about her or this old house?"

"She makes the best pancakes." Dominque said lamely. "And this is her house."

Aunt Jemima was a lot more than her pancakes. She was kind. She helped the mothers with their babies. She was the midwife and the mortician. She patched broken arms and healed bruises from fists. She celebrated report cards and collected yearbook pictures. She had a soft bed to sleep on and a warm hug to cry on. She didn't do it for the fame. She did it because she was a nice old lady who cared about her community.

If the neighborhood had a soul, it was right here in this dingy kitchen. This house was a sacred space for lost and lonely souls.

And that was worth fighting for.

The boo hag studied Dominque with those unblinking eyes. "My pancakes didn't taste right. That's how you knew it wasn't her. I thought I followed the recipe perfectly."

"You can't make soul food without a soul." Dominque

wanted to slap herself in the mouth. "Not that you don't have a soul. Of course you do. But she doesn't need to follow a recipe."

The boo hag nodded. "An accurate observation. I will make a note of it. Very well, I agree to your terms."

"Thank you." Dominque smiled ingratiatingly. She gritted her teeth to stay quiet.

The witch rubbed her nose. At least that's what Dominque thought until she peeled her face off.

Brown skin curled away from the boo hag's body like a giant starfish trying to stand on two legs. The skin wobbled and swayed. Bones snapped into place like a weird jigsaw. Muscle, necrotic purple blood vessels, and sinew, thin with age, wrapped around the bone.

The boo hag opened her mouth wide and a pair of eyes scuttled out trailing eardrums along the prehensile synapses. Ears and a nose sprouted like mushrooms as a head rose up out of the writhing skin like a turtle waking up. The eyes burrowed into the soft flesh covering the eye sockets. Fingernails projected from finger bones at the tapered ends.

Patchy gray fur dusted the wrinkled sagged flesh of a warped half-dog and half-woman creature. Then it shrunk into an old naked Black lady.

Dominque dropped the trash bag, rushing forward, arms out to catch the real Aunt Jemima as she toppled. She was heavy but Dominque was strong. Her skin was clammy to the touch, sticky as though covered in a clear viscous syrup. Her hair was thin on her scalp. Her eyebrows were barely there. Her face was slack. Her teeth were missing. The gums were a dusky pink. Her breath was foul as she wheezed, coughing and hacking. Dominque yanked a crocheted brown and green afghan off the plastic wrapped couch to covered Aunt Jemima's nakedness.

The boo hag towered over Dominque, hands on her hips. She had transformed into a White woman with stringy straw-gold hair. Still as wide as a couch turned on its side. She had an ugly and forgettable face that wasn't about looks but the soul inside.

The boo hag wore a floor length dress of brown skins, layered upon each other in a pinched patchwork. A leathery skullcap decorated with teeth, bones, and fingernails. Leather gloves. The skirt moved without a wind.

"You could've asked for anything," the boo hag said, "You really want some old dog with breast cancer and diabetes?"

"Yes," Dominque said, "Thank you for giving her back."

"Don't mention it." The witch harrumphed. "I hate old flesh. It's so fragile. The bones are so brittle."

Dominque did not look up as the witch riffled through the trash bag. She flinched as the witch tried on her sneakers. The long bloated feet warped to fit each shoe.

"Ooh, these are nice," the boo hag said as she put on the special edition Starry Night Air Jordan Retro Ones. The ones based off of Vincent Van Gogh's *Starry Night* painting.

Rage planted heat in Dominque's chest. How did the boo hag know that the Starry Nights were her favorite sneakers? The ones she liked to stunt in? The ones she cleaned carefully to keep the silver, yellow, and blue as fresh as the day she bought them? The ones she spent *fifteen thousand dollars on*. Okay, yes, the price had ballooned into the stratosphere but the pair was in her size and she wasn't walking away without them in her hand.

Figures.

Dominque bit her bottom lip. She didn't care. It was fine. She couldn't wear sneakers anymore anyway. She was a werewolf.

She was lying. She hated and feared the boo hag. She wanted her sneakers back but the witch wouldn't have accepted the trade without knowing it had equal value.

Sometimes doing the right thing felt like a punishment.

"My name is Stacy," the boo hag said. It was absurd enough to be true. Dominque knew girls like her in high school and college. The bitchy bullying co-ed with skinny lollypop legs and bad posture. "You're mine now. You will come when I call."

"But Aunt Jemima's free now, right?"

"Yeah, that juice wasn't worth the squeeze."

"Is she still a werewolf?"

"Obviously. But she'll have to survive on her own. I had to cure her breast cancer, lymphoma, gout, and diabetes just to keep our arrangement. She had quite a collection of cancers." Stacy reached into her hip flesh pocket and showed Dominque a necrotic sweet potato. It took a moment to realize that this was Aunt Jemima's cancers lumped together in a calloused membrane.

Dominque hugged Aunt Jemima protectively. "Thank you for curing her cancer."

"It's nothing. I can cure anything with my medicine bag." The witch tucked the lump back into a flesh pocket. No, it was a large doctor's bag made of skins.

Despite the danger, Dominque was impressed. Skin magic wasn't only horror. It had real applications. Maybe Aunt Jemima had welcomed the boo hag into her home hoping for a miracle.

Dominque offered the trash bag. Stacy reached past the bag and stroked her unruly hair. "I love your hair."

Not even certain death could stop Dominque from Turning and pouncing on Stacy. She ripped up mouthfuls of skin. "*Don't touch my hair!*"

The meat in Dominque's mouth expanded. It covered her throat inside and out like an octopus trying to block her airway. It oozed expanding slime like a hagfish, only it was black as tar.

Dominque recoiled, clawing at her own face to tear the skin off as it covered her nostrils, her eyes, and cinched tighter and tighter around her throat. She fell to her knees, claws gouging the fur of her throat as she heaved on the constricting skin.

Stacy got up, dusting herself off like being mauled by a werewolf was a minor inconvenience. She watched Dominque thrash for another moment then she snapped her fingers. The malevolent skin ripped off hunks of facial skin and fur as it jumped off Dominque and splashed across Stacy's chest.

Dominque gagged, rolled over, and vomited up a big gooey blob of tar into a discreet trash can under an end table. Her facial fur grew back, only instead of dark brown it was silvery white.

Then she Turned human. She tried to become a werewolf again but couldn't. "What did you do to me?"

"Don't be so defensive," Stacy said, "You can't Turn anymore."

"Fix it." Dominque hadn't liked being a werewolf. The Turn was forced upon her but losing it made her want to cry. She bared her flat human teeth and growled. It wasn't nearly so threatening but she was incoherently angry.

"Now that's not very nice." The boo hag pursed her lips.

Dominque braced, terrified out of her mind but not enough to cower. If this was the end, so be it. Her fingers curled into fists. She kept growling and maintaining eye contact. "Fix it."

"Fine. Be that way," Stacy grunted. "You're not good purse dog material anyway."

The boo hag threw the trash bag cavalierly over her shoulder, knocking more figurines off the walls as she turned to the door. She stepped on the ceramic dolls, the crunch scuffing the pristine soles of the Starry Nights. That little act of cruelty made Dominque hate the witch. She saw that nasty little smirk. The nostril flare of triumph as she established dominance. The malignant glee in her pitiless gaze.

Dominque silently said goodbye to her Starry Nights. The silver stars painted on black and blue suede would never recover.

The witch drove off in a poison apple green Camero. By the sound of the engine and the aftermarket paint job, this car was somebody's treasure. The boo hag liked to take people's beloved treasures. That included Aunt Jemima.

Dominque relaxed with an exhausted sigh as the car engine faded into the road noise. She borrowed some clothes from Aunt Jemima's bedroom since hers were tattered on the floor and still slimed with tar. She quickly bundled them into a plastic bag and scrubbed the carpet to clean the stain.

She lifted Aunt Jemima onto the couch. She added more blankets and pillows to support the old lady's limp form. She wrapped her head in a silk sleep bonnet that she found in the bedroom to restore some semblance of dignity. She lay a floral bathrobe on top of the blanket. While she could carry Aunt Jemima into her bedroom, she wanted to keep an eye on the old lady. She'd been through a lot.

Dominque studied Aunt Jemima's face as she smoothed the wrinkles in the blankets. She checked her pulse. It was weak but steady. Her teeth had grown back. Dominque looked around the house. The ravages of time frightened her but so did loneliness. How long had the boo hag been wearing her skin?

Dominque found a broom and dust pan in a closet. She swept the figurines off the floor. The horrible dolls didn't scare her anymore. She put them into a large bowl lined with a plastic bag. The witch's weight had ground the figurines into painted shards.

She cleaned, mopped, and checked on Aunt Jemima. She made sure the door was locked every time she walked past the hallway.

She threw out the food and seasoned the cast iron skillets. The boo hag had washed them with dish soap! She wasn't hungry but she made some pancakes, following the instructions in the cookbooks neatly arranged on a shelf by the cutting board. The pancakes were lumpy but they smelled okay.

Dominque almost dropped the glass mixing bowl when Aunt Jemima sat up.

"You're burning the cakes!"

Dominque bit her trembling lip. "Sorry."

Aunt Jemima squinted myopically at Dominque and then at herself. She gripped the edge of the bathrobe to hide her nudity with a trembling hand. "Where are my clothes? What are you doing in my house?"

The frightened warble of confusion was difficult to hear.

Dominque gestured at the pancakes. "Let me fix you a plate. We've got a lot to talk about."

Jasmine and Tiana

THE WRETCHED HOWLS AND CRASH OF BODIES HURLED against chainlink echoed down the cinderblock hallway. The crowded bullpens were fetid with human excrement, sweat, and blood. The detritus of drug use clung to clots of hair and greasy takeout wrappers. More people were herded into the cages with cattle prods, increasing the stench of frightened humanity.

Jasmine and Tiana huddled together, very sober and very scared. They were not supposed to be here but nobody was getting out of these cages unless they were escorted down the hallway into the screaming darkness. Masked men guarded the cages.

The two friends hugged each other, still in their skimpy sexy Disney princess themed club clothes. Their bright neon green and turquoise wigs brought too much attention their way but at least provided some warmth. Their high heels were ruined but it was better than barefoot.

"I love you," Jasmine whimpered, as the cage door opened and the cattle prods herded people down the hallway.

Tiana ducked her head to hide Jasmine with her big curves. She gave her an anxious kiss on the cheek, tasting sweat, tears, and the last remnants of Jasmine's floral body wash. "I love you too."

Jasmine hugged her back. "Look on the bright side. If we get through this then we'll be werewolves."

Tiana gaped at her. "Werewolves? Seriously?"

"I heard the guards talking. They're feeding us to real monsters. But if we don't die then we'll Turn into werewolves."

"If we don't die," Tiana repeated.

"Yeah." Jasmine's momentary optimism evaporated as they shuffled with the waxen-faced crowd.

They tried to stay in the center of the hallway, away from the men. Other women had gotten pulled into side rooms. Werewolves were better than those closed doors.

The howls got louder.

They couldn't see much beyond the door they were shoved through. No light. The humid chill of cement. Maybe a warehouse basement or a slaughterhouse kill floor. The smell was like a physical slap to the senses.

There was a sense big things moving. The wet slurp of blood. The screams of the dying. The confusion of panicked people running and big things that chased on four legs. Fast, so fast.

The two friends faced the darkness together. They screamed and attacked the werewolf as it charged out of the gloom to grab them.

Delilah watched Jasmine and Tiana through the security monitor. She had spotted their wigs in the cattle chute and watched them valiantly fight the werewolves. She had seen enough dog fights to know that their talent was wasted in the Puppy Mill and Fighting Rings. They survived the Turn easily.

She bribed the guards. The two were shot with tranquilizers and hustled to her 4Runner. She spotted Cruella and Stacy choosing their own favorites from the cages. Werewolves were loyal if you trained them right.

She drove to the Salon. The other beauticians got the clothes and bath supplies out while Delilah brought them in through the back door. This was an initiation of sorts.

It took several baths to wash the fleas out of their fur and give them a good trim. She used special skin care products that transformed them back into their human shape. The bath went quickly because they were too drugged to resist. She dressed them in black t-shirt dresses and black Crocs.

Just as she suspected, these two were gorgeous. Exactly the kind of high-femme pretty that she wanted working in her Salon.

"What's your names?" Delilah demanded. They both roused as the magic shimmered over their skin.

"Tiana. Jasmine." They mumbled.

She printed cute heart-shaped dog tags with 'Jasmine' and 'Tiana' on it and strung them on real gold chains.

"Where are we?" Jasmine said.

"What the fuck happened?" Tiana said, skipping from confusion to hostility with admirable speed.

"You're in the Salon," Delilah said, "I saved your lives. I got you out of the cages. You're werewolves now but you'll be safe as long as you stay off the street and work in the Salon as beauticians."

"Is this a joke?" Jasmine said, "You're joking."

Delilah gestured at the office. "You're going to work here, doing hair, nails, and waxing." She handed them two zebra-striped bags of nail care implements. "Now, show me how you'd do a basic manicure. Unless you want to go back out there?"

Jasmine and Tiana exchanged a look. Then immediately got to work doing some extremely impressive nail art on her fingers. Delilah nodded. "You're hired."

"Don't you want to see what we do?" Jasmine waggled the nail polish brush.

"I know you're good by the way you hold the brush and organized the nail kit. That comes from experience. You'll start as nail technicians. But be careful. A werewolf can grow their claws one to three inches when they're stressed. You'll need to be quick."

Jasmine and Tiana looked at their hands like they'd never seen them before. Delilah didn't give them a chance to ask questions. She opened the door and led them into the main room of the Salon. "Now, let's meet the rest of the team. They'll train you as you go."

Whitney walked over, her hand out to shake. "I'm Whitney. I'm a tooth fairy."

"Like for real?" Tiana said weakly. "Like Tinkerbell?"

"Tinkerbell isn't a tooth fairy."

"Where are your wings?" Jasmine said.

Whitney's smile congealed. "A witch ripped them off."

Delilah ushered them away from the tooth fairy. "That's enough personal questions. In case you haven't noticed, we're all here because it's safer to help werewolves look human than trying to run the streets like a hood rat."

"Excuse me, we're college graduates." Tiana said, offended. "We were at a Halloween party when we got jumped!"

Delilah waved her hand, interrupting. "It doesn't matter what you were. You *are* a werewolf. That is what matters."

The door at the front of the Salon dinged. "Okay, we've got a client. You two hang back then jump in when I say."

The Salon

THE SALON HID AT THE END OF A BADLY LIT STREET IN North Central Austin, behind the Highland Mall. It was sandwiched between new housing developments and old foreclosed shops. The narrow access road was close to I-35's frontage road but was overlooked by anyone who didn't have a magical eye or a werewolf's nose. The Salon backed to a culvert. Werewolves could travel to and from the Salon without ever seeing a human.

The Salon was busy tonight. Eight beauticians per werewolf client worked together like a NASCAR pit crew. They plucked, tweezed, waxed, cut, clipped, flossed, and threaded the werewolf's body. No hair left below the eyelashes. Armpits and leg hair were a hotly debated subject. Pubic hair length was dealer's choice if they didn't want a full Brazilian wax. A dental cleaning was mandatory.

Delilah braided the werewolf's head into Senegalese twists, her fingers in a blur. Whitney the tooth fairy flossed and cleaned teeth. Other beauticians focused on each individual limb.

The client was strapped down into a padded dentist chair. She wore a muzzle that wedged her mouth open. No beautician wanted to have her hand bitten off while cleaning teeth or her guts ripped out during a pedicure.

Jasmine and Tiana raced each other to paint the client's toenails and fingernails a neon green. Werewolves had sensitive feet. The beauticians had to work quick. No time for acrylics. They used UV lights to set the nail polish.

Looking like a human was vital for long time survival. Werewolves often commented on how lycanthropy undid decades of chemical burns and receding hairlines.

But sometimes, like right now, the werewolf panicked.

Delilah yanked Whitney out of the way just as the muzzle broke with a metallic twang. Gears shot across the Salon as the werewolf's teeth snapped shut. Tiana and Jasmine scrambled back, gaping in horror at the big muscles bulging. The werewolf strained against the reinforced leather straps. The braids became fur as her morphology changed. The freshly waxed skin grew fur like overzealous grass.

"Get to the back!" Delilah shouted.

The beauticians had time to free the other clients from their chairs. They ran to the back room and locked the reinforced metal door. No one wanted to get attacked by a hysterical werewolf.

Delilah slammed her hand on the big red button that remotely opened the front door. The werewolf ran out instead of trashing the Salon.

The clients and beauticians relaxed and returned to their appointments.

"This is why you always get the money upfront," Delilah said to Tiana and Jasmine, who were huddled in the back corner of the panic room.

"That was totally wicked," Tiana said.

"Oh my god, I have chills!" Jasmine said, "It's like a full contact sport!"

Delilah nodded, approvingly. "I knew you'd get it."

An alarm went off. Jasmine and Tiana hurried over to the panic room's wall of security cameras.

"We've got a live one," Tiana called excited.

"Ooh, she's wild," Jasmine said.

Delilah joined them at the security cameras to confirm. A young Black werewolf thrashed inside a cage. She stepped into the Salon's trap. "Bring her in."

~

THE TRAP CLOSED AROUND DOMINQUE'S NECK. SHE WAS dragged into the Salon. She lost control and Turned human then wolf then back to human but nothing broke the leash and muzzle over her head.

The beauticians smiled. "Welcome to the Salon. Let's get you cleaned up!"

Dominque was subjected to a full body beauty treatment. Her head was put in a vice and a new muzzle wedged her mouth open. Reinforced straps kept her pinned to the swiveling dentist chair. She fought and choked as she was scrubbed with rough hands. They did not care that she was buck naked. They cinched the straps tighter when she tried to wiggle free. After they wiped her dry, they started waxing.

Her skin burned as every hair was pulled out. She gagged on the pervasive stench as rose oil scented shea butter was rubbed into her freshly waxed skin.

"There's a spell infused into the shea butter that'll keep you from Turning," Delilah said. "Now, let's tame that wild hair." The dentist chair changed positions as Delilah cut then braided her hair while she thrashed. "Hold still, goddammit! You need the protections I'm putting in the braids!"

The triangular Fulani braids created a spiral pattern. The baby hairs were set into swirls with a greasy toothbrush. The longest curls were styled into twin puff balls.

"Fuck you!" Dominque slurred through the muzzle.

"She's tender-headed," Tiana said, dabbing away the drool from Dominque's neck. "Maybe she'd prefer a free-flowing style?"

"Yeah, like an afro or something?" Jasmine said.

"She's hardheaded, that's all." Delilah swatted the sharp end of her comb against Dominque's scalp. "Hold still!"

Dominque gagged and squirmed. Her growls were guttural curses. Delilah cussed the whole time, viciously braiding with angry knuckles.

Jasmine and Tiana were unnerved by Dominque's rejection of the beauty treatment and Delilah's need to force her submission anyway.

"She's new new. These baby teeth aren't even a full moon old." Whitney inspected Dominque's teeth, flossing fast. "Listen up pup, you must take care of your teeth. A werewolf's teeth are vital for her survival. Don't forget to floss after every meal!"

"You'll have to use magic," Delilah said.

"I can only do so much if she doesn't brush her teeth. You're supposed to teach them preventative care."

"I don't think she owns a werewolf grade toothbrush," Jasmine said, pulling out a care package from a drawer of ready made hygiene kits. She leaned over Dominque, angling the toiletry bag so she could see it. "You get your first kit for free. There's a toothbrush, tooth paste, dental floss, tongue scraper, mouth wash, and a mouthguard. I've also put in a nail clipper, a file, some polish. What color do you like?"

"Just pick something!" Delilah snapped. "She's so new that she'll probably throw it all away."

"You don't know that." Jasmine said, holding the kit defensively. "Maybe she'd like purple?"

"Lilac or violet?" Tiana said, holding the two bottles.

"Just pick!" Delilah snarled. "We're behind schedule."

Whitney pulled a wand out of her apron. It had a silver sequined star on the end. She smacked Dominique on the mouth with it. The werewolf yelped then sneezed as magic shimmered like glitter tossed into the air. The spell settled on her teeth.

"It's the best that I can do," Whitney said, stashing her wand.

"She'd break free if she could," Tiana said, painting Dominque's toenails violet.

"We're almost done," Jasmine said, painting Dominque's fingernails lilac.

"What's your name?" Delilah demanded, plucking rogue chin hairs from Dominque's chin.

"Fuck you," Dominque snarled.

Delilah cinched a leather dog collar spangled with rhinestones around her throat. Dominque gagged at the pressure. The beautician squeezed her cheeks so the muzzle bit into the soft flesh. "What's your name? Or do you want me to give you one?"

"Dominque," Dominque slurred.

A name tag was printed and attached to the collar. The straps were loosened. Dominque jumped out of the chair, naked and sweaty. The beauticians gave her wide berth, averting their gaze. This was not the Salon experience that they planned.

"Girls, help her get dressed." Delilah's syrupy-sweet tone was pure poison. She grabbed a broom to quickly sweep up the hair.

Tiana and Jasmine hustled Dominque into a sports bra, panties, and a sundress. It still had its tags from the Fiesta Mexican supermarket. Her feet were stuffed into black Crocs.

Dominque wiggled her toes. She looked like herself in the mirror but it felt like a hallucination. How long would it last? She couldn't even remember when she Turned. The last coherent memory as a human was eating pancakes at Aunt Jemima's. Then it was a blur of smells and sensations until now. "I hate Crocs. Don't you have any sneakers?"

"Oh, she speaks," Delilah said. "How about a thank you?"

"Thanks." Dominque muttered. "So about the sneakers?"

"You can't wear sneakers. You'll ruin them." Jasmine said.

"It's a waste of time and money," Tiana said.

"How much for all this?" Dominque said.

"You already paid with your hair and nails," Delilah pointed to the drifts of hair around the chair being swept into trash cans. "But next time bring cash."

Dominque scratched at the collar. Her scalp ached. She

frowned at the hair on the checkered floor. "What do you need hair and nails for?"

"We make werewolf hair care products with it," Tiana said.

"It's not like we can go to Sephora," Jasmine said.

The bell rang as the Salon door opened.

"We're here!" A smiling woman walked in. No, correction, a witch. "They need a bath and cut, Delilah."

It was Stacy the boo hag. Dominque recognized that tang of otherness wafting. A different face but the same smell from Aunt Jemima's house. Dominque froze, unsure of where to run as the boo hag ushered in a group of Black she-wolves.

"You're right on time," Delilah said with an obsequious smile. Then less warmly focused on Dominque. "This is Stacy the boo hag. She'll keep you safe from hunters and other werewolves. You're part of her pack."

"Yeah, we've met," Dominque said.

"Is that so." Delilah sucked on her lips, nostrils flared.

"Yes, she's my newest gun dog." Stacy said. Dominque flinched as the witch patted her bare shoulder. "You'll sit and wait with the others, Dominque. Then we'll go home together."

"Yes, ma'am." Dominque snagged an Essence magazine from the coffee table and sat down in a corner of the waiting area's wooden benches. Her chair was sheltered by the big green leaves of a japanese peace lily. There was free water and soda in a small refrigerator but she didn't drink anything. Her scalp ached.

Delilah beckoned to Stacy. "If you'd follow me to my office?"

The beauticians strapped Stacy's werewolves into empty chairs. Dominque grimly flipped through her magazine but watched over the top edge. The other werewolves and beauticians gossiped as they groomed like this was a normal day at the Salon. The grip of her fingernails tore the magazine. This was her pack, whether she liked it or not. Stacy had called her a gun dog.

In the back room, Stacy took her time inspecting Delilah's inventory of hair and claw clippings. She read the labels on jars of discarded teeth. No words. Just little purses of her lips and nostril flares to indicate what was good product and what wasn't.

"I'll take all of it." Stacy set down a Dior purse full of rolled hundred dollar bills.

Delilah watched her sourly as the witch emptied the shelves, drawers, and cabinets into her magical medicine bag. Then Stacy went into the connected walk-in refrigerator. The dead humans hanging from hooks on the ceiling were for the staff lunch and dinner. Stacy skinned them and left lumps of bones and meat.

The Salon had plenty of ingredients to sell to any buyer with the right amount of cash or something equally valuable to trade. Delilah knew those ingredients went to bad magic. She just didn't care. Werewolves were monsters. Humans and witches needed ingredients. Win win.

The beauticians finished grooming Stacy's pack. Dominque joined the quiet shuffle out of the Salon and into a waiting black BMW tour bus.

Delilah went back to her office to count her money. Skin witches were stingy but they paid in cash and real jewelry. No crypto-currency or checks. No tip. As usual.

More clients bustled in at dawn. The heat of the day was flavored with cigarette smoke wafting in from the inner courtyard where the beauticians took their lunch breaks.

There was a shift change at sunset. Jasmine and Tiana were forced to stay because their clients weren't finished. Whitney stayed too, quietly mentoring the newbies to keep the veteran beauticians off their backs.

Delilah organized newly swept hair, nails, and teeth by size, color, and quality. She mixed hair dyes, replenished the products on the shelves, and updated her inventory records.

The doorbell to the Salon did not ring when the door opened. Wild magic blew dust across the freshly swept floor. The beauticians gawped at Coyote.

Time felt hot and heavy. Delilah pushed through that oppressive magic to get out of her office and into the Salon's main room.

Coyote wore a wide red hat, a long red leather duster, and black leather Louboutin boots. She prowled past the other beauticians to Delilah, grinning with sharp yellow teeth. Coyote smelled like blood drying on dirt at High Noon. There was nothing humorous about the sheer menace squeezing Delilah's heart.

"Good evening, Coyote," Delilah said, "How can I help you?"

"I like you. I'm giving you a warning." Coyote's eyes glowed like hellfire in the shadow under her hat. "Do not sell to the Witch Market. You make hair products for the Salon only. No side hustles or backdoor dealing. Listen to my warning."

Coyote strutted out. The thunderous pressure eased as the door silently closed. Delilah sat down on her work station's chair.

"I told you not to sell that bag of hair." Whitney said, breaking the stunned silence. "The Witch Market is bad news."

"You ratted me out?" Delilah said. "You're fired. Fuck off."

"Gladly," Whitney angrily packed her dental equipment.

"Who's Coyote?" Tiana said.

"That wasn't a werewolf," Jasmine said.

Whitney glanced at the other beauticians through the mirror's reflection. "Coyote is no one you want to meet twice. If you stick around, you'll be missing in your own mirror."

"Is Coyote a good guy or a bad guy?" Jasmine said.

"Coyote is the Wild West that never died. Delilah knows better but she let money steal her soul."

"I said get the fuck out, you rat traitor!" Delilah shouted.

"Fuck you!" Whitney slammed the door with a jangling crash.

Delilah texted Stacy. Whitney needed to be dealt with. She vowed to change her ways but knew she wouldn't. The money was too good. The other beauticians and clients exchanged worried glances.

Genna and Troy

Iphigenia 'Genna' Bellwether stood on a glass enclosed porch and enjoyed the evening's heat. The full moon cast shadows on the gray dirt and ornamental plants set in clay planters. Austin's cityscape was an orange tiara on the dark rolling hills in the distance.

An owl languidly soared out of the live oak trees clinging to the sharp cliff edge next to the porch. The tree roots and some strategic support beams kept the mansion from tumbling down the cliff face of Cat Mountain into the distant ravine hidden below by dense trees. The entire first floor was all windows, which gave the disorienting feeling of floating in thin air.

To the rest of the world Genna was a voluptuous light-skinned Black woman elegantly dressed in haute couture. Her breasts and backside looked fantastic in her form-hugging sapphire blue and yellow gold dress. Her stacked gemstones bracelets and rings caught the light from the party inside. Her black sequined boots made her toes ache. Her hair was a loose mane of curls down her exposed back.

But Genna wasn't human.

She stared up at the moon. Some werewolves needed to howl but she had learned to be quiet and to keep her location to herself.

Genna felt a disturbance in the air behind her and pirouetted, gracefully dodging the long boney fingers which snatched at the air instead of her curls.

"OMG! I love your hair!" The Influencer reached for Genna's hair again with the selfishness of a child that never learned boundaries.

Influencers were a type of energy vampire. By the fetid halitosis of her breath this one was new Turned. She stank of vomit and the Monster energy drink that she had gargled in the bathroom. There was fried chicken grease and hot Cheetos dust under her buff acrylic manicure.

The Influencer was dressed as a realtor, a beige pin-striped suit with a cream top and pointed Manolo high heels. She even had the little pin representing the Austin Board of Realtors next to her Kendra Scott single pearl necklace.

Genna and the Influencer were alone on this particular stretch of porch. On the other side of the windows there were vampires eating the guests. The other partiers were glamoured to think that the carnage was boring and unproblematic.

The Influencer was so sure of her power that she extended her fangs and unhinged her jaw to intimidate. Her pale blue eyes glowed with malevolent hunger. The Influencer lunged, any pretense of humanity vanishing.

Genna transformed into a werewolf in a blur of speed. Magic shimmered like moonlight on diamonds as her jewelry and outfit became dusky black fur the color of shadows. Her muscles were sleek. She tackled the Influencer. Her powerful jaws clamped on the vampire's throat before she could scream. Her claws hooked on the Influencer's exposed ribcage through the thin fabric of her suit then pulled the vampire apart in one long steady yank. The wet snap of bone and the splash of blood then guts were background noise to the hungry snarls as she ate the vampire.

What really pissed Genna off was the greasy smear left by the vampire's hands in her fur.

"Don't Touch My Hair!" She howled.

Her howl rattled the windows. The subsonic vibration shattered the glass and the glamour, revealing that everyone was some kind of vampire preying on each other.

Troy ran into the living room. He was fast and lethal with his sword and his gun. The buttons of his black guayaberea shirt popped open. The linen fabric fluttered around his tattooed torso as he shot and slashed. The vampire horde attacked from every direction via trap doors built into the walls, floor, and ceiling. They intended to drag Troy into the true lair inside the cliff. The whole mansion was a facade.

The vampires attacked Genna and died. She was quieter about her kills. The porch filled with bodies.She lifted her muzzle out of a vampire's chest cavity to watch Troy dodge and kill with balletic grace inside.

Troy was the magical direct descendant of Achilles, the greatest warrior of the *Iliad*. His blood was rich with battle magic. He was a gorgeous sensual lover and when he was hunting? He was magnificent. A beautiful monster. A dragon slayer. Blood soaked into the ecru couches and smeared the driftwood gray wood floor.

Troy searched the mansion's many rooms and honeycomb lair for stragglers. Then he strode out onto the porch, weapons sheathed. His black pants and shirt were soaked with blood. Sweat and blood glistened on his chiseled stomach and pectorals as he inspected the dead carpeting the wraparound porch.

"I love the taste of vampires." Genna growled in hungry ecstasy. Organs hung like wet Christmas ornaments from her big teeth. Blood dripped down the fur on her chin.

Troy adored Genna. He was always impressed by her elegant kills. In Sweetwater, they called her Black Belle, the killer of killers. Genna's human body, while beautiful, was a mask and a shield made of diamond-hard skin. But his favorite thing was seeing her in werewolf form. Her sleek black fur. The way she wore the night like a skin, at one with her magic and the wild world.

"The mansion is clear," Troy said.

"Were there any innocent victims?"

"Just converted revenants. It was a vampire party. There were blood suckers, energy vamps, harpies, and a few other types. Influencers, investors, and realtors. You know, Colonizers. Business has been good for this real estate cabal."

Genna's ears perked up. "It was a genuine vampiric real estate cabal? Did they let you into their secret lair to recruit you to their fraternal order?"

"It was a room full of animal heads and cigars. I'm not a big Lagavulin drinker." Troy transformed into a wolf. His fur was as red as fresh arterial blood. His muscles were decorated with scars. He crushed a vampire's skull between his teeth. "I sent the cabal's info to your Glamazons," he said around a mouthful of bone and brain. "You'll own everything by sunrise."

The Glamazons were Genna's paramilitary army of lawyers, makeup artists, and PR specialists who shielded her from the minutia of human existence. Her family had been wealthy and Black for four hundred years. Staying off the radar was family policy. Being a werewolf was just another secret in the vault. Troy's family legacy was monster hunting. He was equally determined to hide in plain sight.

"You're beautiful," she said. "I'm glad I married you. The hunt is more fun."

Troy's fur fluffed as he flexed, pleased by the compliment. "I'm glad you Turned me. I like being a werewolf."

He nudged his kill closer in shy thanks. Genna accepted the offering, pawing through the vampire's torso to eat the liver. He always saved the liver for her because it was her favorite organ.

Life in general was fun. For all her wealth, magic, and influence, falling in the love with Troy was like finding the perfect amount of dynamite to blow up the cage of obligations that kept her trapped in Sweetwater, Pennsylvania for thirty years. These days, Genna only returned to Sweetwater in her nightmares.

She knew that one day she would have to go back. But not

today. Today she was free to build a new life with her beloved husband somewhere she wasn't Black Belle.

Magic dusted the air like fresh snow and volcanic ash. Genna expanded. She became a fire-breathing dragon, slurping up the vampires as they charred at the proximity to her power. Her wings extended and then retracted, wafting the air. Her scales were black like obsidian and fire opals. Her tail ended in the shape of a spade with twin scales that could turn into an ax blade.

Troy matched her vibe. He transformed into a dragon with blue opal and lapis lazuli scales. Lightning danced along their scales, horns, and spines.

"Are you sure that you want to live in Austin?" Troy said, "I'm happy wherever we are."

"I found a place. It's perfect. It's called the Briarpatch. The vampires owned it. Now we do."

"Perfect?" Troy repeated, a smidgen of doubt marring his tone.

"Perfect for us. We're needed there. I feel it in my bones." She stomped on the porch emphatically. "I can't explain it."

"No, I get it. So there's nothing to do but feast."

"Precisely."

They finished their meal and groomed each other. Their mutual affection shown in the gentle teasing touch. Wolves and dragons mated for life. They Turned back into humans and kissed. They used magic to reknit their clothes and clean off the blood. It was cheating but also reduced the chance of designer sunglasses melting down their faces or pants burning off their legs.

Professor Onyx

Professor Onyx found a werewolf hiding in a dumpster, three in different parts of the same junkyard, and several pretending to be street walkers under a highway bridge. There were werewolves hanging out by the nightclubs on Sixth Street. Werewolves sneaking food at tailgate parties near the University of Texas stadium. They had only transformed once.

Professor Onyx lured them into a conversion van with fresh kills (three ex-boyfriends, two cops, a pimp, a handsy uncle, a businessman, and a family-sized bag of cool ranch Doritos).

None of these girls knew the werewolves who bit them. To them the Turn was like contracting a sexually transmitted disease from an assault. They focused on adapting instead of vengeance, living their human lives while they starved. They teetered on that edge of desperation and hunger which pushed new werewolves out into the open. She had saved them from themselves.

She passed out name tags to Jarritos, Fanta, Schwepps, La Croix, Pepsi, Sprite, Sunkist, Malört, and Yoohoo. "Welcome to the Dragonfly pack, Youngbloods. My name is Professor Onyx. I am your pack leader. These are your new names."

"I don't even know what Malört is," Malört said.

"It's a liqueur from Chicago." Professor Onyx said, deadpanned. Jeppson's Malört was a disgusting brew. It had anise and wormwood in it.

Malört waved her name tag and pouted. "Why do I gotta listen to this old-ass bitch?"

Professor Onyx snatched the name tag away. She opened the door to the van. "If you don't like it then get to stepping."

Malört didn't move. She was a scared, spoiled, hyper-sexualized child alone in this uncaring world. They all were.

Professor Onyx shut the door. She climbed into the drivers seat and put the van in gear. The werewolves focused on eating.

Was saddling a new recruit with a bad name a petty abuse of power? Absolutely. She saved any stray werewolf she found. Period. But that didn't mean she had to like them or give a shit about their feelings. Malört would be a tiresome addition to the pack. This bitchy pup was already on her last nerve.

"Will you teach us how to be werewolves?" Jarritos asked while gnawing on the leg of her ex-boyfriend.

"Every Youngblood must pass Werewolf 101 before they are allowed to hunt with the pack." Professor Onyx said, her afro whispering against the headrest. "Rule Number One: Trust your gut. Don't die. Floss your teeth. Don't get caught. Don't get fleas. Don't get pregnant. Are any of you pregnant or mothers?"

Malört shuddered, her eyes wide and haunted. "No, ma'am."

WEREWOLVES MET AT BRUSHY CREEK DOG PARK AFTER hours. It was a large fenced-in area, easy to get to, and no one would ask questions about a lot of dogs running around off leash. Some stayed in human form and others as dogs. Many werewolves did not transform into wolves at all. Or even big dogs. The heart was wild but the body was a Chihuahua.

Many werewolves in the toy dog section were bitten by a werewolf locally called Satan's Butthole. Nacho, Taco, Guac, and

Cilantro did their best. They ran the life of the idiot woman who owned the toy werewolves in the puppy mill.

Word got around. Puppy mills were bad news.

Nacho the Chihuahua had a change of heart when one of the cage cleaners kicked him down the stairs. He bounced on every step. A normal Chihuahua would be dead. Nacho survived. Taco, Guac, and Cilantro weren't so lucky.

Nacho ran on three legs to the dog park to spread the news about the puppy mill. Nobody wanted to help an evil ankle biter who farted when he was nervous.

But Professor Onyx did. She lurked outside of the fence, eavesdropping on dog park gossip to learn current events.

"I'm looking for the barn where they keep the fighting dogs," she said. "That's where they take us."

"I'll tell you everything I know," Nacho said, nervously farting as the rest of her pack, Troop Dragonfly, padded out of the underbrush.

The Dragonflies listened. Professor Onyx made Nacho show her the way. His information was correct. He unlocked the door and turned off the alarms. Her pack slipped inside of the barn.

Professor Onyx found several werewolves in fighting dog cages. They had been in beast mode for so long that they had forgotten how to Turn. She returned to the rings. She watched the dogs fight. She studied the humans screaming over the protective wall. They shook cash and beer cans in their fists.

She remembered the cages and the ring. The manic blood and pain. The needles and the beatings. She had many scars and leash burns under her black turtleneck and jeans. She wore a leather coat even though it was hot inside of the barn. She focused on organizing her gold necklaces as one female dog killed another. Her face was a mask to hide the effect of that death yelp.

Professor Onyx left the barn. One of the dog catchers wore Axe body-spray. She followed that acrid cologne to a construction site. The meeting was in a guarded trailer. The armed humans died fast with their throats ripped out.

She burst into the meeting while the Dragonfly pack hit the dog fighting ring, freeing the dogs, werewolf and real. She pulled out her magic wand, an enchanted AK-47 with witch killing bullets, from under her leather coat. She blasted the monster hunters out of their kevlar. She cackled as their bloody corpses danced for her until they dropped.

She searched the office for paperwork to ascertain the locations of other puppy mills and dog fighting rings. A shotgun blast caught her in the chest.

She was knocked out of the trailer's doorway. She fell backwards, missed the short steps, and landed on her back. She rolled but her guts were out and catching gravel like chicken pieces rolled in cornmeal.

"I'm gonna *kill* you, sucka," she gasped, blood in the spittle foaming around her teeth. Her body shrieked as it healed but slow, too slow. Another gunshot in the back knocked her flat. A different gun. A Glock. A third gunshot blew her intestines across the gravel.

She curled into a fetal position and tried to breathe. She used her afro as a coverage. She fought her striating vision to stay awake.

There was more gunfire in the barn and parking lot. Her pack had freed the fighting roosters to cause maximum confusion. Maybe they hoped to hide. Maybe they ran. Getting shot sucked.

Two cops approached. Their big boots crunched gravel as they cautiously circled her prone form. Either this was a sting operation or the cops were in the barn gambling until they heard gunfire. Professor Onyx cursed herself for not noticing them until now.

"Turn your body cam off," a cop ordered.

"What the fuck is that thing?" The other cop muttered.

"Turn your fucking camera off now, Ramirez!"

"Why? Trenton, we need to tell people."

"No, we don't. That's a werewolf. Not a woman or a dog."

"But she's Black!"

"It's still a fucking werewolf, dumbass! We need this one alive to tell us where the pack is hiding."

The second cop stopped muttering a prayer in Spanish. He repositioned himself so his gun pointed at the other cop. "Wait a goddamn minute, you knew that werewolves existed? And you didn't tell me? That's fucked up!"

"For Christ sakes, not now, Ramirez!"

"I'm your partner, Trenton. Fuck you!"

The momentary distraction was all she needed. Professor Onyx flung herself at the cops. Her claws slashed their throats as she slammed their heads onto the ground. Her fingers sank into their necks. Their guns stayed clutched in severed hands. She ate them, hauling off their Kevlar. The more she ate, the more she healed. She destroyed the body cameras.

Her intestines healed. The little pieces of gravel wormed out of her muscled torso. She lifted her ragged black turtleneck to brush and pick the shrapnel out of her smooth skin.

She investigated the cop car, using their badge numbers to hack the system. She had left enough of their faces intact to unlock their phones. She found what she was looking for on Officer Trenton's cellphone.

She drove the cop car to the second location. She sniffed around and found a trail to the puppy mill and caged werewolves.

Professor Onyx taught the were-pups how to kill as they hunted down every member of the puppy mill's supply chain. Malört, Fanta, and La Croix were surprisingly capable killers. They attacked anything that moved. The other new Youngbloods went down in the dog fight and gunfire.

"I get it now," Fanta said, her tail wagging. "We're saving people. We're frontier justice."

"We're doing the Lord's work," Malört said, virtuously.

"Thank you for saving us," La Croix added, obsequiously.

"You're welcome." Professor Onyx nodded at the barn. "Get your fallen pack sisters. We can't leave any evidence behind."

"Yes, ma'am!"

The three trotted away. They worked together, wrapping bodies in tarps then piling them into trucks. The Dragonflies stripped the barn for anything useful then burned it down.

There was a crematorium at the puppy mill. The Dragonflies gathered the ashes and scattered them in Walnut Creek.

Professor Onyx led a funeral for the fallen. A homily, few scripture verses, then singing *Amazing Grace* and *Ave Maria*. She led the pack in a howl. The three Youngbloods sobbed. The Dragonflies were solemn. This wasn't their first funeral.

Life could be mercilessly brief as a werewolf.

Rainey

THE LOVEBIRDS DIDN'T MIND THE RAIN BECAUSE THEY walked together. They discussed the August Wilson play that they had just seen at the black box theater. Every word was wreathed in happy smiles. *Ma Rainey's Black Bottom* was a different experience live instead of watching the movie with Viola Davis and Chadwick Boseman. They delighted in each other's company. Then the werewolves grabbed her and dragged her into the park.

He ran after her screams, his new loafers slipping on the wet grass. His terror pushed him to charge blindly through the sharp branches and tripping rocks. He had no thought but to reach her, choking on the despair that he was already too late. He pushed himself to run faster.

"Tyrik!" She screamed as the werewolves pounced on him sideways. They toyed with him, easily dodging his wild punches and kicks. She was pinned under the weight of the werewolf eating her alive. She watched Tyrik by arching her back. Her upside-down view added to her heartbreak.

His wretched bellow of pain when he saw her galvanized her to move, to disregard her own injuries, and stab the werewolf in the eye with her thumbnail. She scrambled up, feet sinking into the mud. She needed to reach him. He caught her, hugging her in desperate joy. They kissed as the monsters ripped them apart.

~

THE WEREWOLF WAS GENUINELY AMAZED TO BE ALIVE. She squeezed the rain and blood mottled theater program for *Ma Rainey's Black Bottom*. She swallowed the urge to cry as she smoothed the laminated paper with shaking furred hands. It was all she had left of Tyrik and her life before the Turn.

He hadn't been her boyfriend yet but he didn't hesitate when she was stolen.

They fought so hard to save each other that it never occurred to them that this was an initiation test. The pack was impressed by their ferocity. The bites and scratches were shallow and strategically placed to maximize infection without dying in the process.

The Turn felt like boiling acid in her veins, her morphology changing between woman and wolf. Then back again.

But Tyrik did not make it through the Turn. His bones twisted and snapped like brittle branches. His skin bubbled and wept vital juices. He screamed as he Turned inside-out until there was nothing to scream with. Just quiver and ooze.

She stared at him, wanting to vomit.

It began to rain just enough to turn the ground into slick mud. Rain dribbled down exposed organs and seeping shards of broken bones. She squeezed the program, trying to preserve the memory of Tyrik and not this horrible oozing ball of meat.

"What's your name?" The pack leader demanded, a name tag and a permanent marker poised.

"What?" She said, dazed. She wasn't the only newly Turned person huddled among the ferns. This was routine.

"Your name or do you want me to give you one?"

She dodged the pack leader's attempt to touch her shoulder, batting him with the program. "It's Rainey."

"Nice choice." The werewolf scribbled the name and slapped the tag on her chest. The sticker's adhesive clung to her fur.

"Wait! What about Tyrik?" She gestured at the nightmarish mound of flesh. "You can't leave him like this."

The werewolf clicked his tongue against his teeth. "Aw, yeah, that's too bad. He's stuck in the Turn. We gotta eat him."

"Excuse me?"

"Once you get stuck in the Turn then you'll never get out of it again." He nudged her. "You do it. Or I can eat him if you want. Otherwise he's stuck like that forever."

She wanted to say no but she couldn't. Not with the pack watching. She hated their callous indifference. She didn't want them to touch him.

She ate Tyrik, bones and all. She told herself that it wasn't murder. That it was an act of love and mercy to end his suffering.

She buried her hopes and dreams with the theater program under the ferns.

~

Rainey never expected to find happiness as a werewolf. She put her head down and focused on survival.

It worked. She quickly forgot about anything not werewolf related. Maybe her life before hadn't been such a big loss. Ghosting her family had gone without notice. Sad but true. Tyrik had been the best thing about it.

She never forgot about him. She never forgave the pack either. She quietly vowed to avenge him.

Then the Ragers attacked. They were huge, terrible, and wild werewolves. The whole pack was no match against their ferocity. Rainey fled. She had no intention of sacrificing herself for the pack or getting eaten.

She lived like a stray dog. There was plenty of roadkill and dead bodies to eat. She did not enjoy the taste of drug dealers and addicts but many died from gun violence, overdose, or suicide.

Their bodies were dumped into ditches behind the trap houses or in dumpsters to rot.

The rest of the time, she wandered. There wasn't much to do but enjoy the sunshine and silence.

She went home to see her mom. And was shocked to find another trap house.

Rainey had gone to college to escape her mother and this life. She hadn't been back since. Too focused on paying off student loans and credit card debt. She built a life far away from her mother. Then the Pandemic happened. The last wellness check that became a screaming phone call was Thanksgiving 2021.

It enraged her to see the state of her family home. Her mother had disappeared. Her brother had too. Maybe dead. There was nothing left of her family but this rotted shell of a house.

Rainey used the trap house as her hunting ground. It was easy and a punishment.

Then a big she-wolf found her eating a drug dealer one clear full moon night. Rainey startled away from her prey. She hadn't heard or smelled the intruder's approach. She growled but the elder wolf remained calm.

"I'm Professor Onyx. Interesting meal choice."

"I hate drug dealers. This used to be my house," Rainey said, defying this strange werewolf to comment about the graffiti on the walls and the dirty furniture and trash on the crusted carpet.

"I hate drug dealers too. Want to join my pack?"

"Whatever." Rainey couldn't think of a reason to refuse.

Suddenly Rainey's life of wandering had a purpose. She could still do good as a werewolf. She liked how Professor Onyx gathered stray werewolves like a sheepdog searching for lost sheep in an urban wilderness. The elder wolf cared and her pack did too. The Dragonflies had a code that they strictly followed. They taught lost pups self-respect and how to do more than survive.

Professor Onyx was good company. She never asked Rainey about her past. Rainey almost told her about her mom, her brother, and the pills. How the despair of living got too much sometimes. How her mom was better at hiding her addiction than her brother. He never got off the pills long enough to have a life that wasn't looking for more. Her mom tolerated heinous things from her boyfriends just so she wouldn't be alone. How choosing to be drug and alcohol free had saved Rainey's life but never stopped the isolation or loneliness.

Rainey was just as desperate to find someone as her mother. Thankfully, Professor Onyx was a genuinely good person. She loved that Rainey's training tactic for Werewolf 101 was reciting Maya Angelou poems. The Dragonflies did too.

One day, they found Missy wandering down a bike path in Brushy Creek. Both were excited to have another Black werewolf in the pack. Missy's baby fur was so soft that Rainey couldn't stop giving her big squishy hugs.

Missy was bedraggled and haunted by her past. "I haven't had the best of luck with packs."

"I know what you mean," Rainey said.

"All we're asking is that you try." Professor Onyx said. "Welcome to the Dragonfly pack."

Missy

In retrospect, it was a mistake to go check on Breanna alone. Missy had plenty of time to think over past mistakes as the Turn twisted her guts and her teeth fell out.

Missy dressed in matching jerseys like Missy Elliot, was usually the biggest girl in the room, and could out-dance anyone. She won tonight's Halloween's dance contest with her rendition of 'The Rain' by Missy Elliot, complete with an inflated garbage bag costume, sunglasses, and glittery gold bike helmet. Breanna had missed the party and sent a text that she needed Missy's help. Missy stopped by her apartment on the way home.

Missy had always been a goody-two-shoes, the designated driver, the straight-A student, and the babysitter that kids actually liked. She mistakenly believed that if she was kind to others then they would treat her with the same generosity of spirit.

Breanna despised Missy's amiable nature. She maliciously mauled her for being so naive and stupid. Missy would've died if Breanna hadn't spent so much time tormenting Missy with bites up and down her arms and legs while spewing hateful slurs.

Instead, she Turned.

Breanna attacked, frightened and furious. Missy was a big werewolf. She didn't waste time either. She killed Breanna, brutally fast. Then pulled her body apart. Then burned each piece in a fire pit behind Breanna's apartment complex. Then scattered the ashes in Lady Bird Lake.

Breanna's hatred frightened Missy. She had never felt that way about anyone. It made Missy question her life choices.

She listened to 'I Don't Know Anything' by Mad Season on repeat to make herself fall asleep. But her body woke her up. She shredded her sheets as she Turned again.

Her roommates made the mistake of checking on her by breaking down the barricaded door. They thought she was on drugs. Missy woke up among their half-eaten corpses. She cleaned up and destroyed the evidence.

~

MISSY KNEW THAT SHE COULDN'T GO HOME TO SEE HER parents. No family visits during the holidays, weddings, or funerals. It was hard. She couldn't explain to them that she was a werewolf now. They might try to fix her.

The nightmare of eating her folks like she had eaten her roommates made sleep a torture. Not that she was sleeping much anyway. She felt guilty. Their families didn't even know that they were missing. Their boyfriends thought that they'd been ghosted. Online friends forgot about them too.

She had tried living on the streets. Even if the Texas night was hot, it was a constant fight for survival against monsters, humans, and animals. Cars were terrifying. Dogs hated the smell of her and chased her, barking hysterically if she was in human form.

By the third night, Missy realized that she was not for the streets. She risked discovery by returning to her apartment. Only to find her apartment already occupied by werewolves!

Big scarred monsters licked the blood off the walls from fresh kills. She watched the pack through the slats in the blinds of the garden window. She was scared but also fascinated.

Loneliness pushed a whimpering sigh from her lips. The pack froze, human and dog forms went rigid with alert.

Missy cringed away from the window. She tripped and fell into an overgrown boxwood hedge in her haste to escape.

The pack had scouts. They had watched her this whole time. Now she was surrounded. Missy crouched in the scrub grass and dandelions, trying to be as respectful and nonthreatening as possible.

"Welcome to our pack, little sister," a scout said, cautiously touching noses. "Thank you for sharing your den with us. Please join us for a meal."

Missy was escorted into her own apartment. It was unnerving but her tail wagged hopefully. A werewolf needed a pack. Now she had one.

~

"I'm the alpha male." The male werewolf growled at Missy. "You have to sleep with me."

Missy backed away. "Um, no thank you. I'm not into men."

"You're a werewolf now. There's no more of that."

"I don't want to." Missy hated how her voice wobbled.

"Are you telling me no in my own den?"

"This is my house, I mean den, I mean rental. None of you pay rent or fix anything. And you keep peeing on the walls!"

The werewolves prowled forward. They bared their teeth and snapped at the air. The alpha male scratched at the carpet. The pack herded Missy away from the door and back down the hallway to the bedroom where the rest of the harem obediently lounged naked and attentive on her bed. She hated it. But what she really hated was seeing another male wolf pissing on her wall.

"Stop that!"

The self-proclaimed alpha male attacked Missy with a roar. He expected a show of force to be all he needed to make her fold like laundry. It had worked with the rest of the pack. She was supposed to roll on her back and beg for his forgiveness.

Missy ripped his head off. She was scared. She kept seeing Breanna in his bullying behavior. She yanked his guts out. Then twisted his limbs off, throwing them at the rest of the pack.

She grabbed a gallon of bleach from under the bathroom sink and dumped it down his throat even though he was already dead.

"You never clean anything! Fuck you! It's my name on the lease! What about my deposit? How am I going to pay for anything? Fuck you!"

She stuck his torso in a pillowcase and punched it. The rest of the pack watched, impressed by her barbarism. No one had dared to challenge the alpha male before. Missy returned their mute respect with rage. She hurled the alpha male's remains at them.

"Get the fuck out of my house or I'll kill you too! Take this sack of shit with you!"

The pack didn't need telling twice. They grabbed the wayward limbs, put them in garbage bags, and quickly filed out. The harem hunched, ducking to avoid her angry glare as they scuttled to the door.

Missy slammed the door after them. She surveyed her ruined rental. She sat on the only part of the couch not ripped to shreds. She was exhausted but first she needed to clean. She had to use milk and vinegar instead of bleach because the stench of chemicals made her nauseous. Having a pack was nothing like the movies.

There was no way that she was getting her deposit back.

MISSY WAS NERVOUS. SHE HAD THE SCENT OF A PACK IN her nose while walking down a bike path through a greenway. Fear slowed her down. What if this new pack was mean?

It was a warm windy day. She lay on a sunny porch at the back of park. She listened to the breeze and the dry leaves skittering across the pavement and whispering in the grass.

The pack watched her sunbathe. Three young females braved the flat grass park while the older members crouched inside the brush of the forest.

Missy was still and relaxed. The welcoming committee stayed in the grass. Slowly they sank into the warm peace of their surroundings. More of the pack joined the sun bathing. They decided to invite her. Missy was welcomed in sunshine.

"Hello, I'm Professor Onyx," an elder she-wolf said.

"Hi," Missy said, wagging her tail with anxiety.

Professor Onyx was the most intimidating werewolf she had ever met. Her fur was mostly black with streaks of gray, brown, and tan in it. Her body was lean. And she was old, both in werewolf and human years which emphasized her power. The older a werewolf became, the stronger they were in their lycanthropy. She hadn't realized that until now.

"I'm Rainey," the other Black werewolf said. Rainey was a little older than Missy. Maybe early thirties. She was a grown werewolf but much younger than Professor Onyx. Her fur was brown and gray like the dried grass around them.

"Would you like to join our pack?" Professor Onyx said. "We're called the Dragonflies."

"Okay," Missy said, because she was tired and they smelled good. She wanted Professor Onyx and Rainey to like her and was relieved to get an invitation.

She was introduced to the Girl Scouts and Youngbloods. Fanta, La Croix, and Malört were her age. Professor Onyx had found them at a tailgate party. They looked exactly like the White co-eds hanging around a UT and Texas A&M football game.

Fanta was an ex-cheerleader, a finance major who got Turned while taking a leak outside during a house party.

La Croix got Turned while skinny-dipping at Hippie Hollow.

Malört was shooting coyotes at a ranch until one Turned and mauled her hunting party.

"You're lucky that you look like Missy Elliot," Fanta said, "I thought for sure that she'd name you Hennessy or some shit."

"Why?" Missy was shocked.

"Because you're Black," Fanta said.

"Why is that relevant? We're werewolves." Somehow, Missy expected racism to evaporate with the Turn. Lycanthropy had certainly changed her perspective. "And I don't drink Hennessy."

"The pack leader names you," La Croix said. "I'd rather be White Claw. I mean, come on. It's right there!"

"Bitch, don't get me started!" Malört snapped.

"Oh my god, get over it," Fanta said. "Nobody cares!"

"Fuck you bitch!"

The three bickered. Missy backed away.

Rainey later told Missy the truth on the drive to the den, in the privacy of the Tundra. "Professor Onyx likes you so you get to choose your name. But if you piss her off, she'll name you after a drink. She's got zero tolerance for disrespect."

"Malört must've really ticked her off." Missy laughed.

"Malört's lucky that she didn't get eaten."

Missy's glee died in her throat. "Eaten?!"

The Witch Garden

Dominque crouched and plucked weeds dressed in a loose t-shirt, bra and booty shorts. Before she was a werewolf, she never wore such skimpy clothes. She carefully tucked a leafy plant limb back into its metal trellis. The feel of dirt between her toes and fingers was comforting.

She secretly loved when Stacy the boo hag was not in the witch garden. It felt like a happier place, the buzz and rustle of magical wildlife was loud. She did not mind choring.

Mist rose off the magical wards over the witch garden. It kept the plants hydrated and healthy through the Texas extended summer. Vegetables and fruit trees which had no business growing in the same area thrived and fought in the witch's garden.

The weather inside the witch garden was a perpetual non-season. It was like autumn because everything was in full fruit. Like spring because the flowers bloomed. Like summer because it was always dry. Like winter because the air was crisp and clear when it should've been rife with pollen. The pitiless bright sun outside the ward beat upon the barrier but inside the garden was its own defined night and day.

An unkindness of ravens in the mulberry trees croaked a greeting. A few swooped and fluttered, inviting her to play. She liked ravens. A murder of crows cawed on the other side of the wild-flower fields in the apple trees, arguing over territory.

Dominque ate as she gardened. She dug through the compost bin for yummy mushrooms. She picked oranges, figs, peaches, apples, pears, pomegranates, and mangos.

A female salamander scuttled out from under a leaf. Her scales turned a patterned green-brown. Dominque stayed still. Either there were four different types of salamanders in this garden or they went through a metamorphosis.

The salamanders started on the ground, quick and fast like geckos. Then grew feathers, resembling the geese that they ate. Then molted the feathers, leaving a weird kind of algae residue growing along their spiny backs from nose to tail. The last stage was the salamander burrowing into the soil to wrap around a root ball. Dominque nearly fainted with surprise when she found one while weeding.

Another salamander scuttled over the zucchini a row over. This one was big and purple like an eggplant.

A stab of movement. Dominque leapt back, Turning completely into the wolf by the time she landed.

Stacy held the purple salamander in her hand. It wiggled, turning white with black along the tips of its scales. She stabbed it with a metal needle right below the jaw. The salamander screeched in pain as its limbs strained. The tail stiffened and curled.

Dominque Turned back. "Stop! Don't hurt it!"

The boo hag ignored her and walked to her work tent. The tent looked like one of those ready-made micro-homes, with a designer's garden shed and mismatched windows.

Dominque followed Stacy, goaded by the salamander's thin squeals. Inside the tent were wooden cabinets and cubbies with a long stone slab in the center. Stacy fit the bottom of the spike into a slot in the stone. The salamander tried to free itself from the long metal spike it was spitted upon. Stacy calmly opened a drawer, pulled out a small canvas roll, unrolled it with a practiced flick of her wrist.

She slid a metal trough under the salamander. Then she stretched the salamander to its full extension by pinching the tail with a pair of metal chopsticks. She scraped the algae off the salamander's back with the flat of a scalpel and a wire toothbrush. Every movement was smooth with practice.

Dominque's ears flicked. She was unable to detect what was inside of the drawers. She stared at the salamander. Then at the scraped clumps on the tray which had a familiar color and consistency. "Wait a minute, is that the wasabi colored stuff that you put in Salon's skin lotion that keeps us human?"

Stacy gave her a measured and hostile look. "Everything comes from somewhere, Dominique."

The salamander's high whine wound tight around Dominque's heart. She hated the way its legs flailed and its claws desperately windmilled to grab anything nearby. "Are you going to let the salamander go once you get that wasabi?"

"No." Stacy rotated the salamander on the spit to get better access to its left side.

"Are you going to use every part of it?"

Stacy thumped the table with the fist holding the scalpel. "Yes, I'm going to eat it."

Dominque picked at the dirt under her nails. "Then why don't you scrape off the wasabi once it's dead?"

"Because the potency is a twentieth of what can be harvested while it is alive." Stacy snapped. "Why am I explaining this to you? Werewolves are too stupid to comprehend true magic."

Dominque wanted to lunge at the table and snatch the salamander away. She hoped that stalling would distract Stacy and give the salamander more time. The boo hag acted cranky but liked to brag. "There's been a lot of salamanders in the garden."

"It is an infestation. They feed on my wards. They're manageable as long as they don't get too big. I drained their magic so they stay in this juvenile size. They adapted as I hoped. Now their entire cycle is accelerated and contained."

"Why do the salamanders grow wasabi? Is it abnormal? Like a

congenital disease? Or is it connected to the sped-up life cycle? Does it kill them? Is it a fungus or some kind of parasite?"

"Which question would you like me to answer first?"

"All of them."

Stacy pursed her lips. She pressed the salamander's tail down on the tray and cut the entire end off with the scalpel. The salamander, which had slumped into a stupor, started screeching and flailing in earnest. "The salamander has formed a mutualistic symbiosis with the fungi to digest the garden's magic. Usually it takes at least a decade for this quantity of algae to grow and by then, the salamanders are sixty meters long."

"Sixty meters?" Dominque tried to do a metric conversion in her head and failed. "So that's really big? Like a football field?"

"Dragons are very big when they reach full maturity."

"You mean, these are dragons? Like real dragons? For real for real? And you're killing them to make hair gel?"

"Stop glaring at me, Dominque. I'm not going to feed you any scraps no matter how much you beg!"

Dominque straightened. She almost walked out. Almost. But the salamander's yellow eyes were on hers. Not asking to be saved. But to be witnessed. She couldn't refuse that intelligent stare.

Dominque stayed in the doorway, fuming. She endured the salamander's pained squeaks, the scrape of the scalpel, and the sharp suction from wrenching the spines out of their mooring with pliers. She watched because it was all she could do. She tried to see some kind of sense in the salamander's torment. There had to be a purpose beyond brutality as Stacy flayed the salamander. The death screeches stopped with a twist of the boo hag's hands that pulled the head and entire spine out of the body.

Then the salamander's corpse burst apart. The threads of muscle coiled themselves around wooden spools. The globular yellow fat plopped into a clay jar. Claws, teeth, and bones leapt into other jars that stored similar pieces. The scales looked like cheap glitter floating in vials. The eyes were carefully scooped out with a silver caviar spoon and dropped in vials of oil.

"Why did you do that?" Dominque whispered.

"Death is a conduit. Pain is too. Skin magic wastes nothing. The salamander's essence remains in its ingredients."

"Wait a minute, the dragon's not dead? You trapped it inside of its pain for the maintain the potency?"

"You're not as stupid as you look."

Dominque stalked out across the garden, fleeing Stacy and the tent. She stomped her feet to scare away the salamanders hiding under the cabbage leaves.

She could not forget that this was a cage. She had to stay useful. To stay obliging and stop asking questions. Stacy might be friendly but she was not Dominque's friend. This was a farm. Everyone was fattened up to maximize their potential.

Dominque went into the kennels where the other werewolves were asleep. Her whimpers woke up Karen and Sarah. They came into her kennel, warming her with their bodies. Dominque sniffled. They cuddled her closer.

"She's killing baby dragons," Dominque whimpered. "I couldn't do anything."

"That's why I don't go into the garden," Sarah said.

Karen groomed her with maternal kindness. "Get some rest. It'll be better in the morning. We'll get through this together."

Dominque fell asleep praying that someone would kill Stacy. If there was any justice in this world, the boo hag would pay for her wanton destruction.

She woke up to find Sarah and Karen gone. She huddled alone in her kennel. She went to the shed in the witch garden. She found them in jars.

Stacy planned to bottle her tears. Karen and Sarah had emptied themselves into mason jars via their tear ducts. But Dominque did not cry. Nothing but grim silence. Stacy sent her back to weeding, annoyed by her resilience.

Dominque gathered salamanders in a bucket as she weeded. She dumped them behind the compost pile and whispered, "Run, run, as fast as you can. Find a way off of this cursed land."

Brother McGruffin

BROTHER RUFUS MCGRUFFIN STRAIGHTENED HIS TIE and tilted his fedora to a jaunty angle on his afro. He brushed his muttonchops and beard. Then he swaggered over to the group of young men. He wore a brown plaid seersucker suit with a brown leather jacket on top. His pointed snakeskin boots shone.

"Say Youngbloods, lemme talk to yah for a minute."

The young men were barely teenagers. The age was in their hard cynical eyes. Their hands drifted to hidden weapons while their phones aimed at him. "Fuck off, Unc."

Brother McGruffin was undeterred, smiling like a storefront preacher beginning a sermon. "How'd you Youngbloods like to be werewolves? Stop waiting for that bullet. Be real monsters."

"Ain't no such thing as werewolves, Oldhead," the one in the Steelers hoodie said. "What you want?"

"I want to make you bulletproof, Youngblood." Brother McGruffin's big gold-plated grill gleamed inside of his beard.

"I got all the protection I need right here, Unc," the one in the Raiders hoodie said, reaching for the gun in his waistband.

"Ah, but if you were a werewolf, bullets wouldn't touch you." He tilted his head so the streetlight caught the animal shine in his pupils. Then he winked. "Do we have a deal?"

"Fuck it. I'm game." The one in the Bulls hoodie yanked his sleeve back. "Do it."

The Youngblood pack attacked hard and fast from different directions. The werewolves broke a few arms when yanking the guns from the boys' hands. They might be bulletproof, but Brother Ruffin didn't want innocents catching strays. Or any cops sniffing around.

He had studied these boys. They were tough. Street-smart and book-smart. The planners. The heavies. The survivors. Ruthless and cunning. Just like him.

The young men fought hard as they were dragged down an alley and into an empty lot beyond it. The rubble of a torn down house and wild grass around it hid the werewolves. The agonized bellows mixed with barks and snarls.

Brother McGruffin sat down on a stack of milk crates like it was a throne. The moon rose high above the condos.

The pack dragged the new recruits over to let them bleed at his feet. The wounds healed slowly. The young men would be pissed off when they woke up but rage made the first Turn manageable. Then they would thank him.

BROTHER MCGRUFFIN YANKED TWO YOUNGBLOODS apart, holding the fighting werewolves tight by the back of their necks. He was an ancient and powerful werewolf. The primordial rage in his snarl stopped them cold. He yanked them around, turning them to face Freedom Corner.

"Do you see this place? Not here! You don't fight here. No drugs, no guns, no fighting. None of it. Not at Freedom Corner!"

Freedom Corner was located in the middle of Pittsburgh, Pennsylvania. Every brick had the name of a Civil Rights activist carved into it. For every name written down there were hundreds of other folk who had lived and died fighting for justice and freedom. They didn't get written about. They never made the news.

They were Forgotten. Yet still, they were part of the change that made Freedom Corner possible.

Brother McGruffin did not like it when the Youngbloods fought on Freedom Corner. Yes, there were still territory disputes, rivalries and snubs that turned into fights, but not in this sacred space.

There were other memorials and monuments like Freedom Corner across the country, but for Brother McGruffin, this was favorite because he knew the names on the brick. Once upon a time, before he was Turned, he was a freedom fighter. He had been there when Pittsburgh was desegregated.

"Do you know what Freedom Corner is, Youngbloods?" Brother Gruffin demanded, glaring at the whole pack. "This is where we gathered to go march with Dr. King. We heard him speak. We were there with Brother Malcom, with Fred Johnson, and more. So many more. I heard the *I have a dream* speech with my own ears. I froze my tail off that cold day in D.C. when Obama was elected president. I have been to the mountaintop, and I've seen things! You must respect this place! It is your heritage!"

The Youngbloods squirmed uncomfortably in his powerful grip. Youth didn't always win against wisdom. Brother McGruffin was as close to a father that they had. Still, that didn't equal obedience.

Brother McGruffin shoved the two Youngbloods away. He walked over to the wall, tracing the names in the brick with a calloused thumb. Sometimes he cleaned it, scrubbing the graffiti and gum from the stone. Sometimes he slept on the bench.

He looked like a storefront preacher at the best of times. But in reality, he was a prayer warrior, still fighting for Black Excellence. Lycanthropy was his ministry. He dragged his pack across the country from one Civil Rights memorial to another, recruiting and Turning young Black men. He taught them Black history that was often forgotten if it was ever learned.

Freedom Corner was his altar where he could pray. The bricks were all that remained of old friends, now long gone. Nothing but memories to keep him company. Many of the social justice warriors hadn't lived long enough to see Barak Obama become president or Kamala Harris become vice-president. But then they hadn't seen other things that made him doubt his own sanity.

Time was cruel like that.

"Say it loud: I'm Black and I'm proud!" Brother McGruffin commanded.

"We're not Black anymore. We're Big Dawgs like DMX!" a Youngblood said. He woofed and several other Youngbloods joined in and pounded their chests.

"You are still Black," Brother McGruffin snarled. "That's your culture. It's the way you were raised. The skin that you're wearing. The way the world sees you and treats you." He slapped his chest. "I've been Black a long time. I accepted you into my ministry because I believe that you are worthy of carrying on the legacy. *Say it loud! I'm Black and I'm proud!*"

But the Youngbloods wouldn't say it. They looked away, lips twisted and shoulders bunched in anger.

"There's nothing special about that, Unc," a Youngblood muttered. "Wakanda's cool but it's not real."

"I'm not talking about Wakanda. I'm talking about right here and right now. You and me. Say it loud: I'm Black and I'm proud!" Brother McGruffin commanded. "You've got to believe it. Your ancestors lived and died so you could stand here today. Rejoice! You are worthy!"

"Ain't got nothing to be proud about," the Youngblood said, "I'm just a n—!"

Brother McGruffin barked a warning. He hated that word and wished that he could yank it out by the root, knowing that he couldn't. He hated how freely it was used. He hated the misplaced belief that saying that nasty word, calling yourself it, and using it towards other people somehow defanged the word and made funny.

But some words, especially that one, would never be funny. It was old and nasty. It stained the soul like toxic tar.

Brother McGruffin had seen a lot of ignorance masquerading as camaraderie in his time as a werewolf. Whether the hard R was used or not, that word was still poisonous.

Brother McGruffin approached the Youngblood slowly. He gave the twitchy pup time to adjust to the invasion of personal space before he wrapped him in a paternal hug. "I will teach you how to love yourself, Youngblood. You are worthy. And I'm gonna keep telling you that until you believe it."

He let the Youngblood go. No need for anyone to get the wrong idea about his affection. He focused on the pack. So young. Mostly fatherless. Looking for guidance. Expecting rejection. It broke his heart, but he kept that compassion to himself.

He pointed to Freedom Corner. "That is why I brought you here. To tell you. To show you. You're gonna learn today!"

He wanted his Youngbloods to find freedom and dignity in lycanthropy that they couldn't as humans. But his way was old and hard. Just as fixated on race as his enemies but coming from the opposite direction. His philosophy hadn't changed since 1971.

The Youngbloods exchanged a look of resigned animosity. They didn't like each other but they were Brothers in the Youngblood pack. Or else Brother McGruffin killed and ate them.

Humans driving past Freedom Corner dismissed the pack as part of a gang at first then saw Brother McGruffin wildly gesticulating from on top of the bench directly below the Freedom Corner logo. The assumption changed from a gang to a group on a Black Heritage Tour.

The Youngbloods stayed and they listened, very aware of the cars. They were embarrassed by the old wolf's passion but they circled him protectively. He might be weird and scary but he was all they had.

~

IT WAS THE ANNUAL WEREWOLF CRAWFISH BOIL cookout. The Cajun cuisine was abundant and so was the beer. Fold out tables were covered in Cajun cuisine. The scent of fried oysters and alligator wafted from the portable fryer.

Werewolves hunched over mounds of spiced crawfish, cut up potatoes, corn still on the cob, sausage with their fingers. Some didn't even bite the heads off. They just popped the whole crawfish in their mouths, their powerful molars ground the shell into pulp. There was ice cream, peach cobbler, and other desserts to add to the feast.

But some wanted to dance. A bluetooth speaker and a great playlist was all they needed to get the party started. The werewolves line-dance in the moonlight.

It was an Old-School dance party music. Otis Redding, the GAP band, James Brown, Aretha Franklin, and other greats blared from the standing speakers.

Brother McGruffin washed his hands, checked his facial hair, straightened his tie, and tilted his fedora to a jaunty angle on his afro. He wore a blue plaid seersucker suit with a matching vest and a long paisley shirt. His stacked snakeskin boots shone. He added a red carnation to his lapel for the flare.

He swaggered over to Professor Onyx and offered her a calloused palm. The twist of his wrist showed off his diamond encrusted Rolex and the big gold rings on each finger. "Hey there, foxy lady. May I have this dance?"

Professor Onyx had put glitter in her afro and wore a silver jumpsuit that was so tight that it looked spray painted onto her curves. She smirked and accepted his invitation. "I'm Professor Onyx. Walnut Creek Park. Austin, Texas. Pack leader of the Dragonfly pack."

"I'm Brother Rufus McGruffin. Freedom Corner. Pittsburgh, Pennsylvania. Pack leader of the Brothers pack." He made an extravagant bow. Some ladies wanted the smooth talk but he was a little tongue-tied as she pulled him into the dance area.

Brother McGruffin two-stepped with Professor Onyx on the

portable dance floor. They showed off their best moves and delighted to find commonality.

"When were you Turned?" He asked. Werewolves didn't age like humans. They stayed youthful. But only someone born in the same era knew how to dance in a Soul Train properly.

"Oakland. 1972. At a Free Angela Davis march," she said while spinning and swaying. "I got bit by a werewolf pretending to be a cop dog."

Brother McGruffin frowned. It had been a long time since anything surprised him into thoughtful silence. "I was too. Same street. Same time. Same march. It must've been the same dog. Or the same pack."

"I thought you smelled familiar." She gave him a look with a little smirk that had enough heat in it to make him sweat.

He was in love. She was looking for a good time. It was a full moon tonight. They left the open air concert to find a little privacy. The hard ground and the shelter between her parked Tundra and his Lincoln Towncarn by a copse of live oak trees was perfect.

Others used the same busy shadows to find pleasure in moonlit company. The shape did not matter. But Brother McGruffin and Professor Onyx wanted to savor the moment and the skin-to-skin connection. Meeting another elder wolf was a rare and beautiful thing. Feeling a sexual attraction was even rarer. Both preferred to have sex in their human shape, another sign of an elder not wasting their energy on the rush of the Turn.

Love for werewolves was like fireworks over a battlefield. For a moment every scar and muscle was painted in beautiful color. Fast hands and urgent mouths. Ecstasy in every gasp and guttural moan. The rush of *now now now.*

Brother McGruffin savored the wet pleasure of Professor Onyx's thighs wrapped around his ears. Every shiver and howl was a gift. He stroked himself eagerly. The urgent way she shoved him onto his back, positioned herself, and sank down to slowly fill herself with his length made him tremble. He loved her brown skin and magnificent breasts. Her afro glittered in the moonlight like there were stars captured in her curls. She went slow to build pleasure. Exquisite torture, arching back. On top and in control.

He worshiped his goddess with joy. But when she was satisfied, she dressed, and drove off. Brother McGruffin dressed slowly, feeling oddly bereft that she didn't stick around to cuddle.

Damn. That was one helluva woman.

The Briarpatch

GENNA AND TROY EXPLORED THEIR NEW HOME. IT WAS different from her other real estate ventures because it was a house for herself and Troy. It was theirs.

They weren't in a hurry. They had nowhere to be. Just walking together through the grass. Listening to the wind through the olive leaves as they wandered down lanes of olive trees and wild growing pecan trees.

Their new home had an old name. It was even on the survey. It was called *The Briarpatch*. There was a list of grainy historical documents that came with the purchase of the mansion. Once upon a time, during the Jim Crow era, in post Civil War Austin, the Briarpatch had been a Freedom Community.

Freedom Communities were sanctuaries for freed slaves, migrant workers, sharecroppers, and born-free Black folks. There was a church, lots of farmland, a few shops, and a little township. The real kiss of death had been a railroad being built through the town square.

After a two hundred years of gentrification, shifting housing markets, failed factories, slaughter houses, a railroad line being built and then diverted, and other defunct operations, all that was left of the Briarpatch was an old Christmas tree farm built on a toxic waste dump.

Twenty years ago, an ambitious realtor bought the land and converted it into an olive orchard, a sunflower field, and built an ultra-modern and yet old fashioned Spanish-style mansion. Unfortunately, getting a local oil company running didn't go as he planned. The Briarpatch was a huge money pit.

The seller was too broke, impatient, and afraid of the shifting political climate to stay in Texas. The wildness of the land had reinserted itself without anyone to pick the olives and sunflowers and make them into oil.

The Briarpatch was a great place to run as a werewolf without the worry of smartphones and security cameras.

Genna knew real estate and realtors. She listened to the rumors as the sale went through escrow. Humans believed that the Briarpatch was cursed *and* haunted. There was a mass grave under the Christmas tree farm. It wasn't hard to guess what happened to the Freedom Community that lived in Briarpatch. The same thing that happened to the people living in Black Wall-street in Tulsa and other communities.

Genna smelled werewolves the first time she toured the property. Troy found abandoned buildings sunk deep into the ground like headstones. The Christmas tree farm was quite literally a tar field too dangerous to traverse. Troy used his monster hunting experience to stalk several packs. He was concerned with home security but Genna wasn't worried. She was amazed to find so many werewolves living among humans, vampires, and other magical folks.

There was something about the Briarpatch that called to them both. So they bought it. The seller was so delighted by Genna and Troy's offer that he didn't haggle. He just signed, washed his hands of Texas, and moved back to New York City.

Troy transplanted sacred olive trees from his ancestral land in Greece. Genna planted a variety of trees from Sweetwater. Also a herb garden. The trees were very shocked by the Texas summer but Genna and Troy watered them continuously to help them adjust to the tough clay soil.

Hand in hand, Genna and Troy wandered out of the olive trees and into the sunflower field, a sea of swaying yellow and green. Bees and birds flitted through the blossoms. There were several apiaries. Genna loved bees. Troy loved the honey roasted peanut butter she made.

The air shimmered around them. The rows of olive trees transformed into a field as reality slid away like a heat haze.

Genna and Troy pulled out their weapons in smooth lethal unison. Troy had a handgun and sword. Genna had a rifle and a knife. Back to back they watched the world changed. Ready for anything as magic swallowed them whole.

The Jackalope

in the technicolored hell are we?"

The acid rainbow landscape gave her a migraine. Troy's tattoos shifted like iridescent snakes underneath his tanned skin. She felt odd. Like her skin was too tight. Her insides strained to burst out. She wanted to run, howl, kill things just to feel blood between her teeth.

She shook herself off, trying to dispel the bloodlust. She glared distrustingly at the swaying flowers as they chimed like bells.

"Welcome! Welcome! Welcome!"

If the flowers recognized her true nature then who else might?

"We got to get out of here." Genna said.

"We stay together," Troy said.

"What kind of magic is this?"

"It's the Wild Wild West," Troy was also struggling but he was better at hiding it. "That's the thing about Texas, it still remembers what it was. My dad always said that he became Pacos Bill whenever his boots touched Texas soil. It never happened for me. Until now."

"So you're what? Turning into a legendary cowboy like your dad?"

"I don't know. What if we Turn into wolves? That might help."

They hurried into the safety of a bush made of cotton candy pink leaves and opalescent roses. Turning was easy. Too easy.

The antsy feeling immediately settled down when they had fur. Only instead of Genna's dusky black fur and Troy's red coat, they were rainbow colored like the forest.

"We look like *Alebrijes*," Troy woofed, delighted. "Just like in *Coco*."

"Good, we blend in," Genna said, her ears up and alert. She pawed at the ground which oozed black tar under the candy floss grass. "But seriously where are we? And how did we get here?" She cautiously sniffed the tar. "It smells like the Briarpatch."

"You're absolutely right! This is the real Briarpatch!" A were-wolf wearing a pink Easter Bunny costume with an antler head-band. She popped her head out of a purple briarpatch bush and stood up on her haunches to see past the magenta leaves and long thorns.

"Greetings Iphigenia Bellwether, aka Black Belle, aka Genna. And Achilles Billson, aka, Troy, aka, Pacos Bill the Thirteenth. Welcome to the Briarpatch. My name is Amaya!"

"Black Belle?" Genna repeated sourly. "No one calls me that since I left Sweetwater."

Troy just growled, ears up and body tense.

"As you can see by my antlers, I'm a Were-Jackalope. Yes, I turn into a wolf *and* a rabbit. Genetics and magic can do some funny things, I can tell you!" Amaya had the super perky attitude of a flight attendant on her first day of the job. All enthusiasm and no spacial awareness. "Thank you for eating that pesky cabal of Influencers. They've been gatekeeping us for years. I'll be your tour guide—yikes!" Amaya yelped and sprinted away.

"Troy, no! Don't chase the jackalope!" Genna barked but Troy was already racing through the teal and marigold yellow trees and orange underbrush.

Genna loped after them. The plants continued to sway and

sing greetings. Even the sunbeams fell directly on her so she was blinded by bright white yellow. It didn't hurt but it definitely felt like a spotlight. Her fur shimmered and refracted like diamonds, casting little rainbows on the landscape as she picked up speed. Magic in such abundance was dangerous. She hadn't seen it since she left Sweetwater.

Meanwhile, Amaya juked and dodged Troy's teeth. Both running full out, focused on the chase. Then Amaya spun around and gored him with her antlers as she dove between his legs. Troy stumbled, howling. Amaya sprinted into a briarpatch bush of thick twisting blue thorns. Troy snarled and leapt after her but the briarpatch was too dense to penetrate.

The invisible trap closed on his leg.

He reared back and transformed from a wolf into an enormous blue dragon. His mighty wings created a dust storm and flattened the landscape. Lightning arched off his horns and spines. His great tail swept uprooted trees into the air as he fought his confines. But the enchanted metal sank deeper into his ankle the harder he tried to escape, peeling his skin down to the bone.

Troy raged, pulling more and more elemental magic until the whole area was buffeted by a hurricane.

The Taste of Magic

THROUGHOUT THE BRIARPATCH, WEREWOLVES PAUSED. They sniffed the air, tasting the change. Whether they were in human or beast skin, they went still. Something had happened.

The sky crackled with energy. Lightning flashed high in the dark clouds. The wind kicked dried leaves down the streets. A storm was brewing.

Professor Onyx tasted magic on her tongue. The tang stung her nostrils. She could feel the tension down deep in her gut. The clenching of private muscles as her internal organs quivered like struck tuning forks. Her fur bristled and hackles raised.

She forced herself to breathe. To think past the initial panic and parse out the scents on the storm.

Magic. Big Magic. A direwolf. No. Two direwolves. A mated pair.

Being a werewolf meant learning that magic had its own ecosystem. Werewolves and vampires preyed on humans but they weren't the top of the food chain. Direwolves were an apex predators that ate werewolves, vampires, unicorns, and pretty much anything they wanted.

Direwolf was a term for magical wolves and dragons. There

weren't many of them left. But that didn't mean they were extinct.

Usually direwolves worked hard to lay low and hide their nature. The only time they flexed their wings was during an attack against another magical enemy.

Professor Onyx glanced at the Dragonflies. They shivered. Their fur bristling. The Youngbloods scratched themselves and growled while the Girl Scouts whimpered and pressed against their den mothers for safety.

"What's going on?" Missy's tongue was out as she panted to calm herself down, her ears sideways, and her tail tucked between her back legs. She was the most affected which spoke to a heightened sensitivity the others didn't possess. Rainey's hackles were raised but that was in reaction to Missy and Professor Onyx not the storm.

"Let's get back to the den," Professor Onyx ordered.

"What about the hunt?" La Croix said, "We haven't eaten. The longer we drive these stolen cars the more risky it is."

Professor Onyx glared at the Youngblood. She didn't like this pup but now wasn't the time to let personal distaste distract her from the real danger. "Rule #1 of Werewolf 101. Trust your gut. Something's not right about this storm. We get back to to the den and we wait it out. Nobody's going to out in this weather if they can help it."

Lightning flashed in turquoise clouds. A tornado was growing. They didn't need telling twice.

They got in their stolen cars and drove back to their house in Foxglenn, a subdivision built inside of Walnut Creek Park.

The storm hit while they were on MoPac. Professor Onyx gripped the steering wheel of the Tundra, maintaining speed as rain slapped the truck. Through the side windows it looked like they were driving underwater. The werewolves in the truck bed hunkered under the tarp.

Rainey and Missy were inside the Tundra with Professor

Onyx. They stared at the road, willing the Tundra to stay on the road while the wind howled and lightning striped the darkness.

"What's wrong with the storm?" Missy said.

"I don't know," Rainey said.

"I do," Professor Onyx said and didn't elaborate.

Missy scratched herself, trying to stay calm. She closed her eyes, folded her hands, and prayed that whatever was wrong passed them by. That the Tundra didn't skip in the sudden rain puddles. That they arrived safely home.

The rain eased its onslaught. The truck stopped wiggling. The storm hadn't passed. They could see other cars struggling to stay on the road, some had their flashers on. A motorcyclist had parked under an overpass because it was too dangerous. Yet Professor Onyx couldn't deny that it was suddenly easier to drive. She wasn't blinded by the rain covering the windshield.

Professor Onyx glanced at the rearview mirror. Missy whispered prayers while Rainey scanned their surroundings. She focused on the road. "Rainey, when we get back, tell the Dragonflies to pack up. We need to get out of Austin for a while. We've got enough Youngbloods to start Werewolf 101. I want them to have room to run."

"On it." Rainey texted the other Dragonflies for a moment. "Okay, Velma and Simone found a place in Wimberely. Permission to execute?"

"Permission granted."

Counterattack

Stacy the boo hag hurried through Troy's magical hurricane, her leather dress flapping around her legs. Her headscarf was decorated with homemade protective amulets that kept her safe from his fury.

She created a lasso of beaded barbed wire, focus on his long neck. She grinned with eager anticipation.

A direwolf! A real life, full grown dragon! Big and male and pissed off. His human skin was his weakness. Troy was the most beautiful dragon she had ever seen. Big and strong. Blue lightning turned the sky turquoise. His magnificent wings created cyclones. He had the power of Hurricane Katrina in his magic. The power of hunting and death.

He wasn't just a dragon. He was a dragon *slayer* who had been magically transformed into his prey. His virility was displayed in the size of his tusks and spines. She couldn't wait to pull them out.

She yanked on the lasso. Troy bugled his rage as the enchantment wrapped up his back leg and pulled him out of the air. He hit the ground hard, creating small fires as lightning arced into the sodden plants. Smoke surrounded his bulk. He dug at the ground with claws and wings. His tail beat batted the downed trees.

No one was more shocked than Stacy was when Genna came up from behind her and stabbed her with a knife down to the quick. It burned as it cut. The strikes fast and powerful. Cutting the lasso. Breaking the enchantment. The magic snapped like a rubber band.

Troy transformed from a dragon to a man. He sat up to clutch his leg as the lasso burned off his skin. The metal trap melted in his molten grip.

Meanwhile, Stacy tripped on her skirts, trying to dodge the knife. Genna did not give her time to regroup, slashing and stabbed and kicking and punching. Genna kicked Stacy in the chest, slicing her again to the core with a foot claw. Genna flipped up in the air, spinning while Stacy was knocked flat. Her clothes came apart as the living creatures she had sewn into the folds of her dress escaped her control. Stacy rolled, dodging the stomp that would've crushed her head like a dropped watermelon.

Genna's fury was fueled by protective rage. She had spotted Stacy and quickly Turned back into her human shape. She had been raised and taught magic by boo hags. She knew where to cut so it didn't grow back.

Stacy scrambled away, dodged, and blocked her killing strikes. She was forced to retreat, discarding several escape plans because Genna was too fast and lethal to hoodwink.

Stacy ran. Genna chased.

Stacy reached into her magical medicine bag and hurled everything at Genna. No longer spells. Just books. Furniture. Test tubes. Scalpels. Tables. Anything and everything to give her an extra needed second to escape.

Another slash. Stacy screeched. She hurled her entire tent at Genna, unfurling the canvas and wood like a cloth octopus.

Genna recoiled. The tent missed.

That was all Stacy needed to jump through magic, expend a tremendous amount of energy to teleport away.

Genna snarled and pointed the knife after Stacy. She was incoherently angry and frightened. She silently made herself a promise to kill that boo hag but kept it to herself. There was too much magic in this strange dangerous place to shout vows.

Genna circled back to Troy. As much as she wanted to kill that bitch, his health was her priority.

On the way back, she breathed fire on the stuff Stacy had thrown at her to make sure there weren't any hidden bombs or listening devices. They burned up. Then the quick growing plants curled the charred remnants and dragged them into the tarry ground.

Troy was trying to be brave but he was hurt bad. She crouched down and checked his leg. She knew boo hag magic, how it sunk into the skin and poisoned the blood. She undid the barbed curses and healed his wounds but this was first aid.

"Sorry. I saw the rabbit and just went," Troy panted.

"It happens," Genna said. He hadn't been a werewolf for long but most monsters couldn't control themselves when prey sprinted past.

"We need to get out of here." Genna was scared. "This is plantation magic. That was a plantation witch. A boo hag. The nastiest I've ever seen."

"That rabbit led me right into a trap. Do you think she's working with the witch?"

"Nah, Br'er Rabbit was just using what she can to get you off her back."

"Br'er Rabbit?" Troy repeated, enunciating carefully. "I've never heard of it."

Genna stared at him with chagrin. "You haven't?"

"Hey, we'll get through this. I'm okay. See? Don't worry. You saved me. You're my hero."

Genna did not return his smile. He was unnerved by her horrified silence. Genna wasn't a monster hunter. Sometimes he treated her like a civilian because she didn't react like a hunter to stress. But as she effectively bandaged his wounds using plants and vines that grew within reach, he was reminded not to treat her like a civilian but a highly specialized warrior who had survived alone in Sweetwater, an incredibly inhospitable magic land.

She helped him stand. "There's a path of flowers over there. Let's follow it."

They walked together through the singing plants. Troy tried to hide his pain.

The Forsaken Forest

GENNA AND TROY MOVED CAREFULLY, WEAPONS OUT and minding every step. The flowers of the Briarpatch continued to sing. Rainbows sparkled and trees danced, shaking their branches. She could feel the heat rising out of the ground. It made her knees and feet sweat.

"Is that a bluebird on your shoulder?" Troy said. "I think the trees are singing to you,"

"To both of us," Genna said, quiet with dread as she gently brushed the bird away. "I guess they know that we bought the land and want us to feel welcome."

"How could they know that?"

"It's just a theory, Troy. The local wildlife seems pretty happy that we just kicked the boo hag out of this territory. I always thought that forests were fairly tolerant and adaptable. Hell, Sweetwater was upset when I left and I burnt the forest down."

"So this witch has been up to something fearsome and foul."

"Or worse."

"What's a boo hag is?"

"Boo hags are old plantation magic. Skin magic. Back in the slavery days, all of those people from different places with different belief systems mashed together in subhuman conditions. That's a lot of rage looking for an outlet."

"I felt that when she cut through my ankle like a hot wire through butter. What else?"

"A skin witch takes living skin. She can wear it. She can ride you. That's where the term 'nightmare' originates. She can transform into different people or transform the way someone looks. It's just the surface level unless she's also mastered bone and blood magic. Then she can do terrible things, like turn you inside out."

Critters hopped, fluttered, and pranced around them. Manic happy grins warped turtle and possum faces. The flowers led them into a pine forest where tar pits oozed and bubbled.

Troy tried to stop favoring his leg but the pain was getting hard to ignore. "Why'd the boo hag let us buy her land?"

"To eat us," Genna paused and watched critters dance back down the flower path. They waved enthusiastically. Genna waved back. The flowers closed their blossoms. The music quieted down.

The trees in this part of the forest did not sway and shake their branches like cheerleaders waving pompoms. They loomed.

Tar pits bubbled and hissed under the pine trees. A thin scrim of red pine needles carpeted the tar and exposed roots just enough to give the illusion of flat land.

The two were alone. After the noise and painfully colorful landscape, the dark shadows beyond the normal looking trees was menacing.

"We're at that defunct Christmas tree farm," Genna said. "Which puts us in the physical world on the other side of the sunflower field."

"I see the sign," Troy pointed at a half buried sign so rusted and sun-bleached that it was unreadable. Someone had scratched into the rust with a rock.

It read: The Forsaken Forest.

"I didn't see that during the appraisal," Genna joked bleakly.

"Neither did I. Maybe we weren't supposed to see it. Maybe this is where the true magic lies."

Genna gave Troy a look. "No, I don't think that's correct."

He shrugged. "Then you tell me. I'm all ears. I don't know boo hags or this forest's magic. You lead. I follow. Just talk to me."

"I don't know if I'm right."

"You've been right so far."

Genna pursed her lips. She was unnerved, not by his compliance but by the entire situation. "The land *wants* us here. It's happy. It doesn't want to kill us but it'll happily drink our blood. It doesn't think like a human. It's like a big neglected dog. It doesn't want to kill us because then it'll be ignored again. It wants us to go somewhere that's inside of the Forsaken Forest."

"How do we get past the tar?"

Genna walked over to the side of the path and crouched down. She plucked a few dandelions. "Whatever happens, I love you."

"I love you too," Troy said. "You got this."

She inhaled a deep breath and blew the seedlings off the dandelions. They watched the seedlings swirl into the air and drift into the forest.

The seedlings landed in the quietly steaming tar. The dandelions grew supernaturally fast in the toxic ooze. Their jagged green leaves and yellow blossoms dotted the gloomy interior.

"Okay, we step only where the dandelions grow." Genna said, guiding Troy's hand to touch her shoulder. "Watch my back."

"Always," he vowed.

They entered the forest together, stepping only where the dandelions grew. She paused to pluck more and blow seedlings across the tar. It was difficult to resist the urge to step off the dandelion path and onto the roots but Genna didn't trust the conifers. She felt them watching.

She was reminded of the book, 'The Giving Tree' by Shel Silverstein. She had always hated that book. These trees felt sullen and angry. They wanted her dead. To take from her like the little boy took from the Giving Tree.

"These are Taker Trees," Genna said quietly. "Don't let them touch you."

Troy grunted and squeezed her shoulder. She glanced at his hand. It was swollen, the nail beds were purple and each finger was swollen like a sausage. He sweated hard and it stank of infection. When she touched his wrist, he flinched.

She risked twisting around, not moving her feet, but enough to see him and gasped. He was a mottled yellowy green-gray like the flesh of an oxidized avocado left out on a kitchen counter. Parts of him were a shrunken neurotic purple. His leg had swollen like it had elephantiasis. He hadn't complained.

"Holy shit!" Genna gasped.

He stopped her from touching him further with a squeeze on the shoulder. "Keep going. We're almost there."

But they weren't almost anywhere. The dandelions grew in a yellow path that led them deeper and deeper into the Forsaken Forest. The trees stretched in every direction. The trunks' regimented rows created an optical illusion.

The Forsaken Forest was almost the real world. Magic was so close onto the landscape like a layer of plastic wrapped around a head. Enough to suffocate.

"Hold on to me." Genna commanded, shifting so his hands gripped her shoulder and her waist. He needed to put more of his weight in his hands to stay balanced. His quiet agony fueled Genna's desperation.

She reached out and sank her fingers into the air, extending her claws. She felt the plastic flex, confirming her suspicion that there was an obfuscation ward in their path.

Genna swiped at the air, pulling the spell back like it was a shower curtain.

The trees wrinkled and bent, revealing a military canvas tent built next to a gardening shed on the other side of a garden. There were baskets and dried herbs. Lots of dead animals and skins drying in bright sunshine. The dandelions grew a trail right up to the canvas entrance.

Genna recognized the tent. The boo hag had thrown it at her during her escape.

Her triumph was stymied by Troy stumbling. He grabbed her shoulder harder, fighting to stay upright. He didn't say a word but his breath was reedy through gritted teeth and whistled through his flared nostrils.

"Okay, okay. We're almost there." Genna said.

"Sorry," Troy wheezed.

"Hush." She grimaced, regretting her hard tone. She lifted his arm over her shoulder. He flinched when he put weight on his armpit. She felt the lymph nodes, swollen to the size of oranges under his arms.

"I can walk," he said. "Lead the way."

She still had a few dandelions gathered along the way. She breathed on them all, needing a wider path.

Ordinarily she would avoid a boo hag's lair of power but Troy wasn't healing.

The Boo Hag's Tent

The walk through the Forsaken Forest into the boo hag's garden was a forced march. Troy's rapid decline frightened her. She had never seen him even catch a cold until now.

Genna helped Troy inside the boo hag's suspiciously ordinary tent.

It was a Civil War era field hospital tent. She felt like she had stepped back in time as she surveyed the roughly hewn furniture. The walls were just stretched canvas. More folding beds. Mismatched tables covered in jars. Dried herbs hanging from the ceiling support struts. The tools were archaic and needed to be cleaned.

She guided him onto a worn canvas stretched across the sun bleached wooden frame of an old fashion military bed.

She gave him so water from a flask that he kept inside of his duster. He coughed and gagged, his lips swollen. His face distended. His eyelids couldn't even open. It looked like an allergic reaction. Troy's body was fighting the curse. His water flask was usually a cure all but not here.

Genna rubbed her hairline. She searched the tent, feeling ill.

Everything the boo hag had thrown at her was inside the tent, neatly arranged. Hadn't she burned it up? What was it doing in here?

Inside those sturdy wooden boxes were werewolf parts. Teeth, nails, hair, and skin. Stacked like jerky sticks. Or collected in jars. Bags of hair and fur separated by color. Scalps on the walls like wigs.

Also dragon pieces. Their spines and claws were gouged out of sockets. Scaled skins stretched on wooden frames. Jars of dragon blood. She held up an entire skeleton dipped in silver. The dragon's magic was drained so it physically shrunk to the size of a gecko then it was skinned, declawed, and deboned.

No wonder Troy hadn't been able to ward against the trap. It was specifically designed for his kind of magic.

Missy Bootsie, the boo hag in Sweetwater who taught Genna skin magic, had primarily used human and wild animals. Every witch had their preference. This one clearly liked dragons, were-wolves, and humans.

The back of the tent was divided by a beaded curtain made of folded beer bottle caps. Past the curtain was a white tiled room, like the inside of a kill floor or a gas chamber. Hooks on the ceiling. Drains in the floor. Walls of metal cages. Obviously where the preparation happened. There was no smell. Cleaned by magic. Nothing wasted. Nothing left to rot in the drain or collect in the corners or the grout.

Genna retreated to the main room. "I think the trap was made in here so it can be undone here." Genna used her own knife to searched through drawers full of unsheathed cleavers, knives, and scalpels out of the way.

"When I find that fucking rabbit, I'm gonna skin it," Troy wheezed.

"You can't kill the rabbit that runs the plantation." Genna searched the shelves for something remotely familiar. "Br'er Fox never wins against Br'er Rabbit in the Briarpatch. The Rabbit is always the clever hero who out foxes the fox. It's an analogy for how slaves had to outwit the plantation owners and every other White person to survive since they couldn't use force."

"So I'm like Wile E Coyote chasing Bugs Bunny?" Troy groaned, holding his thigh.

"Cause and effect, Troy. The jackalope welcomed us and you attacked. That's why she led you to the boo hag's trap."

"You believe that?"

"I do." She found a small garden through another curtained door.

"So this is my fault." He groaned, clutching his leg.

Genna hurried back over to his cot. She cut his pant off his leg and peeled the bandages and poultice that she had made from Briarpatch plants. She studied the wound with dismay. The raised veins in his leg was purple black. Blisters oozed green pus. And it *stunk*.

Not just of rotting flesh but of vile magic. Poisonous curses spawned from an evil mind full of hate and self-loathing. Her bandages earlier had prevented the curse from spreading up his leg so the sour magic had focused on rotting what it touched. His skin had become weirdly porous and spongey. When she pushed on it, the pores oozed black tar.

"Holy shit. This curse is fast." Genna cussed, tying a tourniquet at the top of his hip. She raised her knife. "There's no time. I've got to amputate your leg. There's cleavers but I'd rather use my own knife."

"Use my sword." Troy yanked his sword out of his sheath. "It's the only thing that'll cut through my body ward."

Troy's sword was one of those well loved and well used blades that had been worn down to a hunk of lethal metal. It had been repaired so many times that it wasn't a broadsword or a saber or a xiphos. It was simply Troy's sword. As much a part of him as his gun, knife, and magic.

Genna took his sword. She didn't give herself time to think as she lifted it up. She just focused on the curse and what needed to be done. She aimed, did a tight pirouette to gain momentum, and chopped down into his thigh with all of her strength to get through his femur. She cut his leg off with surgical precision, bone and all. No attached skin at the bottom of his thigh either. She used lightning to cauterize the wound.

Troy's wretched howl hurt her heart as he clutched his amputated thigh, curling up into a fetal position as it spurted bright red blood. A glance confirmed that she had cut above the infection point. The tourniquet stayed cinched in place.

The cursed leg fell onto the ground with a wet splat. It collapsed into a tarry ooze with parasitic curses wiggling like maggots to the surface, looking for a host to devour.

Genna breathed fire on the cursed leg, the sword raised to stab anything that might squirm free. Lightning chased up the blade. She plunged the blade into the ooze. The curse shriveled with high pitched squeaks. The way the maggoty magic elongated as they died made her nauseous. On anyone else, this would've killed them before help was possible.

Troy held still as Genna breathed fire on him. The cot and the interior burned up. The shed and its baskets of ingredients did too but the tent did not. Not even smoke gathered at the top. The werewolf and dragon pieces smoked and collapsed into ash.

Troy's leg grew back, like fast moving vines. His skin was pink without his tattoos and dewy as the day he was born. He rubbed his thigh.

They hugged, needing to confirm that the worst was over. She inhaled his scent. He smelled good, healthy, and curse free.

He kissed her cheek. "Quick thinking, Doc."

"That was close," Genna said shakily. "I'm sorry."

The scream in her chest eased. He was okay. She had done it.

He nestled her against him for a deeper hug. "You should become a witch doctor. I can't be the only one who needs help. This boo hag has some serious mojo."

Genna grimaced at the tent. "Medicine has changed a lot since the Civil War."

"Not for werewolves it hasn't. They're still picking bullets out of their bodies and cutting off limbs. It's not like they can walk into a hospital and get real surgery. You need magic and healing know how." He gestured at his leg. His tattoos regrew down his skin. "This is the fastest recovery I've ever had."

"It's not me. It's the tent." Genna frowned at the canvas. "Maybe the tent wasn't originally the boo hag's so it doesn't feel any need to prevent outsiders from using it. Maybe it really was a medical field tent before magic turned it into something else."

"Or maybe, it's exactly what you need it to be." Troy caught Genna's hands, ducking his head so that they were eye to eye. "Sweetheart, this isn't a coincidence. You found a way to get my own magic to heal itself and reject the curse. That's not the tent. That's you doing what you do. You've got a gift."

She shrugged. "I'm just glad it worked."

"You're right." They looked around the tent. "I guess this is spoils of war," he added. "You should take it to the local Witch Market and help people."

Genna couldn't think of a reason to refuse. This place was a not a good place or nice. She was surprised that anything as positive as healing a curse actually worked.

Genna kissed Troy's sweaty forehead, smoothing the sheets over his cot. "You get some rest. I'm going to find that rabbit."

Troy smirked thinly.

Defeat

S TACY THE BOO HAG STAGGERED INTO HER WEREWOLF den, spooking her pack awake. "Fuck. Fuck! Fuck!!!"

Dominque and the other werewolves cowered in their cages, watching the witch stomp around and rage.

Stacy yanked opened the cages. "Get out! Go! Git!"

She used magic to drag the werewolves out of their cages and fling them out of the wards into the real world. She slammed the door behind them, ignoring the plaintive and panicked whines and barks.

The Ragers living under the culvert by the highway trotted out. They were always hungry. Her pets' barks became panicked howls as she yanked her protection free of their bodies.

The Ragers also yelped and writhed as she withdrew her magic. They attacked her pets. Stacy didn't stick around to find out who won the fight. The werewolves had her scent and Genna Bellwether would be on the trail.

Stacy needed help and she needed it now from someone with enough magical firepower to make an enraged direwolf change her mind.

She sensed Amaya hiding in the grass. The jackalope was fast but Stacy was pissed off. She reached into the grass and yanked Amaya up by her long ears. "I got you bitch!"

The werewolf wore an Easter Bunny costume that enabled her to transform into a jackalope. It was easy enough to transform that skin into a real rabbit body and truss Amaya up inside of it.

"You think that you could kill me? Think again!" Stacy lifted Amaya up to eye level by a fistful of ear. She easily avoided the big feet that tried to kick her in the face.

"It's not my fault!" Amaya squealed. "He was after me! Don't blame me!"

"Oh, I blame you! This is your fucking fault and you're going to die, you stupid rabbit! Where is Coyote?"

"How should I know?"

"Too bad! So sad! That was your one chance to save your skin. Now we're going to visit the fur farm! What nice fur you have. Cruella's going to love it. You're going in the bag!"

The jackalope screamed and thrashed but couldn't break free as she was stuffed into Stacy's magical medicine bag.

Inside the bag Amaya was poked and prodded. Her blood was drained and recycled. She was tested and experimented on.

The medicine bag could cure anything but it also needed test subject. A magical were-jackalope was perfect. The medical journals wrote themselves as they recorded Amaya's reactions to curses, blessings, healings, and poisons. Medicine, skin care and makeup were created and tested.

Ordinarily torturing the jackalope would make Stacy happy but she had needed help and ingredients. Amaya was not enough.

Stacy felt scalded by the near miss. She thought that Troy Billson had the only magic worth taking and that Genna Bellwether was just his meal ticket. The female direwolf hid her true power well. She needed more power, lots more.

The Fur Farm

Furs hung in neat rows in the warehouse. The furs had been dyed and organized into a hairy rainbow. Large vats of dye bubbled and steamed. The air stank of chemicals and urine. Some furs still had heads, paws, teeth, and tails. Their glass eyes were clotted with dried chemicals from the acidly humid fumes.

Metal cages rattled as the pulley system lifted and dropped struggling magical creatures into the vats. Bubbles streamed around the cages then were lifted back up, dripping color and acidic remains. No bones or meat left. Just fur.

Stacy the boo hag shoved Amaya into a cage. Amaya tried to break free but there was an enchantment that kept her in rabbit form. "She's all yours, Cruella."

Cruella pursed her cadaverously thin lips. She patted her black and white wig. Some witches liked to advertise their power. Cruella looked like Glen Close in the 1990s '101 Dalmations'. The same manic stare, same fashion-forward dress. She stroked Amaya's fur. "What a beautiful coat. I must have it." A darting glance and a nasty smile. "You wouldn't bring her if you didn't want something."

"Tell me where Coyote is," Stacy demanded.

"Why do you need to know? Can't you patch yourself up

with that medicine bag?" Cruella eyed the beaded bag on her hip. "Or isn't it working anymore?" She sniffed. "What *have* you been up to, Stacy?"

"Just tell me or I'll skin her myself."

Cruella yanked Amaya's cage out of Stacy's hands. "Don't be so hasty. I'll tell you."

The witches talked. Amaya tried to use their distraction to pick the lock but failed. The cage was designed to contain magical monsters like herself.

Stacy left, hurrying fast enough to show the limp.

Amaya fought as Cruella sawed her antlers off to the nub. "Ooh, this still has dragon blood on it." The witch hooked Amaya's cage into the pulley system between a vixen and a were-wolf. Amaya bounced and kicked in her cage.

The vixen's magic was familiar. Amaya had to focus past the smells and sounds and use her eyes. "Zora? Is that you? What happened?"

"I got got, what does it look like?" The vixen glared hopelessly at Amaya. "What the hell are you doing wearing the Easter Bunny's fur, bitch?"

"I was rolling out the welcome mat in the Briarpatch for Genna Bellwether and Pacos Bill's grandson then he attacked me! I went to Stacy for help but she turned me into a rabbit and dumped me here. What the fuck is going on? How could she do this to me? I thought we were friends!"

"Stacy ain't your friend, bitch." Zora chuckled meanly. "What's going on is that you're in a fur farm and you're fucked."

"How did you get here? Aren't you supposed to be too clever to get got?"

"A bunch of foxes went missing. I followed the trail right into a trap. Here I am." Zora glared at the cages as she leaned against the metal. "I thought I'd save them but I'm gonna die with them. Ain't that some shit?"

"We've got to get out of here." Amaya searched the inside of her cage.

"Gee, why didn't I think of that? Look around. This witch skins werewolves. She knows how to keep us caged." Zora's voice shook, trying hard not to cry. "She's got so many fur farms. This is just one of them."

"At least we're together?"

"Ain't that some shit?"

Amaya stared at her and she stared back. The metal churned and creaked. Their cages swayed. The death screams of boiling monsters got louder the closer they were carried to the vats. The acidic steam burned the nostrils and worsened the tears flowing down their faces. But they never looked away from each other.

Their cages were dropped into a boiling vat of magenta dye. Amaya screamed as she boiled and drowned. The chemicals eroded her features and tried to take her body too. They regrew, melted, and regrew as her magic fought back. The neighboring cages were wreathed in bubbles. All of the monsters were desperately trying to escape and survive.

She couldn't die like this. Roger was the Easter Bunny. She had borrowed his skin to show Genna Bellwether into the Briarpatch. It wasn't supposed to be her time. But she needed out of this fur farm.

She embraced the Easter Bunny's magic but nothing changed. She kept boiling.

Genna ran along a catwalk, the metal grates rattling under her boots as she picking up speed. She vaulted over the vat's edge, and dove into the boiling dye.

The vat erupted into a pink geyser. The others did too, creating a toxic rainbow. Monsters were swept out of their cages as the metal eroded. They scrambled free and sloshed out of the warehouse. Chains broke. The already prepared furs disintegrated.

"My furs! Get back here!" Cruella shrieked, but there were too many to grab. The warehouse groaned as Genna's magic ate its way through the spells.

Genna climbed out of the vat panting and spitting, Amaya

and Zora clung to her back like baby possums. The heat steamed off their skin as the dye dried.

Amaya's skin was the color of chocolate covered raspberries. Her hair was the dark red of pomegranates. Zora's hair was as pink as a hibiscus flower. Her brown skin was like chocolate covered strawberries. The dye slid off Genna's body without staining her skin.

She set them both down. "Are you all right, Br'er Rabbit and Br'er Fox? This place is a maze. It took me ages to figure out which cage you were in. I'm so glad I reached you in time!"

Amaya and Zora gaped up at her, gasping for breath and wiping the dye from their eyes.

"You're not even wet!" Zora exclaimed.

"I was wet. I just dry fast," Genna said, gesturing at her black athletic-wear and tactical boots.

"You saved us. Thank you." Zora said but Genna was focused on Amaya.

"That was a mean trick you pulled on my husband, Br'er Rabbit. I saved your life so we're even. Don't mess with us again."

"Fuck you," Amaya said.

Zora glared at Amaya. "Bitch, you're always doing too much!"

"What was I supposed to do? He tried to eat me!"

"Would it kill you to say thank you? She just saved our lives!"

"Fine! Whatever! Thanks!"

"You're welcome." Genna said which made Amaya even madder. "Now, where's the boo hag?"

"How the fuck should I know? She put me in here!"

"She didn't tell you anything? No leads?"

"I don't owe you anything." Amaya scowled. "She's looking for Coyote. There! That's all I know. Now we're even!"

An angry screech above them interrupted the conversation.

"Give me your fur!" Cruella attacked, her skinning blades out and whirling.

Amaya and Zora scrambled away, slipping on the puddles under them but Genna ran straight at Cruella. She grabbed her wrists, stopping the whirling. There was one frozen moment, Genna held the witch with muscle and magic, her body taut. Then she snatched the skinning knives out of Cruella's hands. The witch's expression changed from rage to raw fear. That little 'oh shit' moment of realizing that she wasn't going to win this time as she looked into Genna's inferno eyes and saw the dragon fire.

Then Genna flipped her over and body slammed her into the ground. Cruella was used to magic catching and shielding her from harm. But she couldn't access it with Genna's burning magic short burning her synapses. Her furs burned. Her spells burst messily out of her skin like a popped water balloon.

Genna yanked Cruella's head up, arching her back to the limits of her spine. She kept her still with a knee in the back. She swiftly dragged the skinning knife across the edge of Cruella's hairline.

Amaya and Zora watched Genna scalp then skin Cruella. Then pull out her bones and organs. Every movement was ruthless and fast.

"Holy shit," Zora muttered, "Bitch, you better not fuck with that direwolf or her man no more. That one knows how to kill magic. You don't know shit like that unless you've been through some shit."

"Fine, fine," Amaya groused, scared and pissed off about it. No wonder Stacy was on the run.

Genna breathed fire into Cruella's mouth. Cruella burned from the inside out. So did her enchantments that kept the fur farm running. The power went out. The machines creaked and collapsed in on themselves.

Amaya and Zora ran. Genna caught up with them. "You're going the wrong way. That's not the exit!"

"I have to save the other foxes!" Zora snarled. "My Skulk is still trapped in fur farms. I have to get them out of the cages."

"Fuck that, I've got to get home to my kids!" Amaya yelled,

taking off in the direction that Genna pointed. She leapt over falling machinery.

Genna and Zora ran together. The vixen glared at Genna as they reached the stairs. Zora stopped her with a hand to the chest. "Thanks but you've done enough, direwolf. Get out of here."

Genna scowled, incredulous. "What are you doing? The building is falling around us. I can help save your skulk."

"No, you need to follow the rabbit." Zora shoved her away and leapt down the stairs. "Go. Now."

Genna hesitated. She was confused by Zora but not enough to ignore the sound of veracity that rang through her at the vixen's command. She spun around and ran after Amaya.

The largest vat's cracked when a pylon landed across it, sending a wave of acid pouring through the factory. There was no more time.

Genna ran, dodged, juked, and jumped over the falling metal. She charged through the exit door since Amaya had closed it. The door hit the stairwell outside. Genna surfed the last few feet on the door before hitting the cement, rolling to her feet, and running across the parking lot.

The warehouse collapsed like a great groaning beast. The howl of tortured metal echoed across the parking lot.

Amaya had turned into a jackalope and was already on the far side of the field beyond the parking lot that backed the fur factory.

Genna couldn't keep up. Panting and sweating she jogged to her purple Mustang. Thankfully, she'd left the keys in the sun visor. She revved the car and drove off.

The waxing gibbous moon highlighted the colorful smoke billowing up into the night.

She drove the long way back to the secret tent in the Briarpatch. The tent had transformed Troy's coat. He slept on a queen sized bed with carved wooden posts. The tent had also grown a bedroom and shower. There were richly colored carpets, pillows, and rare landscape paintings in gilded frames that looked like windows inviting her to climb into new strange and fantasic worlds.

Genna ran her hand along the beautifully lacquered counter made of six different types of wood to look like pale flowers were painted on the edge. Some of this furniture was from her castle in Sweetwater.

Troy was still recovering so they had camped out in the tent for now. But it was more than that. This felt like home.

She showered off. The last of the fur farm and Cruella's death magic washed down the drain. She knew that the tent had a built-in redistribution magical system.

Troy woke when she climbed into the bed. "How'd it go?"

"I saved Br'er Rabbit."

"Of course you did." He kissed her cheek. "She's more likely to tell you the truth if she owes you her life. Smart move."

"She didn't know where the boo hag was. Or at least, she didn't think saving her life from different skin witch at a fur farm was enough of a reason to tell me the truth."

"Another skin witch? Is it a coven?"

Genna snuggled deeper into the bed. "I should've asked. I just got so angry that I scalped the fur witch and burned her alive. I didn't think about asking questions."

"Did the jackalope say anything else?"

"Just something about the boo hag looking for a coyote."

"Not *the* Coyote with a capital C?"

"You know them?"

"Yeah, I do but this is Texas. The Wild Wild West never died." Troy hugged her and kissed her cheek. "No use borrowing for trouble when we've got enough on our own."

She hugged him back, still needing to convince herself that he was healthy and okay. He was physically weak, needing time to recover, but okay.

"I saved a vixen too but she didn't want my help. She told me to chase the rabbit."

"And you listened?"

"Yeah, it felt like the right thing to do. I'd just pulled her out of a vat of boiling dye that literally melted everyone but the rabbit and the fox." Genna started up at the struts in the ceiling. "This boo hag is the real deal."

"Should we leave the tent?"

"No, it's ours. Just like the forest and the land by right of conquest and combat. Also my stuff moved itself in here."

Troy snuggled closer. "I thought that bedpost looked familiar."

Genna yawned sleepily. "One way or another, we're supposed to be here."

Troy didn't answer. He was already asleep, snoring in her ear. It was loud and a little annoying but she was happy to cuddle against his muscular warmth. She chased away a few tears.

The fur farm was another awful place. She wished that she had saved more than just two monsters.

Coyote and Anansi

NIEDERWALD, WHICH MEANT 'LOW WOOD' IN GERMAN, was a stretch of land between Austin and Buda where mesquite trees grew. There was a town but this specific area was never built upon. There was a few billboards of ownership that periodically changed hands but nothing ever came of those projects. Nothing ever would.

This was Neither World, hiding in plain sight of the highway and humans. It wasn't day or night. Perpetually sunset or sunrise, depending upon which direction Stacy was headed.

Stacy walked and walked and walked. She followed her shadow and trusted the directions that Cruella gave her to find Coyote's tent.

The longer she walked through Neither World, the heavier her medical bag became, dragging her down to the scrub grass. She stopped to gather prickly pear cactus fruit in her bag, preparing a gift so she wouldn't arrive empty handed.

Her good intentions evaporated the longer she searched and perpetual sunset became perpetual High Noon. The sun baked her blistered skins. Her hat wasn't the right shape. She used up several skins as she drank the water from their bodies. She ate the prickly pears and the cactus.

It was like Coyote didn't want to be found but Stacy was desperate and determined. She couldn't go back to the Briarpatch. Not with Genna Bellwether there. Stacy had seen her death in Genna's eyes and that scared her into walking faster. She finally had a moment to digest her defeat.

She had to find Coyote. She had to get help.

She found Coyote in the Violet Crown, an old neighborhood on the other side of Austin's river, Lady Bird Lake.

There was a dented silver airstream attached to a pristine 1966 Red Ford F100 truck parked in the driveway of an anonymous A-frame house. The house was on a blind curve. The orange sunset sat right on the winding road. Prickly pear cacti grew in a secondary privacy fence. So many ways that humans noticed and forgot about Coyote's house.

In the backyard was a tall teepee out in plain sight for anyone to see. A verdant garden grew, using red hoses to drip water on the plants. On the other side was the edge of an old cemetery. The headstones were so worn that they were barely taller than the grass.

It was all so human. So normal. She had scoured the goddamn hills of Neither World and here Coyote was, siphoning free Wifi from the neighbors!

Stacy stomped into Coyote's tent, straight into a spiderweb. Bone wind chimes rattled and skins drummed as she yanked on the sticky webbing. "Let me go!"

Anansi the Spider sat in the rafters, spinning a yarn. Coyote was annoyed by the interruption. Anansi told such great stories.

"Tell me your story, morning glory. Are you ignorant or just stupid?" Anansi said, watching her upside-down.

Stacy wailed as her life was unraveled, written in blood on her skin. Coyote and Anansi read with minimal interest and flipped to the end, more interested in Genna and Troy than this arrogant colonizer who complained like they were managers at Starbucks instead of ancient mythical beings.

Stacy wept but hid nothing. Only the truth would set her free. Or at least she hoped.

Finally, Anansi let her go and climbed up into a hammock at the top of the tent. Coyote sat down at a loom, returning to the story he wove into a blanket. They spoke to each other in Old Growl, the ancient language of direwolves and sabertooth tigers. Stacy tried to parse out what they said but failed.

"I told you my story," Stacy shouted.

"What do you want?" Coyote's teeth snapped at the air in annoyance.

"I want you to help me!"

"Help you do what?"

"Kill her! Take my land back!"

Coyote laughed. "What'd you think would happen when you tried to skin a direwolf in front of his mate?"

"Not to mention giving Sister Rabbit and Sister Fox to Cruella?" Anansi said. "They are the Briarpatch."

"I caught a dragon." Stacy sulked. "I had a right. And that damn rabbit started it."

"Troy Billson is not a dragon. He is the son of Pacos Bill. He has the Spirit of the Wild West in his veins. He is not just anything. Neither is Genna Bellwether."

Stacy glared at the fire burning at the center of the tent. "Will you help me or not?"

Anansi walked along the top of the tent. "Genna had cut her deeply, Coyote. I recognized that technique. That's Miss Bootsie the boo hag's signature cuts."

Stacy gasped. "So it wasn't just a lucky shot? A boo hag betrayed her own kind to teach her secrets? What was this world coming to?"

"She kicked your ass too." Coyote chuckled.

Humiliation flushed her skin. Asking Coyote and Anansi for help was probably a mistake but she was desperate. She needed a power-up. But what would they want in exchange? She had lost everything but her life in that altercation.

"What did you bring us to ask for help?" Coyote said.

"That medicine bag looks nice," Anansi said.

"No, it's mine." Stacy gripped her medicine bag, fingering the beading. It wasn't fair. She had done everything right. That trap was made perfectly! "You're supposed to be on my side!"

"Then you shouldn't have eaten those prickly pears," Anansi said.

Coyote got up from the loom. "Give me the bag."

Stacy straightened up, clutching the bag. "But it's mine!"

Anansi snorted. "No, it isn't. You stole it off an old coyote."

Stacy scowled. "It was payment for services rendered."

"You took it because you wanted it," Anansi said, "You took it because you were powerful and he was old. His wife tried to stop you, didn't she? That's her beadwork."

Stacy squeezed the bag. "You didn't have a problem before."

"That was before," Anansi said. "You could have learned how to use the bag.

"You don't know how to use it," Coyote said, "It's not a weapon. It's a medicine bag. It's supposed to heal."

"But I need it!" She gasped as Anansi wrapped her up so only her arm holding the medicine bag was outside of the cocoon.

Coyote took the bag. His skin changed. He became a she. Stacy cringed. He smiled, wearing Genna Bellwether's face. Then he walked out of the tent.

Anansi went back to spinning his yarn. Stacy was Coyote's guest. Eating someone else's guest inside their own home was rude.

Stacy slunk out of the tent and back out onto the street, narrowly avoiding a speeding F-150. The truck was trying to get around traffic. It lost control, went over the curb, and plowed straight into the house, missing Stacy by inches.

The human climbed unsteadily out of the truck. A few empty beer cans tumbled out as he staggered away. One anxious look at Stacy. She got into the truck. The house groaned and snarled as she reversed. She stomped on the gas.

Cars honked as she backed into traffic but no one hit her bumper. Stacy drove away, leaving a hole in the house.

Neighbors walked over to inspect the damage. Cop sirens wailed in the distance.

The house owner came out of the air stream. He checked his truck first. Then his house. He looked around the broken stone and exposed wires with dull shock. There was already plastic and half-done flooring of a house mid-renovation.

"You're lucky that you weren't home," a neighbor said. "That truck went right into your living room!"

"Now I have to get new new floors." He rubbed his baseball cap backwards.

The backyard no longer had a teepee. No sign that it had ever been there.

Anansi walked through the cacti and tugged on a thread. It reached all the way to the Church of the Forgotten.

Pastor Faith woke up from a cat nap. She was sunning herself in a patch of colored light in the minsters office below the stained glass window. She watched a spider crawl along the outside of the window for a few disinterested moments.

A whisper of an idea tickled her ears. "You will have visitors soon, Pastor Faith."

Imani yawned, stretched, and padded out of the Church to investigate in the form of a black and white tuxedo cat.

There were dandelions growing a yellow trail from Forsaken Forest to the edge of the Church property. She sniffed the dandelions and the Taker Trees. There were Anansi spiders in the the branches, weaving webs to catch ambient magic and small creatures.

The cat groomed herself then walked back through the briarpatch hedge which circled the property.

Delilah

The Salon had plenty of ingredients to sell to any buyer with the right amount of cash or something equally valuable to trade. Delilah knew those ingredients went to bad magic. She just didn't care. Werewolves were monsters. Humans and witches needed ingredients. Win win.

Stacy bought Delilah's entire inventory of hair and nail clippings and discarded teeth. She used it to heal, feeding off the life energy of the werewolves the clippings came from. She reached for her medicine bag but there was nothing but empty air. She squeezed her hand into a fist. She stuffed the stolen truck with the rest of the inventory.

She was alive. That was important. She hadn't expected to get out of Coyote's tent. That near miss with the truck was a message. She used the knockoff Coach duffel bag Delilah gave her as her new medicine bag.

Her tent was gone. Her inventory was gone. Her bag was gone. She had to build everything from scratch. She needed to be creative.

She found a Louis Vuitton shoulder bag full of non-sequential bills buried under a mesquite tree. Cruella had told Stacy where to find the lost stash of drug money as payment for Amaya.

"Did you hear about Cruella?" Delilah said, accepting the bag of blood money. "Word on the street is that she got got."

Stacy pursed her lips. Rumors had traveled fast thanks to Anansi. "Any idea who?"

"Maybe the Easter Bunny."

"The Easter Bunny? Seriously?"

Delilah shrugged. "Everyone blames the Easter Bunny but I know for a fact that Roger was at the Speakeasy tap-dancing through his set because I was sitting at the tables."

"Then who destroyed the fur farm?"

"Who knows? Watch your back. Maybe the Tooth Fairy."

Stacy nodded and hurried away. Genna Bellwether had already found Cruella and Amaya. She needed to move faster.

Delilah watched the truck speed off sourly. No, tip. As usual. She went back to her office to count her money.

Delilah would sell anybody out. There was always a sucker who thought that she lied or joked when she called it a biblical obligation to steal strength with a haircut. Stacy and Cruella were her best clients for her side hustle. That's how she knew when the fur farm burned down. Hopefully whoever got Cruella didn't know where the fur came from.

The doorbell to the Salon did not ring when the door opened. Wild magic blew dust across the freshly swept floor.

Time felt hot and heavy. Delilah pushed through that oppressive magic to get out of her office and into the Salon's main room. She stared with the beauticians gawping at Coyote.

Coyote wore a wide red hat, a long red leather duster, and a beaded medicine bag on her hip. She ignored the other beauticians. The leather of her clothes squeaked expensively as walked up to Delilah, grinning with sharp yellow teeth. There was nothing humorous about the sheer menace squeezing Delilah's heart.

"I know what you're doing, Delilah." Coyote leaned close. "You've just served the last customer for your little side hustle.

This is the only warning you or any of your beauticians will get. Do not sell to the Witch Market."

Coyote left. Delilah staggered to her work station and sat in her chair. She took a long drag from her vape but marijuana could not shift the gravity of this close encounter.

"That was Coyote," Whitney said, breaking the stunned silence. "The headhunter. The scalper. Here in our Salon."

"We're the only werewolf Salon in Austin," Delilah said, "We're famous. It's not a big deal."

"Nah, Coyote was pissed. I told you not to sell that bag of hair. You can't spend money if you're dead."

Delilah glared at the tooth fairy. "You sold me out, you bitch."

"I didn't say anything!"

"Then why is Coyote here, huh? I know how you like to run your mouth. Always talking. I bet you told the Easter Bunny and he told Coyote. Pack your shit and get out!"

"You don't need to tell me twice." Whitney gathered her dental implements.

"Can somebody tell me what Coyote is?" Tiana said. "That wasn't a werewolf."

"Coyote is no one you want to meet twice, Youngblood." Whitney glanced at the other beauticians through the mirror's reflection. "She was born free in Texas during the real Wild West right here in the Briarpatch. Can you imagine what it was like to be Black and Tejano? Her people didn't leave. They stayed. She's the only one left. If you stick around, you'll be missing in your own mirror. If you're smart, you'll clear out."

"I said get the fuck out!" Delilah shouted.

"Bitch, bye!" Whitney slammed the Salon door with a jangling crash. The other beauticians and clients exchanged worried glances.

"But I just got my license," Jasmine whined.

Delilah cleaned her station. She vowed to change her ways but knew she wouldn't. The money was just too good. She texted Stacy on a burner phone. Whitney needed to shut up. Forever.

Werewolf 101

Professor Onyx called Amaya to confirm her suspicions about the magic storm. The jackalope had an ear for gossip. "What do you know about the magic storm?"

"My bad. I accidentally started a turf war between witches," Amaya said. "But that's not the bad news."

"How in fuck isn't that the bad news?" When witches fought for territory, werewolves died in the crossfire.

"Delilah's been selling to the Witch Market."

"Sugar. Honey. Iced tea." Professor Onyx whispered, too horrified to manage real cussing.

A witch could do terrible things with a single strand of werewolf hair or a fragment of a tooth. But wholesale access to the only werewolf salon in Austin? This wasn't bad. This was catastrophic.

"How long?"

"At least since she opened the Salon. Maybe longer. Whitney knew but she's disappeared. I think she got got. Coyote showed up at the Salon and she was *pissed.*"

"Is this other witch in on it?"

"You're not listening to me. Black Belle is not the problem. Delilah is. If anything, the new witch is the solution but it's too soon to tell. Take the pups you've got and run. Lay low. Teach them Werewolf 101 while you still can."

Professor Onyx hung up, feeling ill. Delilah had encouraged her to grow out her afro to its current majesty. She stupid for trusting the beautician. Not all skinfolk were kinfolk.

~

THE DRAGONFLIES MOVED INTO A MASSIVE ECO-friendly and self-sustaining mansion inside a privately owned forest in Wimberley. Nobody noticed that werewolves had eaten a rich tech bro living off the grid. The maintenance staff hated the guy and were happy to accept a large paycheck to leave quietly.

The Dragonflies were proud of Professor Onyx, complimenting her foresight. She didn't care. She wasn't losing her pack to witches.

"We shall begin Werewolf 101," Professor Onyx proclaimed.

Today's class was held in a mixed use building. This particular room had cement walls and cement floors. There were bullet holes in the walls. There was a reinforced door and a reinforced window. The elder Dragonflies were on the other side of the window taking notes on the Youngbloods' performance. The Girl Scouts got to run in the woods.

Missy wished she were with the Girl Scouts instead of trapped in this miserable gray room that stank of sweat, urine, and anxiety.

Rainey played Youtube recordings of Maya Angelou, parsing through the AI fakes to find a real video. She connected it to the bluetooth speaker. "Okay, Youngbloods, listen up! Focus on the voice of Maya Angelou. You are stronger than you know!"

The werewolves groaned and squelched through the Turn. Getting the transformation right took practice.

The overhead fluorescent light glistened over breaking bones and viscera coated fur. Human teeth bounced off the dirty floor. Claws scrabbled on slick cement.

The other teachers walked among the struggling Youngbloods. They guided Turns with gentle encouragement to reduce panicked mistakes. Practice made perfect.

Rainey bellowed poetry. She had memorized 'Still I Rise' and 'I Know Why The Caged Bird Sings' because they were her favorites. She chanted them like a mantra.

Rainey had always imagined Maya Angelou as her grandmother. She had that special voice of the wise matriarch who loved you no matter what you did. Now, those poems anchored Rainey.

The pack had demanded that Rainey contribute so she passed along the same poems. Some of these Youngbloods didn't even know who Maya Angelou was! That was motivation enough. They were gonna learn today!

The Youngbloods shakily got to their four feet and shook themselves off. They howled in triumph at the moon. "Still I rise!"

~

"TODAY YOU'RE GOING TO LEARN HOW TO ROAR," Professor Onyx said. "Sometimes you can end a fight before it begins by showing dominance. This works better with wild animals, like bears and wolves. Sometimes it works with humans. Other times, you get shot. Rainey, front and center."

Rainey half-Turned, her jaw and stomach white, her muzzle and down her back a mottled gray and brown. Her tail brushed the ground. Her ears and snout were a mottled gunmetal brown.

Missy's stomach clenched. She still didn't enjoy watching other werewolves Turn. It looked so painful. The skin stretching until it ripped like an overfull water balloon, blood and viscera oozing out. A few Youngbloods looked away out of politeness and revulsion. Older Dragonflies had no problem with Turning or nudity. The Girl Scouts didn't either.

"The rest of you start half-Turning too," Professor Onyx said, lips pursed with impatience. "It's not a race but it will be. You need to look like a Hollywood werewolf every time."

The Youngbloods shifted away from each other to make space. Ten minutes of organic groans, whimpering, cracked bones and blood, they were in rough half-Turned shapes, their bodies lopsided. Some with legs that would not support their weight and leaned on oversized gorilla arms. Missy slipped past half-Turned into beast mode or human. She struggled to stay balanced.

Professor Onyx rubbed an eyebrow. "Rainey, are you ready?"

Rainey took a deep breath and roared so loud that it rattled the lights in their fixtures. The force of the roar rippled down her neck and shook her furred curves. Her tail puffed out. Her back fur stuck out. The pink ridged tunnel of her mouth was framed by bulging sharp teeth. In this closed practice room the roar came from every direction, including directly underfoot.

Missy yipped in terror, snapping into beast mode mid-leap. She was not the only one scrambling to get away, kicking and fighting to get through the door, which was locked.

"No no no! Come back!" Professor Onyx said. "Don't run. You have to roar back."

The other teachers herded the Youngbloods into a recalcitrant line. Rainey swaggered in place with smug satisfaction.

Professor Onyx paced in front. "You have to learn to run *to* the roar. Not to run like prey. Roar back and attack!" The last word was a deafening roar that made the Youngbloods cringe. "Fanta! Back in line!"

Fanta had peed herself and stood slightly behind the rest, ashamed. Missy scratched herself, relieved that she hadn't lost control of her bowels. She studied the air vents, wondering if she could feasibly climb up into the HVAC and escape this miserable room. Her feet and hands were clammy instead of her fur, sweating through her paws. She wished that she had ear plugs.

"Let's try it again," Professor Onyx said, "Everyone in line stay still. You have to get past your fear and control yourself. You have to think. Even when you're staring into the jaws of death you have to think instead of panic. Panic makes you forget about cars. Panic makes you stupid. Rainey, again!"

Rainey winked at the Youngbloods, inhaled and roared. Only half the line stampeded.

La Croix lunged straight for Rainey and got swatted across the room. Malört and Fanta jumped in. Professor Onyx blew a whistle, the shrill tone cutting through the mayhem. Missy slashed another Youngblood in the face when she lunged. La Croix bit her throat and got eviscerated. The violence pulled the teachers into a dog fight.

"Enough. Back to the line!" Professor Onyx barked but it took several teachers to pry the Youngbloods apart.

The third roar lacked much power. The Youngbloods were exhausted and Rainey was winded.

"Okay, okay! We're going to try this another way," Professor Onyx said, "Missy to the front."

Missy didn't move. The teachers turned her way.

"Missy, you're up," Professor Onyx repeated.

Missy grimaced, wiping her hands on her thighs. Her tail was tucked firmly between her legs. She was convinced that she would get eaten. She was in half-Turned mode. It didn't seem as difficult as roaring in public now.

"I want you to roar just like Rainey did," Professor Onyx said.

"Just roar? No crash out?"

"Think of a roar as shouting 'Fuck you!' as loud as you can," Rainey said. "Think of a time when you were hellfire mad. When someone did something to you and you wanted to end them. You're so pissed off that there's lightning in your veins. You could breathe fire and spit nails."

Missy stared at Rainey. So did the Youngbloods, surprise and understanding across their furred faces.

"Yeah, that's it. Don't make yourself small." Rainey nodded, encouraged by Missy straightening out of her cringe. "Imagine it's someone you hate the most and they're talking some shit. Who do you hate?"

"I don't hate anyone," Missy said.

But that wasn't true, was it? Breanna hated her. That's why she got Turned in the first place.

"Remember to breathe," Professor Onyx said.

Rainey pantomimed exaggerated breathing. Missy concentrated. She took a deep breath. Her head sunk to the level of her shoulders, her claws gently flexed, ready. She pawed the cement. The fur down her spine rose into spikes. Her tail fluffed.

She snarled, lips curled up away from her teeth. It was a good snarl, real and strong. It promised everything that Rainey had said and more. But not one person on the line did more than flick an ear.

Missy recoiled, snapping her mouth shut so hard that her teeth clicked. Self-consciousness and recriminating. The space between Missy and the walls, ceiling and the other monsters had expanded. Nothing but air to hide in. What was she doing? Making noise? She couldn't do something loud.

"A good try," Professor Onyx said politely. "Do you want to go again?"

Rainey was silent which made it worse. Marlört yawned. Missy hurried to the line. She wanted flee to the door, away from their appraising gazes. She kept her head down, grateful to be at the far end of the line. She focused on keeping her fur smooth, her tail loose instead of tucked, her ears forward.

"Fanta, you're up," Professor Onyx said.

Fanta shivered to attention and walked over to center.

"Now, try to breathe. Think about what Rainey said."

Missy cringed through the rest of the roars. She never ran. Her feet stayed glued to the line. Her head stayed low. She watched the others. She wished that there was a clock to tell how much time had passed.

"All right, good," Professor Onyx said. "I want you paired up. Rainey with Missy. Help her turn up the volume."

Rainey strode up to Missy, clamping a hand on her shoulder. "Hey, that was a good snarl."

"Yeah, right," Missy said hollowly, wishing that there were an odd number of Youngbloods so she could be unpopular and practice by herself.

Rainey was *loud.* Even her breathing, her movements, the jiggle of her breasts as she leaned too close, crowding Missy with a friendly determined smile of overbearing encouragement. "So you get quiet when you're mad. That's fine. It doesn't have to be loud. It has to be real. And yours, I felt right here." Rainey jabbed her thumb into her sternum. "You've got the fire. You're not about that flash. I respect that. Now you have to let that fire out."

Missy took a deep breath through her nose, counting to ten.

Rainey took a few dancing steps like a boxer in a ring. "Start moving. Planting isn't going to do you any favors."

Rainey roared. It was awful. Even more brutal up close because she committed her entire self to the roar. Spittle dappled Missy's cheeks. Rainey's bass bellow pounded through her ribs, electrified her body, made her hair stand on end. She could not out-roar Rainey. She was not scary. And that pissed her off.

Missy snarled, softly, lips raising off her teeth to expose her pink gums. Her muzzle wrinkled like a slept-in comforter. Her ears pressed against her head.

Rainey roared again. Missy snarled back. A cycle of menace, neither backing down.

Missy leaned into that sound even though Rainey's eyes were starting to lose their humanity. She needed to back off. To start cringing and deescalate. But the anger, that sizzling fury was still there. She was so damn tired of bullies and her own weakness. Rainey bulked up.

Professor Onyx blew the whistle from the other side of the room. That sound was like a starting gun.

Missy and Rainey launched at each other. Missy dodged the jaws, leaping and twisting up the fur. Rainey reared back, in agony as Missy jabbed her thumb claws into Rainey's eyes. Rainey caught Missy in one great paw and spiked her into the ground so hard that she blacked out.

The Lake of Calm

"FINISH EATING." RAINEY SAID. "FIELD TRIP!"

The Youngbloods groaned. It was dawn. Breakfast was too early but at least it was quiet. Missy wanted to go back to bed.

"Aw come on, Rainey, we sat down." Fanta said. It was safe to whine at Rainey. She didn't bite faces off.

Rainey walked over and patted Fanta on the back. "This is a nice thing. I promise."

The Youngbloods followed Rainey out into the quiet. The running itself was not the problem. Missy was continually surprise at her own enhanced athleticism.

She sunk into full beast-mode. The Turn no longer hurt. Werewolf 101 Turning practice actually worked. Turning was a muscle. The more she Turned, the easier it became.

The dirt under her feet was slick and a rock punched the arch of her foot. She grimaced and wobbled into a half-Turn. She slowed down to shed her sweaty clothes. The other wolves hobbled into their own Turns.

Rainey tilted her head back. She closed her eyes, her fur ruffled by the wind. She howled, a pure jubilant sound. The others half-Turned and joined in, their throats exposed to the sky as they howled.

Howls echoed down the hallway from inside the building as the Dragonflies answered Rainey. Some were sleepy and annoyed. Some in agreement. Some garnished with silencing snarls. The Girl Scouts joined in, higher pitched warbles.

The song faded.

Missy stared at Rainey. The Youngbloods panted with amazement, tongues lolling out, ears flickering in independent directions, and tails wagging.

"That's what a howl feels like?" Fanta said, eyes round. "No wonder wolves do it all the time."

Rainey rubbed against Fanta then all the Youngbloods, affectionately ruffling hair, nibbling necks, and hugging anyone within reach. "You're such good pups."

Missy's bushy tail wagged in pleasure. Other Youngbloods had their tongues out, panting and relaxed.

"Howls have a rich and complex nature," Rainey said. "The more you practice, the better you can communicate across great distances. Two wolves can sound like twenty."

Missy grinned like an idiot too. This was a pack. Her pack.

Rainey sprang into a long-legged lope. Missy eagerly scrambled after her, bumping and jostling the other Youngbloods as they hastily gave chase.

Rodents and small mammals scrambled up trees and further into burrows to avoid the sudden werewolf stampede.

They were deep into the forest now. The pack ran down a channel created by a fissure between two limestone cliffs. Two trees bowed to create a natural archway. Rainey and the faster Youngbloods sped straight down the center.

For the hell of it, Missy deviated, running to the other side of the trees, curious at another path. She climbed up the knobby geometric roots, claws digging at dirt and protruding rock. She nimbly scrambled her way along the cliff face. The Youngbloods were ahead, narrowing to get single file through the mouth of the fissure. Missy loped after them to catch up.

The pack stopped to take a break in a canyon. Missy snuffled around, digging at a fallen tree for some acorns underneath. She rubbed her back on the knobs of a pine tree. She wiggled into a new position to scratch another part of her back. It felt *great.* The knob she leaned against kneaded into another layer of muscle, fur, and fat.

Youngbloods howled. Missy joined in. Their voices echoed off the canyon. Rainey trotted on. They followed.

The cliff walls finally opened up into a large hilly landscape with a small lake. A few Youngbloods ran straight into the lake. They frolicked in shallow water and hunted for fish. Canadian geese, herons, and ducks flapped away from the water.

Other Youngbloods chased each other along the plain. Some had peeled off into the forest to hunt. Others pawed the shore, focused on their own conversations. The tree covered cliffs behind them blocked most of the wind which whistled hollowly through the fissure. The lake reflected the sunrise like a giant puddle of spilled paint on a brown shag carpet.

"Oooh, this is nice!" Fanta said.

"We call it the The Lake of Calm," Rainey said.

"That's a good name. I feel calmer already!" Missy rubbed against her, tail wagging. "Thanks Rainey." Rainey was the goddamn best teacher in the pack.

"You can come here whenever you need to, okay? I know Werewolf 101 is overwhelming. Don't ever feel like you're alone or nobody cares. Because we do. If you can't talk about it and need a change of scenery, let one of us know you've gone for a run to the Lake of Calm." Rainey focused on Missy. "Missy, I want you to show the Girl Scouts the lake."

Missy's grin faded slightly. "Oh, yeah, sure."

The Medicine Bag

Genna learned how to use the medicine bag by going to hospitals. The tent could disappear into the bag. That wasn't the problem. It was figuring out how to parse through the deluge of information that the medicine bag provided without rhyme or reason.

She wore maroon scrubs and a doctor's white coat with her stethoscope across her neck and her doctor's bag at her hip. She pulled her hair up into a high pony tail and enchanted prescription glasses to hide her power. She drove a silver Subaru Forester. She wore sensible scuffed sneakers.

Genna looked like a doctor. The costume fit like she had worn it on a thousand rounds. She had her Happy Meal list but first she needed to get a lay of Austin's hospitals, clinics, and hospice centers. She expanded the search to Sun City where a lot of retirees lived.

The medical staff needed to see her as a traveling doctor, working in and out of the facilities. She was efficient and forgettable and always on call.

It was hard to match the profiles in her Happy Meal list to the elderly women watching reruns of *Murder She Wrote* in wheelchairs in bland nursing homes.

Fifty years ago, these same women had burned crosses into the yards of frightened Black people. They helped with deportation and cutting education to poor neighborhoods. They protested at abortion clinics. They screamed hate and threw things at little kids trying to go to school. They used their White privilege to grind anyone under their high heel and crush them like the burnt end of a cigarette. And their husbands, fathers, sons, and bosses were encouraged to be the worst versions of themselves for the good of the community.

These women longed for the 1950s when everyone 'knew their place' and stayed in it. When segregation made sense. Time and illness had winnowed these women down into querulous old harpies. Their families had dumped them in these nursing homes like old shoes forgotten in the back of closets.

The staff hated the harpies, receiving the brunt of their nastiness while changing diapers and feeding them medicine. The harpies were never grateful. Always hateful as they pecked and sniped and screeched.

Genna did not need to sneak into their rooms. She walked down the hallways. She methodically worked down the list of names. She made sure that each death was unremarkable. Few families cared beyond the money that came with life insurance.

Troy was an ordained minister. He looked good but unremarkable as he handled the families. He adroitly ferried the bodies away in an old hearse. He owned a funeral home and crematorium. It was all above board. No one checked what the ashes were. Carbon was carbon.

It was a hard cynical way of looking at the world but Genna wanted justice, however belated, for the people these harpies had lynched by mobs that they started.

There was a name that kept cropping up. Stacy. The last name would change but many had the same first name or nickname. It was an odd coincidence.

Genna made a note of it and kept hunting. And while she was making the rounds, she found a patient that she recognized.

Lily wasn't old. Her face was wrapped in braces and bandages. Her jaw was wired shut. She was young but she was placed in the same long term care facility as the harpies.

"Poor thing," the nurse said, "Her man smashed her face in with a beer bottle. I guess his guilty ass drove her to the hospital when they got into an accident. He died. She hasn't woken up."

"I know her," Genna said.

The nurse gave her a world weary look and bustled away. Genna stayed. The medicine bag pulsed gently against her hip.

She touched Lily's hand then recoiled as magic reacted. She put on gloves and cautiously touched the dry skin again.

Lily's insides were ripped up and quietly bleeding. There was a thing inside of her body. It was a long muscled body like a worm. It had barbs along its contours that kept it in place.

The medicine bag supplied Genna with a syringe and small tincture. She injected it into Lily's IV.

Lily started to jerk and thrash with increasing ferocity. The heart monitors blared and beeped as she flopped.

The nurse rushed back in. "What did you do?"

Lily's throat thickened. The hinges of her jaw broke. The nurse recoiled, keening with high pitched terror as the spine covered worm crawled out of Lily's mouth.

The stench pumping out of Lily's mouth was like the bottom of a slaughterhouse drain. It was choking and pervasive. Genna's stomach roiled. She slapped her mask over her face.

Then heard gagging. The nurse was still in the room, vomiting into a trash can. Genna grabbed her, pushing her out the door and slamming it shut.

The worm stretched longer and longer. The spines flexed out and in, reacting to exposure in the air. The stench got worse.

The medicine bag supplied Genna with a bamboo blowdart and several poison-tipped darts with red feathers. She aimed.

Genna knew how to wait as the worm pulled the rest of itself long prehensile body free. If she grabbed it too soon then the spines would extend into Lily's body again, ripping it up as she hauled it out.

Droplets of viscous ooze pattered on Lily's cotton smock and the bed linens. The worm was sweating. It flopped then curled on Lily's chest, and between her thighs, resting. The slick skin flexed. A thin whistling wheeze from the lamprey mouth. The effort of exiting the body had exhausted the worm.

Genna put the blowdart to her lips and exhaled sharply. Three darts hit the parasite along its ridges. The parasite reared back, screeching and thrashing. Then flopped down. Its dark red skin changed to an oozing tar. Then it dissolved into a nasty stain on the sheets.

Lily's monitors began to beep a steadily healthier beat. The color returned to her skin. She opened her eyes, groaning as she rubbed her throat. She looked around, pawing at the oxygen mask in her nostrils. She spotted Genna by the door.

"Black Belle?" Lily whispered, swallowing hard.

"You were cursed." Genna carefully approached to the bed. She checked Lily's pulse and scent. She smelled right. "Can you tell me happened?"

Lily trembled, she grabbed Genna's hand. She pursed her dry lips. She coughed, unable to speak. Genna filled a cup of water with medicated water in a flask from the medicine bag.

"This water will taste like lemons and mint. It will heal your internal injuries. I'm looking for the one who made that curse."

"I'll try," Lily croaked.

Genna listened to Lily's story, giving her water to sip when she coughed. Lily was alive but weak. She fell asleep. Genna checked her vitals one last them. Then she opened the door to leave. The nurse was still there.

"I'd thought you'd run off," Genna said.

"I don't leave my patients behind." The nurse glared at Genna, sweaty but belligerent. Then past her to Lily. She bustled over, immediately checking the patient's vitals. Then checking them again. Occasionally shooting Genna a look. She lifted the stained sheet. "What was that thing?"

"A parasite. It's gone now."

The nurse shuddered. Then she shooed Genna to the door. "Thank you, doctor. I'll take it from here."

Genna gave her business card. "Call if you see anything."

"Believe me. I will." The nurse said with absolute sincerity.

~

GENNA TOLD TROY ABOUT THE PARASITES THAT NIGHT over dinner. "I've never seen anything like it but the medicine bag knew exactly what to do."

"That was a Slipskin. They're skin parasites. Your friend was banged up on the inside because she'd been worn by a Slipskin. Without their skin they look like a detached cat penis."

"I know. I remember when one crawled out of Lily's mouth. So tell me about Slipskins."

He hesitated then faced Genna. He couldn't lie to her. Never could. Never would. "They're are attracted to boo hag magic. They feed on the trace amounts left behind after a boo hag rides her victim. They don't have any strength besides jumping from one host to the other and eating them from the inside out."

"Do you think that it's the same boo hag that attacked you? Or do you think it's me?"

"I think it's that boo hag. Your medicine bag gave you those darts and that injection that completely negated its power. That only happens when they come from the same source."

Genna rocked back in her seat. "It might not be the boo hag. It might be the medicine bag."

"It's a powerful tool. But no. Slipskins feed on skin magic. Your friend was ridden by a boo hag."

The Club

THE NIGHTCLUB WAS CROWDED BUT DOMINQUE FELT her ass get grabbed. The fingers squeezed her rump like he was one-handing a basketball.

Dominque spun around and slapped the man hard across the mouth. The power of the strike coupled with her claws wrenched his jaw off. His bottom lip and cheek still hung to the torn edge. Blood splashed the guys around the him, their girls, and the bartender behind them.

That frozen moment of shock was just enough time for Dominque to dive into the crowd. The blaring dance music, densely packed bodies, and strobing neon lights hindered her progress. She yanked her bright neon green wig and cap off. Thank God she's braided her hair tight. Now she looked slutty but forgettable in her little black dress and knock-off gold Air Jordan sneakers. Just another woman hustling for the door.

She made it outside. The bouncers watched her hurry away without interest. She had parked several blocks down the street. She ran as fast as she could without creasing the toes of her sneakers. She reached her car and drove away. She checked the rearview mirror but no one seemed to be following as she merged onto the I-35 highway.

She drove for an hour. Her grip on the steering wheel loosened as she left Austin behind. She listened to 'It's Gonna Be Trouble (Finding Myself Interlude)' by Tall Black Guy. The Neo Soul beat calmed her down. She drove to San Antonio. She booked a random self-checkin airbnb while getting gas.

The airbnb was a little A-frame house in a quiet suburb. It was cheaply remodeled and unimaginative white. She showered off but there was little blood. She stared at herself in the mirror as she unbraided her hair into a loose puff. She looked human. Except her pupils reflected the light in flat disks and the human skin under her fingernails.

She washed her dress and brushed her wig while she sat wrapped in a towel. She cleaned her Jordans. Her hands shook.

She had forgotten that she was a werewolf. In that moment, the Rage eclipsed thought. She slapped that man like she'd slapped anyone who grabbed her ass.

She ordered Gorditas, enchiladas, and burritos from delivery from the nearest taqueria. She ate. She paced. She got on her knees and prayed that the man died instead of Turned. She cried.

There was a knock at the door. Dominque dressed quickly, even though her clothes were still damp. She expected the cops. Instead it was Stacy the boo hag. "I'm here!"

"How did you find me?" Dominque demanded.

"Don't worry, everything's been taken care of," Stacy said, walking past her into the rental. "You're welcome."

Before Dominque could demand how, a SUV parked in front of the rental. The man exited the SUV. So did his friends, their girls, and even the bartender. Dull eyed and obediently trooping into the rental.

Stacy inspected the empty food bags. "You ate everything."

"I didn't know that you were coming." Dominque hugged herself, unnerved by Stacy's sudden arrival and the listless way the people stood in the living room.

"You should be thanking me. I took care of everything."

"Yeah, thanks." Dominque stared at the man. His face was reconstructed. No damage. "Why did you grab the bartender?"

"He got splashed with blood. You made quite a mess in there." Stacy laughed as though it was a great joke.

Dominque shook her head. "You said that you'd cure me."

"I did cure you. No more howling at the moon. You can't Turn or infect anyone else. That's why I took your wolf skin. But you're still a werewolf. There's no cure for that."

"Do you have to kill them? What if they have kids?"

"This isn't a fairytale, Dominque. Wake up."

Dominque flinched. She wouldn't cry, no matter what.

Stacy clapped her hands briskly. "Now, get your things. We're going back to the club."

"Why?"

"Do you think I left anything to chance?" The witch waved at the airbnb. "I'll have to take care of this too. God, you're messy. You don't think. There were cameras."

Dominque stared at the corners of the room but didn't see anything. "Are you sure?"

"I didn't survive this long leaving anything to chance." Stacy strutted into Dominque's personal space. "You put all of these people in danger when you went to a human club. What did you think was going to happen? No, that's the problem, isn't it? You didn't think. You went because you wanted to feel good. To get jiggy with it." She mockingly started dancing badly, swinging her arms like a White girl. "You're not one of them. You're just too stupid to let that go."

Dominique looked at the meat puppets instead of Stacy. She obediently cleaned up. She didn't think that she had left a mess until Stacy extracted a thick clump of hair from the shower drain.

The witch ate that soap scummy hair, humming as she chewed. Dominque got a cramp in her stomach but stayed quiet.

She didn't need to fake being terrified when Stacy got into the passenger seat. The meat puppets got back into their SUV.

"Drive," Stacy commanded. The meat puppets' SUV drove

away from the rental. Dominque followed the taillights. Her palms were slick with sweat on the steering wheel.

How much power did it take to puppet another person driving in a different car at ninety miles an hour on a crowded highway at night? Did distance weakened the spell?

Stacy connected her phone to Dominique's car stereo. Taylor Swift's *Antihero* played. Dominque had been a Swiftie fan until now. She tried to keep directly behind the SUV as they merged onto I-35 and the speedometer passed 80 mph.

The SUV suddenly swerved and jumped four lanes. It drove directly into a cement wall in a construction zone. There were no water barrels. Just uncompromising cement.

"Drive," Stacy said as traffic reacted to the accident. "They're dead. I made sure it looks like they died on impact."

Dominque choked on a sob. The taillights blurred from the tears in her eyes. The car wobbled. Stacy smacked her shoulder.

"What? This is what you wanted!" Stacy shouted, too close and too loud. "Stop crying! You don't even know them! Who the fuck cares? I'm not the bad guy. They'd still be alive if you hadn't decided to forget what you are. You're not human. That's over. Done! So stop acting like I'm the bad guy! Now drive!"

Dominique hunched away from Stacy and kept driving.

They reached the club. Dominque parked in the VIP section. The bouncer opened the door. The music played. The dance lights painted the eerily still crowd. They were now meat puppets.

There was no blood but an empty hole in the crowd and the bar were the incident happened. Dominque wove through the crowd, trying not to touch anyone or look into their dull faces.

Antihero suddenly blared over the trap music. Stacy's eyes glowed as she smiled at the crowd. She stretched her hands out.

A door opened. In trooped the rest of Stacy's pack. Dominque tried to catch Jasmine and Tiana's eye but the beauticians ignored her, fury and fear in their faces.

Dominque bit the inside of her cheek with dread when she

saw some werewolves still wore pajamas. They had been asleep before Dominque dragged them into her mess.

From another door, the Ragers came in. Even in human form, these werewolves were raggedy dangerous men. Dominque stood protectively in front of her pack but the Ragers ignored her, focused on the humans in the club.

The boo hag stretched her arms out. "Dinner time!"

The spell clouted Dominque between the eyes. She was yanked into a Turn. Slobbering on herself, ripping her clothes off in her haste. Her toe claws shredded her sneakers. Her big teeth bulged from her gums. She pounced on the unresisting bouncer and dragged him inside.

The music kept playing. The feeding frenzy had werewolves attacking each other and the furniture, ripping and tearing. Foam and fabric slopped with blood. The lights reflected off of busy hunched furred backs and glistening corpses.

Stacy perched on a bar stool and drank a vodka. Her skins swelled and pulsed as she fed on the magic and carnage. She needed this.

The Human

THE HUMAN WAS AS PALE AS UNCOOKED BISCUIT dough. Missy watched the forest of brown hairs around his dusky pink nipples, the folds of skin stretching as he inhaled. The rolls of fat under his barrel shaped torso were decorated with hair, acne, freckles, and moles. There was rash on the back of his knee and bruises along his biceps and thighs. Melanoma decorated his early-patterned bald spot.

He was beautiful.

She inhaled his intoxicating scent. His fascinating lack of muscle, fur, and claw. His enticing body had a few tattoos on his biceps and belly. The rhythm of his heart danced through her body. Her stomach growled. She drooled on herself, panting.

The man pushed himself up to a wide-legged stand, puffing with defiant fury. "I'll fucking kill you!"

The Youngbloods pounced. Then recoiled, yelping and spitting. Blisters formed the moment their claws and teeth penetrated his skin, as if they had stuck their hands in acid. They rolled and scuttled away, clutching their mouths with scalded hands.

"Easy, girls, easy. Eat these. It's a bezoar." Rainey and other den mothers crouched down and hand fed each Youngblood a bezoar.

The bezoar was greasy and tasted like the compacted grass. Missy chewed gingerly while the inside of her mouth peeled away. Her lips swollen to rubber tubes. Her eyes swelled shut.

The man's body was broken from the impact of the whole Youngblood class landing on him claws and teeth first. He bled steadily from cuts and bites. He wheezed until Professor Onyx walked over and stomp his head into bone shard and mush. She peeled the plastic bootie off her boot. A few persistent pieces of hair and brain clung to the plastic.

"What the fuck is happening?" La Croix moaned.

"That man was protected with magical spells." Professor Onyx said. She pointed at the corpse's tattoos. "You see this symbol right here? This man was a dog catcher. He planned to sell to you pups to the Witch Market. Maybe they'd skin you or put you in a dog fight or a breed you in a puppy-mill until your vagina prolapsed."

"We've seen that," Fanta muttered to Missy. "That's where we would've been if she hadn't picked us up. We had to put a lot of dogs and werewolves down."

"You're kidding," Missy said.

La Croix and Malört nodded with Fanta, their eyes wide and haunted. "It's hell on earth."

"You remember," Professor Onyx said, standing over them. "We captured his crew. They were very chatty. We've had him on a steady diet of homegrown food. But still he's a bag of poison because he's marked with a witch's protection."

"Why did you make us eat?" Fanta said.

"What's a bezoar?" La Croix said.

"How do you not know what a bezoar is?" Malört said, "You get them in the guts of a deer or a cow."

"They're a rare magical cure-all," Rainey said, frowning at her wooden box. "It took us months to collect this many. Whenever you take down a deer or a cow, look through their guts to see if you can spot one."

Professor Onyx shooed the Youngbloods into a corner. "Now,

let's try it again. You won't get a bezoar this time. Get close to the corpse but be careful. Missy! You're up."

Missy crouched by the body. She put her forearm firmly in her mouth. She knelt down closer, the Turn flexing her skin. The bulge of her pants grew into a compressed tail. She stayed kneeling, sniffing the body. A wet snap. She groaned agony. She had bitten through her own forearm bones.

"Hurting yourself won't win the game either." Rainey took a black bandana out of her pocket and fashioned a sling. Missy minced to the back of the class, holding her arm.

Fanta licked the corpse, recoiled, clutching her throat while her tongue eroded. Rainey made her swish with water. "Even a lick will get you."

La Croix screamed as her fingers melted like candlewax. None of the Youngbloods fared better.

WHEN THE TEACHERS WERE SATISFIED, THEY LED THE girls to a large natural hot spring. They brought in baskets of food, clean University of Texas basketball shorts and t-shirts, and bathing toiletries. Professor Onyx and Rainey sprinkled baskets of herbs into the hot water.

"This will heal your bodies but the curses that you ingested will turn into rocks." Professor Onyx said, "They'll squirm out of your skin or you'll pass them like a kidney stone. Drink lots of water."

"Can't wait," Malört said.

Rainey waggled the toiletry kit. "They're easy to get out. Help each other by plucking the rocks free with tweezers."

The Youngbloods bathed, no longer self-conscious of their nudity. The smooth black stones, the buckets of cold water, and the little stools to squat on at the bathing stations were like a Japanese bathhouse.

Missy's arm was still wrapped in Rainey's bandana. Gingerly

she wrestled one handed with knots. The fissures of pain had her sweating. Breathing hurt. She was accustomed to rapid healing. This constant pain was frightening.

Fanta sat on a neighboring stool. "Your arm's still broken?"

"I've broken my arm before," La Croix said, sitting on the other side of Fanta. "It sucks."

"Maybe it's different if you injure yourself?" Missy said.

Fanta coaxed Missy into letting her inspect the damage. "Damn, you really bit your arm in half!"

"I hope I didn't so permanent damage." Missy pushed a curl clinging to her forehead out of her eye and flinched at the pain.

"It's too soon to panic. Here, I'll help." Fanta washed Missy. The suds got everywhere. Missy held her arm elevated. She didn't enjoy Fanta's fingers sliding between the folds of back fat and under her breasts. It felt like an inspection. Especially on her butt and belly. Fanta's breath changed with fascination, arousal sending those hands down to her thighs.

Missy slid away from Fanta without meeting her gaze. "Thanks. I'm good."

"Hey, come back. I'm not done washing you," Fanta frowned, hands out, reaching for Missy's breasts. "Aren't you a lesbian?"""

"No thank you!" Missy said, forcefully. Enough to echo against the stone. The other Youngbloods stopped washing. Missy hurried into the hot water. She washed herself again, hunching down to cover as much of her chest as she could with her hands. Fanta's touch made her feel gross.

"Jeez, weirdo," Fanta said, an angry blush covering her from neck to nipple. "I'm trying to help."

"Sorry," Missy mumbled, not sorry and not getting out of the water either. "I'm freaked out about that guy."

"Hey, I get that," La Croix said while Fanta glared at Missy. "He smelled so good. I don't remember what he looked like. I *had* to eat him."

"I know it's stupid but I thought that they were lying." Malört said. "There isn't a cure for this, is there?"

The Youngbloods finished cleaning themselves and climbed into the hot spring. No one talked. Just stared at the suds and the potpourri scenting the water. The loss of their illusions aged them, deepening the lines around mouths. A few washed their faces to hide their tears.

Missy poked at her forearm again, the swollen purple hematoma made ugly flowers on her brown skin. Lightning agony arced through her body with every slight movement and the fluctuation of the water. But she was healing impossibly fast. No human could achieve such a thing.

"How the hell are we supposed to hunt humans?" Fanta demanded. "I lost my mind just standing in the same room."

"I think that's the point of the stress test," La Croix said, "Only the best get to hunt. They can go out, keep their shape, hunt, kill, and bring humans back to the den without getting caught. Everyone else stays home and cooks or does other stuff because they can't be around humans."

"Is anyone else freaked out that witches are real and curses can kill us?" Fanta demanded. She had tweezers out to pick small stones from her skin. "I'm kinda grateful that the teachers know what to do. It keeps me from crashing out."

"I think we need Jesus," Malört said virtuously.

"I think you're full of shit," La Croix muttered.

"Fuck you, bitch! Rot in hell!"

"You first, bitch!"

Missy sunk under the water to tune out the bickering.

Stress Tests

Professor Onyx brought a scary authenticity to the stress tests. She used the same draconian tactics that police used on protestors.

She walked around the classroom with her super-soaker water gun on her shoulder cocked like it was an AK-47. The teachers wore hazmat suits and rubber gas masks hanging loose around their necks.

The Youngbloods and Girl Scouts were herded into a new room by the teachers. The stench of anxiety was stifling. A few rippled in and out of Turns. Many shed fur across the floor.

Today's class was in another cement box of a room. Missy had once volunteered at an animal shelter that had a working gas chamber. She had quit because she couldn't save the sweet pets from euthanasia. The cement walls had the same vents and smell.

Missy wondered what the guy who owned this mansion used to do in here. Maybe he wasn't a victim. Maybe he was a really bad guy. Maybe the Dragonflies had done the world a favor.

"The stress tests are practical lessons in pain." Professional Onyx nodded at an unfamiliar wolf. "Simone, if you would?"

Simone stepped forward. She was a willowy brown woman with close cropped hair and a scar across her face that warped her lips into a permanents sneer. "This is your smell test. We are expanding the limits of your endurance. As a reminder, this will hurt but you won't die."

"Do we have to stay in human shape?" Malört said.

"Yes, that's the goal," Simone said. "We have highly developed senses of smell. Humans don't. You have to stay in human shape and pretend that you don't smell anything."

Simone yanked her hazmat hood over her head, pulled the cords tight, then put on her mask. Then she lifted a small ceramic pot out of a box. The other teachers quickly zipped their hazmat suits and helped her set up.

The Youngbloods backed away. Missy's palms and armpits were sweaty. A teacher pulled levers at a panel on the wall. The whole room shuddered.

Simone lit the clay pot in the center of the room and ignited the wick by breathing on it. Then hurried out, pushing the fleeing teachers though the door before slamming it shut.

The floor slid open and raised up, revealing panels. The Youngbloods fell a short distance and landed on different poisonous-to-werewolves plants. Green lichen that burned Missy's bare feet. There was wolfsbane, mistletoe, citrus, and other scents. Some had purple or yellow blossoms. Pollen puffs rose around their feet. The clay pot stayed on a little immovable plinth.

The stench came on slowly, growing bigger and bigger. Missy pressed her face into her hands. She swallowed another cough. She tried meditative breathing. She pawed at her nose, scratching swollen eyes. Blisters formed on her tongue. The itch made her shake. Her throat tickled. She fought the urge to cough. Fanta was purple-faced and dry-heaving, hanging onto Malört. La Croix was on her hands and knees vomiting.

The Girl Scouts and the other Youngbloods were on the ground. They screamed and coughed. Green snot oozed from their noses. Their eyes bloodshot from crying. Their tongues were covered in purplish-white ooze.

A new horrible burning steam began to fill the room through

tiny vents in the ceiling. It mixed with the smoke. There was no suppressing the cough now. She sneezed and coughed so hard that her back muscles strained.

"What the hell is this a gas chamber?" La Croix shrieked before doubling over to wretch. "Are we going to die?"

Missy lost control and Turned. She shed fur. She gnawed at her ankles, her thighs, and her paws. Chewing and chewing. Her lungs writhed.

The plumes of evil purple and green smoke increased. Missy was doused. She scuttled back, wheezing and choking. She dug at the wolfsbane even as it burned her skin.

She lost track of time. She had to endure. After so much time relying upon her sense of smell, she felt blind.

Mace could stop a charging werewolf. No chance of attacking when you couldn't breathe.

THE SOUND TEST WAS WORSE THAN THE SMELL TEST.

The screeches, groans, squawks, and scrapes were a cacophonous symphony. The teachers hauled on janky fraying ropes attached to winches and a network of dried bamboo, metal, and more rope, rusted metal and groaning pipes. The whole structure shrieked with every quarter turn. The squeak was as loud as a scream, tortured metal fought the rope. The incredible, straining, kinetic energy as they twisted one squealing winch and a resisting pulley got worse. The twanging groans of brutalized metal, the whine of compressed wood threatening to splinter, and the strain of twine pulled to its limit. The structure shuddered, threatening to collapse under the strain.

Missy squeezed her ears. Her sinuses were still inflamed from the smell test. The sonic agony affected her whole body.

The Youngbloods huddled in the center of the room, surrounded by noise. Several had reached that point of the Turn where skin and muscle bubbled and twisted. They crouched low, ears back, screaming at the noise. Missy pressed against the other Youngbloods. Everyone was in too much pain for trivial personal animosity.

A tap on the shoulder woke Missy up. Rainey wore head-phones usually found at an airport operator. Missy had to read her lips when she said, "How are you doing?"

Missy raised a shaky thumbs up then Simone plugged in a circular saw and started cutting wood at the far end of the room. The nearest newbies scrambled away. More squealing metal made worse when she started cutting through planks of wood. The smell of sawdust added to the smells.

Professor Onyx switched on an industrial vacuum cleaner sucking up the sawdust. Then a row of blenders with metal ball bearings inside them. Missy finally understood why the dogs hated the vacuum and blender.

A FIREHOSE HIT MISSY IN THE SIDE, SWEEPING HER OFF her feet. She rolled across the room with the other Youngbloods. They hit the wall and were plastered by high pressured water. She couldn't breathe. Her skin was on fire from the barrage. La Croix slipped and was pressed into a fetal ball by the firehose.

"This is crazy!" La Croix shrieked. "Stop it! Stop it! Stop it!"

Missy tried to protect her head. Through the onslaught of water she saw Professor Onyx. She had to endure.

PROFESSOR ONYX RAN AFTER MISSY, POUNCED ON HER, and wrapped her up in a strange neon yellow and black contrap-tion that stuffed her legs into a sling, forced her hands on her lap, and clamped her head in a round helmet.

Missy couldn't breathe, or speak, or see. Her shoulder was

fractured from the force of being bound. She could not move or lift her head. She writhed, having a full-blown panic attack.

Professor Onyx quickly unwrapped Missy from the full body restraint. There were marks on Missy's chest, hips, and torso for the straps. "How do you feel?"

"F-fuck you." Missy hugged herself.

"This is called the Wrap. It's a full body restraint device. I found it in a pig's truck." Professor Onyx always called cops 'pigs' which confused Missy sometimes. "The pigs call it 'the Burrito' since they use it on immigrants. They don't care if people suffocate and die on the deportation flight." Professor Onyx talked as she bundled the Wrap into its black canvas bag. She walked off to show La Croix her new toy.

Missy huddled on the ground, panting and shaking. Her shoulder healed. She rubbed painful circulation back into her fingers and toes. Experiencing a modern police restraint was an awful reality. Professor Onyx knew how to make a lesson stick.

GENNA SPOTTED PEDRO THE FROG IN THE CROWD ON 6th Street, chatting up women in a rumpled suit. Pedro wasn't his real name. He looked like a frog with his bulging eyes and gross shiny lips that he licked whenever he talked to a potential victim. He rubbed his hands, trying to act and Black. He wasn't. Pedro was just another White asshole trying to score a girl half his age.

She used a tiny electronic pulse to unlock his BMW. She hid in the backseat of his surgically clean car. Then locked it again from the inside.

She listened to the rain patter against the car as she waited for the Happy Meal to bring his next victim. Some guys didn't stop until somebody stopped them.

IT WAS A DARK WET NIGHT. THE STREETS REFLECTED the orange lamplight and the neon glow from restaurants and bars crowding 6th Street. There wasn't nothing easy about 6th Street or the surrounding traffic of downtown Austin.

Pedro the Frog chuckled to himself as he wove through the congested traffic of gentrified East Austin, and into a new housing development. Miss Piggy sat in the passenger seat, playing with the curls of her blond wig.

Miss Piggy thought that frogs and serial killers were sexy. Pedro told her what he planned to do and she thought he was joking. Okay, he could be Kermit until she knew he wasn't. That got her into his BMW and miles away from help before the mask slipped. Then she whimpered, cringing against her side of the BMW. Fumbling with lock. He grabbed her shoulder, squeezing that arm fat and finding muscle.

She spun and punched him in the eye, fake nails breaking as they clawed. That stung. His fist knocked her head against the window with a dull thunk. Her blonde hair was a sexy mess clinging to her eyelashes. Her perfume was sugar-coated daffodils.

"Don't make me kill you in my car," Pedro said, showing the gun in his hand.

Oooh, he wanted to kill her but anticipation made his dick hard. She cried softly as he drove into the underground parking lot of the high rise apartment building. The place was so new that the cement was still pristine. Several floors were empty, waiting for plumbing and occupants.

Miss Piggy did not move. She hunched. Her sparkly sequin dress was too tight to move. Her bad posture annoyed him.

"Stand up straight!" he barked.

She jerked up, shoulders down, back straight, chin up, boobs ready to escape her low neckline. She had told him all about her years as a fashion icon and a runway model. The first Black woman to achieve blah blah blah. He stopped listening.

Her feet kept sliding in and out of her heels during dinner. Her knees hurt, slowing every lift off a chair. That's how he knew that she would be slow.

She had lied about her age. As if he couldn't see the sag of her jawline. Her makeup was flawless. She looked just like the Miss Piggy muppet. It was hilarious.

Pedro was repulsed by his own attraction to Miss Piggy's

thickness. She reminded him of those dancing hippos in *Fantasia*. And he was the crocodile ready to devour her whole.

A flicker of movement in the rear view mirror. The guitar wire slid over his head and yanked against his throat. He jerked, fighting to move. His fingers clawed at the metal string digging into the soft skin of his neck. His own pocket had been picked to get the garrote. He grunted, heaved himself forward, his long tongue lolling out and slapping his face. But the enemy was strong, twisting the wire together, winding it tighter and tighter.

He punched the car horn. Miss Piggy caught his hand. She wrapped it around her safety belt. She whimpered and sobbed as she searched his jacket. Miss Piggy got the gun and the knife. His knife. The one he had in a secret holster inside of his jacket. She stabbed him, not well. The knife's point caught in the fabric and skittered on his chest.

She helped his killer. He stared at her with hate-filled eyes. This fat bitch had set him up?

Blood seeped from broken skin. His tongue flapped. He clawed at his seat and behind him.

"Stab him again," the other assailant commanded. A woman's voice. A *Black* woman!

He redoubled his efforts but his vision was striated. His wrists were bound, jerking in the safety belt. He swatted Miss Piggy with both fists. She dropped the knife and fell back to her side of the car with a yelp.

A curved knife, no, a claw sunk into his Adams apple and ripped it out. Blood splattered the inside of the windshield and across the dashboard. His strength drained with the blood pouring down his front. The wire bit deeper, slicing through his esophagus, his arteries, and then catching on bone.

Miss Piggy fumbled the knife, lifted it with both hands and slammed it into his stomach. Then yanked it out. She stabbed him again and again. He was dead but she kept stabbing.

"This is ridiculous," the masked woman muttered, shaking

her head as she pulled the wire off the corpse. "Have you never killed anyone before?"

"Fuck you!" Miss Piggy wiped blood out of her eyes and hair. She pointing the knife at the woman in the black hoodie and black mask. "How long were you back there?"

"I'm not after you. I was waiting for him." Another beleaguered sigh. "You're lucky that I was here. He would've butchered you like a pig. Are you going to report it?"

"I didn't see nothing."

"Then get the fuck out of the car."

"But how will I get home? If I call an Uber then there's a record that I was here."

"You talk too much, Miss Piggy."

Miss Piggy tried to hide her flinch. She fumbled the door, knife wobbling in hand. She got out but her purse spilled its guts across the parking lot floor. She hastily scooped it all up. The knife was snatched away by a black gloved hand.

The car door slammed, catching strands of her weave. Miss Piggy fell on her ass, her heels falling off. The woman was covered in a hoodie, baseball cap, cloth mask, black bandana, and sunglasses. Her oversized jacket was stolen straight off of Pedro's back. She didn't seem to care about the bloodstains.

Missy Piggy stared up at her as she walked past, heading for the elevator. She glanced back at the car. "He's still in there?"

"What do you think?" The woman pressed a key fob against a panel. The doors slid open with smooth elegance. Missy Piggy hurried in and stayed in the back. She watched the woman's profile, rubbing her arms.

She should be running. But where? There was nothing but construction in both directions. She hadn't paid attention to where she was going. She bent towards the woman's strong presence. She followed her through the parking lot and up the stairs.

They walked together down a luxurious hallway to an elegant white door. The key fob opened the electronic lock. Missy Piggy was herded through the elegant but menacing foyer into the living room. The galley kitchen looked unused except for a fancy espresso maker and a blender on the granite counter.

The bedroom bed was a huge altar to sex. Wrought iron posts with hooks were riveted into the ceiling to cage the mattress. Miss Piggy didn't even like sex with women but the fear had her pussy pulsing with need. She was sweaty, and shaky, and okay, if the woman had even hinted at the bed, she'd be on it, legs spread wide open. This was the kind of bed for some serious kinky shit and that knife still had Pedro's blood on it.

The woman began to search the walls and bookshelves. She was so relaxed. She found several rolled stacks of cash in a drawer filled with designer watches. She glanced at Miss Piggy, tossed one her way. She pocketed the rest.

The woman lowered her mask enough to show her nose. She sniffed and sniffed. Then stopped at a random part of the wall. She pushed it and found a hidden seam. She used a second key fob. There was another quiet beep. A mechanized pocket door slid open and into the wall, revealing a hidden hallway.

This hallway was austerely lit. Utilitarian. But it smelled bad. Like really bad.

Missy Piggy's skin prickled. She didn't want to leave the bedroom. She didn't want to go down the hallway.

The hallway dragged at her attention. The smell reminded her of her uncle's fridge. A power outage had left the fridge full of meat in a hot garage for two weeks. Her uncle opened the fridge up on Juneteenth and the smell of rotting, thawing meat had slapped her nose like a fist. The cookout turned into an abrupt party at the overcrowded municipal pool, far away from the stench that permeated the whole house.

That was the smell in the hallway.

She gagged but couldn't run away now. She was already here. She flinched at her own reflection. She paused in horror, hastily fixing her smeared makeup and frizzed weave. She pulled her dress down her thighs and tried to cover more breast.

This apartment was just like her fantasies of dangerous men.

Cold and impersonal. Everything crisply vacuumed and cleaned but clinical instead of inviting. The sexy bed. Even the hallway.

Miss Piggy went into the hallway. She kept walking, terrified but she had to keep going, had to see, even when her instincts screamed at her to run, run, as fast as she could home.

But what was home? Just a postage stamp size studio apartment with a black mold stain on the low ceiling. Microwave Mac and Cheese on paper plates with red drink, a sleeve of Oreos, and a big stack of unpaid bills. She couldn't afford her life. That's why she wanted to escape it for a night. To play with danger. To be sexy instead of a total failure. She wasn't anything like the Miss Piggy muppet who was stylish, confident, and sexy. She was just a big boned and pathetic hot mess.

Miss Piggy was also angry. Under that fear was a toxic rage. Why did Pedro the frog have to be such a creep? Why couldn't he be like Prince Naveen or Kermit? Why couldn't this be pretend not real? What had she done to deserve this? Was she just a little too desperate? A little too needy? A little too fixated on a *Princess and the Frog* fairytale to save her from her problems? Did that mean she needed to get butchered?

Her hands sweated as she stood in front of the door. The heavy door deserved to be the front entrance of a castle not here in a fetid hidden hallway in an upscale skyrise.

The doorknob was ominous and out of place. She could smell the wrought iron. She wiped her palms on her hips.

The door was locked. She stared at it, confused.

"You forgot the key," the woman said, directly behind her.

Miss Piggy squealed like a pig. She clapped her hand over her mouth, staggering away from the woman who had followed her like a shadow. She watched the door get unlocked with a skeleton key. She could hear the metal grating against the tumbler. Her heartbeat was fast in her ears.

Miss Piggy gripped the woman's wrist, stopping her from turning that big scary key in the big scary door. "Don't."

The woman looked at her. "We've come this far."

"Don't. Please?"

"There's women like you behind that door. I have to save them." Confirming that she was a vigilante street justice warrior.

"Look, I'm grateful and all but if they're in there then you can't help them anyway." Miss Piggy added strength to her grip even more sure that this was not the way. Not everyone could be Catwoman. And the foul stench could only mean dead bodies at odds with the pristine interior of the apartment. She didn't think Pedro could control himself enough not to murder on the first date. This place was where he cleaned up the mess he made.

There was a growl, low and deep from the other side of the door at head height. The scratching of claws against wood, impatient like a big dog demanding to be let outside.

"Let me out."

The woman pressed her hand against the door. "Hello in there. What's your name?"

"I'm sick of your games, asshole. You don't fool me."

"Pedro the Frog is dead. We killed him. We're here to get you out."

"Who's we?"

"It's me and Miss Piggy."

Nicknames were never ideal. And she was dressed like Miss Piggy. But a nickname meant that she was included in the club. Whatever this awful club actually was. A bunch of vigilante women saving each other from terrible men? She'd join in a heartbeat.

"What's your name?"

"Call me Black Belle." The woman said with only a slight hesitation. The way she smirked at the name made Miss Piggy wonder. Black Belle was as beautiful as she was scary, and she was very very scary.

"I'm Whitney," the voice said, "Whitney the tooth fairy."

"We're going to get you out of here, Whitney."

"I'm hungry, Belle."

"I know, but I've got him downstairs in the car. The others are on their way."

"I'm hungry!" There was a hard impact that made Black Belle and Miss Piggy press against the opposite wall.

"Let me out!" The roar couldn't come from a human throat. The door shuddered but was reinforced so there was only noise. No creaks of stressed metal or whine of cracking wood.

Miss Piggy ran. She got down the hallway, through the bedroom, tripped on the living room's carpet, skinned her knee, and kept running. She needed to live. She had to live!

She hit the door, fumbled it open, then ran to the stairs instead of the elevator, not trusting it. Her frantic heart felt ready to leap right out of her chest. She kept running, a hand pressed on her boobs to keep them from popping out of her dress. Her high heels clacked on the cement stairwell.

She reached the first floor, ran across the cold lobby to the sliding door. She didn't have a car. Her shoes were not made for running but it didn't matter. She clattered down the driveway and onto the dark road.

Then she saw dogs. No, not dogs. Werewolves! Their eyes reflecting the parking lot light. Their limbs too humanoid to be regular dogs.

Missy Piggy kept running. At this point, she'd believe anything.

The werewolves tracking her barked and howled excitedly. But Miss Piggy was fast and determined. She ran. She juked. She dodged bites and claws. She didn't let them back her into the trees or a shoal.

The werewolves got frustrated. They attacked. They missed. She jumped off the edge of an embankment, slipping and sliding down the soft earth. She rolled to the bottom of the slope, picked herself up, and kept on running through the construction site.

The pack hesitated on the soft edge of the slope. "Enough. Let her go!" Rainey barked. "Come back."

"Aw man! We can catch her," Fanta said.

"I almost had her," Malört complained.

"No, you did not," Rainey said.

"I can't believe that fat-ass out ran us," La Croix growled peevishly. "In heels!"

"But now you know that hunting a human isn't easy." Simone said, "You need to work together as a pack."

"I sure as shit wouldn't hunt with you," Velma said.

Missy was over by the BMW, sniffing the blood. She tried to open the locked car. She squinted at the bloody corpse through the heavily tinted windows. She spotted Genna helping a scrawny dirty woman out of the elevator. Genna gestured at her urgently to get away.

Missy backed up. Trotting over to Rainey and the petulant Youngbloods. The BMW's trunk quietly opened and closed again. The car started to sway.

The pack watched a werewolf ripping up the corpse inside.

"Hey, I know her," Rainey said, "That's Whitney the tooth fairy. She used to work at the Salon."

Simone came over. "Holy shit, you're right. That's Whitney. What's she doing here?"

"She looks bad," Velma said, "Real bad."

Rainey was on the phone with Professor Onyx. The Youngbloods crowded around the BMW, fascinated and hungry.

"Save some for us!" Malört shouted, banging on the window.

"Shut the fuck up," Velma shoved her away from the BMW. "That tooth fairy will eat your bones."

"That's a tooth fairy?" La Croix exclaimed.

"Yeah, the real kind are all glitter and wings," Velma said, "So don't fuck with her."

Missy looked around. She spotted Genna as a dark shadow loping after Miss Piggy's disappearing figure. She caught up but didn't pounce. Instead she guided her through the mounds of gravel and half-made buildings.

"Get the pups out of here," Rainey said, still on the phone. "I'll take care of Whitney."

Velma and Simone nodded. Velma barked. "Okay, hunt is over. Back in the van!"

Whining and complaining, the Youngbloods obediently trooped back to the vans waiting down the road. Simone and Velma drove. Missy was crammed in the back seat in the corner. She turned around, straining to watch the building as the vans trundled down the lonely winding road. "Is Rainey going to be okay back there by herself?"

"Professor Onyx is on her way with the others," Velma said at the wheel.

"Shouldn't we wait?"

"Rainey's better off on her own. You pathetic losers are a liability. You couldn't catch a fat girl who literally looked like Miss Piggy. I knew this was your first hunt as a pack but this is fucking embarrassing."

"Miss Piggy was running from something," Missy said. "She smelled really scared and weird. Like blood and bad stuff."

"That doesn't matter. You had one job. You failed. So you're going home with no supper. Losers."

Fanta nudged Missy. "Why do you care about some random human?"

Missy shrugged. "I thought we'd be hunting bad guys not scared girls."

"Meat is meat, Youngblood." Velma said, "Stop humanizing the human."

Strait-Legged Bacon

THE STRAIT-LEGGED BACON BARBECUE JOINT WAS packed. Humans and werewolves sat elbow to elbow, focused on their heaping metal trays of expertly prepared meat.

Genna savored the beef rib stretched across her tray like a dinosaur bone. She also had juicy brisket, pork ends, jalapeño sausage links, and for sides there was tater casserole, Brussel sprouts sautéed in a sweet serrano pepper sauce, and pinto beans. She had banana pudding for dessert. She washed it down with a Pacifico Beer. Troy feasted on his own tray.

Strait-Legged Bacon, the owner of this fine establishment, was a Hawg with four nicotine-stained tusks. He wore a beaten straw hat, a suit jacket, and a big apron on top. A little cigarette hung from the corner of his lip.

"How ya'll doing?" He rumbled as he set another beer down.

"Everything is delicious," Genna said, and meant it. "I came to tell you about your niece, Miss Piggy."

He put his hand on her shoulder. "She got away. She's home now. Safe and sound. She had a tale to tell. I bet you're hungry, Black Belle."

Genna stared up into his dark knowing eyes. "Always."

"I'll fix you another plate. You like the beef ribs?"

"They're the best I've ever had."

He pulled out a small beaten black notebook from the inside of his suit jacket. "Werewolf Wednesday is coming up. I've got mouths to feed. And they won't ask questions about who's on the plate."

"What is Werewolf Wednesday?"

"Folks like us gather for fellowship. You don't need to be part of a pack. Just come and eat. It's good for the community. You'd be welcome. Both of you."

Troy nodded. He hadn't asked but it was good to get that question answered. "It's next Wednesday?"

"It used to be every full moon but then Folx started showing up every Wednesday. Ya'll think you can catch a few for the grill?"

Genna and Troy raised their beers, making a promise.

"Let me get you that tray." He bustled away.

Troy stroked Genna's wrist. "I saw the way his nostrils flared. You still smell like the Happy Meal."

Genna sucked on a filament of meat stuck between her teeth, mortified. "I'll take care of it."

She pulled out a a beautiful round cobalt blue perfume bottle out of her purse. The bottle was a genuine René Lalique. She dabbed the perfume on her wrists, behind her ears, and a few other places. The scent had ambergris, rosemary, frankincense, lavender, and other things not so easily defined.

Troy inhaled sharply, overwhelmed. He drank his beer. He noticed other werewolves sniffing and looking around. But their eyes passed over her like she had just become invisible.

"Better?" Genna asked.

Troy nodded. His pants felt tight. "The glamour is in the perfume."

"It's my own special blend." She grinned at him, proud of herself. "There's a bunch of cookbooks in the tent and the bag. I already had the perfume but this elevates it to a whole new level."

"A good hunter makes their own weapons." They touched beer bottles, saluting each other.

"Werewolf Wednesday sounds like a place to meet our kind of people."

"We should've asked how to get in. There's probably a secret door or something."

"Or maybe finding it proves that we're supposed to be there. Like we found the Church."

Troy drank his beer thoughtfully. "We'll need to get him meat for the grill by Monday or Tuesday so it's got time to cook."

"How many do you think we need to make a good impression?"

"As many as can we get by Monday or Tuesday." Genna told him the Happy Meal list. "I want to learn more about the medicine bag. Be careful out there. Come back to me."

"You too."

Troy was eager to prove himself that he wasn't ill anymore. He had his own list, evil guys in the monster hunting community who needed to be taken out. The hunt worked better filtered through Genna's cipher.

Troy was an exceptionally gifted monster hunter but Genna's skill at tracking a target down and seamlessly taking them out was masterful. He knew that she was exhausted but listening to her cry at the Church galvanized him to up his game. He wanted to prove to her that she could rely upon him to bring home the bacon.

Tooth Fairy

GENNA WANDERED AROUND THE MEDICAL TENT. THE library was full but the empty counters above the medicine table waited. For what, she didn't know. The tent was alive and communicating but she didn't understand what it said. Just like the medicine bag.

She had no idea what she was doing.

She took a dab of perfume and put it behind her ears, her wrists, and the nape of her neck. Then she set the beautiful blue bottle on a shelf. The perfume bottle looked lonely on the carved wooden shelves but it was the only real potion she had.

There was a buzz, it rattled the inside of Genna's ears. She turned around.

Whitney the tooth fairy looked like Whitney Houston. She wore the same sparkling golden dress from the *Cinderella* movie with Brandy. Same curly brown hair. She had immaculate teeth in her mouth, strung into necklaces, and in mason jars. She set them onto the counter. "How many teeth do you want?"

"I don't want teeth," Genna said carefully. "I'd like to start a dental practice next to the clinic. You know, flossing and teeth cleaning."

"I don't have that kind of time," Whitney said. Her dragonfly wings fluttered, displaying her annoyance. It made the stored teeth dance in their containers. "I'm not a dentist. I collect children's teeth. That's it."

"What about dental floss?" Genna showed her a store brand packet. "This floss for humans doesn't work with werewolf teeth."

"I'm not interested. I'm busy enough as it is." Whitney waved her magic wand with a sequined star at the end. "What are you going to do with this tent?"

"I want to help werewolves. Lycanthropic surgery. You know, pull bullets out and stuff."

"You saved my life. I can see that you won't misuse the teeth, unlike *some* people." Again the teeth danced in their jars.

"I don't know bone magic." Genna said, deciding that honesty was the best policy. "I don't know how to use teeth, much less misuse them."

Whitney flew into Genna's personal space. "You saved my life, Genna Bellwether. That miserable toad tortured me. He ripped my wings off. He starved me. I had to live on the bones of his victims. I couldn't get out. I tried, believe me." She fluttered higher. "I can never repay that. All I have is teeth. Take them."

Genna nodded. "Are you expecting payment for these teeth?"

Whitney's hands were dry and calloused as she grabbed Genna's face, smushing the cheeks. "Do you know what I was? What I did? How I became the tooth fairy? I will tell you."

Magic shimmered. Genna saw a long hallway. Barrels full of teeth lined the side of the dank room. Screams echoed from the people bound to chairs.

"They took our teeth to make dentures. It was my job to sift through the teeth for the best ones." Whitney's smile was ghastly. "I took children's teeth but there's a price. The bones. They knew."

Genna squirmed, feeling an odd vibration in her core. She could not break Whitney's hold on her face. "Can you let go please?"

"How did you find me?" Whitney demanded. "How do you know what I am? Are you a boo hag? Tell me!"

"I was taught skin magic by Miss Bootsie the boo hag but I'm not a boo hag." Genna said, trying to relieve the pressure of her teeth rattling in her gums. "I learned blood magic from vampires but I'm not a vampire."

"That's not an answer."

"Pedro was on my Happy Meal list. I was hunting him when I found you. I smelled something on him. I smelled you."

Whitney released her vice grip on Genna's jaw, she flitted around the top of the tent in wild figure-eights. Her spastic movements reflected inner turmoil. "You can't explain it, can you? The reason why you must hunt and find us? That is the price of your power, huntress. Why are you in this tent?"

"I want to heal. I want to do more than hunt Happy Meals."

"But you're not a healer. You're Black Belle, the killer of killers."

Genna took a deep breath and exhaled slowly. "I want to heal."

Whitney hovered above her, wings flapping so fast that they were invisible humming air. "Leave these jars on their own shelf. I will fill them."

"Okay." Genna said, her tongue tracing over her teeth to make sure that they were still there.

"You will pay me in Sacagawea and Harriet Tubman coins."

Genna blinked, surprised. She owned a mint that printed these coins. "I can do that."

She reached into her pocket and held out a coin. She always kept one for luck. Whitney took the coin and put it into a leather bag. She hefted the bag. Coins clanked inside. "Pleasure doing business with you."

Whitney stashed the purse and buzzed out of the tent.

Genna walked stiffly over to a cot and sat down. Her jaw ached. She opened her mouth wide, letting her fangs extend. Her tongue again explored each tooth. Magic hummed like a hive of bees lived in the marrow of her bones. Genna picked up a tooth and suddenly she knew what to do with it. Carefully she set the tooth back in the jar and closed the lid.

Jars of teeth filled the empty shelves. There were little labels of ages and descriptions on the jar. Human teeth, werewolf, vampire, witch, and animal. The tent had tried to warn her that the tooth fairy was coming.

Silver Test

THE PANTRY WAS EMPTY. HALF THE CABINET DOORS were broken wood clinging on bent hinges. Missy stared at the splatter on the ceiling. It could have been ketchup. It was not. There was a handprint in the center of it. A few den mothers poked the overturned Tupperware containers and stew pots for anything leftover but every container had been licked clean. One lobster pot had a bite through the edge.

Professor Onyx took a hair pick out of her afro and started fluffing her afro. Missy was at the back of the crowd but that small movement had her ready to flee.

The pack's collective fury stung the nose.

There was a tendril of guilt wafting off the Youngbloods. There had been a midnight binge party and she wasn't invited. As if Missy needed more evidence of her lack in popularity.

"Who did this?" Professor Onyx asked.

Missy had been asleep. She was innocent but this was not the time to speak up.

"It's me. I'm bulimic," Fanta squeaked, backed into the walk-in fridge by the line of scowling werewolves. "I didn't mean to. It's not my fault."

Fanta's stomach was bloated. Grease and flecks of various

foodstuffs were in her hair and down the front of her ripped hoodie. Her tattered clothes hung off her body now that she had returned to human form. But everyone was covered in masticated food except Missy.

"The binge eating and vomiting can be mistaken for an eating disorder created as post-traumatic stress." Rainey said, calmly. Nearly robotic. "You were supposed to be honest with us."

Professor Onyx continued to fluff her afro.

Simone came in from the smokehouse. Her focus was on the inventory Mead notebook in her hand. The Youngbloods parted out of her way, backing to the edge of the kitchen.

"Damage report?" Professor Onyx said.

"Six month's worth of food for the whole pack. It wasn't just the meat. Veggies, fruit, bread, you name it. She chewed up the cans of beans. I'm estimating a year's worth of inventory was consumed."

"So everything we'd saved up is gone or just unusable?"

"Gone gone." Simone tapped the notebook with the heel of her pen. "The mansion's trashed too. We'll have to move locations or do a complete renovation because it's all fucked. The meat smokers are trash. Pantry shelves are kindling. The fridges are toast. The walls are ripped out. There's live wires. I turned off the power. We're running on the batteries right now."

"Thank you, Simone." Professor Onyx stopped fluffing her hair. "Velma, get Brittany."

The Dragonflies stopped scowling and glanced at their leader. Mean little grins grew across every lip.

"Yes, boss," Velma said, with sadistic delight. She practically skipped out of the kitchen.

Missy closed her eyes and prayed.

BRITTANY WAS SHOCKINGLY THIN. HER PALE SKIN HAD an awful bluish tinge. She wore a black synthetic wig too far back on her hairline, revealing a wispy peach fuzz. She wore skinny black jeans and a loose black Boris Karloff Frankenstein t-shirt which emphasized her boney shoulders and hips. Her black lipstick, black eyeliner, and thick fake eyelashes added to the cadaverous hollows in her face. Her eyebrows were too thick for her narrow face, two black caterpillars clinging to the milky cliff edge above her jaundice yellow eyes.

She stood behind a table of ominously understated cedar boxes. Each box was beautifully handcrafted with dovetailed sides. The box was too big to carry a deck of cards.

"This is Brittany," Professor Onyx said. "Brittany has the highest silver tolerance in the pack. She's our expert poison eater. She creates the medicines and antidotes that we need to survive."

"Thank you, Professor Onyx," Brittany said as Professor Onyx retreated to the far side of the table. "Let's talk about silver."

She opened the three boxes with a flourish. A set of silver marbles sat in with crushed blue velvet inside. Another in yellow velvet. The third in red.

"First, I'll show you what pure silver does to us." Brittany picked up a silver marble from the red section, opened her mouth, stuck out her long red tongue, and placed the marble on the curved tip of the tongue.

A hole fizzled in her tongue around the marble. Her tongue turned from red to pink to neurotic purple then black. She caught the marble as it fell through her shriveled tongue before it hit the table. Brittany grinned, lifted the slimed marble while she waggled her ragged black tongue at the squealing Youngbloods and Girl Scouts. She bit the end of her tongue off and spat it out. Her tongue grew back, bright pink. She waggled it at the class.

"The silver marbles have three different colors. Each color represents a different amount of purity." Brittany gently lifted the blue layer out and set it down. Then a yellow layer. Then a red. "Red is pure silver."

"And we're supposed to eat them?" Missy said.

"And shit them out," Brittany added, in case it wasn't obvious. "Then clean them up and put them back in the box."

Missy stared at the boxes, grossed out.

"But why?" La Croix whispered.

"This is not a lab. This is real life." Velma said. "What we know is what we have experienced. We have an antidote for silver, a healing pattern, and cleansing rituals that purge silver from our bodies without long term effects or scarring."

"Spontaneous combustion is not on silver's list of reactions," Brittany added.

Missy exchanged a frightened glance with Fanta. "So what does make you explode?"

"Curses," Professor Onyx said, "Eating a grenade. But mostly magic."

Malört raised her hand. "Is silver poisonous because it is holy and we're damned?"

The rest of the class shifted restlessly while the teachers glared at Malört.

Professor Onyx strutted over to the werewolf and slapped her in the forehead. "The power of Christ compels you!"

Malört fell over, screaming and trying to get the large silver ankh burning the skin between her eyebrows. Professor Onyx kicked Malört's feet out from under her and pinned her to the ground. With a free hand she flipped open her butterfly knife and used it to pry the cross out. She dropped it onto her gloved hand and stood up. She kicked Malört in the solar plexus. The wailing turned into gags. "Get the fuck up. And act right."

Professor Onyx returned to the table and set the silver cross down. She nodded at Brittany. "Sorry for the interruption."

"No problem," Brittany tapped a cadaverous purple veined finger and an even longer nail tapped on the boxes. Her grotesque brown smile had too many long sharp teeth in purple gums. Her eyes were like runny eggs. "Any more questions?"

Malört stood between La Croix and Fanta. She desperately

combed her bangs to hide the blistered ankh print on her forehead. Missy sucked on her lips to keep from laughing.

THE SILVER TEST WAS A DIABOLICALLY SIMPLE AND effective. Missy never wanted to experience anything like this again. Ever.

Each Youngblood and Girl Scout swallowed one marble after the other. No teacher cared about age or who was sorry. Everyone punished.

If they weren't willingly ingested then the teachers strapped them down and force fed them. A gloved hand over their mouths so the marble could not immediately be spat out.

She sagged against the wall, her stomach and throat raw, while other girls shoved to get to the sink taps of the bathroom. Her head clanged and seethed with a migrant. She expected her skull to crack open and spill brains like an overheated popcorn bag spitting hot kernels. Several Girl Scouts threw up in the corners of the room, not able to hold it in until the Youngbloods finished vomiting into the toilet.

Missy's hands shook, the tendons slow to heal after the silver burned a hole through the palms.

Brittany lectured them while they shivered and threw up.

Silver deteriorated the body like acidic snake venom. Necrosis in the immediate area while the rest of the body puffed in an anaphylactic reaction. The lips corroded, blistered skin inside and out of the mouth, throat closed, the tongue puffed, as did the eyelids and nostrils.

The weaker marbles had a slower and more pervasive impact. The body broke out in grotesque pustules, clustering under the armpits, back of the knees, inside of the thighs.

The skin split, leaving fissures of oozing meat and dry skin. Her abdomen cramped. Her skin had come off the one time she tried to swab away the rectal bleeding and vaginal discharge. Her joints ached, fingers and toes twisted like arthritis. Her teeth fell out of her bleeding gums. That had been a bad moment, when she swallowed a canine.

Missy yanked a paper towel from the dispenser and wiped her mouth. She stared at her awful reflection. Her lips were blistered, the inside of her mouth stripped and scalded. She glanced at the others but her eyes focused on a slumped body limply clutching a toilet, her legs twisted awkwardly under her. Missy pushed off the wall and staggered over to push the half closed stall door open.

Some of Fanta's brown hair hung in the toilet, pooled on the surface with red chunks of chewed flesh. Her lips inflamed, rubbery. Eyes disappeared in the pockets of her swollen face. The bottom half of her face had eroded and the gooey remains of her eyes ran down the side of her nose.

Missy shook Fanta, so scared she could barely breathe. "Fanta, hey, Fanta?"

"Leave me to die." A small wheezing groan flooded her with weakness.

Missy staggered back to her empty patch of wall. She flopped back against the wall, exhausted, weeping with relief. Her eyes burned. She dabbed her face. Her tears were mixed with blood.

She absently rubbed her thighs. Beneath the loose sweatpants clusters of sebaceous cysts covered her inner thigh. Each grape sized pustule was a silvery-purple so dark it was a greenish black, striations of blue spider-veins and inflamed magenta skin. She tried ignoring the cysts at first, but they would burst instead of recede, then grow back. Again and again. By the ache in her left leg, another had burst.

She reached under the elastic band, past the soft interior lining of her pant leg. The stink of blood tacky with pus. Missy rubbed her fingers, holding it up to inspect the discharge. She gagged.

The smell was faintly like parmesan cheese. The pus was a yellowy-white no longer greenish-brown of rotten avocados. But the free flowing blood was a healthy bright red instead of the noxious dark red it had been all week. She wiped her fingers clean on toilet paper.

The silver was slowly filtering out but not fast enough.

Missy was exhausted. Sleep was not possible when there was no place to lay comfortably. Of course they had to sleep in the communal room too.

The smells and whispers of disgust adding to the humiliation. They had to defecate in a bucket and sift for silver marbles with bare hands. Wipe them clean then boil the damn things in a pot and put them back in their velvet lined box.

There was a dimple for each marble so Brittany knew exactly how many were left.

The last few had come out all at once the third night. The absolute worst was when her pelvic girdle dissolved while she screamed at a decibel never before reached.

Professor Onyx and the rest of the pack stood over the groaning Youngbloods and Girls Scouts. They were unmoved by apologies and pleas.

She walked across the bathroom. Her boot pressed Fanta's head into the toilet.

The others watched Fanta struggled and choke. Her hands hit the toilet bowl and scrabbled at Professor's motorcycle boot. She lifted her foot once Fanta stopped moving. Then she kicked the half-drowned Youngblood off the toilet and stomped on her solar plexus.

Fanta woke up and spewed vomit water across herself, getting some in her eyes. Professor Onyx stepped back.

"You don't steal from your pack. You don't eat more than your share. Do you understand?"

A few whimpered. Velma barked, "Your pack leader asked you a goddamn question! Are you going to steal from your pack again? Or do we need to feed you more silver?"

"No," the Youngbloods and Girl Scouts whimpered.

"I can't hear you!"

"No!"

Brittany grabbed Fanta's head by a fistful of hair, strands clinging to the slime down her mouth. "This lying ass bitch will do it again. I just know it."

"No, no, please!" Fanta whimpered. "I won't. I swear. Please! You've got to believe me!"

Brittany yanked Fanta to a stand, forcing her to stagger around and face Professor Onyx. "Permission to teach her a private lesson? La Croix and Malört too."

"What!" Malört shrieked but La Croix couldn't pretend.

"How'd you know it was us?"

"We could smell it," Professor Onyx said, "Velma. Simone."

"You can't do this!" Malört snarled.

"I can do anything I goddamn want."

Velma and Simone grabbed the other two offenders and frog-marched them back into the horrible little room.

Missy pressed her throbbing forehead into the wall.

THE SO-CALLED ANTIDOTE WAS WATER. LOTS AND LOTS of water. Drinking buckets of it and pissing it out.

Missy's stomach was so fragile that in the beginning, water felt like it was laced with acid. But eventually, it started to be just water and the tedium of yet another bathroom trip.

She chose to stay out in the woods, guzzling water from the Lake of Calm. The Girl Scouts went with her but many Young-bloods wanted to stay holed up in their rooms, recovering.

Missy and the Girl Scouts ran and hunted. They foraged for cures, using actual Girl Scout handbooks and old folklore learned from their grandmothers. The forest was a treasure trove of resources but using them correctly was all guesswork. Missy was willing to try anything to feel better.

Their recovery was quicker because they let themselves run wild.

"Why did we get in trouble too?" A Girl Scout demanded. "I didn't do nothing!"

"Neither did I," Missy said, "That's why we got off light."

"No we didn't!"

"Why do you think they haven't come out of their rooms? They're still taking the silver test."

The Girl Scouts stared at Missy with horrified rounded eyes. They wanted hugs for reassurance and vowed that their innocence.

"I know. I know," Missy petting their fur. "You're all such good girls."

Rainey watched them from the ridge. She didn't join in. Missy was relieved.

Slipskins

Genna and Troy found the Slipskins' lair in an office building an hour outside of Austin. The building was an unmemorable sky rise.

They walked around to the service entrance, following the signs for the HVAC room. He picked the locks to get to the basement. He put his hand on the humming metal body of the intake units. He concentrated, letting his magic drift through the pipes like dust, floating on the faint breeze of recirculating air. Genna checked the entrances, hallways, and the basement while he pushed his magic through the building.

"There's a hunter trick for killing a Slipskin infestation," Troy said, "I'm counting at least a hundred full grown parasites. I can kill them all but there won't be any left for questioning."

Genna sucked on her teeth for a moment. Troy waited. She nodded. "Do it."

Troy's brown eyes turned phosphorus blue and flashed with lightning. The Slipskins jerked as though electrified, their bodies bubbling from the inside, then exploded. The emptied skins collapsed like piles of dirty laundry. Then evaporated into smears.

"Thorough," Genna said, impressed.

"You have to be with infestations this large. They're too good at blending in with humans."

She waited for Troy to climb the stairs. Neither wanted to go in alone.

They entered the main office. The entire floor was open. The ceiling had canned LED lights. The shelves in the middle divided the space into quadrants. There were vases of fake flowers attempting to make the space less claustrophobic and depressing. The vision boards covered every wall, like a belt around the middle of the room above the desks. There was a chemistry set. A portable centrifuge. A bathroom with a shower stall.

She took the medicine bag off, set it down in the center of the room, and opened it up. "Stand back."

Troy retreated.

The whole room shimmered like a car reflecting sunlight as it passed an opened window. The whole room emptied. Except for Genna and Troy, and the money that they found in a strongbox in the floor.

"Let's get out of here," Genna said, closing the medicine bag. "I want to take a bath. This whole place is gross."

"Yeah," Troy said. He bagged the money, jewels, and passports.

They exited the building, got into the Bronco, and dove off. The recovered treasure was sealed in an enchanted box.

"So what do you think about the hunt?" Troy said, needing to talk about anything.

Genna stopped frowning at the highway. She held the medical journal that the bag gave her. She petted the embossed cover with her thumb. "The medicine bag made an inventory. It's mostly just inventory records of hair, nails, and teeth. There are warehouses full of them. Mostly human and werewolf. The cookbooks are full of hair and skin care recipes. From what I've seen, the Slip-skins don't need any of that. They don't even need money. So why is it easier to get the jewels and cash than the cookbooks? Why keep them at all?"

"Maybe they're like security dogs protecting inventory? Is there an address for a warehouse?"

She flipped through the journal and typed an address into her smartphone. "This is part of the equation. I don't know how."

"A hunt is like that," Troy said philosophically. "Sometimes you don't know what's important and what's not. You gather what you can and keep moving forward."

"I'm glad I could help Lily."

"Where did you know Lily from? Sweetwater?"

"It's weird that she's in Austin."

"If the boo hag is riding people in Sweetwater then she knows who you are too. Do you think that it's Katie?"

"It's not."

Troy waited for Genna to say more about the vampire princess. After a long silence he tried again, "Are one of those cosmetics factories nearby? We should check it out."

Genna typed in a new address in the Waze app on their burner phone.

The warehouse was a makeup and hair product factory. Nothing magical. Just humans handling the processing and packaging. Genna hesitated then she caught the scent of Slipskins. She sorted through the administrative office while Troy killed the parasites. They both hoped to find regular humans but everyone was marked by contagious magical infections, parasites, and boo hag magic.

The files in the administrative office led them to a private hospital deeper into the Texas scrub brush. They found the real inventory in a town called Sweetwater, Texas.

Werewolves were strapped to gurneys with so many IVs attached to them that they looked tangled in spiderwebs. Some were missing arms and legs. Others had the soft fur of a freshly regrown leg.

Hundreds of fetal Slipskins filled their bellies in a large embryonic sacks. They writhed and squirmed. Finally they chewed up their birth sacks and slowly ate the werewolf host.

There were sickly humans too. They checked themselves in, believing this was a regular hospital. Then became carriers for a single Slipskin.

Genna and Troy killed the Slipskins and burned down the buildings.

The drive back to Austin was quiet. They took a break at the Czech Stop, eating freshly baked kolaches and pastries off the I-35 highway in West, Texas. Occasionally an idea would rise to the surface of conversation.

"I've got an approximate start date when the Slipskin infestation hit the factory." Genna said, "The beauty product plant was one of those old nasty places that never stopped animal testing. Tons of code violations. They had a long stand-off with PETA. They dumped toxins in the water and the air. You name it, they did it. The record keeping used to be real unorganized when it was run by humans."

"And then everything changed like magic?" Troy snapped his fingers.

"No, the Pandemic happened." Genna showed him her tablet but he waved it away, preferring to hear her translate the raw data. "I think that the boo hag used Lockdown's the shelter-in-place quarantine to infiltrate the company's employee population and the local hospitals. Nobody noticed."

"I bet they did notice and got got. Slipskins are carrion eaters like vultures. They're the clean up crew not meat puppets."

"This might be completely unrelated to the boo hag we're hunting. It could be someone else."

"We keep hunting."

Genna nodded, eating a cinnamon roll. She was exhausted by the sheer volume of Slipskins. The antidote that worked on Lily had killed everyone else.

If the boo hag was behind this, then she had a much wider reach than anticipated.

Weapons Class

Professor Onyx read 'Beloved' by Toni Morrison in one hand and spun a matte black butterfly knife in the other. She waited for the students to shuffle in before closing her book and her knife.

On the vinyl record player the long acoustic intro of 'Papa Was a Rolling Stone' by the Temptations played.

Class was in an old gun range. There were bullet holes peppering the back wall and slots in the ceiling.

"Now for the weapons portion of your training," Professor Onyx said. "First will start with knives and guns. Then we'll move on to explosives like claymore mines, flash-bangs, pipe bombs, and flame-throwers. You need to get used to them now before someone throws a grenade into your car."

"Excuse me?" Several of the Youngbloods squealed. "You're throwing grenades at us?"

"It will hurt like hell but you'll still heal."

"What if we lose a limb?" Missy said.

"It'll grow back."

"You're seriously going to blow us up?" Malört said. "Like for real?"

"You'll heal."

"From grenades?" La Croix exclaimed. "The blast radius alone will kill us! How is that even possible?"

"You're werewolves. You're extremely hard to kill. You'll heal from most wounds but telling you isn't the same as experiencing it."

"Hard pass," Fanta muttered.

Professor Onyx flipped her knife. "You haven't plumbed the depths of what werewolves can do. That's the point of Werewolf 101."

"So you're going to stab, shoot, and blow us up as some weird-ass training exercise for our own good?" La Croix said. "That's insane!"

Professor Onyx pointed at the wall with a long red manicured thumbnail. "Do you think anybody out there gives a shit about you? We're werewolves. You've gotta be tougher, meaner, and nastier or the males will chew you up."

Missy grimaced, thinking about the alpha male who had expected her to roll over. She glared at the tables. "I don't want to do this. How are we supposed to simulate being shot in a real world setting?"

"Would you rather get shot by the pigs for being Black and nearby?" Professor Onyx said, strutting over to the opposite side of the table. "That's how Brother McGruffin trains his Young-bloods. He uses them as bait to hunt trigger-happy cops."

"Um, no thank you." Rumor had it that Professor Onyx had a boyfriend, an old hard-ass like herself but the Dragonflies were strictly female only.

Missy licked her lips nervously and whispered to Rainey, "Brother McGruffin really trains his pack on the streets?"

"Hell, it works too." Rainey scoffed. "All you have to do is walk up to a raw recruit and say, 'Want to be werewolf?' And that's all it would takes."

"Because they're people of color?" La Croix said.

"And poor?" Malört said.

Professor Onyx, Missy, and Rainey exchanged looks while the

other teachers began lecturing about social impact of today's economy, the intersection between racism and poverty, and other 'helpful' factoids that failed to call the Youngbloods out on their racism.

Missy was glad that Professor Onyx and Rainey were there. Even if their lips were tight with anger. Not arguing. Giving the rest of the pack enough rope to hang themselves.

"Okay, pair up," Professor Onyx said, "Missy. You're with me."

Missy stared at Professor Onyx. The whistle blew. The other girls lunged. Missy hesitated. Professor Onyx stabbed her in the chest so hard that she was lifted off her feet, gagging on the pain.

The curve of Professor Onyx's fist. The strange feeling of her heart attempting to beat with metal in it. Her lungs full of blood. Missy Turned, snarling, snapping, clawing. Bloody spittle frothing over her teeth. Professor Onyx stabbed her in the mouth through the back of the head. Sharp agony.

Missy woke up when she hit the ground. The elder wolf's expression had not changed once. She wiped Missy's blood from the two long knives with the crook of her arm. She challenged Missy with raised eyebrows.

Missy scrabbled on the ground. She swayed upright. Just in time to get shoulder-checked. Missy landed hard, rolled, sliding in a trail of her own blood. She pushed herself up again.

Fanta was on the ground, a strangulated huffing. Her neck had been broken, her head facing too far to the left. Missy stared down at the bone pressing against the skin. Rainey had broken Fanta's back.

"All right kiddies, go pick up your weapons!" Velma shouted, holding a metal whistle like a gym teacher. "That's why we teach weapons. Most of you still think you're human."

The girls reluctantly limped past the teachers, their wounds healing, wiping blood off their mouths. Missy shivered. She wanted to run.

"Hurry up," Professor Onyx barked. "When are you going

to stop reacting like humans? A knife in the gut is an appetizer. Stop freezing. Keep fighting. How do you think you can hunt?"

"Maybe I'll just eat old people who died in their own houses or suicide jumpers," La Croix muttered. "I've done it before."

Missy was revolted. La Croix wasn't the only one who ate the dead.

Professor Onyx blew the whistle. Everyone lunged. Missy tried to dodge. She got stabbed in the side.

"God, it hurts," she gasped, coughing up blood.

Professor Onyx sliced her up. "Yes, it does."

Missy hoped that the sharp pain of knives would reach a strange kind of monotony. It didn't.

To her amazement she was able to dodge and bite. Professor Onyx was easier to deal with than other teachers whose scent made her skin crawl. That didn't stop the teachers from beating her like a sandbag and slicing her up like gyro meat.

By sunset the Youngbloods were exhausted by the pain. They lay together in wolf form. A few whimpered quietly. Others were cutting themselves.

Missy stared at the orange and pink clouds and thought about her apartment. Those quiet mornings of drinking coffee and eating cinnamon rolls from a bakery. She wondered how the apartment was doing. She had forgotten to keep track of what day it was.

Her rent. Oh, God, rent! Her job. How in fuck was she going to pay her bills? Why had she ever left?

That further depressed Missy. Nobody noticed as long as the bills got paid. She wept quietly until she fell asleep.

MISSY'S SKIN WAS SORE FROM HEALING. WEAPONS injuries healed differently. Internal bleeding had to be managed. Missy spent the evening in the supply closet, eating from her stashed snacks and licking her wounds. She woke up in a pile of shrapnel.

She found some frozen alaskan king crab in the back of a freezer in the mansion's cavernous garage. She made croissant bread. Then jumbo crab grilled cheese sandwiches with crab bisque from scratch. She had learned this recipe from an online video. Then cooked it often enough that she didn't need a recipe. It was comfort food.

She started with sautéing the veggies. Then sprinkled in the spice, salt, pepper, and paprika. Then added the crab with the shell on with seafood stock.

La Croix, Fanta, and Malört came into the kitchen while she stirred.

"How can you cook?" Fanta muttered. "I'm still shitting bullets."

"I'm hungry," Missy said. "I'm sick of eating humans."

La Croix sniffed and sneezed. "Is that gumbo?"

"No," Missy said.

"Is there enough for us?" Malört said.

"No. Fuck off," Missy said.

The three glared. Missy ignored them, waiting for the fight. But she wasn't sharing. Period.

"Bitch," Fanta muttered as they slunk away.

Missy focused on cooking. Once the bisque was done, she combined heavy cream, the cooked crab meat, shallots, chives, salt, pepper, shredded cheddar and mozzarella cheese. She spread it onto the croissant bread. She added more crab meat. Then toasted it until it was golden brown.

She ate the entire pot of bisque and the whole loaf's worth of grilled crab meat sandwiches. She didn't even sit down. Just stood at the counter and ate.

A few Youngbloods and Girl Scouts came in and then left. Even Professor Onyx and Rainey checked on her. Missy didn't care. She wasn't sharing. There were five other kitchens in the mansion. They could make their own food.

Then she cleaned the kitchen and made several sourdough loaves, leaving them in the fridge to rise. Baking made her feel better.

~

As bad as the knives were, the visceral pain of a gunshot was unrivaled.

It was the next day. Weapons class had moved outside. It was the middle of the day, absurdly bright. High Noon. The same tables full of weapons were neatly set on the dry grass in the shade of a forest.

The Youngbloods faced off against the scarred up Dragonflies. The pack elders who had seen it all and done it all. Just like Professor Onyx. Dolly was Missy's least favorite of the new teachers.

"Now, some of you have racial based reactions to guns," Dolly began.

"What makes you think that?" Missy said loudly.

"Because you're Black." Dolly gave her a look.

"And your mamma breast fed you meth, you white-trash snag-gletoothed bitch." Missy snarled. "Fuck you and your ratty blonde wig. I hope you die slowly in a dumpster fire and I get to watch, you wet-brained flea bitten cunt!"

"What did you say?" Dolly snarled, stepping forward with a growl.

"You heard me!"

The teachers stepped forward but Professor Onyx guffawed loudly. "She got you pegged, Dolly. Let's stop with the racial discrimination. No one likes having guns pointed at them. Plain and simple."

Dolly bared her nicotine gray teeth. The rest of the Youngbloods glanced Missy's way. She raised her chin defiantly.

"Are you okay?" Fanta said.

"I'm fucking tired of getting shot," Missy snarled. "This is bullshit."

"Ain't that the truth," Malört said.

"I know that's right," La Croix said.

"It's playtime kiddies!" Dolly bellowed, cocking a shotgun loudly.

Most of the Youngbloods fled but Missy didn't feel like running. La Croix, Fanta, and Malört stayed. They stood together half-Turned as the Dragonflies leveled guns of different caliber like gun fighters at a quick draw. Missy shivered as she stared into the black eyes of handguns and rifles could not be suppressed.

"You'll heal. You'll heal. You'll heal." Missy whispered to herself. "Just keep breathing."

Then a painful force slammed into her shoulder, knocking her off her feet so fast she spun around as she fell over. She gasped for breath, choking on blood.

She lay in the dirt. The shotgun shell wormed through her body. Her nose was overwhelmed with the stench of blood, pine and mud. Panting she rolled face down in the pine needles and dirt, a rock grinding into her cheek, trying to stand, trying to shift the blood out of his lungs. Her breath bubbling as she tried to cough. She needed to make a tourniquet. The other Youngbloods were on the ground too.

Missy dug her fingernails into the dirt. The blazing need to live, the fury of pain, the fear as sneakers crunched through the forest fused together. There was a swagger in their step, triumphant. She healed in a burst of speed. The other Youngbloods also staggered to a stand. Only to get shot down again.

Bright pain flowered in Missy's shoulder as her arm and ribs regrew, her lungs healing so she could cough up the blood and shrapnel. She stayed on the ground, her skin itching as shrapnel wormed out of her pores and plunked on the ground.

"Get up!" Dolly kicked her in the belly with toe claws, gutting her so she flew across the field like a misshapen football. Her intestines unspooled behind her like wet streamers. Missy hit a tree branch, an intestine caught on a limb, and she hung like a piñata.

Dolly laughed as Missy struggled to free herself. Her body regrowing intestines which further tangled her on the branch. The teachers took turns taking potshots while she wailed. The branch snapped. Missy fell onto the hard roots and rocks. Dolly shot her again then walked off.

Missy lay in the dirt, waiting to die. Instead, her body healed, her intestines regrew while the old mangled ones shriveled up and fell off. She clawed her way up into a stand, using the tree trunk for balance.

She got back up. She got shot again.

Guns and knives. Knives and guns. Nothing stopped the seemingly endless bullets. The Dragonflies replaced each other whenever someone needed to reload. If they weren't shooting the Youngbloods then they were knifing them.

The knife and handgun combos were difficult too. The Youngbloods slowly learned. They stopped flinching or freezing at the sound of gunfire and started fighting back. Some succeeded for minutes at a time.

Finally, Professor Onyx blew a whistle three times. Class was over. Time to eat.

The mud was churned into a slick slurry of blood, trodden grass, and bullets shells. Missy flopped on her back, gasping. "Fuck this shit. Fuck this fucking shit. I really hate those bitches."

Rainey came over, crouching down to pick a bullet shell stuck in Missy's scalp. "It'll get better."

"No, it won't." Missy curled away from her, hugging her knees. "Leave me alone. I hate getting shot."

"Everybody hates getting shot."

"No, I mean, I'm scared of it. My cousin was shot. She was in her house making a grilled cheese. A fight next door got ugly. A bullet went through the window and caught her in the ribs. She bled out before anyone found her."

"Aw Missy, I'm so sorry," Rainey sighed as she sat down in the grass. "You should've said something."

Missy flexed her shoulders. "I haven't thought about Aunt May-May in a long time. I remember thinking it was a joke when they said she was stuck to the floor. There was complaints about a burning smell. The stove was still on. The grilled cheese almost burned the building down." Missy rubbed her eyes which only made the gritty feeling worse. "I don't want to die like her or get shot. I don't want any of it!"

"We've all got stories like that. If it's not someone we're related to, it's someone we knew."

They lapsed into silence, watching the sunset as clouds passed and listening the grass rustle. Missy was naked and didn't care about the ants and mosquitos crawling across her skin, mistaking them for more bullets exiting her skin. She didn't feel better but at least Rainey stopped talking.

PROFESSOR ONYX STOOD AT THE BOTTOM OF A ROLLING hill. The desiccated ground was firm. She picked up a rock, fashioned her scarf into a slingshot.

Professor Onyx wore a sports bra, bike shorts, her steel toed boots, and a centurion helmet with a wolf's mask. Her saber was in a sheath but she didn't wear a belt. She just held the sword. She had styled her afro into a tall 'fro-hawk. She looked like a gladiator from hell.

If this were a video game, Professor Onyx would be her favorite character but Missy did not want to fight her for real. Ever.

"Come on you slackers. Nut up," Velma growled.

The Youngbloods were at the top of the steep hill. They wore old police body armor and held rifles, handguns, axes, and shields. There were swords but everyone picked guns instead.

Missy still held her assault rifle like it was a snake about to bite her. "I don't like this."

"No shit," Fanta said.

"She's just standing there," La Croix said. "We're supposed to attacking her, right?"

"She's a sitting duck," Velma said. "Fire!"

Professor Onyx ran up the slope as the Youngbloods fired. Muscles pumping. It looked like magic but she was just really fast. A few bullets hit but didn't slow her down.

"Shoot her, goddamn you, shoot!" Velma bellowed. "Easy target!"

Except shooting Professor Onyx wasn't easy. Her mesmerizing grace as she clawed up the steep rocky slope. The lack of hesitation. The intensity. She ran straight at them and every Youngblood missed their shot.

Professor Onyx reached at the line, kicked La Croix in the face, grabbed a rifle, and swung it like a bat into Malört's head. She stole her ax. Missy shattered Professor Onyx's ax with a hail of gun shot. The point blank gunshots failed to even break her skin. Missy gaped, in horror and was bludgeoned with the flat of the ax.

Professor Onyx cartwheeled, stabbed, shot, stole weapons, sliced, and hamstrung her way down the line. Velma screamed at the Youngbloods right up until Professor Onyx shot her in the heart and head too.

The elder wolf chased down those who fled into the forest. Then ran back, stole two rifles, climbed a tree, and shot everyone who tried to stand, whether they were teachers or Youngbloods. Then came back again to replace the rifles with handguns. She was relentless, knowing precisely how long it took to heal from a bullet wound. The complete disrespect of picking through the fallen to take their guns only magnified the difference.

Missy lay on the grass. Bullets whizzed overhead. "She's a one woman army."

"Get up you lazy bitch!" Velma kicked her in the hip.

Missy glared. Once upon a time, Velma had been her favorite

character in 'Scooby-Doo' now it was ruined. Velma was even more intolerable than Dolly. Why did the teachers have to suck so damn much?

It was a dusty sunset. The orange sun reflected through the smoke. The teachers picked their way through the scorched pitted field. Missy crawled with her one remaining arm, her legs were wet shrapnel catching dirt as she dragged herself away from the screaming and moaning.

Professor Onyx put her foot on the small of Missy's back. She strained to keep moving.

The elder wolf dropped a charred squirrel in front of Missy's face. A gopher. A rabbit. Three raccoons. An opossum. "Eat. Your body does the rest."

Missy ate, whimpering as she chewed. She passed out from the agony of regrowing her legs and arm. The internal injuries healed. The shrapnel wormed from her skin.

The teachers dumped more and more dead animals in front of the Youngbloods. The whimpering ebbed.

Ten minutes later, the Youngbloods swayed in a ragged line. Blood down their breasts and completely healed.

Professor Onyx and the teachers surveyed them, hands on their hips. "You get it now?"

"Yes, ma'am," La Croix said while the rest nodded. "This final girl is tired."

Missy watched the iridescent haze of smoke on the sun. She ate a skunk. She didn't even care about the stench.

Missy made chicken and dumplings from scratch. This time there was enough to share with the Youngbloods.

Malört covered her mouth as she savored a dumpling. "Oh damn."

"It's like happiness in a bowl!" Fanta said.

"Period!" La Croix snapped her fingers.

Missy waved at the kitchen. "You can thank me by cleaning up."

They gave her a look. She ate another tender mouthful of chicken and raised her eyebrows. "Do I look like your cook?"

There was much scoffing and resentful banging but they did what they were told. Missy savored her meal.

Tacos

It was Werewolf Wednesday. A lot of werewolves had taco trucks that didn't ask questions about the meat in their empanadas and tacos al pastor.

They met at Walnut Creek Park. An inflatable movie screen was erected. 'Jurassic Park', 'Godzilla', and 'the Mummy' played while werewolves ate tacos.

Genna learned how to make tortillas from corn masa. She delighted in using the taco press. Troy was chopping garlic, serrano and jalapeño peppers for guacamole.

Everyone who contributed to the feast got to eat for free. Genna and Troy had several kills slow cooking in spices at several trucks.

"I love barbacoa!" Genna groaned through a full mouth. Troy hummed with agreement.

They tried tacos at every food truck and table. They ate grilled street corn covered in mayo, spices, and butter. They drank watermelon Aqua Fresca, Jamaica, and Horchata. Then went back for seconds, thirds, and fourths.

It was nice but strange to walk through the crowd of werewolves and be unnoticed. No one cared about anything but tacos.

Not about Genna being rich and famous. Not Troy being a former monster hunter. Or that they were an interracial couple.

Genna and Troy paused on the ridge by a baseball field. A pickup game between two werewolf teams was underway. The Hillcrest Howlers and the Pflugerville Flyers. The players had dyed their fur their team colors because they kept ripping through their uniforms. It was hilarious but the werewolves cheered and drank beer, serious about their team.

Genna and Troy kept wandering. Past the playground full of kids and den parents. Past the crowded public pool. Down the cement path that led into Walnut Creek Park's walking trails.

They had no particular plan in mind. Just enjoying a good meal and good company.

"Grab my ass again, motherfucker!" A female werewolf howled. "I'll rip your throat out!

Snarls behind them froze them in place. Several dead werewolves were on the ground. The Youngbloods had burst out of their clothes. Males and females stood braced, teeth and claws bared. Fur bristling.

Whoever lunged first, it didn't matter. The Youngbloods attacked. Genna and Troy stepped back into the trees, out of view. Elders fought like they were pups.

Genna and Troy quickly Turned and loped away from the fight.

It was time to go.

Den Mother

THERE WAS NO CELEBRATION WHEN WEREWOLF 101 ended. No pizza party or a little certificate. Not even a gold star sticker with 'Good Job!' The teachers simply loaded the Youngbloods and Girl Scouts into stolen Yukons and off they went with the Dragonflies.

The job was to find new werewolves. To the Girl Scouts, it was like gathering up stray puppies hiding under dumpsters. The older Youngbloods were still nervy to be outside again. Missy was too. She looked around, waiting for something to happen. For the crickets to stop singing. But nothing did. This was different than that Missy Piggy hunt. Nobody was cocky or wanted to stray far from the van.

"Okay, everybody out," Professor Onyx commanded. "You can run in the park but don't go into the neighborhoods. Stay in the green space and play with the kids."

The waxing crescent moon was hidden behind clouds. No stars were visible either. Werewolf children chased each other, laughing and yipping excitedly across the baseball field in Walnut Creek Park. Den mothers watched on the ridge or hunted among the trees.

Lala was a new werewolf. The oldest of the finds. Lala was

pretty but empty, like a knockoff barbie doll. Fanta, La Croix, and Malört had convinced her to stop hunting coeds from the sorority that kicked her out and join a real pack. But Lala wasn't gelling with the other Youngbloods. She wasn't gelling with anyone.

Missy tried to make friends but Lala ignored her as she stomped over to Professor Onyx. "I'm not wearing a dog collar." Lala flung the dog collar at Professor Onyx, who caught it. "I'm not fucking a dog!"

"Um, name tags stick to fur," Missy said, attempting to put herself between Lala and the elder wolf but it was already too late. Professor Onyx tackled Lala. She had zero tolerance for disrespect.

Missy rolled her shoulders as a death yelp shivered through the air. Professor Onyx got down to the business of eating. Cannibalism didn't bother the elder wolves. They had starved. They weren't squeamish about roadkill either. Food was food.

Other den mothers moved their new recruits out of the way. The warning and the lesson mixed together. The Girl Scouts kept playing in the swing sets and playground.

"Damn, I really liked her," Missy said, which wasn't true but she *wanted* to find something likable.

"She wasn't a good fit." Rainey said as she picked up the offending dog collar. She went to her rolling duffel bag suitcase where she had alphabetized drawers of collars. She put the collar in the 'L' drawer with a brisk snap.

Missy nervously surveyed the rows of nicknames. Rainey's brutal organization also had beginning and end dates. The older the name, the more werewolves had lived and died under that nickname.

Troop Dragonfly kept receipts. There was always someone who enjoyed taking notes. Rainey worked with a team. She was focused on Black recruitment.

Rainey checked her notebook. "Oh, I'm supposed to tell you that you've been voted in as the newest den mother."

"Me?" Missy exclaimed, pointing to herself. "But I'm not—I can't—do I have to?"

"Relax. You're arts-and-crafts. Basically a glorified babysitter. You don't have to lead a hunt or anything. Yet."

Missy didn't relax. She tried to ignore the sounds of mastication. Could she do that? Could she eat a disrespectful pup? But refusal wasn't an option either. She had to be a team player or else they might start asking questions.

"I'll do my best," Missy said, unhappily accepting the den mother's sash. Fanta, La Croix, and Malört were tasked with hunting.

Being a den mother was its own challenge.

Werewolves had kids. Some kids got Turned. They needed an outlet and to be around other monstrous kids. The den parents sent the girls to Troop Dragonfly. Missy didn't have time to wonder about the boys because there were so many girls.

Gender equality wasn't the priority. It was survival. Like it or not, many male werewolves would try to mate with any female. Most of the girls got their first period at ten or eleven. And after that, they were as vulnerable to the manic sexual appetites of frenzying males during a full moon as those that reached adulthood. It was heartbreaking and violent.

Missy agreed with Troop Dragonfly's mission to help these girls have a childhood as it were possible.

Missy wasn't the fastest or the strongest but that was okay. There were only two other Black werewolves in Troop Dragonfly. Rainey and Professor Onyx couldn't be more different and yet now that she had passed Werewolf 101, she was one of them. They welcomed her with open arms and gentle smiles. They ate together and always had a seat with her name on it. Missy felt wanted. Hunting with them was an indescribable joy. She didn't enjoy hunting with La Croix, Fanta, and Malört.

Troop Dragonfly structured its hierarchy like a Girl Scout troop. They even baked cookies, which Missy loved. She specialized in making pineapple upside-down cake with coffee cans on an open fire.

There were a lot of young pups in the pack. Little girls with haunted eyes. Missy was horrified and heartbroken for them. Some had been werewolves for years, figuring out things on their own. Missy hadn't felt blessed until she listened to their whispered stories. They found comfort in earning badges and structured hunts.

Missy sewed patches onto sashes. She up-cycled cardboard and paper to make trophies and prizes. She crocheted dolls out of old sweaters found in donation piles. She ran with them, commiserating as they went through their own Werewolf 101 classes. The nuance of survival as a werewolf made her an attentive student, even though she had graduated.

She hunted, flossed, groomed herself, braided her own hair, trimmed her own nails. Werewolf flexibility made waxing a lot easier. No Salons or beauticians was a new rule.

Missy loved sitting in hair braiding circles, sharing gossip and listening to the den mothers tell stories. When the den mothers told her to hunt rats, rabbits, and opossums, she did. Hunting deer and wild boar was more difficult than she expected.

Real stray cats, dogs, and coyotes hated werewolves. Usually they ran away but a few times, she had to kill.

But Missy hated hunting humans. She watched people living their lives, going to the grocery store or gym like it was a normal day. They had no idea how close real monsters lived.

The other Youngbloods and den mothers had no problem eating humans. Missy felt guiltier after every kill. But she couldn't deny that humans were delicious. There was something about the flavor of their blood, the buttery marrow, and tender flesh that was unrivaled. She couldn't eat enough.

Missy kept her feelings to herself. She wanted to stay with the Dragonflies. There was safety in numbers. She tried to hunt bad people to make herself feel better.

~

Something was wrong. Missy could feel it in the air like the taste of rain. She looked around. The evening was purple and pink striated clouds stretching to the horizon, reflecting off the river.

She had taken the Girl Scouts on an overnight trip to Big Bend park for some hunting exercises. Mist drifted over the river and the trees along the banks. In the distance was the orange mountains. The rocks were brown and the ground was cracked in patterns like rattlesnake skin.

They were on Juniper Canyon Trail, taking a water break. Missy wasn't the only den mother. She watched La Croix, Malört, and Fanta but no one else seemed to feel that itch on her skin.

"There's a hurricane coming. We need to go now." Missy didn't wait for permission. She packed up the lanyards and art supplies. The den mothers shrugged and didn't ask questions. Werewolf 101 rule #1: Trust Your Gut.

Missy drove the van. The other den mothers kept the girls occupied. There was plenty of fresh cobbler cooked and prickly pears roasted on the open fire to keep their bellies full.

La Croix asked why Missy wasn't driving with the headlights on but she said, "They're watching us."

"Who?"

"I don't want to find out."

La Croix nodded. "I called Professor Onyx and the others. They're at the camp site. If someone's there, they'll take care of it."

The den parents weren't pleased that their vacation from their little monsters were curtailed.

"Missy smelled a hurricane coming," La Croix said, backing Missy up, a hundred percent. Fanta and Malört nodded.

Missy was right. A squall hit Big Bend a few hours later. And in the middle of the storm, a group of dog catchers snuck into the camp. They expected to find a bunch of frightened little girls. Instead Professor Onyx's magic wand perforated them.

The next day, Missy was awarded her first badge in Witch

Craft. The ceremony and applause embarrassed Missy. Even Fanta, La Croix, and Malört gave her bouquets of flowers and gift cards to Starbucks and Whataburger.

"I didn't do it for show," Missy said.

"We know," Professor Onyx said, "That's why you earned that badge. You trusted your instincts and we didn't lose a single girl."

"Plus, we found the dog catcher's home case," Rainey said, "They triangulated your position using gaming apps to see which users are nearby."

"Smartphones," Professor Onyx growled.

The Girl Scouts cringed, guilty, scared, and in trouble. "We didn't know!"

"You didn't think!" Professor Onyx snarled. "You're lucky that Missy was there."

The whole pack gave Missy the first bite of the meal. There were other little congratulatory signs. She accepted them with grace.

~

"Don't do it. Stay hidden." Missy warned, noting the telltale nostril flare and unified predatory turn of the head. She was almost surprised that the Youngbloods listened. A few glared at her but went back to watching the playground on the edge of Walnut Creek Park.

The playground was crowded with children and a handful of adults.

The pack was hidden down the slope behind the cypress trees. There were walking trails on either side. A dry creek bed where the edge was soft and full of white rocks. Humans walked their dogs and biked past but avoided this area so close to the dark drop-off. No one listened to the birds who had vacated this part of the forest.

A little girl, maybe three, wandered away from the swings, out of the playground, and into the wild sunflowers and weeds. Bees buzzed. She giggled to herself, little pudgy hands reaching out to stroke leaves and grip flowers. She crouched down, yanking up little white flowers, gathering them and dropping them. She followed the flowers away from the playground and down the slope.

She was far too close to the pack and getting closer. Missy swallowed, her mouth dry with nervousness. She glanced up at the playground but nobody noticed the little girl's absence.

The Youngbloods were taut with hunger. Yet they obeyed Missy's soft commanding growl. It was like holding the pack by a leash with the tensile strength of a spiderweb. Yet they did not move.

The little girl climbed down into the narrow creek bed, scattering flowers in her wake. She jumped from rock to rock, giggling to herself. She crouched to put a flower in the shallow water. She wobbled, teetering on a stone. Then fell.

She missed the water and hit the rocks. Her limbs trembled and went still. The faint scent of blood and urine as her body died was a bright firework in Missy's nose.

"Wait!" Missy said, "Parents!"

The Youngbloods obeyed. They watched the playground fill and empty. It got hotter and hotter. The sun beat down on the forest.

Another girl, a bossy eight instead of wobbly toddler, climbed down into the creek. She picked up the dropped flowers along the way. She found the corpse.

She poked and prodded the body. Lifting the legs up and moving the arms with the callousness of a child. Then she squealed at the blood on her hand.

She washed her hands off in the creek, wiped them dry on the corpse's front, and climbed back up the slope. She ran to an adult, drinking coffee flavored whiskey on a bench.

The woman picked the girl up, grabbed her bag, and hurried to the parking lot. Her minivan drove off with a roar of the engine.

Hours past. Nobody else found the girl's body. Not the mountain bikers. The dogs smelled the werewolves and weren't interested in approaching a fresh kill rotting in the sun. Flies crawled over the body. The playground emptied and filled.

"I don't think anyone's coming," La Croix said.

"Me neither," Malört said.

"Circle of life," Fanta said.

"My mom used to forget me at the playground all the time," La Croix added. "Especially if she'd been drinking."

Missy hated that they were right. Worse, they were letting it be her decision, absolving themselves of responsibility. This was exactly why she didn't want to be a den mother.

But the Youngbloods had waited. They had obeyed. She had to reward them. Nobody was walking away. Only she had lost her appetite.

"Okay," Missy said. "Keep quiet."

The Youngbloods rushed the corpse. They grabbed the body and dragged it back to Missy. She had to take the first bite, barely a nibble. The sun-warmed skin had only begun to bloat. She let the Youngbloods have the rest while she kept lookout.

Missy went back to watching the playground, praying that somebody would come looking. No one did.

Missy had never felt like a monster before. There was always a perfectly logical reason that she could explain her actions away. But now she knew that she was damned. The taste of blood was on her tongue.

She did not like being a den mother.

Troy

Troy loved being married to Genna. He loved the companionship, the conversations that flowed in and out of everyday activities. He chose to stay faithful. He chose to stop inviting new people into his bed. He chose to do what his father never would: be loyal. No side pieces. No extra nookie. No little something-something in the back alley behind the gay bar.

He still had fun. Only Genna knew about it. They negotiated the terms of their open marriage. Both were bisexual. Neither expected the other to play straight.

Nobody watched Troy like Genna did. Hunger and desire twinned together. He could never tell if she wanted to rip his clothes off and fuck him or rip his throat out and eat him. The delicious tension had him ready to go with a single brush of the hand.

Genna's lips were soft and her teeth were sharp. She stroked his crotch through his pants, the lightest of feathering touches, again and again. He was as hard as a rock. Need strained against self-control. She whispered against his neck, growls prickled his sensitized nerves.

She gripped his dick, all command and control. Troy's knees nearly buckled right there. He loved her dominance. He worshiped her strength. He could be vulnerable and submissive. She never saw him as lesser.

In fact, she encouraged him to shed the trappings of toxic monster hunter behavior and be himself. To admit that he liked it when she bit him and scratched him. To admit that her monstrousness ferocity was a huge turn on. He loved it when she pinned him down, pushed his legs wide, and slid her finger or a dildo inside of him. Not hard but gently, shattering his soul with loving power. Putting him back together again and kissing his tears.

She could make a handjob into the most exquisite torture. Have him writhing and begging as she grinned piratically down at him before spitting into his own mouth. She loved it when he moaned, soft and plaintive. Caught up in pleasure.

Then she slid a finger inside, tickling and teasing. She tugged on his balls. So many sensations. Then she added magic, lightning sparking and igniting his body.

It was too much.

He filled her hands with cream and burst into blue lightning. They were in the magic tent so his power didn't burn anything. Instead it grounded in the tent walls and floor.

Troy came back to his body on the comfortable bed. He watched Genna carefully dispose of his seed. His body hummed with pleasure. She came back and snuggled. He held her with loose limbs. His eyelashes brushed her cheek. "Was that a test? Did you want to make sure that the tent could handle us?"

Genna stroked his hair away from his face with a smile. "Nah, I just felt like pleasuring you."

Troy snuggled closer. God, he loved his wife.

Genna stretched. Sex magic was a powerful tool. The medicine bag rearranged its beads and offered her new medical journals with sexy-fun ideas.

She loved Troy. She loved the way he looked at her, the gentleness in his touch, and the sincerity in his actions. Pleasure used to be a competition but now, she could enjoy the sensations.

The Witch Market

Genna arrived late to the Witch Market which had a special connection to the Farmers Market in Avery Ranch. It was the largest Farmers Market in Austin. It had moved from Lakeline Mall's parking lot up to Avery Ranch.

It was ten am on a Saturday and it was already blistering hot.

She set up a booth at the Witch Market. But the only available tent was in the back by the row of portable toilets and mesquite trees. The stink of feces and chemicals squatted in the tent.

This wasn't the boo hag's magic tent. That was still in the Briarpatch going through a decontamination process. The only way to get it was to walk through a door. Genna had crafted a beaded curtain just like the one inside the boo hag's tent.

She hurriedly unfolded tables and flyers and a wrestled a folding chair out of its sleeve.

She took Troy's advice to keep the magic to a minimum. "The Witch Market at the Farmers Market is a good way to meet the magic folk of the area. You need to get a lay of the land. You don't know what they want. Or how what you're offering fits into the local culture. Whenever I'm hunting, I take my time. I let the locals come to me."

"You're not staying?"

"That would send the wrong message. They still see me as a monster hunter." Troy didn't talk about his recovery but he still needed time in the medical tent.

Genna sat alone. People hurried past, focused on the toilets or getting away from the stench. She was nervous. She had carefully written symbols for medicine, healing, werewolf, and safety into decorative border.

She fiddled with her business cards. Maybe she needed a price list. Or bottled tinctures. She had never worked a booth before. Hell, she'd never petitioned for money. Even her fundraisers were run by other people.

Genna's tent looked nothing like the other tents. Plain white on white with ecru colored business cards. Tasteful and forgettable. Maybe she should've tried the country club. Let word get out.

"You that Becky with the Good hair that's fucking that White boy, ain't you?" The group of women dressed in single pastel colors entered the tent. Each wore a single color from her wide brimmed star hat to her low heeled mules. Their suit dresses were pristine. Their glasses had strands of pearls that caught in their wigs.

"Um, hello," Genna said, "I'm Genna Bellwether. That's my husband you're talking about. Thank you for visiting my tent. Who are you?"

"We're prayer warriors from the Church. I'm Princess," The warrior in peach sneered. "What's a high yellow bougie bitch doing here? Do you think you're better than us?"

Genna gestured to the neat but sparse items. "I am a healer. I can help curse curses and pull bullets out of werewolves."

"We don't need you. We've got Delilah and the beauticians at the Salon. Are you trying to take food out of their mouths?"

"I'm just trying to help."

"That's mighty White of you." Princess sneered.

Rage flashed like lightning. "I'm not White. Or mixed."

"Yeah, right. I see you. Becky with the good hair. You better watch your step." Princess harrumphed and strutted away. The rest of the prayer warriors bustled after her with a few parting looks that Genna couldn't read.

Genna rearranged her flyers. Black prayer warriors protecting a church. They knew that she was magic. Were they witch finders? Genna did not want to tussle with local puritanical zealots.

There were no other visitors to the tent. The heat got worse and the stink felt like a physical presence. Genna sweated and sipped the last of her water bottle. She was not prepared for any of this.

Just as she had decided to pack up her tent, Coyote walked in wearing her face, her favorite red leather trench coat with floral embroidery, a wide-brimmed red fedora, most upsettingly, her favorite Louboutin boots.

"Hey! Those are my boots!" Genna exclaimed. "And my clothes!"

She had been genuinely upset when her box of clothing and boots hadn't made the transition to Austin. She had blamed the TSA.

"I look good, don't I?" Coyote said, grinning.

"You look like Carmen San Diego."

"Wasn't that your Halloween costume last year?"

The tent was too small for a dragon and an ancient spirit of the Wild West. Their human masks stretched thin as they bared their teeth, not smiling but not hostile either.

"Why are you wearing my face?" Genna demanded. She was focused on the wrong thing.

"Because you're rich and it's fun," Coyote said.

"I'm not rich anymore," Genna said.

Taking over the real estate cabal's funds had wasted what little money she had left. Buying the Briarpatch drained her down to gas money. Before the boo hag's attack, Genna believed that it was just business, but now she was sure it was a curse.

Coyote picked up a flyer from the table. "What's this I'm hearing about werewolf surgery?"

"Somebody has to pull bullets out of werewolves."

"And you think that you're the one to do it?"

Genna shrugged defensively. "I've practiced human and veterinary medicine. I know flesh and blood magic."

"You don't know bone magic," Coyote grinned at her. "You killed all those werewolves in Sweetwater. Do you think word wouldn't travel? Are you trying to balance the scales? "

"I did what I had to do."

Coyote walked around the tent, patting the beaded doctor's bag on their hip. "Pretty sparse. Were you planning to bite them to fix them?"

Genna sucked on her teeth. "No."

"So you didn't have a plan. You have a magic medicine tent that you can't use. You're just a do-gooder with a savior complex."

"There's lots of ailments that werewolves believe will just magically go away. They're too dependent on their hyper-healing."

"And you know so many werewolves?"

"I'm a coywolf. I know that I've had to treat myself because there aren't doctors."

"What about witches like Miss Bootsie?"

Genna shook her head. "Miss Bootsie didn't know everything."

Coyote set the medicine bag on a counter. "Everything you know is wrong or out of date. I will teach you how to heal werewolves properly. Lycanthropic surgery is no easy matter. If you're going to do it then do it right. You must learn bone magic on your own." Coyote opened the bag.

What happened next was pain. Agony was Genna's blistering sun, shining moon, and universe. She was warped by the knowledge carried inside the medicine bag. Knowledge came at the price of her memories, her wealth, and her good intentions.

Genna was a dragon but a fledgling compared to the ancient

spirit. She should have been afraid instead of brazenly acting like they were equals. Her arrogance amused Coyote instead of infuriated. Genna was exactly what Coyote expected. A warrior princess high on her own importance, some of it earned and some not.

Three years ago on Halloween, Genna had killed White Fang the direwolf king. He was no friend to Coyote or Anansi. They thought it was funny as hell that a young direwolf had killed the icy bastard with her fire. Now Genna was in Austin just when the Briarpatch needed her kind of help. That was not a coincidence. Coyote had seen Anansi weaving the path.

Coyote had been Turned a long time ago. The stink of skinned buffalo herds rotting in the late afternoon sun. Coyote's people had traded their skins for animal to survive starvation. They ate their sacred herd, knowing that they had damned themselves but were intent upon killing the White men who massacred the buffalo. Coyote was a headhunter, a scalper, a trapper, a trader, and that magic flowed into Genna through the medicine bag.

Stacy had used the medicine bag for the wrong reasons. Sewing lives to help herself not the community. The medicine bag could heal anything but it was up to the user to prioritize what to do first.

The test was wielding the medicine bag. Coyote waited to be disappointed but Genna had meant what she said. Back in Sweetwater, she spent most of her time healing animals and killing the cruel. She was perfectly positioned to help Briarpatch recover from Stacy's cruelty.

Genna was used to power. Born into it. The medicine bag was a tool.

Satisfied, Coyote left the tent wearing someone else's face and the clothes off Genna's back. The red hat, coat, and boots were neatly folded on a cot.

Genna crawled across the tent, dragged herself up to the counter, and fumbled the bag closed. She slumped back onto the ground, panting as the tent became her ideal field clinic. Furniture, carpeting, and tools grew like overzealous mushrooms.

She slumped onto the carpet, panting and shivering. The stink of the bathroom no longer bothered her. She was too grateful to be alive.

The Refrigerated Truck

THE YOUNGBLOODS FOUND REFRIGERATED TRUCKS AT the back of a warehouse parking lot. Eight semi-trucks waited with similar cargo. Only a few bored humans in uniforms milled around, checking inventory. One of the doors was left open. The air conditioning wafted into the hot air. Three scouts snuck into the back and stared at the stacks of dead human bodies on metal shelves.

"Look at the tags," Fanta said, "They've been here since the Pandemic!"

"So there really were trucks of dead folks who never got a funeral," Missy said. "That's so sad!"

"Damn, that's some cold shit." Velma said, disingenuously.

"We should get back and tell the others." Missy said, annoyed.

The scouts retreated to the pack. They were excited.

"It's a fucking goldmine!" Velma said excitedly. "We're about to have Thanksgiving feast!"

Missy wasn't so enthusiastic. "Something's not right about this place."

Velma scowled. "What do you mean? You're the one who said that those bodies weren't claimed."

"Okay but Rule #1: Trust Your Gut. Look around. Those

doors are open. You can smell the dead from here but there aren't any buzzards or flies. It's too quiet. Something isn't right about this place. I say that we leave the trucks and go."

Fanta and Velma were not happy. The rest of the Youngbloods muttered. They were hungry but also wary. Even when they were human, they trusted their instincts. If something wasn't right then they weren't sticking around.

Fanta and Velma weren't happy to look bad. Velma glared. "You're not the top dog, Cinnabon."

"Don't call me that!" Missy growled back. "I don't care what you think. Something isn't right about this. It feels like a trap."

"Let's go tell Professor Onyx," Fanta said nervously. "She'll know what to do."

"That'll take too long," Velma said.

"What do you mean it doesn't feel right, Missy?" Fanta said. "I didn't smell anything weird."

Velma scowled with open-mouthed offense. "Not you too!"

Fanta shrugged. "I want to know. They chose us to be scouts for a reason."

"Yeah, and I'm your supervisor," Velma snapped, "And I say that we just found enough meat to feed the pack for a month."

"There's something about this place that reminds me of that weird thunderstorm."Missy gestured at the eerily empty air. "It's too empty. Like someone's holding their breath and trying to be quiet. Let's get the fuck out of here."

But Velma wasn't having it. "I'm hungry."

"What if it's a witch or warlock?" Missy demanded.

"Yeah, she's right, Velma," Fanta said. "We should go."

But Velma wasn't listening. "There's no witch, you chicken-shit babies."

She stomped down the slope. Fanta shrugged again and followed. After a moment, Missy reluctantly did too. The rest of the Youngbloods were content to stay hidden in the trees without committing themselves either way.

The pressure of being a scout weighed on Missy. She didn't

ask for this but she couldn't leave these two dumbasses either. Pack was supposed to mean something. Even for shitty bitches like Velma and spineless cowards like Fanta.

She reached the end of the truck just in time to see Velma unzip a bodybag. The corpse's skin unwrapped from the bones to reach out and grab Velma like an amorous octopus. The magic drank her strength, blood, marrow, and crushed her into a twisted ball as she was pulled into the chest cavity.

Missy yanked Fanta out of the way, hurling them clear of the truck. They landed on cement, rolled to their feet, and ran. Velma's strangled yelps chasing them. The human guards watched. Their heads moved in sync. Meat puppets with extra eyes.

The rest of the pack didn't need telling to skedaddle.

Stacy sauntered out of the warehouse. She was annoyed that her trap had only landed one werewolf. They had such unique skin. She would not waste a single hair on her head.

Professor Onyx and the den mothers listened to the retelling. The Youngbloods were rattled. Losing Velma was a blow to their confidence.

"Missy told her and she didn't listen," Fanta said.

Missy glowered but stayed quiet.

"How did you know something was wrong?" Professor Onyx asked.

"Rule Number #1," Fanta said, "I trusted my gut."

The Youngbloods repeated the same story. Missy just nodded along.

"Let's have tacos tonight," Professor Onyx said, "We'll try a hunt tomorrow."

The Youngbloods perked up. Everybody loved tacos. They ordered from several taquerias so the sheer volume wouldn't arose suspicion or empty the inventory.

Missy ate her fill and went to bed, not talking to anyone. Professor Onyx sent Rainey to go check on her. Rainey found Missy curled up under her bed in wolf form in a nest of blankets. She wasn't asleep but she wasn't moving either. She watched Rainey with wild eyes, a soft growl of warning when she got too close to the bed.

Rainey retreated. She caught Professor Onyx's eye and shook her head. "If you ask me, Fanta stole her story."

"She could speak up if she wanted to but she's prioritizing the needs of the pack over her own," Professor Onyx said, "That's what we want in a den mother."

"I'm going to keep her company and see if she'll come out." Rainey leaned against the wall across from the room.

Professor Onyx went back to the Dragonflies but sat angled to watch the hallway where Rainey waited. She ordered extra food, setting it aside and defending it when other Youngbloods tried to steal it.

Big Mama

"We're going to Church," Professor Onyx said.

"Church?" Rainey yelped. "But we're werewolves!"

"Yes, so we're going to the evening service." Professor Onyx gestured at Rainey. "Hurry up and get dressed."

Rainey showered in record time. She did a full beat of makeup, even glueing on eyelashes. She sorted through piles of clothing left over from past hunts to find something without bloodstains. She found a purple dress. She was so nervous that she nearly broke the zipper of her dress. Missy helped her because her hands kept shaking.

"Hey, are you okay?" Missy asked. "You're intense right now."

"I'm fine." Rainey snapped, filling a flask with moonshine. La Croix and Malört made the moonshine, claiming it was their heritage. The moonshine was terrible but she gulped down a whole mason jar to steady her nerves. "It's been a while since I went to church. I'm nervous."

"Um, I don't think this church is that formal," Missy said.

"Easy for you to say. You hate wearing dresses!"

Missy bit her lip, offended. She walked away. Rainey kept drinking, feeling guilty. "Church. What the hell?" She muttered as she savagely combed her wig and pinned it in place.

Rainey's whole family hadn't been religious except for her grandmother. Big Mama was God-fearing woman who prayed up a storm. Much of Rainey's childhood was sweating in her stuffy dresses, her scalp aching from braids, and her skin shiny from Vaseline.

Big Mama had raised lots and lots of babies. Her house was always overcrowded. The older kids changing diapers and helping with homework. She would put six potty-training toilets in front of the tv that was always playing her stories. Sometimes telenovelas. Other times horror movies. Big Mama controlled the remote.

Big Mama had a personal vendetta against Tyler Perry. She hated his shows, his movies, and didn't care what her prayer circle thought. Big Mamma looked just like Madea and felt like she was being personally mocked. She never trusted 'That Man' as she called him. Angrily smoking her way through a pack of Dunhill cigarettes and drinking her rum and Coke whenever 'That Man' couldn't be avoided. Rainey still didn't watch any of those shows out of loyalty to Big Mama.

Church was a 24/7 lifestyle for Big Mama until the strokes whittled her down to a drooling vegetable. She died at the nursing home, alone. The rest of the family too busy working to pay off debts to visit.

What would Big Mama say about Rainey now?

Professor Onyx waited by the Tundra. She wore a polyester lilac dress that looked hot even without the matching blazer. Low slung heels. A wig covered her iconic afro. Big clip-on pearl and diamond earrings warred against the curls of her wig. Matching necklace.

Her bible was in a hand sewn denim bag. Her hands covered in gloves. A large pin of a dragonfly on her lapel.

The rest of the Dragonflies didn't show up. Only Missy stood next to Professor Onyx, wearing a black and green muumuu. She wore big dangling earrings and necklaces, definitely from the communal jewelry box. It was the fanciest attire that Rainey had ever seen Missy wear.

"I'm sorry," Rainey began. "You look nice."

"No one else is coming," Missy said loudly.

"Did you even tell them that we were going?" Rainey said.

Professor Onyx climbed into the Tundra. Missy scrambled to get into the front passenger seat, shouting, "Shotgun!"

"What about the Girl Scouts?" Rainey had to sit in the back seat. She inched along, smoothing her skirt over her knees.

"This isn't for them," Professor Onyx said. "It's ours."

"What do you mean?" Rainey said.

"What do you think?" Missy rubbed the back of her hand.

"Sometimes it is about race," Professor Onyx said, "I know it's not always easy. Losing Velma to a boo hag made me realize how careful we need to be right now. If you two ever feel unsafe, even from your fellow pack sisters, this is where you run. They won't be about to get through the Briarpatch."

"Why didn't you show me before?" Rainey said.

"It wasn't time." Professor Onyx nodded towards Missy.

Rainey wasn't mad at that. She understood. In a strange way, they both had been waiting for Missy without knowing why. She sat back in her seat. "What's it called?"

"The Church of the Forgotten," Professor Onyx said.

The Church of the Forgotten

PROFESSOR ONYX TOLD RAINEY AND MISSY ABOUT THE Church of the Forgotten as she drove carefully down the narrow dirt trail through the Forsaken Forest.

The Church of the Forgotten was an old Black non-denominational church. It withstood the test of time and unrelenting prejudice by being hidden in the conifers of an old Christmas tree farm. The trees were haunted because they grew over a mass grave. Poplar and oak trees hid amongst the pine, their gnarled limbs still carrying frayed rope and chains.

The Church cemetery was full of freed Black folk and their descendants dating back to the 18th century. Their headstones were carefully ignored because time had crumbled the edges into soft lumps of carved brick.

The Church of the Forgotten crouched instead of stood proudly on the only solid rock in the forest. The ancestors had planted the pine trees around the Church to hide its location. Now-defunct factories, laboratories, slaughterhouses, and refineries had dumped their toxic waste into the pines. The railroads still used this particular stretch as a dumping ground. The bodies of Black, White, Latinx, Asian, and Indigenous were dumped among the pines to sink into the tar pits. There were many animals too. The tar swallowed anything it could. The soil was so acidic that only bones were left.

Missy wanted to explore but there wasn't time as Professor Onyx rushed them from the parking lot, into the doorway and sat them on an empty pew.

The interior of the Church sanctuary was mosaics. It was constructed at the same time by the same underpaid masons who built the St. Louis Basilica. The masons got their revenge for being overworked and underpaid by using all of those innovative techniques to build the Church. Spite added to their artistry and unknowingly infused every stone with a deep resentment against oppression. The mosaics shown like gilded rainbows.

The arboreal themes in the mosaics surrounded the pews with a bejeweled field of wildflowers and trees. A vivid sunset sky overhead transitioned into a depiction of the sky at night. The constellations glowed in the chandelier light. The phases of the moon circled the centermost arch. Pillars of veiny colored marble looked like ivy wrapped tree trunks with enough quartz to sparkle.

Every hand carved wooden pew had its own artistic flare. Missy's pew had carved wooden grapes and leaves that doubled as ergonomic support. She tried to get comfortable but the sermon was weirdly engaging.

Some werewolves lay on the cool tile floor. There was no fear of scratching the stone. The grout was easy to clean in case of accidents or territorial marking.

"Jonah and the whale," Pastor Faith said.

The werewolf congregation hummed and clapped and stomped their feet. Missy was surprised. Maybe the simplicity of the monotonous sermon was its charm. Werewolves had short attention spans. Professor Onyx and Rainey certainly seemed to enjoy it.

"And Jonah and the whale." The minister was a medium height, heavy set were-cat with medium brown skin. Her fussy brown micro-braids were bundled like a rooster's comb at the top of her head. She wore a voluminous black minsters robe with red velvet patches on the sleeves and an orange kente cloth stole across her shoulders. Her hair-do wobbled as she talked.

"And Jonah and the whale." Pastor Faith used different inflections but it was definitely a five-word sermon.

Missy snuck out to wander the Church grounds on the pretense of finding the restroom. There was a small home printed brochure in the visitor's center. She took one and wandered the Yoruba garden's winding stone path as she read. By the candid language, the author didn't expect anyone to read it. Missy searched for the random facts pointed out in the brochure.

The Church of the Forgotten was a basilica that straddled three centuries of architectural headaches. The few things that did consistently work had their own idiosyncrasies.

The boiler was a metal monstrosity with the technological advances of machinery built during the Industrial Revolution. There was not enough heat in the winter. Too much in the summer when it got so hot under the pine trees that the wind pushed the air around instead of cooling anything off.

The vaguely menacing floral wallpaper in the hallways that led to the Sanctum Sanctorum was as flat as the day it was laid but had lead in the glue. If watched long enough the wallflowers would either bloom or wilt under the scrutiny.

Under the parquet flooring was asbestos. A few attempts were made to fix it but the air circulation was so lackluster that renovations poisoned the whole Church.

The slate tiles on the roof turned into stone daggers when they fell. Once a tile killed a witch finder who poured gasoline on the stone to burn the Church down. His body was found nailed to the walkway by the Yoruba prayer garden with a tree sprouting from the remains of his chest.

The hinges of the enormous front double doors were works of Art Deco and Art Nouveau metal art but shrieked like the damned if not oiled consistently.

Missy had covered her ears when the prayer warriors hauled

the obnoxiously big doors opened in an attempt to lure a breeze into the sanctuary.

Outside the briarpatch and holly hedge were hectares of unstable oozing earth.

Missy wrinkled her nose at the slowly bubbling tar pits. It was a miracle that trees grew at all. But that was the magic of the Briarpatch. Turning the toxic and ugly into something beautiful.

She retreated to the Yoruba garden. She felt the magic as she crossed the thick hedge of boxwoods and wild growing briarpatch. It kept her in her human shape.

Here werewolves were welcomed and treated as people instead of monsters. They could be contributing member of a tight knit community. The Briarpatch had several hidden sanctuaries across Austin. The Church was the oldest and most fortified.

The Church accounted for the deaths of witches, werewolves, vampires, and other Black Folx who had been turned into something magical. Usually the Folx were victims themselves, as confused and frightened of their new power as the mob chasing them. They found the safe path through the Forsaken Forest because they needed sanctuary. Werewolf was an umbrella term but the congregation preferred the term of 'Folx' to distance themselves from their lived reality.

The hedge that circled the Church was guarded by stone griffons and lawn jockeys, brass figures of Black people wearing riding suit jacket, white jodhpurs, and black knee high boots. Each jockey held a lantern that surrounded the Church in a warm yellow ring of light after sunset.

The jockeys were given regular fresh coats of paint because the smoggy air was so corrosive. The griffons were ignored, hidden under ivy and briars. They were carved from the same stone that the Church was built upon.

Missy explored the bell tower, the library, the game room, and any door that opened. She liked the Church. It was a reminder that here, werewolves were more than monsters.

Missy sat down next to Rainey.

"You missed the whole sermon!" Rainey hissed while Professor Onyx harrumphed with severe disapproval.

"I think I got the message," Missy said.

"That's all, Folx," Pastor Faith said then she Turned into a black and white tuxedo cat. She yawned and curled up on the worn seat cushion of the minister's throne-like chair.

The prayer warriors took over the rest of church service. The Choir began to sing. The congregation joined in. Werewolves loved to sing. Imani listened to the harmonies as joyful noise filled the Church. The tip of her tail twitched on beat. More Folx sang from the inside the trees, their howls were deep and soulful. Missy joined in with the howl. The sermon might be boring but the singing was complex. There was an alto who sang just like Mariah Carey, arias and all.

After service they ate fried catfish, fried chicken, and other soul food. Aunt Jemima personally served Professor Onyx a plate of candied yams, collard greens with smoked turkey necks, baked macaroni and cheese, cornbread, rice and beans, and potato salad.

"Wow, the choir is really good," Missy said, chowing down on truly spectacular soul food.

Rainey ate another deviled egg with an emphatic nod.

"Yeah, the choir is really something," Professor Onyx said.

She went on to explain that Pastor Faith's idiosyncratic ministry did not follow more straitlaced traditions. The Church of the Forgotten was a quasi-sentient building. The were-cat protected her congregation. She didn't give a shit about anyone's gender or sexual preference or who believed in what. If the Church let you in then you were in. Period.

The werewolves of the Briarpatch liked Pastor Faith. They appreciated that she focused on the communal aspects of Church instead of ostracizing rituals. They protected her from witch finders and any zealots who might question a minister who turned into a cat and could work bone magic.

"So she's a bone witch?" Missy said.

"Don't you dare call her that," Professor Onyx growled. "Pastor Faith is a prayer warrior. Just like me!"

"What's a prayer warrior?"

"She specializes in exorcism and cleansing the bad shit that religious zealots do to us. We need her right where she is, protecting us from spiritual attacks. Witches aren't the only things you need to worry about. Devils are real. Vampires, haints, and tar babies too. So be careful."

"Tar babies?" Missy said. "That sounds really racist."

Professor Onyx nodded at the pine trees. "There's a lot of ugliness inside those trees that wants to crawl back out. They'll infect you. We call it tar because that's what a curse looks like, shiny, evil, oozing tar."

Missy swallowed her mouthful of mashed potatoes and kept further questions to herself. The brochure had failed to explain the magical component to the tar. Not that she had wanted to explore the eerie forest.

"Thank you both for joining me," Professor Onyx said shyly. "I know that you're in the midst of your training, Missy, but I appreciate your willingness to trust me."

Missy nodded, surprised at the compliment. "Oh, sure. I was curious." She lifted the brochure. "There's lots of interesting things to see here."

"What's this?" Rainey said, taking the brochure.

"I found it in the welcome center."

"What welcome center?" Professor Onyx inspected the brochure and sniffed it. She handed it back with a strange look on her face. "Put it back where you found it."

"Is something wrong?" Missy examined the brochure. It looked like a normal trim-folded collection of paper.

"Put it back. It's not for you."

"Can I finish eating?"

Professor Onyx snapped her fingers and pointed at the Church. Missy sulked but obediently left her half-eaten plate. She wove through the crowd filling the lawn into the Yoruba Garden.

She stopped when she spotted Pastor Faith, still in cat form, lounging on the Church steps.

"That brochure is not for you," Pastor Faith said. "Bad girl."

Missy wanted to hide the brochure behind her back. She held it out. "Um, sorry. I thought it was for public consumption."

"Is your name Cinnabon? Because you smell sweet and spicy."

"No, my name is Missy, Pastor Faith." She gestured at the crowd. "I'm a Youngblood from the Dragonfly pack. Professor Onyx and Rainey are over there."

"So you're new new."

"Um, I guess so? This is my first time attending service here."

The cat padded over and rubbed against Missy's ankles who stood stiffly, not sure what to do. "Here's your brochure back."

The cat transformed back into her human shape with a cute little sneeze. Human-shaped Pastor Faith had yellow eyes that were a little too big for her round brown face. Her unsettlingly big grin was like the Cheshire Cat. They were the same height, which made the direct eye contact and the slight brush of their chests extremely uncomfortable. "You can call me Imani."

"No, thank you."

Pastor Faith opened her palm to Missy. Thick claws extended from her fingers. They were painted neon green with magenta tiger stripes with blue edges. Missy gingerly dropped the brochure in her hand, dodging the swiping claws. She retreated quickly.

"Are you afraid of little old me?" Pastor Faith grinned bigger.

Missy backed up. "I gotta go. Excuse me."

She hurried away, got lost in the garden, then had to back track. Pastor Faith was still there, still grinning. "Well hello again."

Missy sweated through her muumuu by the time she found Professor Onyx and Rainey again. She sat down heavily and gobbled up her cold food, not caring about manners. Rainey passed her another plate stacked high with desserts. Missy ate those too. Then another. She gulped three cups of sweet tea.

"Did you learn your lesson?" Professor Onyx asked.

Missy nearly choked on her mouthful of peach cobbler as she nodded emphatically yes. "I'm sorry."

"You okay?" Rainey said, watching the way Missy hunched over her plate when Pastor Faith walked by.

"I'm allergic to cats," Missy muttered.

"All of my allergies went away when I Turned," Rainey said.

"I wish." Missy ate a slice of dry chocolate cake.

They watched Pastor Faith glad-hand through the congregation. Missy was still hungry. She went to the Kitchen since that trays were empty. She wanted to get away from Pastor Faith.

The Kitchen was magnificent. Missy wandered down the hallways and peeked into the closets. Such neatly organized ingredients. Big stoves, smokers, and kilns. She wished that she could live in the Kitchen, dressed in white like the chefs and baking bread instead of hunting humans.

Professor Onyx and Rainey realized that Missy wasn't coming back or clearing her plate away. A small sign of big nerves.

"She's really scared of Pastor Faith," Rainey said as they cleared the table.

"She should be," Professor Onyx said.

Genna and Troy walked out of the Yoruba garden, overdressed and overheated. Their version of church finery did not match the congregation or the Texas heat.

"Welcome to the Church of the Forgotten," Pastor Faith shook their hands like a politician greeting major donors. "I'm Pastor Faith. You can call me Imani. It means Faith in Swahili."

"We're sorry that we're late," Genna said, regal in a blue dress. "We walked here."

The congregation was impressed. It took real navigational skill to walk through the tar pits without getting their polished cowboy boots dirty.

"Please follow me to the Sanctum Santorum," Pastor Faith said, "I'll fix you a plate."

Professor Onyx watched Genna and Troy intensely as the couple were escorted into the Church. Rainey stayed quiet.

Pastor Faith gave Genna and Troy a tour of the Church. They warily followed, the brochures in their hands like talismans warding off danger.

Genna watched the flowers bloom in the vaguely menacing wallpaper. The prayer gardens beyond the stained glass window invited her to sit and read. Troy silently counted werewolves.

"No one knows when the Church became a quasi-sentient building but I think you've got to be on the right wave length or you'll never find it. Spiritually and physically there must be resonance or you'll walk on by." Pastor Faith led them into the minister's office, aka the Sanctum Sanctorum, and indicated that they sit down on the red velvet couch.

Troy chose to stand. "I'm going to check the grounds."

"By all means," Imani gestured at the door.

Genna touched his hand. He softened and bowed like knight in court. He kissed her knuckles. "I'll return to you, my queen."

She raised her chin, every inch a queen. He nodded at Pastor Faith and closed the door.

It was quiet and a little hotter in the office. Pastor Faith tented her fingers. "Something on your mind, Genna Bellwether?"

"Yeah, why us?" Genna said, dropping pretense.

"Why not you? But that's not the real reason you came."

"I almost lost Troy." Genna whispered, too exhausted to keep the tears hidden. "What can you tell me about the boo hag that lives in your forest?"

Imani Turned into a cat. She padded across the room and jumped onto Genna's lap, demanding pets. Genna told her about the boo hag, the rabbit, and the medicine tent.

Troy guarded them both outside the minister's inner sanctum, giving Genna her privacy. He rubbed his leg. That curse had gone right through every defensive spell he had. If not for Genna, he'd be dead or worse.

Genna and Troy strolled back into the Forsaken Forest like the tar wasn't there. The whole congregation noticed the dandelions growing under their feet. Pastor Faith waved them off then stalked over to Professor Onyx.

"I've got a job for the prayer warriors. Are you in?"

"Of course," Professor Onyx said, "What do you need of me?"

Pastor Faith fiddled with the hem of her stole as she relayed the information that Genna had shared and Troy confirmed by showing the scar on his ankle.

Professor Onyx listened, her grim expression getting harder and harder. "If this is true then it is much worse than I imagined. I need the best prayer warriors in the congregation. The ones who won't flinch."

Rainey and Missy were sent back to the den.

"We can help," Rainey protested.

Professor Onyx touched them both gently on the shoulder. "I won't be able to do what Pastor Faith was asked of me if I'm worried about you two. This is prayer warrior business."

Imani quickly discovered that Genna and Troy had told her the gospel truth.

There was a tunnel through the catacombs to the laboratory built under the monastery. The gloom stank of chemicals and desperation. Imani explored every inch while in cat form but now she needed a pack to save the girls being experimented on in the name of Jesus.

Imani hated the room of fetuses and the bodies left to rot on forgotten shelves in the catacombs. She wanted to rip up her pastor collar. So much evil done for the 'good' of Christianity. The witch finders and exorcists weren't doing anything but rape and torture.

One pregnant girl had managed to escape but Imani had to save another strapped to a chair from getting her tongue cut off.

The Church pack were too angry to see past their bloodlust. The nuns were ripped apart along with the male doctors, enforcers, and the guy with the cameras filming everything (those snuff films were how Imani triangulated the Lab site).

The monastery burned. The old stone worked like a kiln, burning feet and paws. The werewolves were covered in smoke, insane with pain. The girls they saved got scratched and Turned during the escape. The prayer warriors herded them down to the river by the monastery.

Imani found the priest sneaking off in a gardening truck. He was unrepentant, a sweaty zealot who believed in hellfire. She landed on him with extended claws and open jaws. Her magic and his death cleared the evil haunting the monastery.

Professor Onyx searched for hidden archives or laptops in the wings of the monastery that weren't yet burning. She stuffed what she could into a backpack, opened a window, and repelled down to the courtyard.

The prayer warriors drove the rescued to the Church. They were bathed in the baptismal pool. The curses washed away in the suds and holy water. The prayer warriors got the rescued bedded down in clean rooms.

Pastor Faith and Professor Onyx sat in the Sanctum Santorum. They sifted through the pilfered paperwork. Other prayer warriors bustled in and out with new information.

<h1 style="text-align:center">Beauticians</h1>

THE SALON HID IN PLAIN SIGHT. IT LOOKED LIKE AN ordinary rundown beauty parlor. Bleached beige stone walls. Faded 80s decals of smiling White women. The only strange thing was that it was open and crowded after midnight.

Troy was outside, deconstructing traps. Now that they knew what to look for, the traps had led them to the Salon.

Genna walked into the Salon. The door squeaked. The bell rang. The subtle sonic magic trying to appraise and ensnare her had the same signature as the boo hag.

All activity stopped. The sudden cessation of hair dryers was loud. The beauticians and werewolf clients stared. The music 'About Damn Time' by Lizzo played from a bluetooth speaker until someone turned it off.

The menacing aura made Genna feel like a gunslinger walking into a saloon in the Wild West. The checkered laminate floor could be old wooden slats. The long floating tables covered with hair care products could be a bar. The clients could be whiskey drinking patrons.

"Hello," Genna said in the silence, "I'm looking for the boo hag."

The werewolves jumped out of the seats in the waiting room. A few needed a beautician to unstrap their confines.

No one said anything. Just rushed out, heads down, not looking at Genna as they scuttled for the door. Some had half-done braids and raggedy bits of weave. It didn't matter. They cleared out.

Now Genna *really* had that OK. Corral feeling.

"Stacy's not here!" One beautician said brightly. She had 'Tiana' embroidered on her smock.

"So you don't work with the boo hag?"

"We don't accept any of her business anymore," Tiana said.

"But this is her shop, isn't it?" Genna gestured at the bell. "That's her doorbell? You use her products?"

The beauticians stared at the pastel bottles of conditioner and shampoo. One with 'Jasmine' on the lapel laughed, a high pitched titter. Then picked up a trash can and swept her counter clear. The other beauticians quickly followed suit.

"No, of course not. We buy all of our products from reputable artisans." Tiana said over the thunder of plastic bottles being hastily shoved into trash bags. "You're welcome to check our sources."

"I would actually."

Jasmine sprinted into a back office and came out with a laptop. Her sneakers squeaked on the linoleum as she carried it over to Tiana who passed it to Genna. "Here you go! It's all here! Everything's above board! No need to audit anyone."

There was also a Louis Vuitton knockoff bag full of rolled cash. Genna ignored the bribe. She focused on the laptop, quickly scanning the excel spreadsheets. "It says Witch Market."

The beauticians were sweating through their heavy makeup. They had that terrified honesty of people used to being threatened. Genna felt bad but not enough to stop looming. She couldn't forget Troy nearly dying.

"You supplied the boo hag with your clients," Genna said.

"We thought she made medicine," the beautician said.

Genna sniffed. That stank of honesty too.

"It was Delilah who sold us out!" Another beautician exclaimed, ignoring frantic shushes. "It wasn't us! We just work here."

"You didn't know or you didn't want to know?"

"I didn't know!"

Another honest answer. Wow, this was the easiest interrogation she had ever done. "Why should I believe you?"

"If you don't believe us then ask Whitney. She's a tooth fairy."

"Where can I find her?"

The beauticians shook their heads. Genuine worry leaking into their expressions.

"We haven't seen her since she quit," Jasmine said, fiddling with her long nails, "She called Delilah out. We didn't listen."

"And you think that Delilah might be feeling vindictive?"

Jasmine shook her head hard enough to make her ombre pink to blue tresses bounce. "I don't know. I didn't know her long. Delilah got out out of the cages but it's all super weird."

"I thought we owed her," Tiana said, "But what if she's the reason we got Turned in the first place?"

Other beauticians snapped their fingers. The scent of seething resentment overshadowed the smell of hair products.

Genna put the gathered hair products into the medicine bag. The medical journal gave her a report of its contents, who had been ground into ingredients, and the times. She took a Mead Journal from the stack of offered paperwork. It was empty except for a few scribbled pages. She pressed the journals together. The writing transferred itself. She offered the journal to Tiana and Jasmine."Here's the ingredient list of your products and the people who got turned into ingredients."

Neither touched the journal. "We believe you."

"Would you like a haircut or a free pedicure?" Tiana said.

"Maybe later." Genna gave her a long look as she closed the medicine bag. She walked out. The bell dinged.

She snatched the bell off its mooring and squeeze it. Her eyes went from brown to wildfire orange with purple lightning crawling along her eyelashes and eyebrows. The bell melted in her hand. She tossed it into the medicine bag and walked out.

The beauticians grabbed their bags, got in their cars, and fled. Except for Jasmine and Tiana, who started sweeping and cleaning. The Salon was all they had. There was nowhere to run.

"Why'd you try to give her a haircut?" Jasmine growled, "That sounded like a threat!"

"It was habit, I swear!" Tiana squealed, grabbing her vape.

ESPERANZA THE TATTOO ARTIST ALWAYS KNEW WHEN A witch walked into her parlor. Boo hags had a special relationship with tattoos. Many brought their own ink or watched closely as she prepared the drawings, the needles, and the ink. She bought ingredients from the Witch Market. They said it was locally and ethically sourced. She believed them.

Until one day, a dragon dressed as a cowboy walked in. She stared at the complex artistry and magic decorating his skin. Even his black stetson and rattlesnake skin boots were magic.

Then his wife walked in. She had no tattoos but the air buzzed around her with the same power. She stroked the leather couch covered in tattoos. Esperanza practiced on the furniture when she tried out new needles, ink, and protective signs.

"Hello, would you like a tattoo?" Esperanza said.

"You should get rid of your ink," The witch traced a design.

"I paid for these inks from a reputable seller," Esperanza said angrily. "I am a member of the Briarpatch."

"You're a good artist," the cowboy said, patting his tattooed forearm. "But your seller bought bad product."

Esperanza wished that this was a lie or a shake-down but she smelled the truth. They were delivering the bad news to innocent witches trying to make a dollar out of seventy-five cents. She told them about Stacy the boo hag. Then she threw out the bad ink.

The Bone Tent

PROFESSOR ONYX DID NOT LIKE WITCHES. THE GIRL Scouts had made the mistake of singing show-tunes from *Wicked* and *K-Pop Demon Hunter* until she kicked the door open.

"Have you ever seen what witches do to us?" Professor Onyx snarled. "Didn't you hear about the Salon? Witches ground our bones and made face cream!"

"But everybody knows that they use animal parts in makeup," La Croix said.

"What's the harm in singing?" Malört said.

"It sounds to me like we need to have a field trip," Professor Onyx said, smiling like a cadaver dog that had just picked up a new scent. "Seeing is believing."

La Croix, Malört, and the Girl Scouts looked at Missy for help but she shook her head. "Field trip."

~

OUTSIDE THE BONE TENT, PEOPLE BUSTLED PAST AS IF this tent was nothing. This shop was positioned at a busy corner where a confluence of markets met. The Farmers and Witch Market were in the front. The Black Market was behind.

There was a car rally going on in the parking lot. Vintage cars puttered down the sloped cement. A huge clothing swap called the Boutique on the other side of the big building.

Skin traders and slavers walked among soccer moms and incense peddlers. Hunters, witches, vampires, werewolves, and magical creatures pretending to be human. All pretending to be human as they hawked their wares from different stalls.

The Dragonfly pack ranged throughout the Black Market stall. A tight maze of shelves and stacked baskets made navigation difficult. Missy hugged her elbows against her sides. She didn't want to explore. She was too wide and genuinely not interested in finding out what was in the dark recesses of the store.

There were bones. So many bones. Death was this tent's primary merchandise. Bones in their raw form filled barrels and hung baskets. Bone wind chimes. Bones carved and painted with designs. Bone masks. Bone jewelry. Bone art.

There were antlers of various animals. Antler chandeliers and lampshades. Hooves made into footstools.

And taxidermy. Baby ducklings in jars. Butterflies and bats pinned on cardboard. Different kinds of animals were sewn together to look like jackalopes and rodents living humorously human lives.

Missy had seen placed like this before but now she could smell it. She wanted to vomit. She was mesmerized by the jars and taxidermy. There were bones everywhere. Every creature had died terribly. The pain of their tortured deaths lingered in the bones and remnants.

Rainey gripped Missy's arm. "Breathe. Just breathe."

Missy took a deep raspy breath. She had been hyperventilating. "I-I-I can't do this. I know we're supposed to be brave for the girls but I can't."

"It's okay. This is a Black Market stall. Be careful. Don't touch anything."

"I won't."

Rainey stayed close. Missy was grateful that she was her

hunting partner. Rainey was muscular like a roller derby star. She was good at killing, quick and ruthless.

Professor Onyx had gone ahead. The rest of the pack stayed in clumps.

There were enraged snarls and startled shrieks from the very back of the tent. Then the entire Dragonfly pack stampeded through the narrow channel of shelves and aisles, knocking over everything in their path. Magic leapt along their hair and clothes like black lightning. Missy could smell it.

Rainey swam against the current. Missy followed. They reached the back office just in time to see Professor Onyx rip the head off a woman and flung it across the crowded office. The mangled remains of a man was at her feet.

Missy had seen Professor Onyx kill before but this was worse. There was blood everywhere. Dribbling pieces of organs and intestines. Exposed living bone. A heart still pumping as it died.

The same curses crackled off of Professor Onyx's fur. Blood dripped from her teeth. Her eyes were too wide. "Get out of here or you'll be cursed like me!"

"It's already too late," Rainey said, "The whole pack has been infected."

"You did what you had to do," Missy said, stuffing down her revulsion. "Whatever comes next, we'll face it together."

"They have a daughter." Rainey picked a framed photograph off the wall.

"She'll come after me," Professor Onyx said. "Don't follow. That's an order. Keep the pack safe!"

She ran out the back door into the Black Market section. Rainey dragged Missy back. "Come on. We've got to go."

"No, first we burn this fucking place to the ground." A strange fox said.

Missy and Rainey turned to see an Asian fox pick up a bottle of soju from the desk. She bustled around like she knew what she was doing. Missy and Rainey followed her orders.

Briskly they ignited several small fires in different parts of the store. Then they hurried out, trailing smoke. The fox ran out after Professor Onyx while Missy and Rainey rejoined the flow of market traffic.

"What do we do now?" Missy said, looking straight ahead.

"We get as far from here as we can," Rainey said.

"What about the black lightning?"

"What are you talking about?"

"Never mind. Let's get out of here."

Smoke rose out of the Bone Tent.

A Magnificent Smell

MISSY FOLLOWED THE LADY IN THE RED TRENCH COAT. She looked like Carmen San Diego at a Paris fashion runway. Missy didn't know much about designer clothes but the way the woman carried herself screamed wealth. She had fuck-you money. The kind that meant she didn't need to work a job that she didn't want. No one could force her and no bill could bind her to a desk.

She smelled magnificent.

Missy followed her, sniffing at her scent. She was confused by her own arousal. Then was distracted by hunger since the lady stopped at a barbecue joint. The big Strait-Legged Bacon sign glowed on one side. The Yellow Rose strip club was across the parking lot.

"You missed Werewolf Wednesday by a day," the lady said, now behind Missy.

She hadn't seen the lady move. Professor Onyx and Rainey would be pissed that she was out of the den wandering around by herself without backup. That was why they were supposed to hunt in groups. But Missy had wanted to enjoy a quiet evening without being a den mother.

"What are you?" Missy said to hide her chagrin at getting caught. "You don't smell like a werewolf."

"What do you think I am?"

The longer Missy looked at the lady, the harder she was to see. Her eyes glowed in the dark, not reflecting the parking lot light, actually glowing from the inside. Orange as a banked fire. Her skin prickled with danger. "You smell big and scary, like that deep sea nightmare fish in *Finding Nemo*, you know the one with the shining light at one end and lots of teeth? It's like I see you, and you want me to see a werewolf, but it's not you."

"That's an angler fish." The lady turned into a coywolf with fur blacker than the shadows. Only for a moment. Then back into a woman. "See? I'm a werewolf. Not a nightmare."

Missy shivered. That transformation had none of the bone popping and skin twisting. It was quick, like a flash of lightning. "Please don't eat me."

"The thought hadn't occurred to me."

"What are you? Seriously. I won't tell."

"I'm a direwolf."

Missy chewed on the inside of her cheek. "Okay."

The lady gave her a long look. "You don't believe me?"

"I didn't say that. It's just, direwolves went extinct 100,000 years ago. So where've they been until now?"

Another look. This time, it was intelligently amused. "Most people don't know what a direwolf is."

"I googled wolves after I got Turned. The pack doesn't care but I wanted to know."

"A direwolf is a dragon. I'm a fire breathing dragon disguised as a werewolf. My husband is too."

"You're married to another dragon? That's so cool!" Missy knew she sounded stupid but what else did you say to a real life dragon? She felt like Bilbo meeting Smaug, only she was not the embodiment of evil. "Why do you stay in human form?"

"I was born in a human body."

Missy nodded. "I get that. I can Turn but being human is a habit that's hard to shake."

"You have a pack?"

"Yeah, I'm new."

"I'm also a doctor. I specialize in lycanthropic surgery. I pull bullets out of werewolves. I heal curses and other ailments."

"That's cool."

"Come find me if you need help. And you should come join Werewolf Wednesday to meet others like us." She reached into her doctor's bag and pulled out a flyer. "Here's the instructions. You have to pass through a magic door that's a security check point. Once you're in, you're in."

Missy hesitated then took the flyer. "I'm Missy."

"I'm Genna. If you can smell my true shape then you have magic too. Like attracts like."

"I don't have magic. I can't do what you do."

"Magic isn't always obvious. Sometimes it's just a gut feeling."

Missy bit her lip. "I saved my pack the other day. I got this bad feeling that it wasn't safe. They believed me. There were dog catchers. They would've kidnapped the girls."

"Great job. Keep trusting your instincts."

"Are you a good witch? Werewolves hate witches because they chop us up and sell us for parts at the Witch Market." Missy told her about the bone tent and the black lightning. And the Salon.

"I've been to the Salon and the Witch Market. That black lightning sounds like a death curse. Be careful."

"Do you think you can cure a death curse?"

Genna stepped closer, sniffing the air. "I need to touch you. I'd invite you to my medicine tent but I should give you a free sample healing. I mean you no harm, okay?"

"Okay." Missy stood very still. Genna's hand gripped her shoulder. Missy stared into those glowing eyes as Genna pressed the heel of her hand against her forehead like she was blessing her in church service. There was purple lightning in the orange and red irises.

The magnificent smell surrounded Missy. The overwhelming scent lifted her up. For a moment, she stood in a field of blooming flowers. There was rainbows and cotton candy colored clouds. Then it was gone. They were back in a dark parking lot.

"Woah," Missy said, swaying.

"Okay, you're healed," Genna said, taking a bottle of antiseptic out of her bag and rubbing her hands. "That was one heck of a nasty death curse you contracted."

"Could you make potion that I could give to my pack?"

"It's not an antidote. I could only redirect the spell because you also have magic. You still have to pay for killing those bone witches."

"What did you do to me?"

"Think of it as getting whiffed by a bus. You'll feel the breeze as it passes but it won't hit you."

"Can you heal my whole pack?"

Genna touched Missy's hands. She squeezed her thumb int the back of both wrists. "I'm sorry. The best I can do is teach you how to divert the death curse from two people."

"Only two?"

"One for each hand." She turned Missy's hands over. A cold spread across her palm as though she had cracked a raw egg so the ovum oozed over her fingers and down her wrists. "There. Make sure you touch them and only them."

"Thank you." Missy stared at her hands as the feeling dissipated. "I'll tell them what you did."

"Are you sure that your pack would be okay with that? I didn't know that witches and werewolves had such a fraught relationship down here."

"Yeah, you're right. Honesty might not be the best policy here." Missy chewed the inside of her cheek. "But thanks for your help, seriously. What do I owe you?"

"You paid me with information. I've been going to Werewolf Wednesday for months and no one told me the truth. Now I know why I haven't had any patients. I'll find a better place to set up shop thanks to you."

"Be careful out there, okay? Not every werewolf is a good dog, if you know what I mean."

Genna smiled and hugged Missy. She was strong and warm. Missy felt very small and very safe. "You too. It was a pleasure to meet you, Missy. I hope you come to Werewolf Wednesday so we can talk more. The barbecue is delicious."

Genna Turned into a coywolf and loped off.

Missy walked thoughtfully through the quiet neighborhood. It took longer on human foot to reach Walnut Creek Park but she wanted time to think before she reached the den.

Much of Werewolf 101 was an indoctrination process to reduce questions and stop independent thought. Until she talked with Genna, Missy had assumed that werewolves could heal from anything and that witches were evil incarnate. Upon reflection, that was a dumb assumption. Not all werewolves were the same so why should witches be like the bone collectors and dog catchers?

The new den was in a large house that looked out at Walnut Creek Park's greenway. She walked in through a back gate and tromped through tall grass.

The pack was eating dinner, some on the porch, some in the kill floors, and others in front of the flatscreen tv watching *Bridgeton* season 2 for the billionth time. Usually she would be right next to Fanta, enjoying the romantasy but she was on a mission. She felt guilty as she walked past the couches but not enough to stop.

Professor Onyx and Rainey ate tacos in the dining room with the den mothers at the long table. Missy put one hand on Professor Onyx's shoulder and the other on Rainey. She concentrated. She smelled Genna's scent again and that egg dripping down her fingers feeling changed direction. Now it spread over Professor Onyx and Rainey.

They gave her an annoyed look.

"You missed dinner," Professor Onyx said, "We're not sharing. No begging."

"Fine, fine," Missy said, making a show of backing off while waving her hands.

She went into the kitchen. There wasn't anything to eat but a can of sardines and some crackers. She put some sriracha and lemon juice on top of the fish and crackers. She ate her sardines and thought longingly of the barbecue.

She had done the right thing. She trusted her instincts. The flyer stayed hidden in a side pocket of her leggings.

Missy smiled to herself. She had met a real dragon. Cool.

Long Shadows In Tall Grass

Long shadows in the tall grass cast by the burning tent hid Professor Onyx from the angry teenager.

"Where are you?" The teen shrieked. "Come out and fight me!" The girl was mad, sad, and wielding an ancient Korean artifact that spat pink lightning. Professor Onyx didn't know magic but she watched a neon-pink spell incinerate a vixen to smoking bones. She wasn't in a rush to take her head on.

Professor Onyx wasn't sorry that she murdered and ate the girls' parents. The girl clearly wasn't sorry about who had been reduced to ingredients in her family's tent. Professor Onyx had walked among the shelves. She found missing members of her pack in the Bone Tent and too many werewolves who smelled like the Salon. Their teeth turned into necklaces. Their hair ground into powder. These black market butchers had to pay. And now, she had to deal with the justifiably enraged teenager she had orphaned.

Professor Onyx wasn't magic. Not like the fox. She had tried to leap out at the girl and passed through her like she was made of smoke. There was some kind of defense aspect to the artifact in her glowing hands.

Professor Onyx hated fighting witches but she didn't back down. She crept over to the vixen's still smoking bones. Only the skull and teeth remained. And hate.

"They killed my children!" the fox shrieked in her head, *"They burned my forest. They skinned us and sold us. They took everything from me!"*

"Help me kill her," Professor Onyx whispered. "I swear I'll rip her apart."

That was all the fox needed. Power crackled like fire. Fortunately, Professor Onyx had plenty of rage. She put the fox's skull on her head. The teeth sunk into the skin of her forehead and eyebrows. The vixen's power was in the smoke.

Professor Onyx ran through the grass, the nine-tailed fox's ancestry gave her speed. She howled. The teen screamed and blast the artifact. Professor Onyx dodged, juking with the artfulness learned from a thousand fights with a thousand enemies. She disemboweled the teen and ripped out her armpits. She tore out her hamstrings and dragged her through the tall grass.

The vixen's smoke filled the girl's lungs. Professor Onyx blinded her eyes. It smothered her while Professor Onyx kept her too disoriented to use her earth magic. The artifact dropped on a rock. It shattered.

"Get back!" The fox barked.

Professor Onyx leapt back. The pink lightning turned to fire. The girl writhed as she burned. Her life and blood were consumed. She turned into ash. The fox skull crumbled into dust on Professor Onyx's head. She shook it off. A hot breeze disturbed the piles of ash. Professor Onyx trotted away. Alive and satisfied.

Rainey and Missy were the first to greet her when she returned to the den.

"You did it! You killed the bad guys!" Missy sang. Missy dropped all pretense and hugged her tight. The soft strength and genuine happiness surprised Professor Onyx as Rainey joined in.

Several Girl Scouts demanded to be included in the hug. Tails wagged. Professor Onyx accepted the pack hug.

"It's good to be home," she said, marveling at that truth.

Black Pearl Necklace

Genna extracted the tusks, the teeth, and claw fragments from a corpse she found among the olive grove. The wild boar's carcass had two full sets of curly tusks. The flies and maggots were gross. The vultures had eaten well. The smell was fowl. Teeth extraction was disgusting but she needed to know who hunted on her land.

She followed the trail of corpses into the Forsaken Forest. No bullets, crossbows, or traps. By the strike pattern, an exceptionally large mountain lion killed adult wild pigs. She smelled werewolves too. The cat fed the packs living in the Forsaken Forest.

The medicine bag helped the extraction process. She used a set of pliers and put the extracted teeth into small glass jars. A label wrote itself across the jar's face when she corked and shook it. She scanned the neat writing. The teeth rattled when she crouched down to put the jars near the cat scent. The medical journal added more information.

Bone magic. Powerful and dangerous. Gryphon.

Genna rocked back on the heels of her boots. A gryphon was a monster connected to spiritual righteousness. Gryphons used churches and other religious buildings as dens. Gryphons were hunted to near extinction like dragons.

More knowledge rocked through her. The medicine bag knew a lot about gryphons and their connection to organized religion. She hugged herself, surfing the tsunami of information.

Genna's instincts howled in alarm. She jump straight up, tucking her knees tight against her chest. The tar trap unfurled several tendrils, intent on dragging her downward. The tar grabbed the boar's corpse instead.

She created a bubble ward around herself like she was Glinda the Good Witch. Her boots landed on hard air as bubble floated above the ground.

The tar aged the dandelions. A breeze freed the dandelion seed pods from their stalks. It wafted Genna away from the kill site. She crouched, weapons ready as the bubble spiraled up through the trees with the seed pods. The tar sunk back into itself. Waiting.

Genna landed on the dandelion path a few miles away but still in the Forsaken Forest. She checked her surroundings before popping the bubble.

"Are you enjoying your walk?" Imani asked. Genna spotted the little tuxedo cat in the crook of a tree branch.

A sunbeam broke through the dense tree cover. She could see under Imani's fur. The cat was covered in thick scars. There were crucifix keloids branded into her skin. Tattoos for containment. Anti-witch blessings and bindings were layered upon the scars. Her neck, wrists, and ankles had thick callouses from chains and manacles. Her back was a network of whip scars and two large scars where her wings were amputated. Genna was horrified.

The gryphon trapped in a house cat's body batted a knot of a tree. "Got something for you in there."

Genna carefully put her hand into the small knothole. She expected the tree to crush her fingers. Instead, she extracted a leather bag. Inside was a triple strand of black Tahitian pearls.

Genna knew jewelry. This was the largest collection of symmetrically perfect black pearls that she had ever seen. No clasp. Just a deceivingly simple knot and a single large black pearl.

Each pearl was heavy with water magic and the oyster's death as it was ripped open and its soft insides were searched with brusque hands.

Genna saw a memory of a Black woman crouched on the shore of a midnight ocean with a bag of gathered bloody pearls. The full moon was bright against her brown skin and the floating corpses of the men that she killed. Magic foamed over her ankles like the hem of her dress. Her braids draped over her face and shoulders like willow fronds.

The woman was a Yoruba practitioner. She built the Church garden, laying the stone path and planting every herb. She guided the underground rivers so the water stayed fresh and clean inside the Briarpatch. Then tar grabbed her and she drowned among the uncaring trees. Imani dragged her corpse out of the tar with bone magic. It still wore this necklace. Imani wept as she washed the bones and necklace in the Church baptismal pool.

"You know that's a fortune in real Tahitian pearls," Imani purred, waking Genna from the memories. "The Briarpatch survives by staying forgotten. I'm counting on your discretion."

"You mean, *you* need to stay forgotten."

"You do too, Genna Bellwether." Imani's eyes and eerie grin glowed in the forest's gloom. "Let's have brunch. There's an oak tree on South Congress. Wear the pearls or you won't find it."

"Sounds lovely. See you there."

Genna fed the necklace to the medicine bag. She nodded at Imani then walked out of the Forsaken Forest and into the sunflower fields. She was relieved to be under the bright open sky.

In the medicine bag was a recipe from a root worker's cookbook for a curse cleaning oil. She harvested sunflowers and olives as she walked to the mansion. She made oil infused with rosemary in her crafting room, following the recipe. She put the necklace in the oil. Tar oozed out like evil balsamic vinegar. She cleaned each pearl with a soft cloth and bone magic. She braced herself when she put it on. Nothing happened. She quickly dressed for brunch.

"Nice necklace," Troy said as she kissed him on the way out.

The Oak Tree

THREE HUNDRED YEARS AGO, THERE WAS A VAST LIVE oak forest that spread across south Austin below Lady Bird Lake. The enormous oak dominating the backyard of a high-end salad restaurant was one of the last survivors of that original forest. Its branches were wider than ordinary trunks.

Its survival was a mysterious miracle.

The truth was, this was Anansi's tree. She had lived in the original forest. She lost trees to gentrification, in-fighting, disease, and bad luck. The ultra-healthy fashionable restaurant brought strategic income and positive visibility to the tree.

The oak tree was protected by many covens and prayer groups. The locally sourced ingredients and the green witches who communed with the tree made this a neutral territory. Only branches that naturally fell were carefully collected and burned. The tree was pruned, loved, and warded against greedy developers. Everyone believed that *they* protected the tree from harm. And they were right. Anansi knew how to spin a story.

Imani relaxed under the tree's shadows as she walked through the backyard gate and onto the pea gravel. The tree had its own power which grounded her by sheer proximity.

Imani circled the trunk. She stroked the edge of the rough

bark as she stepped deeper into the tree's shadow. There was a little wolf spider scampering along the contours of the bark as she stepped through the silvery webs of the tree's defense system.

She transformed into a cat. Her muumuu becoming fur. Anyone who noticed didn't care. The live oak tree was a safe place for the magically inclined.

Imani was careful not to scrape the webs that lined the path inside the tree. The spiderwebs around her sparkled like dew drops in moonlight as they caught the excess magic of her transformation. She padded down the intricate root system and into the warm darkness, navigating the twists of roots.

Anansi guarded the tree and the hidden path. The spiders shared stories and gossip. They listened to the prayer warriors kibitzing on the patio.

Imani followed the sound of wind chimes through the defensive maze of webbing. There were impressions of a walled garden through the thick haze of cobwebs. The music stopped. A gentle warning not to walk further. Imani sat down and tucked her tail over her feet. "Hey, Anansi. How are you doing this fine day?"

Anansi was busy building webbing. Her face was crowded with eyes and turquoise mandibles. "You invited a fire breathing dragon to my tree. After what she did to the Sweetwater Forest."

"You told me to welcome her into the Briarpatch. She can't burn anything down when she's wearing the black pearls. Besides, it's not like the Witch Market hasn't done worse and they're sitting at this tree like it's nothing."

Anansi looked at Imani upside-down. "You like Black Belle."

"She brought dandelions to the forest. Nothing's grown there but death for years. What's not to like?"

"No, you like her because she's hunting Stacy."

"I'm trying to keep the Briarpatch safe."

"I remember when you brought Delilah to my tree. You were so excited that she'd help you too. How did that work out?"

"Not all skinfolk are kinfolk. Delilah was always about the

money. Even if we kick her out of Austin, she'll move to Houston or Dallas and cut their hair. She's got a niche skill."

"You don't think she'll heed Coyote's warning?"

"I *know* she won't stop. The money's too good. Look what she did to Whitney. She's only sorry she got caught."

"How would you punish Delilah?"

"I'd curse her scissors. The more she cuts, the more hair grows. Until she and any of her clients look like Chewbacca."

"Why her scissors and not her?"

"That jive turkey is protected by boo hags. They're not going to leave her out in the open. Anyone who speaks against her gets got. What she did to Whitney was foul. Her scissors are her reputation. Without them, she's nothing but a backstabbing bitch."

"Turn her power against herself. I like it." Anansi's busy hands wove and tugged at the webbing. The cobwebs parted like stage curtains. "Enjoy your brunch, gryphon. Let's see if the dragon lives up to your expectations."

Imani padded quickly out of the tree. Her fur returned to the pastel muumuu. She adjusted her sandals and lifted her braids into a stacked ponytail. She stretched to dispel the tension. Anansi's power was *intense*. The tree hummed with it.

Genna sat alone at a table with her back to the tree. She wore a black maxi dress, a wide brimmed black and white straw hat, and flat silver sandals. The black pearl necklace rested against her brown skin. Her matching black pearl stud earrings was the exact same shade. Her eyes hid behind stylish red sunglasses.

Genna wasn't the only one in black but she drew the eye. Her intimidating demeanor transformed when Imani walked up to the table, dazzling her with a genuine smile. "Hi! I love this tree!"

Imani smirked. "I love the salads here."

The dragon and the gryphon feasted on chopped salads, fried goat cheese balls, freshly baked rosemary focaccia bread drizzled in olive oil, and drank ginger beer and fruity cocktails. They laughed in the sunshine, delighting in their new found friendship.

They knew that Stacy spied on them via meat puppets.

Knights

A PRICKLY FEELING WOKE GENNA UP. SHE KISSED TROY, told him to stay in the mansion. She strode over to the closet that kept her entire armory. She had carried it in a magical pocket from Sweetwater castle until now.

"Are you sure you don't need backup?" Troy asked while she cleaned and loaded her guns.

"Not this time, my love." She quickly changed into her hunting gear. "I've got a friend who needs help."

Troy stood in the doorway of their mansion while she jogged into the sunflower field, grow owl wings and fly into the forest. He resisted the temptation to follow.

~

THE STRONGHOLD WAS AN OLD HOUSE IN A FOREST OF trash and trees. The security lights were motion activated, destroying night vision.

The Dragonfly pack burst in through the stronghold's windows and charged down the hallway, howling and snarling as they clawed up the laminate floor.

Missy froze. Her fur stood up on end as the bad feeling

shrieked through her senses. She grabbed Rainey by a mouthful of the tail and yanked her backwards off her paws.

The machine gun blast blew a hole in the wall and floor so big that the pipes behind the plaster started streaming water. Right where Rainey's head would've been.

Rainey howled the alarm. The Dragonflies echoed the call. Professor Onyx stalked forward in human form. Her magic wand perforated the Knights hiding behind the false wall.

Missy ran. She dragged Rainey with her, out of the stronghold, through the door, over the porch, down the stairs, across the mowed yard, behind the dumpsters, and into the trees without triggering any buried mines or booby-traps.

"I'm fine." Rainey batted at her. "Let go of my tail!"

"You're not fine. You've been shot with a machine gun!"

Rainey shook her off and smacked her chest. "Look! I'm healed. See? The Knights are using regular bullets. Stop fussing!"

"You've got to be more careful. You never know."

"I know that our pack needs us!" Rainey loped away from Missy to the parked cars. She clawed up the tires.

Missy hesitated in the trees, pacing with nerves. She hated guns. Werewolf 101 had only increased her unwillingness to risk the pain. Because there was always pain. Pain of getting shot. Pain of healing. Pain of remembering getting shot. Missy wasn't a masochist. She was chickenshit. She cringed at the gunfire, the grenade blasts, and the agonized howls.

"Get down and stay down!" She yelped when Genna shoved her into a brush and shot a Knight with her rifle. Missy hadn't seen him creeping up behind her through the trees.

"What are you wearing?" Missy squealed. It wasn't the right question but her brain was short-circuiting with panic.

"This isn't my first rodeo. I dressed accordingly."Genna was armed to the teeth. She was scary and stylish, like Trinity if *the Matrix* was a cowboy western movie. All black leather and guns. "Stay down and breathe. I got you."

Missy obeyed. She was so relieved to cede control to someone who knew what they were doing. She didn't have to pretend to be brave with Genna. She could be a coward and try to dig a hole into the ground to hide.

Genna shot the Knights and anyone else who ran from the stronghold that wasn't a Dragonfly. No hesitation, disgust, or fear. She was cool and confident and mega-hot in a scary way. Meanwhile, Missy hugged herself and cried hysterically, trying hard to stay quiet.

Once silence settled on the secluded forest, Genna holstered her guns. "Good. Nothing but humans. No magic."

"Wait, you're leaving? You said you'd help!"

Genna studied Missy for a moment. "Do you need a hug?"

"Yes please!!!" Missy rushed her sobbing. Genna caught her and Missy was transported to a magical field surrounded by rainbows and sparkling light. They were inside of a tent. It smelled like Genna, fresh herbs, and safe. There were floor to ceiling wooden shelves of spellbooks on the walls. Thick carpets underfoot and plants in hydroponic tubes by the windows. A place of sanctuary, quiet, and healing.

Genna Turned into a wolf. Missy did too. They pressed against each other companionably. Their tails wagged slowly.

"Thanks for saving me," Missy said, her chin resting on Genna's back. "I totally lost my cool."

"Gunfights are scary. Your response was appropriate."

"No one else in my pack even hesitated."

"Kill when you need to kill. Don't let peer pressure to win."

Missy nodded, embarrassed. "I like your magic hospital tent."

"I ran a diagnosis. Clean bill of health. No bullets or curses."

"Cool."

The magic faded. They were back in the forest and in their human forms again. Genna offered her a flask. It was cold mint infused water. Missy drank her fill and still there was more. She wiped her mouth and handed the flask back. "Thanks, Doc. I really needed that."

"You're welcome, Missy. Come find me at my tent if you

encounter something that can't be fixed with a pair of pliers." Genna trotted away. She disappeared between two trees. Even her scent was gone. Missy was alone.

Genna was more wolf-like than the Dragonflies. Wild and fierce but also nurturing. But as cool as it would be to run with Genna, Missy couldn't leave Rainey and Professor Onyx behind. She crept into the stronghold, needing to confirm their safety. Like it or not, she wasn't going anywhere without them.

Rainey and Professor Onyx were face deep in a Knight's torso, the body armor and ribcage pulled back to get to the good stuff. There was plenty of Knights and their squires for the pack to eat. Enough to butcher, bag, and take back to the Youngbloods and Girl Scouts guarding the den.

Missy ate, spitting out the bullet shells. The Dragonflies joked and retold their part of the hunt. No one had noticed her absence.

La Croix and Malört had found the Knights' manifestos. They angrily shared with the pack the awful missions that the Knights had planned and their targets.

"We did good today, ladies," Malört said.

"Go team!" La Croix jumped like a cheerleader, arms up and legs out in a split. The pack laughed, relaxed and amused.

"This is a link in the chain," Professor Onyx said, dousing the camaraderie like a bucket of ice water to the face. "Do you have the locations for other strongholds? Did they make contact before we cut off communication?"

"Oh my god, you're right," Rainey said, "We don't know who the Knights contacted when we attacked."

"Even if they did, they'll think it's a rival faction or an extremist," Malört said. "No one believes that werewolves exist."

"We can't depend on that," Professor Onyx said, "We have to act now. Did you find the manifests on where the targets were murdered, deported, and trafficked? Do you have their bank statements? Who's financing this operation?"

"I'm just saying that we should celebrate the win," La Croix said loudly. "We did good today. What's so wrong about that?"

"We celebrate by eating." Professor Onyx said.

"You think you're so special," Malört muttered. "You wouldn't even know about the Knights if we hadn't told you."

"I'm not sacrificing my peace because you're at war with yourselves," Professor Onyx said. "Were some of those Knights familiar? Feeling a little conflicted that your own people are evil?"

The Dragonflies were restless and uncomfortable. Missy decided that now wasn't the time to mention Genna's assistance.

Fanta nudged Missy, giving her a look. "Do something!"

"Like what?" Missy said, incredulous.

"Tell her to chill out. She's doing too much."

"Have you lost your mind? Professor Onyx was eating bigots for breakfast since disco was invented. We're new to this. She's true to this. We do what she says and hit the other strongholds before they have a chance to regroup. The hunt's not over."

"Kiss-ass." Fanta muttered, retreating.

"Oh, shut up and eat your dinner, Fanta. You aren't clever."

Now Missy had the entire pack's attention. The glares too.

"Bigots for breakfast," Rainey repeated, "Sounds like a type of cereal like Frosted Flakes or Fruit Loops."

"Special KKK?" Missy quipped. "It's tragically delicious."

The Dragonflies chuckled. It wasn't funny but they'd laugh at anything to break the tension. La Croix, and Malört didn't laugh. They searched through the computer and binders, occasionally glaring at Missy. Fanta did too. The pack went back to eating.

Missy ignored the glares and grabbed another Knight to eat. The last pangs of guilt that she had put Genna's protection spell on only Rainey and Professor Onyx evaporated. The pack didn't have their back.

The Wookie

Delilah's hair started to grow. And grow. And grow. The hair on her back, breasts, and even ass wasn't fur. It was thick greasy curls.

She waxed, threaded, tweezed, plucked, shaved, and cut. She used old photographs of herself to separate her eyebrows from her hairline. The hair grew back.

Delilah went to Coyote's tent to beg for forgiveness. Coyote laughed so hard that she fell off her chair by her loom. "You look like the hair clogging my shower drain! No, you look like a Brillo pad after scrubbing a grease trap!"

"It won't stop growing," Delilah wept. "I'm sorry!"

"Not yet you're not," Coyote chortled. "I warned you."

"They called me a Wookie!"

Coyote howled with mirth, kicking her feet as she rolled on her back. "You look like Chewbacca's cousin, Dreadlacca!"

Delilah left, feeling small, mean, and worthless. She went back to the Salon. Only Tiana and Jasmine still worked at the Salon to handle clients. Most werewolves were too desperate to care about the Witch Market but other beauticians quit after Stacy failed to shut Whitney up. The damn tooth fairy ruined everything.

Delilah wasn't allowed to touch any clients. Or sweep up or

take out the trash. Jasmine and Tiana watched her like a hawk. They searched her bags and tracked her phone.

"It's not that we don't trust you," Jasmine said, "But we've got bills to pay and you kinda got us canceled by doing fuck shit."

"You did my girl Whitney dirty." Tiana said. "That's foul."

"I'm sorry," Delilah said, "I've changed. That's why I'm here."

"Besides, you're kinda busy with your situation," Tiana gestured at Delilah's hair. "Want me to wax your back again?"

"Maybe later." Delilah was nauseous with humiliation.

"You know that this is stress right?" Jasmine said, sweeping up tumbleweeds of hair. "The more you cut the more grows back."

Tiana went to the sink, cleaning combs and brushes. "At least it's a hair curse. It's not like you got turned inside out."

"Ooh, yeah! Remember when Stacy did that bunch of were-wolves at the club?" Jasmine said. "They melted like barbie dolls in a microwave. So gross!"

"I know, right? Or she could have alopecia. Or rabies."

"Or those Slipskins that eat you from the inside."

"You're not helping!" Delilah snarled. "I'm a hairy disgusting beast. Nobody's gonna fuck me!"

The plucked area quickly grew back. She threw herself into her spinning chair with a sob/scream like Frances Conroy in 'American Horror Story', "Balenziaga!"

Jasmine walked over. "Okay, babe, you need to chill. You reap what you sow. So stop crying."

"Being a Wookie isn't so bad." Tiana patted Delilah's unkempt mane. "You gotta keep things in perspective. I think your hair is pretty. You need some shampoo, deep conditioner, and shape but that's what scissors are for."

Delilah straightened her shoulders. "You right. You right!"

Tiana and Jasmine bobbed their heads, clapping out a beat that got Delilah off her ass and back to the mirror. She stared at her reflection. She forced herself to see past the knee-jerk horror and focused on the fall of that hair.

She snipped and trimmed, working the shape into something. "There! I look good."

"You look damn good," Jasmine said. "You're a hot Wookie!"

"Listen, we've got some clients. Now that you're presentable, would you mind?" Tiana tilted towards the backdoor.

"Yeah, yeah, sure, sure." Delilah said, lifting her purse and sliding the scissors in their case. "I'll see ya'll tomorrow."

"Or you stay home," Tiana said. "Take a vacation. See some friends. We got this."

"The show must go on. The Salon's got a reputation to rebuild. You get that, right?" Jasmine plucked the keys out of Delilah's hand. Despite her long nails, she got the Salon's keys off the ring. She handed house and car keys back to Delilah. "You saved us. Now let us return the favor. You've worked hard enough."

Delilah felt her hair lengthening, reacting to the stress as she backed into the hallway. Jasmine and Tiana followed. Their big smiles did not match their hard eyes or their smells. She told herself that she wasn't running away. The door slammed at her back. The sound of the locks were loud. She hurried to her car, pulling her hoodie and mask over her face.

Delilah hid in her apartment until she was evicted. Then used up the last of her social network's goodwill by couch surfing.

She tracked the Salon and the beauticians on social media. Jasmine and Tiana sold some bougie skin product or swore that Black Belle's miracle hair oil could make follicles grow. The whole video series about best hair disposal practices was stupid but the numbers were starting to rise again.

Delilah searched for a cure for the hair curse. The Witch Market was closed to her. She went to Stacy out of desperation.

"What do you think would happen?" Stacy sneered. "The bone shop burnt down because of you! Whitney killed Pedro!"

"But I had nothing to do with that!"

"It was the Dragonfly pack, ever heard of them?"

Delilah grimaced. Yes, she had. Professor Onyx was out to get her and no one wanted to face her wrath. The Dragonflies had a 95% successful kill rate. "What am I supposed to do? Help me!"

"Not my problem." Stacy slammed the door.

Delilah lived on the streets. She wished that she could cut hair for humans but the damn curse could not be hidden or tamed. The only thing she knew how to do was cut werewolf hair. Where was the compassion?

She tried to properly dispose of hair clippings but the damage was done. Nobody trusted her. She could not afford to live off her tips. She had nothing.

Out of desperation, Delilah went to the Church one Sunday evening. Surely she could find forgiveness and absolution there? Pastor Faith was a good minister. She needed prayer.

But when Delilah went up to the altar during the call to action, she saw Coyote sitting in the pews. She looked at Delilah and smiled. The candlelight caught her lovely tan skin and her luminous black hair. The black pearl necklace gleamed.

Delilah's scream echoed off the rafters. The quiet was shattered. She ran down the aisle to the door.

Genna blinked, stunned by Delilah's abject terror. She glanced at Troy, a little hurt. He shrugged. She felt the attention of the entire congregation. Troy slid his hand over hers, squeezing it gently.

Clothing Piles

DOMINQUE SEARCHED THE MOUNTAINOUS PILES OF clothes that filled the back of the Boutique. Many of the clothes were ripped and crusted with old bloodstains. Other werewolves worked in teams to sift through the fetid drifts for something worth washing, repairing, and ultimately wearing.

Werewolves were hard on clothing. The Boutique ran a whole up-cycling culture to find fashions that hid their true nature and stayed unremarkable to the human eye.

Dominque did not like being a werewolf. The violence and rage left her feeling guilty and revolted. She could not negotiate with her own body. She focused on the Clothing Piles. The ultimate find was a matching pair of sneakers that fit. It was tedious work but it was nice and quiet. Stacy didn't bother her in here.

She ruined several pairs of sneakers with overgrown toe claws. She tried plastic and metal inserts which protected the toe boxes but made it hard to walk. She wrapped her feet. Nothing worked. Stress accelerated hair and nail growth. A few werewolves had tricks but pitied her love of sneakers. Dominque refused to dream different dreams.

She found a pair of Black Air Force Jordans, like a prayer

answered. She cleaned the sneakers and dreamed of escape. Stacy's grip on her skin wasn't always tight. She'd be ready to run.

THE WITCH MARKET WAS BUSY BUT THINGS HAD changed. Stacy surveyed the coffee tent. It was crowded. She snapped her fingers at Dominque and the other werewolves compelled to be her security escort. "Wait outside."

Stacy walked into the coffee tent, shoved past the line of offended customers, and glared at Jitters, the vampire behind the counter. "Where's the Bone Tent? You're in their spot."

Jitters smiled professionally without baring any fang. "The Bone Tent burned down."

"Where's the new location?"

"It's gone. Those people weren't bringing good business to the Market." The vampire gave Stacy a scathing once over. "Maybe you should move on too."

Stacy snatched a humorously antique glass bottle from its display rack. "What the fuck is this?"

"It's snake oil from Black Belle, a witch doctor."

She sniffed it. "It's just rosemary, olive and sunflower oil!"

The vampire shrugged. "It's still neon green."

"This is bullshit!" Stacy stomped out, throwing the bottle on the ground. The werewolves paced around her in a loose huddle.

Dominique noticed a Help Wanted sign taped to a flagpole outside the coffee tent. She didn't have a smartphone to snap a photo. She stared at the sign, memorizing the contact info.

Stacy grew angrier and angrier. The Witch Market booths didn't stock bones, furs, or ingredients anymore. Every skin trader had packed up and vanished.

"Cowards," she snarled. "I'll fix her. Black Belle doesn't know who she's fucking with. This is my land!"

Rabid

Stacy detonated a blood spell. A werewolf went rabid. The pain and madness made the werewolf forget her own name. Her body tried to heal itself but couldn't. She screamed and clawed at herself. Other werewolves tried to stop her and got bit. The madness spread as their skin rotted off their blistered skeletons, whimpering and scratching at an enemy they couldn't kill.

Stacy smirked at Dominque as if she hadn't given rabies to random members of the pack. "Let's see how Black Belle handles werewolf rabies."

Dominque felt ill. She could only watch as the boo hag relocated the rabid, letting their destruction infiltrate the Briarpatch.

Genna sat to her field clinic. The wind blew through the canvas flaps. The flying carpets circled the ceiling since no one else was in the tent. They looked like fabric manta rays. Other magical objects and spell books rustled like a colony of parrots, wanting to be read.

The scandal and loss of the Salon had left the beautician

community in a tailspin. If you couldn't trust your barber and hairdresser then who was there?

Genna brought a bag of free samples to Werewolf Wednesday meetups: dental floss, toothpaste, water filters, and nail files. She convinced several tents in the Witch Market to sell her snake oil, which was rosemary infused sunflower and olive oil from her farm. No one touched them.

"Trust takes time," Imani said, "Do you think that the pews were full the first year that I took the pulpit?"

"Is that why someone ran screaming when they saw me?"

"Oh, that was Delilah. Coyote wore your face into the Salon to confront her for fucking us over and selling us out. Then you saved Whitney. Now everyone thinks you caught her in the act."

"But they still don't trust me."

"Patience. Keep doing what you're doing."

So Genna was alone in a medical tent with no patients. Again.

She chose an old medical journal of a root healer in 1848. The root healer wrote about a boo hag preying upon the plantations and sharecroppers where she lived. It was difficult to parse through the language but Genna kept reading.

She moved on to a coyote medicine man's journal. This one was from the 1970s. The words squirmed as if it didn't want to be read. It resisted her with the querulous strength of an elderly man refusing to take medicine. She tried to sweeten it with pureed banana, some books liked to be fed. Still it sealed its pages.

Genna got angrier and angrier. Ready to break the book's spine and rip it in half. "Stubborn old book. I'm trying to read!"

The book snapped shut as a pair of dentures jumped out of the spine and tried to bite her fingers. Genna dropped the book on the floor, staring at it and sweating with rage. The book growled at her, the brittle paper slimed with banana.

She stomped to the bathroom to wash her hands and arms off then change her shirt. When she came back, the book was on the table, now militantly clean.

The necrotic red cover *The Curse of the Rabid.*

Troy ran into the tent. "We've got rabid werewolves on the loose! My bullets aren't working. It's bad, Genna. Real bad!"

The militant book allowed itself to be read. It had a recipe that killed the contagion so the rabies died with the host's body. The medicine bag and tent had the ingredients. She made the concoction and loaded it the bullets for her elephant gun. Her elephant gun was decorated with flowers and inlaid mother of pearl. It was designed to carry magic bullets and channel her magic without exploding in her face.

Troy drove, unwilling to let her face the rabid alone. She'd armed him, happy for the company.

The devastation they found was awful. Nothing was left of the quiet woodland. Even the tress were uprooted and savaged. Chunks of hairy flesh was mixed with dirt and wood. Nothing alive but the rabid. Genna's frantic thoughts smoothed out as she raised her elephant gun. She fired. The werewolf went down.

It wasn't a fight. It was a slaughter. Genna never missed. She took a few careful samples. The medicine bag confirmed that this particular strain of rabies was incurable. Just as it stated in the red book. Another unnerving coincidence.

Genna called Imani. The cat arrived wearing a hazmat suit but it was more bad news. "These are new to me. Cannon fodder. Good thing that you're a crack-shot. Hell, I'm impressed."

Troy returned, his lips tight with anger. "I got a few stragglers. Same signature. Same boo hag. No survivors or witnesses."

"Hey Troy, did you teach her to shoot?" Imani said.

"Genna was a gunslinger when we met," he said proudly.

"Wait a minute, you're rich. You have an army and body-guards. Don't tell me that you have a gun fetish or something."

"I don't have a gun fetish. Sometimes you have to keep your-self safe." Genna shouldered her elephant gun. "It's a long story."

"You can tell me while we're building the pyre."

"I'd also like to hear it," Troy added. "You've never told me."

"But you were there!" Genna exclaimed, incredulous.

Troy met her gaze solemnly. "Only at the end."

Missy's First Dogfight

Fanta, La Croix, and Malört weren't nearly as opened-minded as they pretended to be. They expected, well, *obedience.* Racism clung to every interaction like a bad hangover. The incident with the Knights had deepened that animosity. And the pack kept pretending things were fine.

"Why's everyone being so mean?" A Girl Scout asked Missy as she put the pups to bed.

Missy let the girls cuddle her like a living teddybear. She pet their soft fur and scratched behind their ears. "You know how you still sleep with your Blankies even though you're big girls now? Well, for La Croix and the others, those mean nasty thoughts are like their Blankies."

"But we're not human. We're werewolves!"

"You have to help them remember that."

The next evening, La Croix, Malört, Fanta, and their followers backed Missy up against a wall. The girls had given them Blankies.

"What the fuck is this?!" La Croix snarled, shaking a Blankie.

"Even the kids think that you should apologize to Professor Onyx," Missy said. "She's the pack leader."

"She's the one who should apologize! Acting like she's better than us! She's nothing but a—!"

Missy pounced on La Croix, Fanta, and Malört.

The three condescending bitches had never taken Missy seriously. The trauma of the Turn and the stability of the Dragonfly pack had mentally regressed them to a trio of middle school mean girls. Every bully needed a fat nerdy weirdo to prey upon and Missy fit the bill.

Missy *had* been the victim of bullying in middle school and high school by a trio of White girls. Therapy and graduating college Summa Cum Laude had helped her move past that trauma. Yet here she was retreading the same shitty path because it was familiar. Still wearing oversized muumuus and tracksuits to hide the shape of her body. Still ashamed of herself for tolerating their micro-aggressions for this long. That ended now.

Fanta got her head ripped off while trying to pull her gun from the back of her pants. La Croix and Malört were nasty brawlers but bit her breasts and backside, targeting her curves. Werewolf 101 had taught them how to kill but they wanted to punish and humiliate Missy for existing. That was their fatal mistake.

Missy picked them up, slammed them through the nearest wall, crushed their skulls between her teeth, and ripped their arms off.

Their supporters tried to dogpile her but she was in a full hellfire Rage. Her claws were rated E for everyone. The Dragonflies locked their doors, unwilling to break up the Youngbloods. Despite being viciously outnumbered, it was obvious that Missy was going to win the dogfight.

"She's killing everybody!" A Girl Scout whimpered as Professor Onyx and Missy herded the pups back to their room.

"Hush," Professor Onyx said, "The grown folks are talking."

MISSY KNOCKED POLITELY ON PROFESSOR ONYX'S door. "Can we talk?"

Professor Onyx nodded and opened the door. She had arranged the furniture, standing screens, and bookshelves to divide the long open-concept space into a parlor, a kitchen, a reading room, and a bedroom. It was impressively homey.

Missy checked the hallway nervously. It was either now or never. She went in. Rainey followed, giving her courage.

The other Dragonflies and Youngbloods had left Missy alone since she killed La Croix, Fanta, Malört and their crew. The silent treatment freaked her out. But if this was a passive aggressive tactic to pressure her into an apology then forget it. She wasn't sorry about killing a bunch of bitches who had it coming.

Professor Onyx put on a James Brown vinyl record. The speakers blared funky music loud enough to make her wince. Rainey leaned against the closed door, raising her eyebrows.

Missy stood in the middle of the room. "I'm tired of eating people. I don't like the person I've become."

"You mean a monster," Professor Onyx growled.

"We're werewolves," Rainey added, "We have to eat humans."

"Plenty of werewolves try to only hunt animals or find some other loophole with fish but it won't work," Professor Onyx said.

"Why not?" Missy exclaimed, slapping her hips with annoyance. "Why do we have to eat humans?"

"We have a specialized diet. We can pad our meals with human food and other prey but it won't sustain us. Plenty of werewolves starve while eating deer and wild boar. It works for a while but you'll always end up hunting humans. Usually by then, you'll be so hungry that you won't be careful. That's where the werewolf legends come from. A lot of misguided attempts to change your nature get more people killed then if you'd maintained a steady meal plan."

"But we don't even eat people who deserve! We're not making the world a better place. We're just...monsters!"

"Look, we all aspire to eat only bad people but it's not realistic," Rainey said, "We don't have the infrastructure or resources necessary to do the research involved in identifying and tracking these people down. It's not like we can go down to the local police station and look at all of those unsolved assault charges. Not to mention who you define as bad isn't universal. Just ask Fanta, La Croix, and Malört."

Missy scowled. "But what's the point?"

"Wait, this isn't about killing your pack sisters?"

"What? No! They had it coming! I'm tried of hunting humans. I've been meaning to tell you this. The timing is bad."

Professor Onyx held up a hand to silence Rainey. She stepped forward into Missy's personal space. "Let's take a moment."

Professor Onyx paced over to the wet bar. She lifted a clay bottle. "This is my favorite tequila. *Dos Artes, Reserva Especial.* They used to hand paint every bottle like it was Telavera pottery. They don't paint the bottles anymore but I've kept the original bottles and refill them."

She poured the tequila into three cut rose glass tumblers. "My grandmother used to have glasses like these. I thought that she was so elegant. I always get them wherever I go."

She handed the glasses to Rainey and Missy. "But now, you can find rose glass anywhere. Nobody wants them. They're just old junk."

She raised her eyebrows. Missy took a reluctant sip. Rainey followed. The tequila was pleasant. The three sat down in the parlor.

"This is about that little girl you ate, isn't it?" Professor Onyx said.

Missy scratched her scalp as her hair grew out of its tight braids, reacting to her emotions. "No one even looked for that little girl. There wasn't a report or cops or amber alert. No posts on social media. Nothing! It's like she disappeared and nobody cared."

"You've been checking."

"I don't get it," Missy said, tracing the patterns etched into the rose glass with her thumbnail. "Somebody must've brought her there. Why didn't anyone noticed?"

"My mom used to leave me behind all the time," Rainey said, "She'd think that I was in the back of the car being quiet. Or she'd be focused on my brother. Or she's be drunk. I had to keep myself from falling through the cracks."

Professor Onyx nodded. "Sometimes the hardest part of being a werewolf is how easy it is to find a dead human. You don't need to hunt. The callous indifference and raw violence of humanity does the work. Just follow your nose and you'll find one."

Missy took another mouthful of tequila. It burned all the way down. "I can't forget her."

"Good."

Missy frowned. "What's good about it? I can't sleep at night!"

"Empathy isn't weakness. You have to stay right with your own soul. Your kindness is your strength. You tried to seek justice for that little girl." Professor Onyx raised her glass. "Well done."

"You tried harder to get along with Fanta, La Croix, and Malört than they deserved." Rainey added. "I couldn't do it."

"Me neither," Professor Onyx muttered. "Congrats on winning your first dogfight."

Both saluted Missy with nods of approval. Missy bashfully raised her glass in thanks and gulped the rest of her tequila.

Now that they were dead, she could feel it. The way they put their fingers her hair and stole her bras, laughing as they wore them on their head like a helmet. Malört's constant need to mock anyone who wasn't rich and White. La Croix calling Mexicans fake minorities. Fanta talking Black. They didn't just vote for exclusionist right-wing dogma. They believed in it.

"Why did you save them?" Missy asked, after a few drinks. "You had to know what they were."

Professor Onyx refilled their tequila. "The werewolf who bit me attacked everyone at that protest. He used the confusion to run up and down the street. Afterwards, a bunch of us were strays, living on the streets, trying to figure out what the hell happened. Politics didn't matter. Just survival. But there were fights. It wasn't perfect. Nothing ever is."

"Yeah, but they were bad people!"

"They were good werewolves."

"How can you say that? After they disrespected you?"

"Exactly. Right there. That's why you killed them." Professor Onyx leaned forward, pointing with her pinkie at Missy. "You were good werewolves together. They tried to get along and you tried. But in the end, you killed them because they didn't respect the chain of command. That's why you're here and they're not."

The Gamer Room

Imani walked into the Game Room. It was the only place in the Church that had a consistent WiFi connection.

Screens covered the walls and tables. Gamers hunched over their phones and computers. The mismatched furniture was worn-out and crowded.

Imani had tried and failed several times to change the room into something else. Instead of using the fast and free WiFi for academic pursuits, this was a shrine to video games, online poker, and fantasy football.

Magic the Gathering, *Pokemon*, and *Dungeons & Dragons* were hotly debated games since sometimes there were real magical creatures who got caught up in the mix and needed to be freed. Was there devil worship or was it just a game? Other boardgames and card games were in different rooms on the first floor, along with dominos, spades, and Uno.

Princess sat in her favorite chair playing Mario Kart. She shouted at the other gamers, trading insults and compliments as her fingers clicked on the controls.

The curse was subtle but Imani was good at sniffing out sneaky curses and parasitic spells. Sure enough, Princess had leeching spells drinking her blood along her digestive track. She must've drunk something that was contaminated. Or someone put a curse in her water bottle.

The spell was skin magic. Hair, nails, and teeth. All it took was one trip to the Salon and the boo hag could get them all. The curses were like ticks, fleas, lice, and bed bugs. They jumped from gamer to gamer. The whole room was too preoccupied to notice that they were plague carriers.

Imani retreated.

Despite her fears, what happened to Roger wasn't what plagued the Game Room but she couldn't perform an exorcism without first handling this situation.

Imani closed the door carefully but she saw the same curses in the poker room, the domino room, and the perpetual Spades tournament that took over the Rec room.

Imani went to the ministers office but stared at her grandfather's old rolodex. Delilah had been the go-to witch doctor for the Church until now. Hair, nails, and teeth. Occasionally menstrual blood or a few strategic blood letting. Delilah's betrayal was a paradigm shift. Her entire contact list was compromised.

Imani walked to the edge of the Church's protective hedge. A path made of bones, claws, and teeth rose up from the tar. It wove through the pine trees like a pale ribbon.

Backbone Road thrummed a greeting. Imani transformed into a black and white tuxedo cat. She trotted into the magic, following the path that led directly to the back of medical tent.

Genna read in her tent, simply but stylishly dressed in a yellow sundress, cowboy boots, and free flowing curls. So deceivingly human while the ancestral magic of the Briarpatch pulsed around the tent. Trees swaying. Flowers blooming and chiming like bells. Bluebirds singing. Magical critters dancing. A fire breathing dragon who *was* a Black queen in her element. Her many skins and powers were like facets on a diamond.

Imani meowed, declaring herself while staying within the protective shadows of an archway made from rib bones. Genna knew how to shoot.

"What's up, Doc?" Imani purred at her own joke.

Genna closed the book and stood up, smiling. "Imani, it's good to see you."

"I've got a job for you at the Church."

Genna grabbed her medicine bag. The tent folded itself up, leaping into the bag's open mouth. Then she transformed into a big purple-black wolf the size of a volcano. Smoke drifted from her halogen eyes.

Imani turned and trotted back down Backbone Road. Genna followed but instead of stepping on bones, her paws touched flowers that grew directly underneath the bones. She kept pace, as though walking on the other side of a mirror's reflection. Nonchalantly traversing pure magic.

Imani focused on reaching the Church. It was a risk to open a direct connection to the field clinic but she trusted her instincts.

Imani turned back into a human as she stepped past the Church hedge. Genna did too.

The Church sanctuary was crowded with sick werewolves. They scratched themselves. Their moans and coughs echoed off the mosaics. The prayer warriors ushered more in. One gave Imani a suitcase full of hundred dollar bills out of the Church vault which she handed to Genna. "Save my people, Doc."

Genna nodded, checked the suitcase, and set it into the medicine bag. "I'll do what I can."

"This is Princess. Start with her." Imani introduced Genna to a cranky teenage wolf covered in rashes wearing a pink oversized t-shirt with a screen print of Kagome from *Inuyasha* on it and rainbow pajama pants.

"Can't I go back up and play the game?" Princess muttered.

"No, you may not! You brought this into my Church you nasty thing." Imani hissed. "Now you're going to take your medicine and you're going to like it!"

Princess grimaced and pouted but wisely shut the hell up. The other gamers whined but no one wanted to mess with Pastor Faith. They were intimidated by Genna's powerful presence.

Genna quickly donned a heavy-duty mask over her face and goggles. She took out a stethoscope from the medicine bag and put it against Princess's sternum. She concentrated, rotating the lenses of the goggles to different colors and refractive light.

The trick to using a magic medicine bag that could cure anything was to prioritize which problem to cure first. It wasn't always as straightforward as rabies.

All the bag did was list aliments. Genna had to figure out what was the illness and what was the side effects. The mask kept the contamination from jumping into her lungs.

Genna took a brisk step back. "They need baths."

"Baths!" The werewolves bellowed then coughed. "No way!"

"This is serious!" Imani hissed.

"As a heart attack," Genna retorted. "These rashes and coughing are symptoms of parasitic blood curses. Their bodies are working overtime. They'd be dead already if they didn't have hyper-healing. The Church can only minimize the damage. Ordinarily there are tablets that you can eat but we're past that stage. The bath will wash the parasites off. Then shots." Genna held up a syringe. "You too, Pastor Faith."

There was an aborted stampede. Even Imani tried to run. Genna's power wrapped them up like they were swaddled in towels. A tidal wave of healing spells washed over the congregation as she dunked each in water and scrubbed with Dawn hand soap. The parasites immediately jumped ship the second they were put in soapy water. Princess screamed at the little creatures pushing out of her pores and vomited up more. The injection felt like ice was poured into their veins.

The next few hours were awful. Imani had underestimated the extent of the contamination. But the prayer warriors helped once they were clean. Everyone working together with grim determination. Princess and her gamers faced the brunt of social condemnation for bring bugs into the Church.

Then the Gaming Room was swept for bugs. So was every room in the Church.

Neither Imani nor Genna rested until everyone was taken care of. Genna wrote down instructions for regular bathing techniques and a recipe to combat any internal consumption of cursed food. Her handwriting was gorgeous.

Imani and Genna walked back to her territory.

"Thanks, Genna," Imani said. "That was… just thanks."

"Want to come in for some coffee?" Genna said, opening her medicine bag so the tent leapt out, unfolding itself.

"Thanks but I've got to get going." Imani yawned hugely. "I've got devils to hunt."

"Devils?" Genna said. "Like real devils?"

Imani raised a hand. "Respectfully Doc, stay in your lane. If you really want to help then figure out who made those curses."

"You don't think it was Delilah?"

"Nah, she was the supplier. Whoever this is knows the Briarpatch. It's like we're stuck in a cage made of one way mirrors. We need to find whoever's behind them. You're here. You can figure out the cure. That's why Coyote gave you that bag. So figure it out."

"Well, then happy hunting. Kill 'em dead."

"Always do." Imani stalked away, tail up and fur fluffed. Genna ducked into the tent. Backbone Road sank into the flowers.

Genna sat at the table in the back office and started writing. She recorded the parasites that she had taken off the congregation. They were different from the Slipskins.

She had never been wanted before. Tolerated. Exploited. Usually she got silence. Begrudging acceptance. But not welcomed. Imani's faith was not misplaced.

Ragers

The werewolf didn't have a name. She didn't have a pack, except for the Ragers.

That's what other werewolves called the bloodthirsty, trigger happy, gleeful frenzying werewolves. She fucking loved the Rage. The joy of ripping a body into messy hunks of blood, bone, and organs. She felt powerful. An ancient monster whose howl sent fearful humans back to their caves.

The Rage gave her the speed and vindication to party hard with other Ragers. They had the same hate in their bellies. The same need for Frontier Justice.

The Ragers hunted hate groups, the real nasties. It was her job to take out the females. The girls who were married/dated/related to those hateful assholes. That included their children. No empathy for the mistakes of youth.

The Ragers only had compassion for themselves. They were victims of violence and injustice. Now they could finally pay back their tormentors. And they did. With a splatter radius.

The Ragers were loyal to Stacy the boo hag but the werewolf didn't trust that bitch. She didn't smell right.

Whenever the Ragers went to see the witch, the werewolf hunted the bus stops.

The werewolf liked the taste of misery and despair. She lurked around the lonely bus stops around midnight. She watched from the orange shadows in the bushes as humans waited for the sporadic bus to come.

Depression had a particular scent. She knew it well. Watching her prey reminded her of how little she appreciated her blessings when she was human. A werewolf had attacked her at a bus stop just like this one.

Before the Turn, the werewolf had been too busy whining about failures in online dating and the tedium of an office job to appreciate the joy of living.

As a werewolf she had to rebuild her entire life from scratch. No apartment. No steady paycheck. No social media.

She tried to join a few packs but they didn't trust her. Not that she trusted them either. Alone was better. She didn't have to share her meal. With Ragers, she could come and go when she pleased. They didn't give a fuck about nothing.

The werewolf caught the scent. She stood up behind the bushes, brushing off her clothes and shaking out a wig. She combed it a few times as she straightened the bangs low over her eyebrows. She didn't want the light to catch in her pupils.

She sat down next to a man wearing a horrible Christmas vest. It was out of season. Too hot for wool. Misery was a thick cologne wafting from his hunched solitude.

"Hi!" Immediately she knew that her approach was too perky. Damn, her interpersonal skills were rusty. "I mean, uh, hey, how long do you think the bus will get here?"

"I want to go home to my kitty," he said.

On closer inspection, the werewolf realized that he was a trans-man. Little curls of facial hair struggled to populate his chin. He had a surgically age-less face. She could smell the chemicals and see the little scars from plastic surgery. He had decent muscles too. This man had worked very hard to transform his body with surgery, drugs, and a gym membership.

Now that was a dilemma. The werewolf was hungry but she

considered herself an ally. If she had a house, she would definitely be waving the trans-pride flag. She never hunted the LGBTQ+ and neither did the Ragers. They had standards.

"I don't want any trouble," he said.

"I'm not a prostitute," she said. "I just want to talk."

He sighed, a long suffering gust of exhaustion. "Why can't you people leave me alone?"

He stabbed her. It was a good stab too, angled so the long blade slipped in-between her ribs to pierce her lungs and heart. Her lacy pilgrim dress was no match for his frightened strength. She hunched over, coughing up blood onto his khaki pants.

"Fuck you," the man whispered, shoving her off the bench. He got up and kicked her in the stomach. He ran down the block, his feet slapping the pavement. The knife still in his hand. He was fast. Definitely a runner.

The werewolf wheezed as she picked herself up. The knife wound healed smoothly. She inspected her dress. Ruined. Her wig was soaked with blood. Dammit.

She had tried to be a good person and he stabbed her. Fuck him. She would keep his knife as a reminder that no good deed went unpunished.

He slowed down into a power walk a few blocks down the street, on the phone and texting fast. She hurried behind the mountain laurel bush that was her primary den. She needed a moment to transform. She was faster that way.

She groaned through the Turn. Then shook herself off. As a wolf, she was the size of a German shepherd, scrawny enough that her hips showed and her fur was thin. She loped after his scent. She caught up with him as a car slowed down and pick him up.

"Drive!" He shouted at the driver and he flung himself inside. He slapped the inside of the door. "Go, go, go!"

"Okay, okay. Jeez," the driver said.

The werewolf stared at the tail lights, furious. He couldn't call a Lyft. That was cheating!

The bus rolled past the stop without pausing.

RAGERS WERE ALWAYS HUNGRY. HATE WAS NOT enough to sustain life. Ragers didn't plan either. They found a group. They ate them in a feeding frenzy. Then moved on.

They weren't any kinder to other werewolf packs.

The Ragers attacked the Dragonfly pack. The skill level was mismatched. A few fought but most of the Girl Scouts ran when the big males howled their challenge.

The werewolf attacked the fat slow werewolf who smelled like cinnamon rolls. Professor Onyx kicked Missy out of the way and broke the werewolf's neck, saving her life from snapping jaws. "Wake the fuck up!"

Missy struggled to her feet. So slow. Trying to digest the horror. The male wolves bit the Girl Scouts to kill. The yelps and struggles in the tall grass were horribly brief. There was no mercy for the young. Only terrible, red-eyed hunger.

"They're Ragers!" Rainey yelped. "Run!"

Missy ran. Professor Onyx and Rainey tried to herd a few pups but quickly gave up to focus on saving their own lives.

The werewolf's broken neck healed. She and other Ragers chased the Dragonflies, catching a few by the ankle, but soon fell back to focus on their eating their kills.

Mile after mile the survivors ran. They loped along the traintracks because it was consistently clean. Professor Onyx led them. Missy focused on forward, too scared to slow down or look back.

PROFESSOR ONYX SIFTED THROUGH HER VINYL RECORD collection. It had been a long bad day after a grueling month. The pack was down to the two members slumped on the couch. A few new recruits cried in their own rooms of the vacant house.

Professor Onyx picked Marvin Gaye's 'What's Going On' because she loved it. The gentle soulful music reached every sensitive ear. The sobs quieted though some Youngbloods smothered themselves under pillows and blankets to create cocoons of misery. The trauma of their first Turn was still raw.

Missy pushed herself off the couch. She strode outside. She dodged Professor Onyx's attempt to join her tired sway by the record player. She went outside on to the porch, shutting the door quietly.

Rainey grimaced. "I forgot how new she is. She's never lost her family before. Even her human family is still alive out there. She never tried to eat them."

Professor Onyx sighed. "It never gets easier to lose your pack."

She coaxed Rainey off the couch. They slow danced together, half singing. Their hands slid across back to become a swaying hug. Skin to skin from thigh to breast. They grieved together. Others left their rooms to join the dance.

Except Missy who was still walking away.

MISSY DID NOT DRINK HER FEELINGS BUT SHE DID LOVE to eat bread. Stress and a fast metabolism kept the consumption of patties and freshly baked loaves of sourdough from rounding her features further.

The problem was being a werewolf had been her whole life until a bunch of big nasty monsters attacked and ate her pack. Now Missy didn't know how to be human anymore. She was afraid to be a werewolf.

She needed a job. Maybe at a bakery. Nothing monstrous about that. Except the job required starting work at 4am.

Missy had learned that the Witching Hour was very real. That was a time for a werewolf to hunker down and wait for dawn not get to work.

She didn't have internet or a fixed address. She had learned that her family didn't miss or even notice her absence. No laptop. No contacts. No transferrable skills. Missy wandered, rudderless.

It was raining, just enough to make walking down a Texas road dangerous. People still sped in weather.

Missy ducked into the Top Notch for burgers and fries. Then a man in line behind her grabbed her ass.

She punched him so hard that he and his buddies slipped on the greasy slick brown tile. They cussed and shoved each other.

She stood over them, ready for them to surge to their feet. For the hateful words to tumble out of their mouths.

She was so damn sick of pretending to be human. She wanted to kill and keep killing. Then maybe she'd feel better.

"I'm sorry," the man said. "Let me pay for your meal."

Missy didn't blink. Murderous rage was naked on her face.

His friends were equally nervous. Their hindbrain was aware that they had pissed off the wrong Black woman. The man tossed a twenty at the cashier and the men fled as fast as they could without appearing to flee.

Missy ordered her food and left.

The cashier and staff exhaled shakily.

The Rager wanted Rainey and Professor Onyx to love her but they didn't. She wanted a nickname and to take the Werewolf 101 class that the other Youngbloods told her about. She wanted to a Girl Scout in Troop Dragonfly.

"Troop Dragonfly is gone," Rainey said acidly. "You Ragers ate them. Or don't you remember?"

"But I'm not a Rager anymore," the werewolf protested. "We had fun hunting together, didn't we? We've got a big group to take care of."

This current hate group on the Rager's list had a lot of women. Families. They were the paranoid paramilitary types who expected someone to burst through their door. And they could all shoot. Even the kids.

The werewolf needed help. Several Ragers had died stupidly.

Attacking head-on. She needed a plan or at least a pack who knew how to think. She had to kill them clever instead of running into a crowded room and start biting.

The werewolf studied her prey. She watched what they did to the few Ragers they managed to kill. She tracked them like her prey were a flock of geese or gun-toting deer.

She approached Professor Onyx and Rainey because Dragonflies knew how to kill without getting distracted by hate. Only, it was just these two cranky she-wolves and raw recruits.

"They've got werewolf killing bullets," the werewolf said. "I've never seen anything like it."

That got Professor Onyx's attention. "Silver bullets?"

"I don't know if they're silver. Maybe?"

The Ragers and the Dragonfly Troop worked together. They hunted down and ate the entire hateful herd, stragglers and all. No mistakes.

"We make a great team," the werewolf said.

Professor Onyx and Rainey were unmoved. The Ragers didn't care either. They had served their purpose. Now it was time to move on. The werwolf begged but neither side would bend to her will. Worse, they thought it was a joke. Then the packs went their separate ways, not interested in further collaboration.

The werewolf was left behind. Alone again. Nameless. Friendless. Confused and resentful.

The werewolf realized that Rage was not enough. She needed a real pack but she had a job to do. The Ragers needed her. The Dragonflies didn't. She stayed, trying to implement what she had learned.

Stacy dumped a bunch of newly Turned werewolves in front of the Ragers' lair. Plenty to eat. A few tried to fight. Most ran. She chased. "Wait, come back! Let's be a pack!"

The pups were desperate enough to run across the highway to get away. A few Ragers got clipped when chasing their prey. The werewolf retreated to the culvert with a disappointed sigh.

The werewolf slunk back to her bus stop hunting ground. The prey was equally miserable about their own lives.

She couldn't figure out why Professor Onyx and Rainey allowed the Dragonfly pack to die after a minor setback. Pups died all the time. Packs ate other packs, many preferred cannibalism to hunting humans. This was the way of the Streets. There was no time for weakness.

She caught the scent of a young werewolf, fat and stress-eating an entire loaf of sourdough bread. The scent was familiar.

She was part of the Dragonfly pack. As round and as soft as a cinnamon roll. She even smelled like baked cinnamon and icing.

The werewolf attacked the cinnamon roll. Missy was stronger than she looked. And she recognized the Rager. Missy killed and ate the werewolf with vindictive glee. Then she picked up what was left of the sourdough. It was soaked in blood. She ate that too, chewing on it contemplatively.

She was caught between two extremes. She wasn't werewolf enough to be a werewolf but she couldn't leave it behind either.

Lunas

Missy watched a pretty Black werewolf in a black and lavender cosplay French maid costume run across an HEB grocery store parking lot, tackle an old man wearing a MAGA red baseball cap, break his neck, and dump him into the trunk of his own car. The white and lavender laces of her petticoat skirts flared as she bent over, revealing bare shapely haunches and a werewolf tail. She rolled the man deeper into the trunk, loaded his groceries on top of his corpse, and pressed the trunk's button so it closed.

At the same time, another pretty Brown werewolf in a turquoise French maid costume punched a muscly Cyber Bro in a tight 1776 t-shirt right in the chest. He too got folded into his own truck. A third werewolf broke the neck of an elderly woman with wispy hair and an All-Lives Matter bumper sticker on the back of her gold mini-van.

The parking lot was full of werewolves in color coded French Maid costume. They moved with the balletic choreography of a flash dance. It was late in the evening but still, Missy was shocked.

She looked around but none of the human late-night shoppers stopped wheeling their grocery carts into the grocery store or to their cars. Focused on their phones. Even the security guard in his segue missed the attack. Either no one noticed or cared that the haters got jumped.

Missy turned to leave and was blocked by a perky werewolf in a kente cloth patterned sailor suit. "Hi, we're the Sailor Luna pack. I'm Sailor Òsùpá. It means moon in Yoruba."

"I'm Missy. Like Missy Elliot." She glanced around at the security cameras. "You should get out of here."

"What pack are you from?"

"The Dragonflies. Or I was. But I'm not anymore." Missy trailed off in a mumble. What the hell was she now without a pack? A lone wolf? A human? A patsy standing too close?

"I love Missy Elliot!" Sailor Òsùpá said. "Come with us!"

"Okay."

The Lunas were cute and attractive. They each had Moon as their name in their culture's language. She climbed into a Honda Odyssey with Chaand, Òsùpá, Tsuki, Gaelach, and Moon-Moon. The rest of the Lunas drove the stolen cars with their new cargo.

She expected the Lunas to drive to a coffee shop or their den. She was not prepared for a sex dungeon in the Speakeasy nightclub. The bodies were quickly loaded into the kitchen. Missy was towed into the nightclub.

The music was live. One act following the next in a variety show. Everyone was a werewolf, from the hula dancers to the one singing Nina Simone while dressed like Betty Boop.

The Speakeasy was full of beautiful werewolves, laughing and at ease. Missy tried to be comfortable but she kept seeing the Ragers. Missy felt ancient and awkward while the Lunas danced and spun in a twirl of neon rainbow petticoats.

Chaand, a gorgeous Indian werewolf in a periwinkle sari with silver moons printed on it, got on stage. She sang in Hindi and played a red and gold sitar under a blacklight. Missy was dazzled.

"Chaand was a music major in college when she was Turned." Òsùpá said, sitting next to Missy in the booth, drinking peach cobbler moonshine. "She could've been the next Anoushka Shankar. Now she can only play for us."

"She's amazing," Missy said as Òsùpá pressed close. "And the sitar sounds so different."

"Werewolf hearing," Òsùpá said. Her lips glowed a halogen pink in the nightclub gloom. "Will you watch me dance?"

Missy nodded. "Yep."

Òsùpá slid her voluptuous curves out of the booth. Her smoldering look warmed Missy's core.

"Well, hello Missy, where's your pack?" Missy choked when Amaya in a sparkling red sequined gown leaned over the table.

The heat died. Missy felt cold as a stone in the Arctic Ocean. "The Dragonflies are dead. The Ragers got them."

"All of them?" Amaya straightened up, withdrawing her magnificent cleavage from Missy's personal space.

"Professor Onyx and Rainey are still alive. Last time I saw them."

"But you're not running with the Dragonflies anymore."

"No." Missy watched Chaand, no longer enraptured by her dulcet voice and the enchanting sitar.

"I'm sorry." Amaya gently brushed her shoulder with a satin gloved hand and walked to the bar. Drinks arrived with a beautiful werewolf in a tight dresse. Missy sipped but her heart wasn't in it. This was a mistake.

Two werewolves in denim vests covered in LGBTQ+ Pride patches, rainbows, and 'I'll Steal Your Girlfriend' embroidered across the back stopped Missy on her out of the restroom.

"Hey, cutie. How are you doing? I'm Possum." Possum was short, sinewy, and rawboned. Her hair was in a crisp fade with smooth waves. She jerked a thumb at the bigger one looming congenially. "This is Tater."

Tater was as big and comfortable as a couch. Her hair was braided into tight cornrows.

"Hi, I'm Missy." There was an awkward pause. Missy knew she that needed to make conversation. Possum and Tater seemed nice enough. They were the first out and proud queer women that she had met since Turning. But she couldn't shake the gloom. "I'm sorry. My pack got eaten. I can't—I don't know why I'm here."

Possum and Tater sucked on their teeth.

"Fuck," Tater said eloquently.

"Yeah, we've been there," Possum said. "Do you need a car?"

Missy blinked. "Yeah, I guess I do. I hadn't thought about it. Oh god, what am I doing to do now?"

Possum clapped Missy on the back, making her sway in surprise at the powerful impact. "You're going to get drunk as a skunk and then double fist two ladies of your choice."

"Um, excuse me?" Missy said, wanting to rub her spine. Possum's friendly punch felt like being swatted with a bat.

"You've never fisted someone before?" Possum said.

"I mean, yeah, I have, but not two at the same time."

"You will tonight. You'll see. The Speakeasy is where you come to forget your troubles. Don't worry about Turning or knotting or anything."

"Knotting?" Missy didn't want to sleep with men in any shape, human, werewolf, or canine. Bisexuality wasn't Missy's thing. Ladies were. Always had been. None of the Dragonflies were attractive. Okay, she felt something for Rainey, but that might be misplaced emotions.

Rainey. Professor Onyx. The Dragonflies.

Again, depression sunk its teeth into Missy's soul. She hadn't said goodbye. She just left. Like an asshole.

Possum swatted Missy on the back again. "I said don't worry about knotting. The Speakeasy has magic. You stay in human form as long as you're in the club."

"Oh. That's good." Missy edged out of punching range.

Tater fished a keyring out of her cleavage. "Do you know how to drive stick?"

Missy nodded. Tater put the keys in her hand. "Congrats, now you're the proud owner of a black Toyota Tacoma. The papers are in the glove compartment. The truck's out back in the parking lot." Tater pointed at the distant exit sign across the Speakeasy.

"Thanks," Missy gripped the keys. "Why would you help me?"

"Because that's what we do." Possum gestured at herself and Tater. "We're mechanics. We make sure that werewolves always have a set of wheels."

"I can't pay you back."

"Nah, it's not about that. You're a Dragonfly. We've seen you taking care of the girls."

Missy took a deep breath but the tears poured and her ears felt hot. Possum and Tater immediately embraced her while quietly berating each other for making her cry.

She let herself be held. She was relieved by their brusque manner, masculine clothing, and Daddy-Domme energy. They smelled like cars, booze, and weed. She had met women just like these two at any lesbian bar in any city and online forum. And they were older than her and Black, which made it extra super great. Possum and Tater knew what they were. Lycanthropy didn't change that. Which made it okay for Missy to be herself. It was a slice of home before the Turn.

"Hey, hey, sorry," Possum said, "It's not your fault."

"I couldn't save them," Missy whimpered, "I couldn't do anything."

"It's like that sometimes," Tater murmured into her hair.

They steered her to a booth. They poured alcoholic drinks down her throat and gave her joints to smoke. Missy obeyed, wanting to stop thinking. Òsùpá danced, electrifying and complicated. Missy forced herself to enjoy the variety show. To clap. To cheer. And soon she was laughing for real.

Possum and Tater practically threw Missy out of the booth when Tsuki, a gorgeous Japanese werewolf in an elaborately lacy tie-dyed French-maid's costume and tall stacked club boots, asked her to dance.

They danced together on the dance floor, getting closer and

closer. Tsuki enticed Missy by lightly tracing the skin on her wrist. She led Missy through the sex dungeon. Past werewolves in leather and strapped to Alexander's crosses. Away from the club noise. The hallways was lit by red shell-shaped lamps.

Chaand joined them in the hallway. "Tsuki, you got to her first." She said playfully. Missy sniffed the jasmine blossoms woven through Chaand's knee length black braid. They opened a door. Òsùpá waited on the sheets, naked and massaging her brown breasts and teasing her dark brown nipples.

Missy stood in the doorway, wishing that she was sober to truly appreciate this moment. "You're so beautiful. I love your cosplay."

The Lunas preened.

"We want you to fist us. It's been so long since we met someone like you," Tsuki said, her lips so close to Missy's earlobe that each breath was a kiss. Tsuki helped her undress. "I wish I had your breasts."

"Um, thanks."

Tsuki put little cotton balls under Missy's fingernails and bandages over the cotton. Then latex gloves on top. "This keeps your fingernails from growing."

Missy stared at her gloved hands. "Oh, that's smart. Now I won't scratch you."

They lay on their backs, kissing each other and stroking their breasts and sides. Tsuki slathered lube on Missy's fingers. "There's always more lube."

Chaand and Òsùpá smiled up at her as Missy awkwardly crawled on the mattress, her gloves up. In the muted golden light from the single lamp in the room, they looked like paintings. A beautiful bounty of lush brown flesh. Missy pressed her nose between their thighs, savoring the heady bouquet. The tickle of nether curls.

Missy was excited. She loved when women didn't shave. If her hands weren't gloved, she would tug and tease. She suckled on breasts and teased nipples with the edge of her teeth.

Missy teased Chaand and Òsùpá until their thighs quivered with anticipation. Tsuki was at her back, kissing along the curve of her ass. She tried to touch her hair but Missy swayed out of the way.

"Don't," she said.

Tsuki back up, hands folded. "Sorry." She knelt, beautiful and chasten. Her long black hair spilled down her breasts and back. Missy kissed her to accept an apology then focused on Chaand and Òsùpá.

It took coordination to fist two women at the same time. Missy lifted their legs to press them against her front, curving their butts up off the bed for a better angle of penetration. Missy gently slid one finger inside of Chaand, then two, and then gradually pushed her whole hand in. Missy cupped her hand, pressing her thumb against the base of her ring finger to get the right shape while Chaand arched and gasped.

Meanwhile, Missy kept teasing Òsùpá, rubbing her clitoris and kissing her knee. She put her hand inside of Òsùpá in one smooth thrust.

Chaand and Òsùpá moaned for her, quivered, and gasped. Chaand liked a slower thrust while Òsùpá rocked so Missy's fist pounded against her cervix. Missy tested their flexibility, pressing their knees downward, her face framed by their calms. Their wet hot interior squeezed her hands.

Sweat dripped off Missy's hairline and down her back as she fisted them at different tempos. She grinned, delighted as Chaand and Òsùpá stopped pretending and actually got swept up in pleasure. She knew when she hit their G-spots because they arched, and writhed, and quivered, and cussed. Nostrils flaring. Mouth opened wider and wider to accommodate their moans. They curved around her, urgently dragging her down and desperately kissing her as they begged for more. Missy pumped both hands, her face smushed into their breasts. She snarled against their skin, her teeth scraping delicate flesh. They quivered for her as she growled.

Tsuki stroked herself in amazement. She had expected Missy to hesitate and need instruction. Now as her pack sisters howled through one orgasm after the next she wanted to go next.

Possum and Tater stood in the hallway, watching and guarding the door. They exchanged a nod. Both had clocked Missy's absentminded confidence. She wasn't the type to brag but clearly she knew how to pleasure a woman. Or three, since Tsuki got tired of waiting.

The Lunas were the first three that Missy fisted. Then it became a fisting train. She-wolf after she-wolf ran in and then staggered out of the bedroom, fumbling with their clothes and shoes. Their absentminded smiles and their hair and makeup in sweaty disarray of the thoroughly fucked.

Several horn-dogs tried to pounce on the scent of feminine pleasure and orgasmic moans, their tongues out and panting as they licked the air. Possum and Tater sent them yelping away with their tails between their legs and hands over their dicks. No one was interrupting Missy's sexy-fun time.

After a few hours, Missy prowled out of the bedroom. The scent of sex poured off her skin. Her glazed eyes were half-lidded. Her lips puffed from kissing. Her face and front wet. Several she-wolves had squirted when their orgasmed. She had dodged but her clothes were still damp with sweat. She felt calm and exhausted in the best way possible. Fucking a harem of beautiful willing she-wolves was like gorging on a feast of flesh.

A she-wolf walking out of another room with her male partner froze when Missy padded past. One glance and the she-wolf yanked her shirt down, baring her large pale breasts. Missy's hands were on those breasts. Her face in the she-wolf's hair, scenting her as she growled, scratched, and teased. The she-wolf moaned, trembling back into her male partner. He held her and stared at Missy, trapped between shock and lust. All she had to do was say something but she let the she-wolf go and kept walking. The couple kissed frantically, retreating back into the room to work off sexual frustration.

Possum and Tater smirked affectionately at Missy, playing off their own attraction. She accepted a bottle of water and gulped the whole thing. "Thanks."

"You're welcome," Possum said.

Missy held up the car keys. "Seriously. Thanks."

"Hey, we're family," Tater said, tapping on the pride flag on her vest. "Are you taking off?"

"Yeah, I'm hungry."

They nodded. They knew that she wasn't headed to Whataburger for a late-night snack.

Missy gave them a nod and continued down the hallway. Possum and Tater exchanged a look, amused. Once Missy got out of her own head, she was dominant as hell.

Amaya's painted eyebrows raised when she caught Missy's scent. Missy possessed the sensual magic of a fertility goddess. The she-wolves enthusiastically worshiped at her altar while the males were held at bay. Only someone with magic could access the Speakeasy's latent sexual energy power.

Amaya followed Missy to the Speakeasy's exit and held the door open. She smiled, more out of habit than anything. "I'm glad you had a good time. Come back again soon."

Missy met Amaya's gaze, the wildness right on the surface. The warm night warred with her overpowering scent. Missy nodded. Then she padded into the darkness.

Amaya watched the black Tacoma drive out of the parking lot and down the street. Slowly she exhaled and closed the door.

"Aw, she left already?" One of the regular horn-dog said. "I thought she was here to party."

Amaya ignored the horn-dog. The Speakeasy was a werewolf nightclub but some males treated it like a human hangout. They dismissed the difference between werewolves who lived in houses, pretending to be human and street monsters like Missy. Amaya was glad that she left. She would've killed any male who touched her without consent. Massacres were bad for business.

Amaya checked in on the Luna Pack who lay in a dog pile in

their den room. Òsùpá was missing her eyelashes and her silk press was a frizzy ruin. Chaand's braid was undone and little petals of jasmine were tangled in the tangled black tresses. Tsuki's pale skin was flushed a lovely pink and kept giggling to herself as she sipped her water. The other Lunas were in similar states of deshabille.

"She fucked the whole pack?" Amaya said.

"And I'd do it again!" Moon-Moon proclaimed. The other Lunas howled and agreed, laughing.

Amaya closed the door. She was pleased by their relaxed happiness. There were many female packs hiding in the Speakeasy's honeycomb of hotels and rooms. The Lunas were sweet sensitive girls who spent more time cosplaying for social media than out on the street. A close encounter with a strong she-wolf like Missy was good for the pack.

She got two beers for Possum and Tater who now sat at a private table. "Thanks for having our Dragonfly's back."

"Shit, she taught me some new moves," Possum said. "That girl knows how to show a girl a good time."

"I wanted to hop on that bed myself," Amaya agreed. "Did she say what happened to the Dragonflies?"

"Ragers got them," Possum said. "How many packs have those assholes eaten?"

"I thought the Dragonflies at least had a chance." Tater muttered. "I can't believe they got Professor Onyx."

"Professor Onyx and Rainey survived but that's all she told me," Amaya said.

"That's more than she told us," Tater said, "She started crying when we asked. It must've just happened."

"Still, losing the Dragonflies and their Youngbloods and Girl Scouts all at once?" Possum said, "That's bad for everyone. If they're not around, who's watching the kids?"

Amaya nodded. She stood up. "I'll see if I can find out more."

Eartha

EARTHA HOBBLED THROUGH THE MIST. THE SKY WAS A uniform gray. Periodically, she cleaned her glasses which fogged with frustrated tears and body heat.

She took herself on a walk. Really, it was more of a limp than a stride. Her left calf was knotted pain. Her toes tingled. Her hip throbbed. Her knee threatened to buckle when she shifted her weight. The sciatic nerve around her tailbone ached. Her side pinched.

The first Turn had not been smooth. Something had gone wrong. Tendons twisted the wrong direction. The old scar on her thigh from the original bite refused to heal smooth. Every subsequent Turn made it worse. So did sitting for too long. Or sleeping. Or standing.

Eartha was not old but the badly healed injuries aged her. She'd lose if any hungry monster or gun-toting human attacked.

She was alone in the mist. Even the birds flew from tree to tree instead of through the wet air. No cars wanted to drive with such dangerously low visibility.

Eartha paused under a large live oak tree to rest a moment. Reluctantly the muscles and tendons relaxed as she hobbled down a new block. The last confusion of which direction her knee bent rotated with a painful click.

Physical therapy and knee surgery were not options. Eartha straightened her back. She limped on.

She was determined to win. Soon she'd be fine.

"Pssst!"

She stopped a storm drain, sniffing hard. She crouched arthritically down and met the eyes of several werewolf children looking right back.

"You gotta get off the road!" One of the kids hissed. "They're after us. You too!"

"Me?"

"Yeah! You're a werewolf, ain'tcha?"

Eartha stood up before her leg gave out. "Come with me. I can't fit down there."

The kids wiggled out of the storm drain, scurried down the tree, and scampered across the wet lawn. There seemed to be more and more of them. Too many to count.

~

"For the children," Martha said. Her followers repeated her words.

The children told Eartha about Martha and her mob as she moved them from one house to another. Martha were set on purging werewolves from the Austin. She blamed werewolves for everything.

They said it was for the children but it wasn't. Not for certain kids. Not even for their own kids and grandkids either. No real child could measure up to what Martha believed.

Eartha couldn't hate like Martha hated. She too had to protect the children. They were so thin that their eyes looked too big for their pinched narrow faces. Their brown skin was gray with malnutrition. They dined on squirrels, feral cats, raccoons, roadkill, and anything edible in the dumpsters.

It snowed that night in Texas. The wind howled wild and cold. The werewolf kids were too scared to make noise. They huddled together as Eartha broke into a vacant Airbnb. She was tired, hopeless, and the left side of her back down to her thigh was worse in the cold. It hurt to walk or sit or think.

Only one of her and all these werewolf children. How could she protect them from Martha's hysterical sadism?

The kids watched her fall into a fretful sleep on the padded recliner in the living room. Their time in Martha's cages had made life before lycanthropy as diffused dream. Cruelty was normal. Kindness was like warm sunshine and clean rainwater on their parched souls.

Eartha wasn't afraid of them. She washed them, rubbed their skin shiny with Vaseline, and braided their hair. She let them choose anything they wanted to wear at Goodwill, celebrating their individuality instead of curbing it. She fed them Whataburger and told them stories about werewolves.

The kids were young but not dumb. They could not lose the only adult who gave a shit about their wellbeing. They snuck out into the icy night, a few left to guard Eartha as she slept.

Martha and her mob did not expect the escaped children to come back to her stronghold, free the ones locked in the garage, hack the system, and execute a coordinated attack.

Eartha woke up in a puppy pile. The kids were covered in blood but their bellies were distended.

Martha's head was on the kitchen counter in a plastic bag. So was a purse full of cellphones, credit cards, and cash. A note read, '4 U.'

GENNA INSPECTED EARTHA'S LEG. SHE WAS TORN between horror and admiration. Eartha's skin was full of Stacy's skin magic. Genna read a hard life made of blood and pain. Her resilience was inspiring.

"This knee has been very painful, hasn't it?"

"It's my sciatica," Eartha waved vaguely at her back. "I've been taking short walks and stretching to help."

A young werewolf tugged on Genna's coat. "Will she be OK?"

The tent was crowded with worried kid monsters. Eartha had tried to make them wait outside but they didn't trust Genna. A few opened lids and drawers, boldly eying Genna with unrepentant belligerence.

"Your leg has twisted around your knee cap. It's facing the wrong way and it's pulling the muscles and tendons. Every time you Turn, it makes it worse." Genna pointed at an anatomical poster of a werewolf body on the wall that the tent helpfully provided. "We need to teach your body a new way to grow."

The kids were loud but Eartha silenced them with a bark. "What do you mean, teach my body to grow?"

"The Turn is the Turn. It's what your body thinks is normal."

"Cut it off and grow it back," Eartha commanded.

"Even if I did, the next time you Turned, it would go back to this." Genna gestured at her warped leg. "You're young and you're healthy. This is basically physical therapy to create a new normal."

"A new normal." Eartha's eyes were watery. She wouldn't cry in front of the children but her distress had several sniffling.

Genna smiled encouragingly. She filled a free-standing swimming pool with potion that she made in front of the kids, letting them sniff and investigate every bottle. She helped Eartha in. She took out a long piece of metal.

"Is that a knife?" A kid wolf asked.

"It's like a butter knife," Genna said, "It's for flossing the muscles." She offered Eartha some medicine. "This will numb the pain."

Eartha shook her head. "No, I want to feel it."

Restringing the muscles of Eartha's leg was like unknotting living yarn. Eartha shrieked and splashed. The kids attacked Genna and the tent dumped them into a magical playpen/containment to keep them out of the way. The tent also inoculated each child from several diseases by giving them a bath. The kids fought the floating scrub brushes and bars of soap.

Eartha grabbed Genna's wrist, sweating hard. "I know I let it go for too long. The children need me."

Genna held her hand and looked her in the eye. The spell was in her voice, in her words which buoyed Eartha up. "You're going to walk out of here in an hour. The pain of your leg will be a distant memory. The children will be fine. You will be fine."

Eartha relaxed back into the tub. Magic sped up the process.

An hour later, Eartha walked out of the medical tent. The kids skipped out around her, happy, clean, and healthy. Genna had given them lollypops and beef jerky. Several children promptly forgave her for the great injustice of baths.

"Say thank you to the nice lady doctor," Eartha commanded.

"Thank you!" The kids chorused, embarrassed and wiggling in place.

Eartha patted their wild hair. She reached into her large purse for a tub of Vaseline. She grabbed the nearest child, slathering her face. "Look at you! We're going home right now!"

Genna waved as they piled into a white conversion van and drove off. Then she went back into her tent, zipped it closed, and locked it. The tent vanished from the clearing as it returned to the magical Briarpatch.

Genna sat down and reviewed the patient files. She never thought about children in general. She didn't dislike them but motherhood was somebody else's path not hers. Troy wasn't interested in being a father either. Another reason he was her perfect husband. They were happily childless.

Werewolf children. Genna hadn't even considered the ramifications of being pregnant and a werewolf. Or a werewolf toddler or teenager. Who raised them? Who taught them how to read while weathering the growing pains?

Eartha's strength and resilience came from being a mother. She prayed and worried on those children. Her large bag was full of grade school textbooks, crayons, and coloring books. To her, they weren't little monsters. They were just lonely orphan children who needed stability.

Those kids had survived some terrible situations. The medicine bag had cured them. Where had they been before the Turn? Who Turned them? Why was Eartha the only adult they had?

Genna had tried to give Eartha some money but she gracefully rejected the offer. "We have more than we need, Doctor. Thank you, kindly."

Every time Genna thought that she understood the Briarpatch, she met another werewolf living by a completely different set of circumstances.

Reunited

Professor Onyx tracked Missy to a dog park. The real dogs vacated that side of the fenced-in field. Missy was in human form, sitting on a bench watching the dogs. Rainey was in dog mode. A shaggy sheepdog mix. She carefully trapped Missy against the bench by leaning against her legs.

"What do you want?" Missy demanded.

Professor Onyx scowled. Missy was supposed to be sweet as apple pie not lemon sour and vinegar bitter. Missing Missy was uncomfortable. There was a hole in her world. "We're family. You ran off. We were worried."

"I can't be a Dragonfly anymore," Missy said, "I'm not like you. I can't keep Turning and recruiting. What's the point of Werewolf 101 when no one survives?"

"Somebody has to find the strays. But we can take a break."

Missy was angry but she followed Rainey and Professor Onyx to the parking lot. Rainey wanted to ride with Missy in the Tacoma. She Turned in the back seat and wiggled into a hoodie and leggings. "We missed you. Nothing felt right since you left."

Missy huffed, glaring at the road. "I missed you both too."

~

RAINEY AND PROFESSOR ONYX SEARCHED THE RACKETS of clothes. Missy was at the far end of the Goodwill hunting through the sparse XXL+ section for something vaguely attractive. She occasionally glared at the elder wolves and displayed her pique by yanking the hangars across the racks with a piercing metallic screech.

"Look, she came back," Rainey muttered to Professor Onyx. "What's your problem?"

Professor Onyx wrinkled her nose at a knockoff kaftan. "There is no problem. I'm happy."

Rainey gave her a look over the top of her sunglasses.

"I am!" Professor Onyx said defensively. She *was* happy. Relief flooded her heart.

When Missy didn't come back all Professor Onyx felt was fear. She ran the new recruits into an early grave tracking Missy down. Not that Missy made it easy either.

Missy could blend in with humans easily. No hint at hunger as she went into human populations without anyone noticing. No dogs barking. Babies going missing. Elders helped across the street instead of eaten.

Professor Onyx was both proud of Missy and wanted to kill her hardheaded ass.

"She's pack," Professor Onyx said. "She doesn't get to quit."

"She's also grown and can make her own decisions." Rainey bundled her finds up into her arms and stomped over to the changing rooms. "That's the point of Werewolf 101."

Rainey sharked an open stall from a honky-tonk gal. This feat had the honky-tonk gal muttering with her gal pals loud enough for the whole Goodwill to hear.

Missy and Professor Onyx drifted over to the waiting line. The honky-tonk gals openly glared. Their hostility was returned with naked menace.

The line dissolved. The honky-tonk gals hurried for a manager to complain only to recoil from the Black woman wearing the manager's badge on her blue polo shirt.

Rainey watched her two pack sisters stalk their prey into the parking lot. She hurriedly tried on her clothes.

∼

PROFESSOR ONYX HANDED MISSY A GUN. RAINEY WAS also given a selection of firearms to choose from. Then Professor Onyx led them to her bedroom that was more like a munitions lab than a place to sleep.

"I'm sorry." Professor Onyx wouldn't look at Missy. "It's been a long time since I had a true pack. I didn't want to feel anything for anyone. Then you left and there was this hole I couldn't fill. I knew Rainey was upset that you didn't take her with you."

Missy had started to tear up but then raised her chin with annoyed defiance. "Why guns?"

Rainey grimaced. "Why don't *you* apologize instead of running your mouth?"

"I'm not sorry I left!" Missy snapped. "Especially since you joined the Rager pack five minutes after I left."

Professor Onyx and Rainey grimaced. "It's complicated."

"They ate our girls! How could you?"

Professor Onyx held up a bullet. "They were hunting a group of gun-nuts who had special werewolf killing bullets. After we ate the humans, I stole their stash of armaments."

"She ate the cook," Rainey added. "And took the cookbooks."

"Now I have his recipes," Professor Onyx finished.

Missy frowned at the weapons. "That's what this is about? Bullets? More killing?"

"You think that we'd join the Ragers for no reason?" Rainey smacked Missy on the shoulder. "Thanks a lot!"

"How am I supposed to know what you two hard-asses are thinking?" Missy bared her teeth, snapping at the air to warn Rainey not to hit her again. "You never talk to me. You just expect me to follow orders like some kind of dummy."

Professor Onyx and Rainey exchanged guilty glances. Missy

relented. She knew that neither of them were good with words. For all of their toughness, both felt things deeply. They did care. She could smell it.

She picked up the gun that Professor Onyx had chosen for her, attempting to hide her fear of it. "So, um, will you teach me how to shoot straight?"

~

Professor Onyx ran. Rainey and Missy loped beside her. She breathed in and out. The tranquility in her heart was like snow on a pine tree park. She had absolute faith in both of her pack sisters. She did not have a target in mind. She simply wanted to run.

Rainey heard something. She took off to the left. Missy and Professor Onyx followed. Rainey's fur was spiked. She did not growl but Professor Onyx read the rage in her stride.

They ran faster.

A group of Roughnecks were tormenting a lesbian couple. They had dragged them away from the cars, using the headlights to see. The shrieks and laughter gave the three werewolves all the information they needed.

Professor Onyx hung back while Missy and Rainey attacked in a whirlwind of teeth and claws.

The Roughnecks had their guns out and firing. Some of them were military. The training took over.

Missy dodged but Rainey was perforated. Her agonized yelp made Professor Onyx see red.

She charged, luring the Roughnecks into shooting each other as they tried to get her. She gutted one. She hamstrung another then threw him into the path of the Roughnecks trying to escape in a Chevy Silverado. Tires chewed up his body. The truck skidded to a stop. Professor Onyx punched through the back window and crawled into the cabin. Their guns only got in their way.

Professor Onyx ate them then drove the truck over the downed Roughnecks trying to crawl away. She howled in malevolent glee.

Missy and Rainey helped the lesbians hobble to a car. The two frightened women did not ask questions. One was more hurt than the other. She drove.

Missy and Rainey searched through the forest, confirming that every Roughneck was dead. Then they joined Professor Onyx in the feast.

Possum and Tater

IT WAS A LOVELY NIGHT TO FIX A CAR. THE MOON WAS almost full. The crickets sang in the car cemetery behind the garage. Inside Tater and Possum worked on a Trans-Am Firebird that had been beat to hell.

This week's car repair was pure fun to get up and running. The Firebird didn't need any body work since there was so much rust and dents that it took a full day just to smooth out the lines. The fire ant colonies populating the interior added an extra dose of misery.

Possum fixed the exhaust system perfectly, not needing rulers to get the pipes fitted exactly straight from nose to tailpipe. Tater wrestled the radiator out. They replaced the engine then fuel charged it with nitrous. They added extra doodads and buttons to make sure it worked. They spray-painted it stain black and the backseat. Tater add period accurate gold decals while Possum painted gold pinstripes.

'I'm A Woman' by Koko Fanta sang from the speakers. Tater took a moment to sweep up. Possum stayed by the fridge, drinking beer after beer. Her phone rang. She picked it up. She listened, grunted a few times, and hung up.

"Is that your ex?" Tater said.

Possum finished her beer. "Does it even matter? The dating pool is so damn small that I've slept with everyone already. Who knew that werewolves were such prudes?"

Possum had a tendency to fight instead of think. Tater was a lot smarter than people believed, usually they didn't see past her size. The two had met at the Lone Star Texas Roundup, which was a car show for pre-60s vintage cars. They had been best friends ever since.

Tater grimaced and kept sweeping. "Hey, I heard that Belle's in town. We should show her a night out."

"I heard that Belle married a cowboy," Possum said, inspecting the Firebird's chassis to make sure that nothing had shaken loose during the drive.

"Belle?" Tater said, "As in Genna Bellwether? I can't believe she married a man!"

"She's bisexual," Possum said. "From what I heard, it's love. She went full yeehaw."

Tater harrumphed, annoyed that one of her crushes had put a ring on it. "Well, I hope she's happy."

Possum and Tater proudly owned their own towing company. They had a special affection for Genna Bellwether because she had funded their entire operation. She had commissioned that they rebuild several vintage cars and paid triple the premium. She sold the cars and kept a purple Mustang.

There was plenty of business. Werewolves lived in their cars when the housing situation got too unstable. They also ate road-kill and killed humans along the road, behind gas stations, parking lots, and other public spaces. Possum and Tater were the clean up crew. They handled the cars, the bodies, and even insurance.

The work was tedious but good. Honestly, being a pair of butch lesbians was a bigger pain than lycanthropy. There was always some hater coming after them. Their logo was rainbow-colored as an extra 'Fuck you.' On the outskirts of Austin, there were plenty of haters. They never went hungry.

Most werewolves found new jobs after the Turn but Possum and Tater kept right on trucking, fixing cars, and towing wrecks.

They celebrated the car's finished repair by doing donuts in the parking lot and testing the nitrous by speeding down straightway backroads.

"Bloody hell, this is a great little car," Tater said. "It looks like the Budget Bandit. You know, from 'Smokey and the Bandit'."

"Fucking fantastic," Possum muttered, still surly about her most recent breakup.

She flipped on the radio just to see if it worked. Herbie Hancock's 'Tijuana Taxi' fought to be heard over the roar of the opened windows and the engine.

Their phones buzzed.

"Hey, we've got a tow." Tater said. "Someone actually filled the form out and everything. The pinned location worked!"

Possum squinted at her like she was embarrassed but didn't want to say it. Which was Possum's version of being polite.

They followed the pinned location on their phone's app. But something wasn't right about tonight's job. The bad feeling prickling the skin kept both sitting inside their big purple vintage towtruck named Beulah. There wasn't anyone but them and the large overturned van on this lonely stretch of highway. The full moon cast strange shadows beyond the headlights.

"What's wrong with this picture?" Possum demanded.

"We're sitting in it," Tater said. "Someone flipped that van on purpose. Fuck this."

She put Beulah in gear. The engine revved and whined but didn't move.

Stacy the boo hag stepped into the headlights' glare. The bad feeling now felt like fish hooks sinking into every nerve. Tater had the presence of mind to lock the doors while Possum grabbed their gun out of its case.

Stacy pouted. The truck's loud engine and the spells spraypainted inside every inch of its metal body warded the two werewolves from her influence. The big wheels chewed up the slick skin attempting to choke the gears.

"Get out of that truck!" Stacy commanded.

Maybe if she hadn't added a bunch of slurs, it would've worked. But instead, she activated the *'I'm Rubber and You're Glue'* counter spell.

Beulah roared. Stacy dodged, rolling to avoid getting run over.

That momentary distraction had the other werewolves focused on the truck. Dominque jumped onto the back of the truck as it sped onto the highway. She held on to the neck of the tow truck's hoist. She wrapped herself in the wire, hitching it quickly so she literally couldn't untie herself.

"Get back here!" Stacy bellowed, "Get her!"

The pack charged, sprinting down the flat highway and racing along the shoals through the high grass. Stacy reached out, hauling with both hands as though dragging in a net. Dominque squeezed the hoist, whimpering and gritting her teeth as the furious enchantment knifed her body.

Possum glanced out the rear window, aiming her shotgun. "We've got a live one!"

"Yeah, I see her but I think she's trying to get away. Put the gun down." Tater shifted Beulah into a higher gear. The engine whined, fighting to move through suddenly solid air.

Possum mashed on a button. The truck belched a noxious cloud.

Dominque gagged and sneezed, her eyes watering. Her tongue hung from her mouth, trying to breathe. It felt like inhaling pepper spray. Her lungs were on fire. The other werewolves yelped and slowed their chase, coughing and sneezing.

Stacy yanked harder. Dominque bled without any cuts. Still she refused to let go.

The chase continued for miles. Possum and Tater had been chased before. The only difference was allowing Dominque's continued passage.

"What do we do? That's one pissed off witch!" Possum said.

"We get across Lady Bird Lake. Witches can't stand open water," Tater exclaimed.

"Are you sure about that?"

"Do you have a better idea?"

"Yeah, we get back to the shop. We've got enough headway to get there. We send that girl on her way."

"That Firebird was supposed to pay our overdue bills."

"We'll find another Firebird."

Tater cussed in Spanish and English but relented. "Fine. Fuck it."

Beulah reached the garage in record time, smoking from being kept in high gear but didn't blow out. Possum jumped out while Tater was parking. She ran around to point the gun at Dominque, ratcheting it loudly. "Get the fuck off my truck!"

"I can't. I'm stuck." Dominque wheezed.

Tater pressed her hand on Beulah. Dominque yelped in surprise at the metal uncoiled like anorexic snakes. The truck bucked her onto the hard cement. She landed on her hip with another pained yell.

Tater tossed the Firebird's keys at Dominque. They hit the ground by her head. "Here. Get in the Firebird and go."

Dominque blinked up at them, slowly taking the keys. "Where am I going to go?"

"Not our problem. Fuck off." Possum stomped her boot. Dominque scrambled to her feet and cringed over to the Firebird. She wrinkled her nose. "Um, I can't drive this."

"What're you talking about? It's in cherry condition!" Tater exclaimed.

Dominque rubbed her collarbone anxiously. "I don't know how to drive stick."

The two gear-heads gave her a long look of consternation.

Dominque shrugged. "I never learned. My car's electric."

"Kids these day," Possum said.

"Don't look at me. My dad taught me how to drive when I was eleven!" Tater exclaimed. "What do you drive? A Tesla?"

"A Nissan Leaf."

"Oh my god, shut the fuck up and get the hell out." Tater held out her hands. "Give me the keys. I can't. I just can't."

Dominque gave the keys back. "I'm sorry."

"I'm sorry too. It's the only drivable car we've got besides Beulah."

Possum reached into a closet and pulled out a large green python coat with furred ruff. "Here. Wear this to hide your scent."

It was too big and too hot but Dominque put it on, petting the collar then checked the label. "Wait a minute, is this Valentino?"

"Retail price at 35 grand. I'd take it to Buffalo Exchange or some consignment store to get a good deal on it."

"But it's Valentino!"

"Does it look like we need it?"

Dominque pursed her lips, trying not to cry. "Um, where are we?"

"Austin is a twenty minute drive that way." Tater jerked her thumb at the cemetery. "If you start running, you'll get there by sunrise. Normally I'd say New Braunfels but you need somewhere populated."

Possum tossed Dominque a beer and a packet of jerky. "Here. For the road."

Dominque caught both. "Please, you have to help me."

"We did. That coat will hide your scent. The food will keep you going. It's pretty flat around here so you don't have to worry about creeks or nothing. Now go and get gone. We don't want to know anything."

Dominque took an unsteady breath. She cracked the beer open, guzzled it down, then belched hugely. She covered her mouth. "Oh, excuse me." Then she threw the bottle away in the recycle bin. She gave them a weak smile. "Thanks." She cinched the coat tight and jogged into the car cemetery while gnawing on jerky.

"That was my jerky," Tater said. "And my Valentino."

"You have plenty of Valentino that you never wear," Possum said.

Tater harrumphed, annoyed but not really. It was smart thinking. Now she had a reason to go shopping. Besides, that flavor of desperation was hauntingly familiar.

They began to clean the truck and all traces of Dominque's presence. They also beefed up their home and garage security. They added protective sigils inside the Firebird.

"I hate this," Possum muttered.

"I know," Tater said, adding another layer of paint to a sigil for the Rubber spell. "I put a healing spell in that beer and the jerky but we should've done more."

"The Valentino is warded too. Now hush up. Someone's coming."

Stacy and her Ragers expected to attack the garage but they couldn't find it. A dislocation spell hid the garage and its occupants from view both in the physical world and magical. Possum and Tater knew how to hide in plain sight. The Gearheads watched their enemies pace and search and get beaten by the boo hag.

Then a gorgeous purple 1969 Mustang Judge drove up the drive and through the magic. Possum and Tater relaxed as Genna got out of her car. She was armed. She nodded at the garage and jogged into the grass.

Stacy's scouts weren't fast enough to avoid Genna or Troy, who had parked his Bronco a mile down the road. Stacy fled.

Tater let out a long breath as gunfire echoed across the car cemetery. "I can't believe you called her but I'm glad you did!"

"I thought you did," Possum said. "Maybe she was in the area."

They exchanged a glance. Genna was magic and she looked out for her friends. It was extra terrifying that she felt the need to personally show up.

"Whatever, I'm glad I didn't have to press the big red button."

Tater put the plastic lid back on the panic button with care. She really liked the garage. She didn't want to blow it up.

"Nice Firebird," Genna walked into the garage. "How're the best mechanics in the world doing?"

"We're fucking glad to see you, Belle! I tell you what!" Tater strode from behind her fortifications to give her a bearhug while Possum got four beers. "Have we got a story to tell!"

Dumpster

Missy showed Professor Onyx and Rainey a flyer
for Werewolf Wednesday that Genna had given her way back
when. Magic hummed in the laminated paper so the text changed
when she touched it. She read it aloud, "Werewolf Wednesday
meet-up. Nonaffiliated welcome."

The elder wolf refused to touch the paper. Rainey used tongs
and dishwashing rubber gloves to hold the flyer over a mirror.

Instructions, directions, and verification codes wrote themselves across the previously blank back of the flyer. Along with the
crest for the Church of the Forgotten who sponsored the event.
Missy was impressed. She hadn't figured out the location.

"It's got to be a trap for idiot pups too stupid to know
better," Professor Onyx sneered. Rainey stayed thoughtfully
quiet, studying the flyer instead of agreeing.

"No, it's real," Missy protested.

"You should know better!" Professor Onyx focused her severe
frown on Missy.

"But we need to meet other werewolves in a safe space. The
Ragers can't be the only one out there."

Missy was encouraged by Rainey's silence. "I didn't go when I
first got the flyer. I kept it because—"

"Because you wanted us to come too," Rainey said. "You didn't want to go alone."

Missy blushed. "I vote we go. Free barbecue."

"I vote yes too," Rainey said.

Professor Onyx rolled her eyes. "Fine. We go."

She checked her magic wand. Making more bullets. The other two cleaned their guns, with Professor Onyx instructing along the way. Going meant preparation.

"We check out the dumpster first," Professor Onyx added. "Then we'll go in."

～

RAINEY CIRCLED THE DUMPSTER OF HALF-EATEN barbecue and bones. Professor Onyx and Missy scouted Strait-Legged Bacon. The flyer instructions were legit.

"There's werewolves," Missy panted anxiously, her tail tucked under her back legs so tightly that she walked funny. Professor Onyx's thick fur was also bristled.

Rainey nudged a trash bag. "There's plenty in here. We don't have to go in."

They gobbled everything vaguely edible until another werewolf slunk into the alley. More came up the opposite side.

The Dragonflies growled a warning. The dumpster was theirs. The newcomers snarled back.

Missy launched herself at the nearest werewolf. Rainey and Professor Onyx quickly backed her attack. They killed the werewolf, sharp and vicious. Then went after the rest, leaving their enemies no time to regroup.

Two minutes later only Rainey, Professor Onyx, and Missy remained. They searched the carpet of dead bodies, eating choice bits of the fresh kill.

"Werewolf Wednesday is not bad," Professor Onyx said.

"Maybe it's both?" Missy said. "Maybe we've been living on the street too long. We don't know how to socialize."

"You jumped first," Rainey said.

"I know! I'm wondering if I was a little too hasty." Missy paused. She spotted Delilah, who ducked down. She barked a warning. "Holy shit, that's Delilah the beautician!"

Delilah tried to flee but Rainey scaled the wall and jumped through the window. Professor Onyx entered through the door. She was the fastest at the fully clothed Turn and didn't pause at the front door. Just rushed past to get to the back hallway.

Missy stayed in the alley, covering the exit and looking for most attackers.

"Don't kill me," Delilah whimpered, stumbling against a wall. Her fur was matted and greasy with trash. "I'm sorry."

Rainey growled as she trapped her against a corner of the bathroom. "You're that black market beautician. You should our bones and hair to witches."

"I'm sorry," Delilah sobbed. "Look at me. I'm cursed. I've changed. I'm sorry!"

"Not yet you're not." Professor Onyx attacked while Delilah pleaded. Rainey let her do the killing while she watched the hallway. Missy waited outside.

Inside the meet-up, the werewolves heard the Dragonfly pack eat Delilah but nobody stopped them. Justice was served.

IT WAS A BEAUTIFUL SUNNY LATE AFTERNOON AT Walnut Creek Park. Missy was having second thoughts about this whole Werewolf Wednesday venture. It wasn't just eating. Pastor Faith expected to talk about their feelings. Hard pass.

Professor Onyx had disappeared among the parked cars and bushes to say hello to Brother McGruffin. Rainey sat next to Missy, stoutly refusing to talk to anyone.

Werewolf Wednesday had more lycanthropes and shifters in one place than Missy had ever seen. The peek through the window last week had been the tip of the iceberg. She had no idea that there was more than one type of werewolf. Nobody was trying to kill anyone!

Instead they ate barbecue and drank beer. It looked like a cookout as long as you didn't look too closely at the grill.

Rainey nudged Missy sharply to pay attention to the large circle of collapsible chairs and their occupants. Their expectant eye contact made Missy sweated with nerves. Genna the witch doctor wasn't there. She didn't recognize anyone.

She played for time by wiping sauce off her lips. "Um, hi, my name's Missy. Like Missy Elliot. Um, what's the question?"

"You're supposed to talk about your favorite hobbies," Rainey hissed through clenched teeth. "Pay attention!"

"Hobbies? Who had time for hobbies when you're not even human!" Missy exclaimed. "I can't even bake bread without getting hair in the dough. That's if I have an oven, the ingredients, and baking pans."

"You bake?" Pastor Faith asked. "What's your favorite pastry? I like croissants."

"Cinnamon rolls and sourdough bread," Missy said promptly. "I love bread in every pastry goodness."

Pastor Faith looked around the circle. "Who else likes bread?"

"Who doesn't?" Rainey muttered.

"I think we'll have to add bread to the Church menu," Pastor Faith said. "The Kitchen has an oven. You're welcome to use it."

"I'd be delighted," Missy said.

Pastor Faith and Werewolf Wednesday weren't so scary.

RAINEY WAS GOOD AT HUNTING. SHE FOUND HER PREY easily. There were plenty of tells, little habits that she could exploit. All she needed was a list of names and she could find them. She liked the research. She killed and brought the targets to the Church, satisfied that these were genuinely bad people and the world was better without them.

The Church had big walk-in refrigerators that she could sue. She found peace in draining and butchering the bodies in the cold enclosed space. She could focus on the task.

"You're really good at this," Missy said, surveying the racks of ribs and deconstructed parts. "You could be a professional butcher at HEB."

Rainey shrugged but inwardly she glowed with pride. She had always wanted to be good at something. Missy was right, there was an obvious difference between her kills and anyone else's.

Pastor Faith looked into the fridge. "I've got a few more in the other fridge that need seeing to if you don't mind. There's a bunch of folk too lazy to do any work. They think killing is all that they need to do but we don't waste anything around here. Every strand of hair and stray bone has to be accounted for. That's how Delilah got us. Nobody cleaned up after themselves."

Rainey nodded, cleaning and sharpening her favorite set of knives. Missy grinned and went back to the kitchen, happy to focus on baking bread and making dough for pizza.

The second fridge had older carcasses. These were badly dressed, if at all. She had to break bones and separate the moldy green slimy parts. Some werewolves like a little rot in their meal but Rainey liked to keep things separate.

She worked and worked. Time had no meaning in a windowless kill floor. She realized that it was time for a break when she started naming the colors of corpses. What was green mold and coagulated purple.

She washed her hands, hung her apron on a hook, cleaned her knives, and changed out of the rubber boots.

She went outside into a balmy evening. It was time for evening worship service. Rainey stayed in the back, embarrassed by her messing clothes and wrapped hair. She sang with the rest of the congregation. She loved singing and the harmonies filling the sanctuary.

As a human she hadn't been religious but now the old time religion gave her peace. She was surrounded by Black folk as magical and monstrous as she was. The Church gave her peace. Butchering corpses gave her purpose.

Rainey praised God, tearfully thankful that finally she had found a place that she wanted to stay.

Starry Nights

IT WAS WEREWOLF WEDNESDAY AND ALL OF THE werewolves were line dancing to the 'Wobble' in the parking lot. Their bodies were illuminated by headlights. The bass shook the cars so a faint rattle echoed with the music.

Violence shivered through Dominque's body. Starting outward at the soles of her feet and her fingers and pooling in the base of her spine. She stared at the witch, her nostrils full of a strange and powerful scent.

The scent. It wasn't just witchy. It was just like the salamanders in Stacy's garden but more robust. A genuine dragon was line dancing. The dragon lady smiled and sweated like she was an ordinary werewolf pretending to be a Black woman.

More importantly, this new witch wore Stacy's medicine bag. The beads had changed to read 'Dr. Black Belle' across the center.

Dominque hid behind a large beech tree, trying to get to steady her breath. She hadn't seen Stacy in months. She kept studying faces, afraid to see those seams. This was worse.

Dominque's night got worse as Tiana and Jasmine walked over, savoring margaritas in their water bottles.

"Ooh, you see her too? That's Genna Bellwether. Or Black

"

Belle. Or Doctor Dandelion. Whatever they're calling her these days."

Dominque wasn't sure why these two beauticians were talking to her or maybe they were chatty drunks. "Are you sure that's not Stacy wearing a new face?"

"That's what we thought once we realized it wasn't Coyote." Tiana said. "Some kind of loyalty test."

"Sounds like Stacy," Dominque grumbled.

"Well, it's a good thing that Black Belle wasn't Stacy because we failed the test." Jasmine took a big gulp of her margarita, sloshing ice across her lips. "Anyway, Delilah's dead. Professor Onyx ate her in the bathroom at Stiles."

"That nasty heifer got what was coming to her," Tiana said. "I can't believe she sold us out to the Witch Market. Now nobody trusts their stylist or their barber!"

Dominque looked up at the silent figure looming over them with glowing eyes. No one moved that fast. Unless they were magic.

"Um, hello!" Tiana said with fearful perkiness. "We didn't know you were famous."

"I'd rather you didn't sell my whereabouts to the press," Genna said mildly. Her poise terrified the werewolves.

"We're dead. So very very dead." Jasmine gasped.

"That's Stacy's medicine bag!" Dominque said, pointing at it.

"Would you shut up about the bag?!" Jasmine hissed.

"A mutual acquaintance gave it to me," Genna said. "I believe you know Coyote?"

"Oh yeah, then how did Coyote get it from Stacy?" Dominique demanded.

"Bitch, is you serious?" Jasmine snarled. "It's Coyote! They can do literally anything they want."

Genna and Tiana nodded. "That's right."

"So, um, what can we do for you, Doctor Dandelion?" Tiana asked.

"Dr. Dandelion. I like it." Black Belle tilted her head. "I'm looking for the boo hag. I believe her name is Stacy?"

"Whitney didn't tell you where Stacy is?" Jasmine said.

"Stacy had Whitney imprisoned for ratting Delilah out to Coyote. I freed her." This silenced the beauticians. Genna hadn't stopped watching Dominque with thoughtful predatory eyes. "You're one of hers?"

"I don't know where she is," Dominque snapped, "I hope kill that bitch. She's been using our hair to do all kinds of things. She has to pay!"

"Something like that."

"Can I ask you a favor? Are there any magical shoes in your bag? I'm tired to ripping up my 1s with my toenails."

Tiana and Jasmine gave her an incredulous look. "Bitch, do you think she's got a pair of ruby sneakers in that bag or something?"

Dominque shrugged angrily. "It doesn't hurt to ask."

"Funny you should say that. I found these sneakers when I was organizing the bag." Genna reached into the medicine bag and slowly lifted out a pair of Starry Nights. The same pair that Dominique had last seen on Stacy's feet as she walked out of Aunt Jemima's house.

The sneakers glittered metallic and beautiful. Dominque forgot everything but the Starry Nights. She took them, just short of snatching them out of Black Belle's hands.

"Oh my god, thank you! Thank you so much!" Tears slid down her face. She hugged them, suppressing a sob. "I thought I'd never see my Starry Nights again!"

Dominque shucked off her ratty Jordans and put on the Starry Nights. Her whole body relaxed. She offered the black sneakers to Genna. "I can make an exchange with some Black Air Force Jordans? They're old but they're real. I got them cleaned up."

Genna took the sneakers. "Tell me everything you know about Stacy the boo hag."

Dominque told her about the garden, the cages, the club, and everything she could think of, including Aunt Jemima. She felt sorry to rope the old lady in but she had survived being skinned. She definitely had a story to tell.

Genna had a peculiar way of listening that had the gravitational force of a black hole. Even Jasmine and Tiana shared gossip collected at the Salon. They talked and talked and talked. Genna listened, asking only a few strategic questions.

Finally, she raised a hand. "Thank you for your honesty. That was very helpful. Be seeing you."

She walked away.

Tiana and Jasmine glared at Dominque with matching expressions of exasperated respect. "I can't believe you traded those janky Black Air Forces for those Starry Nights."

"But she took them!" Dominque protested.

"Bitch, you know good and goddamn well that a witch only takes what she wants not what you want to give," Jasmine said.

"She doesn't want your ratty old dunks anyway. She's here for the *chisme*." Tiana said. "You better be telling the truth or you'll pay for those with more than you can afford."

"She's a real one all right," Dominque said, smirking with glee. "That's what Stacy gets for coming into my house and messing with my family!"

"Oh, *hell* no!" Tiana recoiled, pointing a warding two fingers at Dominque. "Black Belle is one thing but you'd lead us straight to the grave. You stay the fuck away from us and the Salon, you crazy bitch!" She grabbed Jasmine's wrist, making her drop her water bottle. "Come on, Jazzy!"

"You made me spill my drink!" Jasmine protested, stumbling after her as she scooped up the bottle.

"I'll get you another one. Come on!"

Dominque watched them go, her toes wiggling in her shoes. She joined the line dancing crowd. They'd moved on to *Where The Fans At?* Which only half of the crowd knew. She pulled a fan out of her purse and shook it as she danced. She laughed and danced and clapped her hands, spinning around with jubilation.

Finally, she had something to celebrate.

Werewolf Funeral

GENNA SMELLED INTESTINES. SHE TURNED AROUND JUST as the back flaps of the medical tent pulled back and 14 year old boy pushed into the safety barrier. The magic confirmed that the body wrapped in several hoodies knotted together held no curses or parasitic magical creatures.

A hood covered the dead child's face but his ear was the same skin tone as the older boy. Blood clung to the waves of a fresh haircut. The older brother surveyed the tent and Genna with big haunted eyes.

A medical table grew out of the ground like an oversized mushroom. He lay his brother on the table and tenderly unwrapped the sodden shroud.

"I don't want Mama to see him like this. It's my fault. I should've protected him."

Hate pulsed like a heartbeat in his soul. She could see it corrupting his magic. He glared up at her and that darkness burned up.

"I killed them. Me and my friends made sure they got what they deserved."

The tent opened again. A pack of Youngbloods drug in twelve hunters and their sons. Then piled up guns, ammo, cellphones, house and car keys, and cash.

"Is this enough to pay for a resurrection?" He asked.

"Your brother is dead but I can make it look like he died peacefully with no pain."

~

MALCOM CLUNG TO GENNA'S HAND, HIDING BEHIND her like she was a protective oak tree. He peeked around her arm and watched Amaya wail over Zion with wild grief. Her terrible broken howls had the Speakeasy staff hastily closing for the day.

Genna wished that she could raise the dead but there was no cure for the violence inflicted upon these children.

The Youngbloods had fled after escorting Malcolm and Genna to the Speakeasy, afraid of the messy sorrow. So it was Genna who had to break the news to Amaya.

"I'm sorry, Mama," Malcom whimpered, sniffling and shivering. Genna's shirt was wet as he hugged her and rubbed his face into her back. "Don't be made at me."

Amaya blinked and looked around, dazed by his voice. "Zion? Baby, is that you?"

Malcolm stiffened and stepped out from behind Genna. "Mama, it's me, Malcolm. I'm still here."

"Come here, baby." Amaya opened her arms. Malcom ran to her and they clung to each other. Their howls mingled.

Genna tried to quietly retreat but the movement caught Amaya's eyes.

"Thank you for bringing my boys back to me, Black Belle."

"Do you want me to contact Pastor Faith?"

Amaya shuddered, dissolving into tears again but nodded.

Genna fled the Speakeasy. She had to drive to the Church because it had poor phone reception.

Imani waited at the front door. She was dressed in full preacher regalia. The Church's vintage hearse was ready to go.

Genna retold Zion's story. She wished that the preacher was shocked and not just sad. "It wasn't skin magic."

"No, he was just Black and nearby," the minister sighed.

AMAYA THREW HERSELF ON THE COFFIN AS THE WHIRR of hydraulics lowered Zion into the ground.

"Wait! He's still in there! You don't do this! My baby! That's my baby!"

Her hysterical screams shattered the stoic silence. Malcom crouched down, covering his face. Family, friends, Church elders, and Speakeasy staff were fainting, singing, holding onto the grieving mother trying to bury herself with her son. Roger stood like a wizen tree, aged by grief as he watched his wife and his son's coffin.

Genna stood stiffly next to Troy. She wore her most elegant understated black dress. Troy wore a crisp black suit. But everyone else wore white. Their hair was covered in cloth wraps and hats.

Drums played, dragging the mourners into a shuffling ring. They clapped their hands and stomped their feet. They called out to the ancestors and waved fans.

Those in werewolf form stayed in the tree-line and howled mournfully.

Genna did not know whether to stand still, retreat, or join in. She had never attended a werewolf funeral before.

Her feet began to move. Her body swayed. She joined the ring shout because the drums demanded it. Troy followed her into the circle. They clapped and let themselves be a part of the collective outpouring of grief.

Amaya was in the heart of the circle. She danced wildly. Hands flung at the empty blue sky. Her billowing skirts rippled around her as she spun. The headwrap came off so her braises bounced with every leap.

She was beautiful and uninhibited as she danced, pouring her everything into the movement.

Genna was shocked when Amaya collapsed into her arms, sweaty and spent. Genna held her as she cried.

~

AMAYA WANTED TO HATE GENNA. SHE WANTED TO blame her for the deaths of Roger and Zion but couldn't. Out of everyone in the community that Malcom could've asked for help, Genna was the one.

It was quiet the morning after Zion's funeral. The first floor was a garden of funeral flowers in vases and buckets. It was beautiful and sad.

She wished that Roger was here. He was at the Speakeasy, drinking and partying to numb his grief with nubile flesh and a snowdrift's worth of narcotics. Roger had many children by many women. She had never asked him if he lost any others to gun violence or illness.

It was just Amaya and Malcom eating cereal while watching old re-runs of Bob Ross painting a landscape of snowcapped mountains and 'happy' trees by a river. They watched mixed pain on canvas become water frothing around river rocks and clouds in the cobalt sky.

This was Malcom's favorite show. Amaya did not have the energy for Bluey and zany cartoons that Zion preferred.

Malcom was her quiet son. She did not want to break the fragile peace of this moment but she had to ask. "Malcom, how did you know about the witch doctor lady?"

Malcom shrugged. His eyes never left the tv screen. Amaya tried again.

"What did you pay her?"

"I told you. We killed the bad guys and gave Miss Genna all their stuff but she couldn't resurrect Zion. She said she was sorry."

Amaya flinched. She didn't know that resurrection was an

option. "Those Youngbloods helped you out but I don't want you out there running around no more. Are we clear? From now on, you're focusing on school. You need your education."

"Yes, Mama. I'm going to be a doctor just like Miss Genna when I grow up."

"Well, how about that." Amaya did not know what else to say. She was surprised by Malcom's seriousness. "A doctor in the family. I like that."

They went back to watching the painting show. Together in grief and holding on tight.

Officer Calhoun

Professor Onyx went still. Her eyes glistened and her afro shook faintly from the tremors running along her body.

Rainey and Missy stared at her, startled by the raw fear pouring off her like black smoke at an oil refinery explosion.

Not just fear. Her magic was ablaze.

Until this moment, Professor Onyx had been a n implacable living legend. An ancient monster more cunning and ruthless than any other. But now she was suddenly just a woman.

And that scared Rainey. She needed Professor Onyx to be her rock. She was unmoored without her strength.

Missy slipped her gun out of its holster. "You good, sis?"

"Put your gun away, dumbass," Rainey snarled. "That's a cop!"

"He's also a werewolf," Professor Onyx whispered with a leadened expression. "I remember him. He was at the Riots. He bit me. He bit a lot of us during the Marches."

Missy and Rainey both knew that Professor Onyx had been Turned during the Civil Rights Moment. They had been unclear about the details.

They had always assumed that her attacker was dead. Not

alive and swaggering in a dove-gray Stetson with a squad of other werewolves dressed as Texas Rangers.

There was a starched authenticity to his garb. An ugly smirk creased his thin lips. "Professor Onyx."

"Officer Calhoun."

"You remember me. Good. I remember you. I remember all that fun we had."

Professor Onyx's magic wand was out and roaring silver bullets. Missy unloaded a clip. Rainey grabbed them both and got them away while their enemies were busy Turning. They writhed like cockroaches as the magic bullets killed them.

Missy was happy to run but Professor Onyx shook Rainey off and charged.

OFFICER CALHOUN WAS A CRUEL MAN AND HIS BADGE made him into a monster. He killed the werewolf who bit him. He made it his life's work to hunt down and kill all werewolves to save humanity.

He loved eating Black women. Especially those proud African queens who dared to march for their so-called 'rights' as if they were people.

He recruited other cops to his cause. They were just as eager to put Black women in their place.

Calhoun reviled his attraction towards Professor Onyx. He saw her marching to free Angela Davis and kept seeing her in the crowds.

He pretended to be a K9 dog when the cops unleashed them on the protestors. He bit and nipped through the forest of running legs, charged, leapt, and slammed Professor Onyx onto the asphalt.

Her blood filled his mouth but she clouted him with the wooden end of her placard. She fought and bit him!

He yelped in agony of her knife in his guts. The gun in his chest exploded his spine.

If he were an ordinary dog, he would've died. He lay on the street and watched her stagger into the riot. Blood in his eyes as he vowed to hunt her down.

Now he finally found her.

~

PROFESSOR ONYX AND OFFICER CALHOUN RAN straight for each other. He howled with hateful glee, not even trying to dodge the bullets.

Long practice kept her aim steady as she howled, "Die motherfucker! Die!!!"

The pain of body parts galvanized him instead of slowing him down to assess the damage. He smacked the rifle out of her hands and ripped into her with tooth and claw.

He was heavier than she was and older. They were a tangle of killing hate, moving too fast for Missy, Rainey, or Calhoun's posse to join in.

The Posse attacked the two she-wolves with glee. Their red rockets already half exposed in excitement.

Missy and Rainey fought as a sage team, moving with deadly grace. Despite her misgivings about guns, Missy was a crack shot. The Posse was quickly reduced to a few angry stranglers who looked between their dying bodies and Officer Calhoun getting his skull bitten into pulp and ran.

Missy and Rainey chased them down then butchered the corpses just to make sure that there was no residual magic involved.

Then they burned the bodies.

Professor Onyx was too hurt to stand but she lifted her head to howl. Only to fall over, vomiting blood.

Rainey and Missy grabbed her and hustled her to Calhoun's

Escalade. The Tundra was a crumpled remnant full of bullet holes.

~

Professor Onyx wasn't breathing. Rainey tearfully cleaned her fur, ignoring her own injuries. Missy drove, pushing the Escalade to its limits as she roared down the busy highway.

Rainey clutched Professor Onyx as Missy juked around trucks and slower cars. "Where are you going? We can't take her to the hospital!"

"I know that!" Missy snarled with road rage when a F-150 cut her off. She banged on the horn and wove across lanes to take a narrow exit in the middle of a construction area, gravel spitting in her wake.

"Missy! She's dying and you're gonna get us killed!"

"Just shut up and let me drive! I know where I'm going. So do chest compressions or something!"

The two screamed at each other as the Escalade left the high-way, zoomed down the access road, took a sharp dog-leg to a pothole infested country road, sped across acres of sunflower fields, and into the shadowy canopy of pine trees.

"Bitch, you better be right," Rainey muttered as trees whipped past. Then held on as Missy took another blind turn. There was a clearing and a small tent ahead. The Escalade skidded to a stop in front of it.

~

Missy dragged Professor Onyx into Genna's medical tent. "Doc! Doc! 911! She needs help!"

Rainey shuffled in after them. She had the careful posture of the severely injured trying to hide it.

"Dock! You gotta help us!" Missy shred. "She's dying!"

Professor Onyx roused when Genna cupped her bloody cheek. She gripped Genna's forearm. Her lips trembled. Her normally embody mask of feminine dominance creased into wrinkles as bloody tears streamed through the mud. "I'm just so tired of killing racists," she whispered. "I'be been killing them for 483 years and there's always more!"

Genna dabbed the tear tracks with a cotton swab. "I understand. I get sick of eating Happy Meals too."

She crowded Missy and Rainey away from the operating table. "I'll take it from here."

She closed the curtain firmly. Then turned back to Professor Onyx. "Okay, I got you."

Professor Onyx leaned into the tender touch of her warm soft palm. Genna's magic was like the quiet ebb and flow of warm waves on a sheltered cove. Professor Onyx relaxed.

The bullets wiggled free of her body. Teeth and broken shards of claws clattered on the metal table. The air glittered as curses evaporated.

"I'm just so tired," Professor Onyx whimpered.

"You're right, bing a Black woman can be a bummer," Genna said, using tweezers to help a particularly nasty claw free of an infected abscess in her belly. "But being a Black woman is also a blessing. We see the world more sharply. The colors are brighting. We celebrate the good days when they happen. The beauty of living can't be forgotten. Even being a werewolf didn't change life as much as you think it will. You're still a Black woman."

"I'm so tired," Professor Onyx closed her eyes. "Just so damn tired."

"Then rest. I'll keep watch over your pack siss. They're safe with me."

Professor Onyx jerked her eyes open and leaned forward to grab Genna's arm. "Tell Brother McGruffin that I got him. That pig Officer Calhoun is dead! And this time those pigs aren't coming back! I made sure of it! Tell him. You have to tell him!"

She slumped back into an exhausted faint. Genna quickly removed more teeth, claws, and bullets.

∽

Rainey snarled at Missy, the Turn warping her features as her teeth bulged in her mouth. "How in fuck do you know a witch doctor? Did you even ask how much it costs to heal her?"

"No, I didn't. I was too busy trying to save Professor Onyx's life." Rainey's rage was scary but Missy refused to back down or break eye contact. "I'll pay whatever it costs so don't worry. Genna's good people."

"She's not people. She's a witch!" Rainey snapped hysterically. "I don't know what she is but nobody but a boo hag can take bullets out like that."

"What's a boo hag?"

"Are you shitting me?" Rainey roared, incoherent from pain and outrage. "Who do you think Delilah was selling our hair and nails too?"

"I don't know but it wasn't Genna," Missy said stoutly. "She's a doctor. She makes medicine. Now will you please let her help you? Look at me. I'm all better now. Professor Onyx's getting the help she needs."

"You can't trust her! She's a witch!"

"She's a witch *doctor* and she's a werewolf. You've seen her at Werewolf Wednesday. She's one of us. Why is now suddenly different?"

"So you knew?" Rainey backed away from Missy, wild-eyed. "That's the flyer. It was a lure. This was your plan all along. You're working with them!"

Missy trembled but stood firm. "I don't want you to die, Rainey."

Rainey swayed, bleeding and furious. "No excuses!"

"It's not a conspiracy, Rainey." Missy sucked on her lips. She backed up towards the medical tent. "Okay, I'm going to sit with Professor Onyx. If you won't go in then can you go get Brother McGruffin? Genna said that Professor Onyx said that they were both turned by Officer Calhoun, that bad wolf cop she killed."

"Why should I ? Aren't you satisfied with dragging us into the witch's lair?"

"I think they're married. I think he loves her. And I think she's dying so she wants to see him before she goes."

Rainey spluttered but Missy retreated. Sweating and limping, Rainey ran for the Escalade. It was a long drive to Freedom Corner.

~

MISSY SAT NEXT TO GENNA. SHE HAD NOISE CANCELING headphones on. 'The Emptiness Machine' by Lincoln Park blared loud. Genna raised her eyebrows but kept sifting through the shards and bullets that she had extracted from Professor Onyx's body.

The elder wolf was asleep inside of an enchanted vat of honey. There were more bits of shrapnel deeper in her body that needed to wiggle free.

"Are you a boo hag?" Missy asked without preamble.

"No, I'm not. I learned flesh magic from a boo hag." Genna used tweezers to delicately set a sharp piece on a small square card. "I learned blood magic from vampires and bone magic from a tooth fairy. I used those skills to heal. Just like I told you I would."

Missy kicked at the ground. "How much will it cost?"

"Well, you can start by saying thank you."

Missy turned off her headphones as she took them from her ears. She sat up straight. "Thank you, Doctor. Seriously. Of course, I'm grateful. It's just hard to trust. Rainey is so scared of you."

"That might have less to do with me and more to do with the boo hag turning people into meat puppets."

"Professor Onyx didn't say anything but I know I crossed a line bringing her here."

They both glanced at the covered tank. Genna moved the shards around. Information wrote itself on each card. This was recorded in the medical journal. Missy tried to read the writing but it blurred itself. She looked away, feeling nauseous.

"Can I ask you a question?" Genna said while editting her notes. "What do you think a pack is?"

"T's a group of werewolves," Missy wrinkled her nose. "What does that have to do with anything that we were talking about?"

"I don't know what a pack is. I have a pack of two. Just me and my husband. We had more but they weren't werewolves and they died."

Missy took an unsteady breath. She recognized that little warble in Genna's tone. The sound of unresolved grief. Sorrow and loneliness that had no end.

"Are you okay?"

"No, not really."

"Want to talk about it? What was their name?"

"Sneakers. Or Black Air Force Jordan but I called him, Sneakers. He was a big black Friesian-Shire stallion."

"Wait a minute, you had a horse?"

"I had a lot of horses. Sneakers was *my* horse. We fought a great battle together against a vampire queen and a direwolf. We won but then Sneakers died. The whole herd died. Now it's just me and Troy."

"You're sad about a horse? But aren't you a super-werewolf dragon? Why do you care about horses?"

"Sneakers wasn't a horse. That was just a skin he wore to exist in this world. He was a nightmare. I've realized that I brought him out of the shadows because I couldn't fight the vampires by myself. Once they were gone, Sneakers didn't need to be here. But I wish that he'd stayed."

"So you made a nightmare real and you think you're not a boo hag?"

Genna took a deep breath, exhaled, and pierced Missy with a burning gaze. "Whatever you need to say should be to your pack not me. Just as you don't understand why I'm upset that I can't ride horses anymore."

Missy slid off her chair. She exited the tent, driven away by the stormy pressure of Genna's sorrow. Missy was mad at herself. She wanted to be Genna's friend but couldn't seem to say the right thing.

Missy sat in the dirt, picking dandelions. She braided a crown of the yellow blossoms. Then she blew the seedpods. She wished that Professor Onyx made a full recovery. She wished Rainey would forgive her. She wished that Genna would see the good that she was doing for her real people.

RAINEY GROWLED AT THE YOUNGBLOODS, "GET OUT OF the way assholes! This is an emergency. I need to speak with Brother McGruffin right now!"

"Bitch, I don't know you!" A Youngblood snarled while the pack surrounded Rainey.

Rainey struggled to stay calm. She had to complete her mission not get into another fight with another pack.

"Professor Onyx killed the asshole werewolf cop who bit her and Brother McGruffin. That's what she wanted me to tell him but now she's dying and I'm wasting my time. Get out of the way! I need to tell him!"

Brother McGruffin shoved through his pack. "She's dying?"

Rainey bit her lip and angrily nodded. "You coming or what? She's being seen to by Genna the witch doctor."

To her annoyance, Brother McGruffin relaxed and nodded. "She's in good hands." He whistled to his pack.

They hurried to their parked cars. "Lead the way, Sister Rainey. Thank you for telling me. I won't forget this."

She drove the long way to Genna's tent, fuming at the long

train of cars following. Did everyone know about this witch doctor but her? Maybe Missy was right.

The clearing was crowded with cars. Only Brother McGruffin was let inside the tent to see Professor Onyx.

Rainey got in the Escalade and drove away. She needed time to think and there was only one place to go.

~

Genna gave Brother McGruffin and all of his Youngbloods a check-up and healing while they waited for Professor Onyx to recover. Genna had put her in a tank of enchanted honey that healed her, body and soul.

After an extensive explanation of why total submersion was the best way to cure Professor Onyx, Brother McGruffin climbed into another tank next to his beloved. Missy and his Youngbloods guarded the tanks.

Genna retreated to her interior office in the back of the tent. She set the notebook down and closed her eyes. Tears slid down her cheeks. The protective walls kept anyone from hearing her exhausted sobs.

Missy walked in unannounced. "Sorry to barge in!"

Genna hastily stood up, wiping her face. "I thought I'd locked the door. Hi, Missy. Is Professor Onyx awake already?"

Missy rushed forward and enveloped her in a hug. It was warm and fearless and a shock.

Genna could not remember the last time that anyone voluntarily touched her besides Troy. Usually they were afraid. Not that she was big on public displays of affection.

"You're a great doctor," Missy said. "The best!!!"

Genna relaxed and hugged her back. "I'm not a doctor. I just wanted to I do what I can."

"You're still the best," Missy repeated stoutly. "I don't see anybody else doing what you're doing to help us."

Neither tried to end the hug. They both needed comfort.

RAINEY DRAGGED HERSELF INTO THE FERNS. SHE gasped in pain as she dug up the theater program, or what was left of the decomposing paper. She flopped on her back, the soggy program clutched in her hand. She stared up through the trees at the obnoxious bright sunny afternoon. Sunlight filled the forest. Texas winter had no right to be so lovely. Where was a dismal cloudy day when you needed one?

Imani padded out of the ferns in cat form. She tucked her tail around her paws.

"Fuck off, Pastor Faith," Rainey snarled. "Leave me alone to die."

"I hate to break it to you but you're not going to die, Sister Rainey."

"Didn't go into the witch's lair. I'm full of bullets. I can feel it."

"Do you think that she's the only one with magic? There's a real young werewolf wishing on dandelions for your health right now. Missy's got the whole congregation and Werewolf Wednesday meet-up group praying up a storm for you right now. And believe me, the power of prayer works."

Rainey scratched an itch which was a bullet shard pushing out of her skin. "What is Genna Bellwether? She's not a werewolf."

"She's none of your damn business, that's what. You're focused on the wrong things, Miss Rainey. Stop looking back."

"Are you saying Missy's a witch?"

"Did I say that? Or did I say that your boyfriend is dead and you won't find his ghost in these ferns?"

The rage buoying Rainey up popped. She curled up and wept. She clawed at the mud. "He should've lived! He should be here!"

"Tyrik sacrificed himself to save you. Now live for you both. Love like you loved him. Forgive yourself and others for living."

Rainey ignored her but Imani kept preaching and purring.

~

A week later...

Brother McGruffin fiddled with the metal straw and coughed hard as he offered Professor Onyx the cup. "Here's your oat milk chai latte from Genuine Joes."

Professor Onyx sipped the drink from her favorite coffee shop. Cigarette smoke drifted around the porch. Brother McGruffin smoked when he was upset. She was surprised to wake with him sitting in the padded chair next to her on the porch.

Apparently Missy and Rainey thought that he was her significant other. Professor Onyx had never allowed anything more than a casual moonlit fling and a shared meal. Yet here he was, filling the tranquil garden with the stench of nicotine.

She coughed discreetly which turned into a full blown asthma attack. Her back muscles clenched. She floundered, needing air.

Brother McGruffin grabbed her arms but she batted him away desperately. He caught her drink before it tumbled to the porch.

"I'm allergic to cigarettes," she gasped. "Get away!"

Brother McGruffin snatched the cigarette from his lips and flicked it into the grass. He spritzed himself with cologne stashed in his suede suit jacket. Professor Onyx focused on breathing.

Her heartbeat settled down. She slumped against her chair, exhausted.

There was a small box on a table nearby. Genna had pulled so many bullets out of her body that it amazed her. Apparently, the fight with Officer Calhoun had been the battle that maxed out her hyper-healing ability.

Her recovery was slow but steady.

"I killed him," Professor Onyx whispered. She held Brother McGruffin's hand tight.

"Yes, you did, my warrior queen," Brother McGruffin said.

They sat together, watching the flowers from the porch.

~

PROFESSOR ONYX DRUMMED HER NAILS ON THE ARM rest of her chair. She sat like an annoyed queen instead of a convalescing elder. Rainey and Missy studiously avoided each other's gazes. Brother McGruffin had excused himself to escape the tension.

The three she-wolves waited until his Lincoln town car and caravan of trucks and SUVs carried him and his pack away.

"She hasn't demanded payment yet, has she?" Professor Onyx said, glancing at the empty space where the tent sat until Genna packed up and left.

"Um, no, she wanted us to make up." Missy faltered. She had practiced a speech but now she couldn't remember it. Why was this so excruciating? Professor Onyx was better. Rainey was too. The pack was back togther but nothing felt right.

"That's it?"

"She wants us to thank her."

Professor Onyx scowled at the wildflowers.

"She wants all of us in her debt not just Missy," Rainey seethed. "She's a witch. You should never have gone to her in the first place! Now we're in her debt as long as she wills it. You should've gone to the Church!"

Missy bit her lip. She hated the tears escaping her eyes and the wobble in her voice. "Genna is a werewolf surgeon. She knows flesh, blood, and bone magic."

"How do you know all that?"

"Because I asked her! Professor Onyx is an ancient magical warrior. I saw what Genna pulled out of her body. It wasn't just bullets. There were this horrible wiggly curses too. They had these weird spines and mouths and dripped poison. I made the right call. I'm not sorry!"

Missy and Rainey were nose to nose. Their bodies quivered with hostility. Neither had Turned but they were ready to fight. It would've been flattering if Professor Onyx wasn't mortified.

She blamed herself for putting them in this position in the first place.

"We'll go together," Professor Onyx pronounced. "The witch wants a united pack? Well, that's exactly what she's going to get. Now where can we find her?"

"She'll be at Werewolf Wednesday," Missy said resentfully. "It's not like I know her schedule."

"Then we'll speak with her there," Professor Onyx said.

"We should rob a bank and kill some haters so we'll have something to offer," Rainey said.

"Good idea. We'll hunt. Can't go empty handed."

"You're supposed to rest!" Missy exclaimed alarmed. The other two fried her with a glare but she stayed strong. "I know she'll be pissed off if you undo all of her hard work. You don't know what she wants. So instead of assuming, let's just go and ask her."

"I'm not weak," Professor Onyx said.

"I didn't say you were. I said that you're recovering and you won't impress a *doctor* by overexerting yourself. We've got a whole week. Then we see her on Wednesday and we ask."

"Well look who decided to grow a pair of balls," Rainey sneered.

"Fuck off!" Missy snarled.

"Enough!" Professor Onyx barked. "I'm sick of the pair of you. Go hunt and bring back something for us to eat. We'll wait for Werewolf Wednesday and see what's what."

Rainey and Missy prowled away, glaring and growling at each other. Professor Onyx hobbled to the Escalade. She Turned into a wolf, curled up in her favorite corner of the car, and went to sleep.

Could hair ache?

The Kitchen

THE WAXING GIBBOUS MOON BALANCED ABOVE THE Forsaken Forest like a cherry on a chocolate syrup covered sundae. It was a nice evening to be outside but Genna was on a mission. She went into the Church through a side door.

Genna found Aunt Jemima in the Kitchen. It was still Werewolf Wednesday. The elder wolf had chosen to stay in the Church instead of meeting up with the Briarpatch. There were other werewolves spending a tranquil evening using the Church's tv rooms, reading books, and speaking in private circles.

It was easy to mistake the Kitchen as an ordinary cooking place. There were no chopped up pieces of humans lying around, no buckets of guts, no hairy monster hulking over a mixing bowl. The Kitchen's white tiles and metal tables were scrupulously clean. Every werewolf was in human form.

The Kitchen chefs dressed in white. They wrapped their hair in white cloth. Their rank was defined by the colorful beads strung across their head wraps. Genna didn't know what the colors meant but the deferential way other members of the Kitchen staff moved around Aunt Jemima spoke volumes.

The Kitchen was focused on meal prep. Some were peeling mounds of garlic, chopping it up to fill big plastic containers.

Others were chopping onions and peppers. Beans were washed. Cornmeal was being turned into masa for tortillas or cornbread. Rice, couscous, and other grains were sifted. Mushrooms were washed and their skins peeled. Sauces and marinades were prepared. Spices were ground up and set in labeled ceramic pots.

Some chefs talked but most focused on their job. The huge fans above the stoves churned. The slightly chilly air was flavored with the smell of sweat, cooking things, and the gas stoves.

"I'd like to speak with you when you have a moment," Genna said to Aunt Jemima, "Can I help in some way until you're available?"

Aunt Jemima nodded at the group of younger chefs. "Go bother Chef Soledad. Let's see if the good doctor can learn a thing or two."

Genna knew a test when she heard it. She quickly washed her hands, put on a white smock, apron, and wrapped her hair in a bandana. Obviously the white scarves weren't an option for visitors.

The other students ignored her, focused on the teacher. She didn't know any of them.

A chef with 'Soledad' embroidered on her lapel raised her knife. "All right kiddies, let's see which one of you were paying attention. Whoever debones the most and fastest, gets first bite. You've got ten minutes to finish sharpening your blades. Then we start with fish. We'll work our way up the food chain. I want clean cuts. I want the offal organized. I want the feathers plucked. You keep your station clean at all times. Nobody's cleaning up after you!"

"Yes, chef!"

Each student were given a small canvas roll of knives. But that was part of the test. Soledad did not like anyone using her good knives. By her demeanor, the knife specialist barely tolerated the outsiders' presence in her Kitchen.

Every knife in the canvas roll had cheap handles and brittle metal. There was a cardboard box of knives in the corner. All rejects had warped blades, handles, or were rusted. Since Genna did not get a canvas roll, she had to search the box until she found one that felt good in her hand. Other students dug through the knives too. They cleaned their knives with varying levels of enthusiasm.

Genna's found knife had a wooden handle. It was long hunk of metal. The edge was blunt from overuse. Rust stains along the side. The blade wobbled in the handle which was clotted with old grease. It was still tacky despite several scrubbings.

She followed the students to the wet stones and cleaning implements. The rhythmic sound of oiled metal on a wet stone was oddly soothing. She picked up a toothbrush to scrub at a recalcitrant mark of rust.

She knew that trust had to be earned but damn. After Dominque's retelling of Aunt Jemima being worn like a mascot costume, she expected the information to flow just as freely. Not a test.

That said, preparing a blade for cooking instead of killing was kind of nice.

"Hurry up!" Soledad shouted.

Genna eyed the edge of her blade. It wasn't great but better than before. Hopefully it was good enough for today's challenge. She imitated the other students in clearing her space and wiped the knife off with a wet rag then a dry one.

Imani walked into the Kitchen and stopped in front of Genna, her hands on her hips. "I've been looking for you. What the hell are you doing here?"

"Begin!" Soledad barked.

The students charged for the stacks of white plastic bins full of catfish. Genna stepped past Imani and went for the lowest shelf, pulling it from the side instead of the front. She dodged around the crowd and got back to her table.

Imani had not moved. She snatched at the top catfish in Genna's bin. Genna did not snarl. She focused on cutting.

Genna threw the smallest fish at Imani. The slick body hit her in the face. Imani bit it, distracted, her feline instincts warring against her mussed makeup.

"Pastor Faith! No eating. Get to work!" Soledad barked. She set a knife down on an empty space of metal table.

"Yes, chef." Imani took off her ministers robe, revealing a conservative suit dress with capped sleeves. She slunk to the rack instead of arguing. She had the smallest bin, glaring at Genna as she pocketed her rings.

Genna focused on filleting her catfish. The knife pierced the white skin in smooth satisfying slices. The bones were easily removed but she wished that she had put on rubber gloves. She hated the feeling in her hands. None of the students wore gloves. It was strangely unhygienic. Perhaps the long werewolves nails rendered rubber gloves useless.

She followed the other students as they distributed the offal into metal bins. Guts in one bin. Heads in another. Bones in a third.

The first fish was done. Second. Third. Fourth. Imani had eaten the fifth.

Genna wiped the knife clean then carried the separated parts over to Soledad who waited behind another stainless steel table. She was the first student to finish. The chef used a pair of long metal chopsticks to inspect Genna's offering. "Knife?"

Genna offered Soledad the knife hilt first. The chef lifted the knife up. "This isn't a sushi blade. You wasted meat by cutting too broad. You didn't follow the seam close enough."

"Yes, chef."

To Genna's surprise, Soledad handed the knife back. "Put the fish away. Move on to the pigs in that freezer over there." She nodded at a reinforced metal door. "Use that table by the wall. I want the spider steak for dinner." She pointed at the laminated cutting map on the wall. "The spider steak is in the lee of the hipbone."

"Yes, chef." Genna felt the gazes as she put the fish bin in the completed racks in the walk-in refrigerator.

"Ooh, you special," Imani hissed, "Usually Chef makes you cut up three kinds of fish then chicken, the chicken, and then turkeys before she ever lets you work on mammals. If she's really annoyed, she'll make you pluck birds. You must really know how to use a knife."

Genna stiffened. Her grip on the knife subtly changed.

"Pastor Faith! Plucking station!" Soledad pointed at a stack of dead turkeys that still had their feathers. "Enough jibber-jabber."

"You got me in trouble!" Imani hissed.

Genna exhaled slowly and relaxed her grip. She went down the hallway to the cavernous freezers. She hefted the enormous wild boar carcass out of the cavernous walk-in fridge. There were racks and racks of carcasses hanging from the ceiling. She did not see any humans. Just hogs and cattle.

Imani sat in the corner of the prepping room, hunched over a duck, and making a mess of feathers. She glared at Genna who continued to ignore her.

Genna studied the pig carcass. Then the laminated diagrams on the wall.

The knife slid through the pig's cool flesh. The brain, tongue and internal organs had already been removed. Genna cut the body into parts. The feel of the muscle parting along the blade reminded her of hunting Happy Meals in human form. But the hog's body was big, cold, and heavy. It took more effort but that was expected. She focused on making every stroke count. To get the angle right.

She organized the deconstructed parts into bins, following laminated signs on the wall. She stacked the bins on racks. She put the bones in their own section. She sharpened the knife when she needed to. The spider steak was placed on its own bin and set to the side.

Other students worked through their assignments. Some were still on fish and others on fowl of various sizes. Several had joined Imani in the plucking station.

Genna finished the boar. She raised her hand. Soledad walked right over. She inspected of the racked butchered pieces and Genna's knife.

"Again," Soledad commanded.

Genna pulled another boar from the walk-in fridge.

The filleting and deboning fell into a rhythm while Soledad paced the aisles. Some students were deboning chickens but no one else had been given pig to cut.

By the fourth pig, Genna's arms ached and her back hurt. Sweat clung her clothes to her back. Swamp crotch made her leggings uncomfortable. Sweat was a cool constant along the edge of her eyebrows and soaked her bandana. Her fingers were swollen and the knife threatened to jump out of her hand if she cut too close to the bone. She kept cutting until her knife hit a vertebra, tangled on the muscle and tendons. Genna yanked and accidentally snapped the knife in half when she pulled it out.

She stared at the handle and the shard of metal. She set both pieces to the side. She searched for a replacement knife in the box but they were brittle discards. She cleaned several quickly. These were much more difficult to get a good cut from.

The second knife snapped. The third was so small that she had to work hard to get a good cut at all. She switched to the other knives. They broke too. She was stuck with the third knife.

"What's the hold up?" Soledad demanded, walking over.

"My knives broke."

"You should've said something sooner." Soledad showed her the knife drawer.

After the garbage blades, the slick metal that greeted her in their bamboo racks were so beautiful Genna was hard pressed to choose. She selected two knives. A cleaver and one beautifully balanced knife that was glorious to hold.

The pig was cut in minutes. She smirked, excited by the change in pace. The cleaver hacked spines. The knife took care of the rest. The fifth, sixth, and seventh a breeze. She filled rolling cart after cart with bins of butchered meat.

Soledad stopped her on the way to get an eighth. "That's enough."

"Yes, chef."

"Pastor Faith, come here." Soledad gestured. Imani wheeled a two metal carts full of plucked turkeys and chickens. Then walked away.

Genna cleaned her work surface again. Then picked up the carving knife. After butchering pigs, cutting turkeys and chickens was a breeze. She sliced and separated with a small delighted smile. It was almost a game. A pattern made of knife strikes.

She was sorry when she ran out of turkeys to carve. She looked expectantly at Soledad. The chef inspected the trays of meat. She nodded. "Okay. You're done. Good work."

Genna wiped down her table. She washed the knive thoroughly and wiped it dry. She returned the knife on the magnetic strip above the drawer so it could dry. She stroked the edge of the knife, a little sad that she couldn't take it. "This is a good knife."

"Thanks, I made it myself," Soledad said.

There was a stack of spider steaks on a small tray of ice at her work table.

"All these steaks need is some salt and pepper. Cook them in duck fat," Soledad said, placing a wet cloth over the top. "They're yours to eat."

"Thank you, chef." Genna nodded, overwhelmed by the acerbic compliment. It was nice to work and actually see the change.

"Get out of here." Soledad said gruffly and walked over another student to bark about the turkey she had deboned.

Genna walked out with her tray.

<h1 style="text-align:center">Straight Edge</h1>

THE KITCHEN'S CAFETERIA WAS EMPTY BUT THERE were troughs of mushrooms, fruit, and vegetables waiting. Genna hadn't considered that werewolves were omnivorous just like humans.

She checked her Patek Philipe watch. Less time had passed in the Kitchen than she expected. Her body was loose with exhaustion, her fingers barely able to hold a fork. She ate spider steaks cold. Then she wandered over to the food troughs to eat her fill of mushrooms, vegetables, and fruit. She sat back down at her table and drank water.

Aunt Jemima came into the cafeteria carrying a plastic pitcher and two mason jars. "Are you thirsty?"

Genna eyed the retro brown plastic pitcher and its stopper lid. "I'd love some."

The elder wolf sat down across from Genna and poured them both a mason jar's worth. Genna took a sip and choked. She had expected sweet tea or lemonade. Instead it was peach cobbler moonshine. She had taken *way* too big of a gulp. It burned all the way down.

She coughed, clearing her throat and dabbed the corner of her eyes. "That's really tasty. The Kitchen has an impressive still."

Aunt Jemima pursed her lips. "What do you want from me, Black Belle?"

"I spoke to Dominque. She said that you survived being skinned by Stacy the boo hag. I'd like to hear your side of the story."

"I don't remember what that boo hag did to me."

"Why not?"

Aunt Jemima sipped her drink. "Before the boo hag cured me I was too sick to leave my house. I could barely make it from the bed to the kitchen."

"She cured you? Dominque said that you were skinned."

Aunt Jemima turned the jar in circles between her fingers. "You'd be better off curing the sick than killing that witch with that bag. The Salon is still collecting hair and nails even when we know where it's going."

Genna took another small sip and gagged.

"You're not much of a drinker, are you? Do you smoke or snort or shoot-up? Or are you Straight-Edge?"

Genna was surprised to hear that 1980s hardcore punk term for militant sobriety. "I've never thought of myself like that."

"But you are, aren't you? Straight and sharp as Soledad's knives. Coming in here, holier than thou. On a mission to help us poor sinners?"

Genna kept her expression pleasant while her ears felt hot. She was not prepared for this onslaught of hostility. "What if I made hair care products ethically which contained healings? And werewolves were involved in every step of the process?"

"Oh, you think you're better than that boo hag? You're just another White girl trying to be Black. What do you know about our hair?"

"I am Black."

"Are you sure?"

Genna struggled to keep her temper. Boy, did she hate this conversation. She tried to steer it back on course. "I need your help. I'd like you to mix a batch of spices. The kind that makes a boo hag jump out of her skin."

Aunt Jemima studied her. "I thought you wanted to kill the witch."

"I don't want to kill the people she's wearing."

"But you could kill them all. I've seen the way you hold a knife. I know a murderer when I smell one."

"I'm not interested in your opinion of me." The anger wreathed her words in a snarl. Aunt Jemima straightened with offense.

Genna pulled out the cookbook from the medicine bag written by a root healer, and slapped it down on the table between them. She flipped to the correct page with a thumbnail. "Now, the basic recipe to make a boo hag jump skins is comprised of red pepper, black pepper, and salt with honey to make it stick. But I think you might know a few extra tricks to make sure it works."

Aunt Jemima eyed the cookbook. She took a thoughtful sip of her moonshine. Genna continued her pitch, holding tight to her rage. "I've been making rosemary infused sunflower and olive oil at my farm. I think it works better as an emulsifier than honey. The purer the better."

"There's not enough spices in the world to make that boo hag shed her skins." Aunt Jemima put a lid on Genna's jar moonshine and shoved across the table. "You're not better than her. She healed me. What've you done? Nothing but run your mouth. You're not saving anybody. You're just another colonizer trying to take take take."

Genna stood up. She put the jar of moonshine and the cookbook into the medicine bag. "Okay, well, then. Thanks for the moonshine. Have a blessed evening."

Aunt Jemima waved dismissively at the door. "Go twitch your smart-ass on home."

Genna glided out elegantly as if the empty cafeteria was a catwalk. The boo hag preyed on vulnerable people too proud to ask for help. She'd formulate a counterattack on her own.

Yoruba Garden

Genna gritted her teeth, bottling a scream. The air wavered in a heat haze as she strode through the Church.

Are you Black? Are you sure?

Genna didn't know how to deal with Aunt Jemima's hostility. The absurdity of getting called White in the Church had sucked the wind right out of her sails. As if they both weren't full of Black Folk magic sitting inside a magical safe space designed for Black people. Two women pitted against each other. Enemies on sight instead of allies.

Are you Black? Are you sure?

It was so frustrating. She had seen the Kitchen's inventory as she butchered. They had plenty of spices. Why not use it to defend themselves?

Maybe she had missed something. Maybe a local implicitly understood what she, as an outsider, did not. Wanting to be part of a community wasn't the same as being welcome.

Genna took a detour into the Yoruba Garden. She stormed past sage, rosemary, and lavender bushes that hummed with honeybees. She paused to watch their busy activity. She started box breathing, forcing herself to slow down. To let go of the hurt.

Are you Black? Are you sure?

Desperately she thought about Stacy the boo hag. What did it all mean? But she couldn't focus.

"Well hello there." Imani sauntered around a catnip bush, idly picking the leaves. She had bits of feather fluff sticking to her braids. "Fancy meeting you here. Are you skipping the meet-up?"

Genna quickly dashed away a few frustrated tears. "Oh, hey. I didn't see you there."

"You asked the wrong person for help, you know. Aunt Jemima has no memory of her life before getting spat out of a boo hag's coochie. She doesn't even remember her original name."

"Her coochie?" Genna repeated, horrified. "Is that what happened? Dominque said that—"

"Dominque is an angry weirdo like you." Imani offered Genna a knife in a leather sheath. "Chef Soledad likes you and she's hard to impress."

Genna unsheathed the blade. It was pretty, well-crafted, and balanced. "I don't need another knife. I need spices."

"First of all, don't piss me off." Imani slapped the knife in Genna's hand. "Second, every student who passes the class gets a knife. This is a cooking knife not a killing knife."

"A knife is a knife."

"Third, you're on your own. The Church can't get involved. Besides, it's not like you need our help."

"What do you mean? The Kitchen has all the spices."

"Oh come on, like you can't buy a metric ton of spices."

"But these are holy spices baptized in Black soul power."

"You're stalling. You know what must be done."

Genna sheathed the knife with the unconscious grace of the extremely lethal and put it in the medicine bag. "I'm trying to heal not kill."

"Listen, I get it but you are what you are. Now, I've got twenty werewolves waiting to get their hair braided. I need to convince beauticians to go back to the Salon with the promise of a pay bump."

"Is the Salon that the big of a deal?"

"You don't get your hair done at a salon?"

"I've always had my own glam squad."

"Right, you're rich rich. This is why you keep getting asked if you're Black."

Lightning flashed in Genna's pupils. "I'm Black."

"I'm just saying, you've missed out on a crucial part of Black feminine culture and it shows. For those of us who don't have Beyoncé money, the Salon is where you get your hair done, you talk, you help each other out."

"Black femininity is not a monolith."

"Yeah? Well, Stacy is better at integrating than you are. She got the Salon started. She's nice like that."

"Let me tell you how nice that boo hag is." Genna scowled, yanking her journal out of the medicine bag. "Stacy started the Salon to funnel her victims into the Witch Market's network of skin traffickers and fur traders. Anyone who doesn't use the Salon gets hunted by her Ragers. She targets werewolves because they've got more magic and a genuine need to look human to survive but she's more than happy to steal Black and Brown bodies too."

She showed Imani her notebook, pointing at names and figures. "Look, immigration, homeless, orphaned, victims of gun violence, and people fresh out of incarceration. She Turns them and sends them right down her pipeline."

Genna flipped to another page, swatting Imani's hand away when she tried to touch it.

"Her dog-catchers hunt anyone who tries to live as a canine. They die in the fighting pits or puppy mills which ultimately lead to ingredient jars and fur coats in the Witch Market and her cosmetics factories."

Genna jerked a thumb at the Kitchen. "Stacy also visits desperate Black humans like Aunt Jemima and solves their medical problems with the medicine bag."

"The medicine bag's a part of this?" Imani hissed.

Genna moved the bag out of reach. "The medicine bag strictly heals. That's it's true purpose but she uses the healing to bind her victims to her will." She stroked the beaded medicine bag. "I hate what she's done with the bag. It was created to do good and she's used it for such evil."

Imani frowned. "But how does she do it? What happens with the skins after she takes them?"

"She wears them. They're still alive. They don't even know that they're being drained dry until a Slipskin crawls down their throats to feast on their husks. And if the parasites don't get them, she eats them, or turns them into hair and skincare products."

Genna nodded at Imani's scalp. "The pomade that you're wearing is made from your congregation, that's why it smells comforting. So is the shea butter lotion on your elbows. So don't tell me that Stacy's nicer than me. I know what she wants."

Imani patted her scalp. "You know what's funny? The Church knew she was no good. I used to be so embarrassed that it never let her step past the trees. The prayer warriors blamed me for offending our benefactor but now I see that the Church was keeping us safe. The same way it knew that you're one of us even if you're weird."

Genna glanced up at the stone and stained glass wall shadowing the Yoruba Garden. The wind blew through the garden. "I'm glad the Church likes me."

"It does. More than anyone standing on this soil besides myself. That's what pisses Aunt Jemima off. She fell for Stacy's act. We all did. Even me. And now I'm looking at you and realizing what a damn fool I've been."

"But I'm still not Black enough."

Imani shrugged. "Nobody is Black enough. It's an impossible standard created to divide us. You're different. So am I. So what?"

"Be careful. That almost sounds like we're friends."

"We are friends, Genna." Imani nodded at the parking lot. "You should go. You don't need us. Be what you are. Break the chains. Free my people. Save them from this curse."

Genna stared at Imani. "Even if it kills you?"

Imani nodded, raising her chin. Slowly Genna took a step past the minister, then another, moving fast. Not a run. More like a rushed strut.

Imani watched her drive away in a vintage purple Mustang. The engine's snarl was loud in the quiet forest. There was a figure glaring at Imani from the edge of the forest. She wore the skin of another Black woman.

"After everything I've done for you people," Stacy snarled, "How could you help her and not me?"

"Because I hate you," Imani purred in a sing-song way. "You're going to pay for what you did. The wolf is coming for you, boo hag."

"How dare you threaten me? I can crush your entire congregation like that!" She snapped her fingers. Nothing happened. She snapped them again. Still nothing.

Imani kept grinning. Stacy stopped sneering, torn between incredulity and fury. She tried to work a spell but still nothing.

The knife that Imani had given Genna had already severed Stacy's connection to the Church the moment she touched the holy blade. Chef Soledad had strategically used Genna to cut the bodies that Stacy had planted to control the Kitchen. The Gamers were free of parasites. The Church was free of the boo hag's power.

The Yoruba Garden rippled in the wind, scent of herbs made Stacy cough and sneeze. She tripped on roots. She ducked as the trees tried to snatch Stacy up into their branches and drag her under their roots. The boo hag jumped and ran across the tar fields.

Imani went back inside. The Kitchen was busy preparing for the feast. Aunt Jemima angrily stirred something in a cast iron skillet on the stove. Chef Soledad nodded at Imani as she walked past.

Imani picked up a tea towel and took the cast iron skillet away from Aunt Jemima, not trusting what she stirred. The rest of the staff stiffened, offended but also careful. The Kitchen might be their domain but it was inside of the Church.

Aunt Jemima gripped her wooden spoon like it was a knife. Her breath was fiery with moonshine. Her gaze glassy. Her cheeks flushed.

"Something on your mind, Chef Jemima?" Imani asked.

"They'll kill us all!" Aunt Jemima said.

Imani was quiet because she knew how to listen. Aunt Jemima's words were like razors cutting her skin. Old wounds reopened by shame and humiliation. Her self-hatred warping sense.

Imani cautiously sniffed then sneezed. The skillet was full of cut rosemary being slowly stirred into hot sunflower and olive oil. There was red pepper, salt, and black pepper. Along with other spices. Exactly as Genna requested.

Imani set the skillet back on the stove. The wooden spoon trembled. Then went back to stirring. The steam made them both sneeze.

"She's beautiful, isn't she?" Imani said conversationally. "Like a beautiful nightmare. She's got everything you ever secretly wanted. Money, power, great hair, great skin, and she's smart too. She's got eyes like a laser microscope. It makes you feel small. Like you're never going to be enough."

Aunt Jemima kept stirring.

"I did some digging and found out what happened to the last town she saved. And all I can think of, is how bad did I need to fuck up to get on her radar? And the worst part is that she's actually good. All that power and she's a good person. It makes me sick to my stomach. I mean, I try to be good but damn, can I live?"

Aunt Jemima added more red pepper. "It'll come back," she whispered, "I'll forget again. I'll get sick again. What she gave will be taken away."

"It's possible but I doubt it."

Aunt Jemima laughed. It wasn't a pleasant laugh. "You think that straight-edged high yellow bougie girl will be any different than the other one? They're the same."

"There's a difference. I guess you were too busy feeling sorry for yourself to pull your head out of your ass and see past her pretty skin."

Aunt Jemima sucked on her teeth, pissed off. "Is that how you talk to your elders?"

"You are hardly my elder."

"I'm sixty-eight years old!"

"No, you *were* sixty-eight when you got skinned alive by a witch who promised to heal your many illnesses. Then you got magically Turned into a werewolf. Then you were freed from your enslavement when a young foolish Sneakerhead traded herself for your freedom. And that poor deluded girl loves you so much that she put herself in Black Belle's crosshairs to make sure that the boo hag pays for messing with you. If you ask me, you seem pretty ungrateful for all the blessings you've already received."

Aunt Jemima stirred the pot. "There won't be enough spices."

"No, probably not but we've still got to try."

More stirring. Imani wiped her running nose. There were a few discreet sneezes as the spice oil's scent permeated the Kitchen.

"This is powerful stuff." Imani said. "It clears the sinuses."

"I'm not doing this for Black Belle. I'm doing this for Dominque. I didn't think she was still alive," Aunt Jemima said, "I thought Stacy had her. How'd she get free? Or is it a trap? Is she truly safe or is the witch using her as a lure?"

"Could be. We have to see." Imani left the Kitchen. She walked through the Church to a special door in the Yoruba Garden that led to the Speakeasy.

She found Amaya in the dressing room combing out her wigs. "You like Black Belle, don't you? You think that she's going to save our asses and solve all of our problems."

"No, I think she belongs in the Briarpatch."

Imani was not distracted. "You haven't been doing anything, have you?"

Amaya glanced at the secret closet. Imani strode over and wrenched to cabinet doors open. But no candles were lit. No tinctures or potions were recently made. Roger and Zion's framed pictures were on the mantle with wilting flowers.

Imani slowly backed away from the altar.

"You thought I'd done something?" Amaya harrumphed. "I'm not stupid."

"No, but you are lonely and sad. And that can make a person do stupid things."

Amaya glared at Imani through the mirror. "What do you want?"

"I want Genna to find what she's looking for. Tell the Briarpatch to stop beating around the bush. That dragon is running out of patience. She burnt her last forest down. Let's not have that happen here. Are you sure you don't have a secret stash from Stacy or Delilah lying around?"

Amaya stood up, fluffed her breasts in her dress, and stalked through a connecting door. She came back with a hand embroidered piece of art in a golden gilt frame. Amaya shoved the frame into Imani's hands. "This is what I've been doing, okay?"

The words were beautifully stitched and surrounded by a thicket of blooming fabric flowers.

The words read:

"There is no wealth to compare with the health of the body. Honor the doctor for her services, for the Lord created her. Her skill comes from the Most High."

Imani lifted the piece up to get a look at the neat stitches. "You made this?"

"I wanted to thank her," Amaya snapped defensively. "It had to be real. No bullshit."

"But you haven't given it to her."

"It's not like I can walk right into her tent, now can I? She doesn't like me."

"To be fair, you almost got her husband killed."

"I'm sorry, okay?" Amaya took the framed needlepoint back. "I'm on her side. I just can't be obvious about it."

"Neither can I."

They focused on the artwork instead of each other.

"You're real good at needlepoint," Imani said, "Where'd you learn to sew so well?"

"I used to make my own dresses because nothing ever fit." Amaya gestured at her dynamic shape. "In the Speakeasy there's always some costume ripping and tearing. Needlepoint relaxes me." Amaya slid the frame back into the closet. She rubbed the closed door. "Don't tell her."

"I won't." Imani sucked her teeth. "I guess we'll all be ringside for this fight."

"Hold on to your butts," Amaya quipped.

The Whopper

It was still Werewolf Wednesday. The Strait-Legged Bacon barbecue joint was its usual level of busy. Smoked meat filled every tray. Genna suppressed a jaw-cracking yawn.

"How was your day, dear?" Troy asked as they ate barbecue.

"It was long and it's not over. We've got a Whopper to deal with tonight."

"Then we had better eat up. We'll need our strength to take on a Whopper."

Genna designated the term of Whopper to anyone powerful enough to be a mortal threat. Like Pipsy Montgomery and White Fang. Stacy was dangerous and powerful enough to knock Troy off the board. It had been hard to keep him in the dark but he had encouraged his own ignorance. The boo hag's influence permeated every aspect of the Briarpatch. Genna wondered if Coyote had worn her face to tip the scales in her favor or to drag her into this fight.

Genna and Stacy had already crossed swords. A death match was inevitable.

She had spent careful months taking over Stacy's territory with one good deed at a time. Or at least she *thought* that she was doing good. Aunt Jemima's hostility made Genna wonder if she'd miscalculated. Maybe she wasn't as good as she thought she was.

Genna also had the Idiot Brother Blues. When she sat down and dug through the boo hag's records she found that the evil mastermind was her Idiot Brother. The paper trail was haphazard but Genna was good at sniffing out hidden ledgers and pocket folders with the real numbers and accounts.

Once again, her Idiot Brother had trusted his money and power to the wrong people. He wasn't evil but he was definitely a spoiled Black American Prince. The first son. A dangerous and exploitable combination of extremely intelligent, competent, and insecure. Stacy didn't even work that hard. Sex was his weakness.

Idiot Brother wanted Stacy and believed that she was just misunderstood. Her parents covered the losses and protected him from legal fallout. Stacy skipped off with a fortune. The evil laboratories, the fur farms, the puppy mills, the dog fighting rings, and the Witch Market could all be traced back to a single line in Idiot Brother's bank statement under 'Groceries' and didn't mention the pain he'd caused.

The Briarpatch werewolves were the faces of countless victims. Genna had to fix this.

First that meant confronting her Idiot Brother. It was a phone call but the argument sucked the whole family into the drama. Genna was vilified. Idiot Brother was under too much pressure and too fragile to take responsibility. Again.

Worse still, several people in Sweetwater had directly funded Stacy's exploits. People that she had considered allies or at least, not enemies. She wasn't prepared to see how easily Stacy had fed upon the disarray.

And Genna had missed it. All of it. Too busy trying to distance herself from her own grief. She had tried to stop feeling anything for anybody. To create a new life far away from Sweetwater. To stay helpful but numb.

Perhaps the reason Stacy hadn't tried to directly tangle with Genna again was because she didn't need a head-on collision to win. Genna was alone. No money. No allies. Her family ignoring her calls because she had called her Idiot Brother out.

She was rushing towards a headlong collision against an enemy with a thousand faces.

"When's the last time you ate a Whopper?" Genna was eager to talk about Troy's exploits and stop thinking about her most recent failures. Troy was born into a monster hunting family. She learned a lot just listening.

Troy frowned thoughtfully as he ate a forkful of brisket "Hmmm, I'd say Pipsy and White Fang."

"What about before we met?"

Troy started talking about a hunt for a Mothman that took him from the back woods in Vermont to a swamp in Alabama. It was interesting. Unfortunately, Genna was exhausted.

Troy startled her out of a doze with a gentle touch on her hand. "We don't have to hunt that Whopper tonight. You should get some rest. Whoppers aren't your average Happy Meal."

Genna clutched his hand, hungrily searching his loving expression. They hadn't had sex in ages. Yet he was still here. He hadn't left. He stayed. "Sorry. It's been a lot."

"Is this about those elder wolves you healed?"

"I supposed it's a compound effect. Professor Onyx and Brother McGruffin were the most complicated patients I've ever treated. I really had to work hard to heal them. Then I chased down a real lead on our Whopper. But I was already running on fumes. "

Troy grinned. "You said *our* Whopper."

"You're my hunting partner."

"I know. It's just the first time you've said it."Troy kissed her knuckles tenderly. "I'm proud of you. I knew that you'd be a great witch doctor."

"Healing is harder than killing but I'm not hunting bad guys. The Whopper will keep on skinning until someone permanently stops them." Genna shook her head. "I've got a plan but I don't know how to lure the Whopper out into the open. This isn't like

Sweetwater. No one wants to help me and I can't even blame them."

"Why not ask the Dragonflies and the Youngbloods to pick up the slack as payment for services rendered? You saved their pack leaders' lives. They owe you. Besides, werewolves need to eat. This is their turf. You can teach them your hunting cipher in exchange. Brother McGruffin seems like a good guy."

Genna jerked up straight in her seat. "I'm not sharing my hunting cipher." Her hunting cipher had kept her belly full and off the radar for decades. This was a big ask.

"Okay, then something else," Troy said, immediately backing off. Genna's brittleness was hard to navigate. "I'm just saying, the point of these meet-ups is collaboration. You can't be the only one who wants the Whopper gone."

"I will ask around but the cipher is off the table."

"You don't trust them? What about the Glamazons?"

"They don't trust me either after Sweetwater," Genna said. She honestly wasn't sure that she trusted anyone.

"I'm sure they'll come when you call. You just have to ask for help." Troy wished that he could massage away the grim set to Genna's beautiful shoulders. He wished that he hadn't fallen into the boo hag's trap. She couldn't ask him for help because he was compromised. She had been so hopeful about moving to Austin and now, she was grasping at straws.

Professor Onyx stared through the restaurant window at Genna and Troy. The couple sat at their own table, smiling at each other, chatting and leaning across their meal with convivial nonchalance.

Rainey felt a deep pang of jealousy as Troy kissed Genna's knuckles. Once upon a time, she and Tyrik had been that lovey-dovey.

"You mean to tell me that she's married to a cracker-ass cracker?!" Professor Onyx exclaimed. "Why didn't you tell me?"

Missy and Rainey gave her a long look. Others had heard her loud and clear. They ducked their heads and hurried inside. Nobody wanted to be a part of that conversation.

Rainey shook her head. "Wow. Just wow."

"First of all, who cares who she's married?" Missy scowled. "Second, you can't be this racist. Times have changed. We have to evolve."

"You two don't have a problem with that?" Professor Onyx demanded. "Look at them!"

"No, I don't care!" Missy snarled. "I have a problem with you!"

Rainey stepped between them. "Look, we've all got problems with Black Belle but it doesn't change anything."

"I don't have problems!" Missy said stoutly.

"Fine, she walks on water," Rainey snapped. "Chill. We owe her so we're going in together. That's the agreement. We do it *together*."

Professor Onyx and Missy harrumphed, mad as hell.

Brother McGruffin was inside with a few Youngbloods. His excitement to see them dimmed until he saw their scowls.

They got their food, letting the noise of Werewolf Wednesday replace any conversation. They filled their trays and followed Professor Onyx through the milling crowd. Brother McGruffin nodded at a few greetings and Missy smiled tensely but their entire focus was on the Dragonflies' approach to Genna's table.

Professor Onyx could not take her eyes off of Troy. She had ignored him before but now, the monster hunter looked too much like Officer Calhoun for her peace of mind.

Missy, Rainey, and Brother McGruffin flanked her with their trays. They expected her to sit down at the empty space of the long table instead of loom over Genna.

"Good evening," Genna said genially gesturing at the large table and the empty seats. "Would you like to sit down?"

Silence stretched. Missy bit her bottom lip, mortified by Professor Onyx. But what could she do or say?

Professor Onyx set her tray down next to Genna and sat. Brother McGruffin took the chair next to Professor Onyx across from Troy. "Howdy cowboy, how've you been?"

"You know, living," Troy said, not eloquent but pleased. She watched the two men shake hands. She internally grimaced. Maybe she needed to get past her own prejudices.

Rainey and Missy crammed into Troy's side of the booth. Professor Onyx raised her beer at Genna and nodded. Genna raised her beer. They clinked bottles. Respect.

"What do we owe you?" Professor Onyx asked without preamble or taking a bite of her meal. Barbecue could wait.

Troy caught Genna's eye. She ignored the signal. Just because he thought sharing the cipher was a good idea did not make him right.

It had taken her decades to get the Happy Meal hunting system right. Money, time, and learning the hard way that her techniques in tracking down serial killers could easily fall into the wrong hands (like Katie McBride's hands). And she needed the cipher. It was hers.

But she couldn't deny that she did need help. That meant admitting her limits. After the debacle in the Kitchen and the family phone call, she needed to reevaluate her entire strategy.

Genna was used to having unlimited access to money and complete obedience. Now she had to try something new. She had to ask for help.

"You have something." Professor Onyx leaned into Genna's personal space. The unblinking eye contact was uncomfortable at this close range. So was getting a nose full of her scent at throat biting distance but it was wolf sign of trust.

Genna loved Troy but he still thought like a human, even in werewolf form. She needed monsters. But could she trust the Dragonflies?

"Tell us, Doc. That's why we're here. Let's not waste time. Who's the target?"

Genna loved it being called Doc. Maybe just maybe, the Briarpatch could be her new home if she killed the witch. She could finally be that healer for werewolves because they needed her mixture of skills.

But the knife from the Kitchen weighed heavy. The Briarpatch didn't want a doctor. They wanted someone who knew how to kill a boo hag. They wanted their Salon to be reputable. They wanted to be treated like people not ingredients.

She took a deep breath and let go of the illusion that she was in control of the situation. "I plan to kill Stacy the boo hag. She controls the Briarpatch. It is the maximum levels of danger for all of us but that's the target. I just don't see a way that continued coexistence is feasible."

Professor Onyx smiled. Rainey and Missy had never seen such a happy, toothy, sunshine beam of unbridled joy. Frankly, neither had Brother McGruffin. And she had bestowed this gift upon Genna who had no idea what an honor she had just received and didn't smile back. She was too busy expecting Professor Onyx to refuse.

"So let's go," Professor Onyx said, "What are you waiting for? Let's get this *jive turkey*!"

Genna took a big bite of her beef rib. She broke the rib in half with the absent-minded strength of a dragon. The power and sharp crack was loud even in the crowded room. The werewolves were impressed.

Professor Onyx pursed her lips, annoyed but chasten. It had been a while since she had to actually listen and allow anyone, let alone another dominant Black female call the shots. Genna was used to serious power in every world she inhabited. Professor Onyx might not like her choice in husband but she respected the way Genna handled the situation.

Genna knew the enemy, planned to killed her enemy, and knew that everyone in at the Werewolf Wednesday meetup had heard her declaration of war. She also wasn't going to make Professor Onyx look bad in front of her community. This was a careful alliance.

Professor Onyx ate her barbecue and tried to contain her excitement. This was going to be fun.

Missy exhaled with relief. Rainey and Brother McGruffin exchanged glances. Troy ate, happy that Genna had listened to his advice.

"What's a jive turkey?" Missy asked. "Is she a turkey? Do we know that?"

"It's an old slang from the 1970s," Genna said, "Jive means insincere, deceptive, and nonsense. Like talking 'jive' means full of shit. And turkey, in combination with jive, means a stupid, inept, or worthless person who is unreliable, makes empty promises, and is generally dishonest."

Everyone at the table gave Genna a look. She shrugged. "What? I speak jive. I love Blaxploitation movies."

"Sounds like a boo hag to me," Troy said loyally.

Professor Onyx looked at Missy annoyed. "Did you get your answer, Encyclopedia Brown?"

"Yes," Missy said, "Sorry. I wasn't talking jive."

"Ooh, so now you know the word?"

"Which Blaxploitation movie is your favorite?" Brother McGruffin asked Genna.

"I love anything with Pam Grier, especially Foxy Brown and Friday Foster. But I'd have to say 'Sugar Hill' is my all time favorite. Dolomite is fun."

"That Rudy Ray Moore is something else!" Brother McGruffin said, pleased that Genna actually had an opinion.

"Also Scream Blacula Scream," Genna added.

"I still like Shaft," Troy said.

"Who doesn't?" Rainey said, "But it's got to be the original."

The conversation turned into a deep discussion about Blaxploitation films. Missy tried to keep up.

Under Pressure

Stacy the boo hag knew that Genna was coming. Everyone kept telling her and Genna had too much magic to be stealthy. It felt like the barometric pressure change as a hurricane approached. Things kept sliding out of her control.

She went to her storage in Chicago and found it empty. She walked around the apartment, feeling the medicine bag's power. It had stripped everything.

She took a deep breath. She was fine. She had other resources. Then she went to the mushroom farm. Genna had also stripped the place clean, but she had left the company and the Anansi.

She was focused on other things. Like her mushroom farm suddenly disappearing without a trace.

The boo hag ran through the cavernous Clinic, searching for something, anything at all. But it was gone.

Stacy squeezed her head as she cussed in frustration. "Impossible! How could this have happened? Who could've done this to me?"

"Who do you think?" Anansi said, a small spider in the uppermost corner of the room.

"How could you told her about my Clinic?"

"I didn't. She noticed because you used her companies and her own money. That's on you."

Stacy wasn't about to apologize or admit anything. But she hadn't know that the Clinic was connected to Genna's companies. She wanted to accuse Anansi of lying but that was even more dangerous.

She screeched another curse and stomped out.

Losing the mushroom farm was the last straw.

Stacy went to the Old Crow for help. She hated herself for asking but did not want to accept that her actions and choices had consequences. 200 years was not enough time on this Earth. She wanted to live! And she would do anything to keep breathing. That included making a deal with the Yahtzees.

The Old Crow was the grand dragon of the Yahtzees that lived in Austin. He ruled the sanctuary for anyone else who felt like America was a little too colorful these days. He was a gore crow, a creature of rot, chaos, and war. He thrived on the malevolent hatred that permeated the current climate.

But the Old Crow didn't like women. Stacy had to prove her worth if she wanted this ancient dragon to lift one bigoted finger.

Stacy decided to offer up a bunch of immigrants who had snuck across the Border as target practice and cannon fodder for a snuff film the Yahtzees was made to feel good about themselves.

What Stacy did not know was that the Old Crow was a member of Genna's country club and the Master of Hounds for the Thanksgiving Hunt. He was a personal friend of Pipsy Montgomery. While he hated Genna for killing the Sweetwater vampires, he was also an elitist. Genna was part of the 1% of the 1%. She might be slumming it but she was always part of the ruling class. Stacy was not.

There was nothing that Stacy could offer that he wanted. He hoped that the two witches would do him a favor and kill each other. He also planned to use their werewolves in his hunt this year.

Genna ignored his phone call. The Old Crow knew that she

wouldn't listen if he didn't give her something. He exposed his team. He didn't care about them. There were always humans who believed that following orders absolved them from consequences. Genna deployed her Glamazons to save the immigrants from his Yahtzees.

They devoured the Old Crow's minions by the light of the moon.

A shadow passed over them. Their guns were out and pointed at the Old Crow as he landed on top of a parked Range Rover. He clacked his beak at the Glamazons. "Call the Queen Bitch. Tell her that I'm waiting so she'd better show up."

They called. Genna came, pissed off. "What do you want, Old Crow?"

"I've got some information that you want and you've got something I want."

He told Genna exactly where the boo hag was in exchange for her sparing his sons from her Happy Meal list.

Genna went home, annoyed that she had to make a promise she couldn't break. Fortunately, Troy was not bound by the same promise.

"I've got another Whopper," Genna said, reaching over to stroke the sword callouses on his left hand.

"Lucky break?"

"No, but it does explain a few things about the other Whopper. You'll have to be careful. Ask friend to come with. Don't mess with the Old Crow or he'll eat them."

Troy was intrigued. That was Genna's roundabout way of encouraging wholesale slaughter. She wanted him to bring Brother McGruffin and his Youngbloods to come along and scatter Stacy's resources.

Uno Night

IMANI WENT INTO THE COMMUNITY CENTER THAT WAS next to the Church and set out tables and folding chairs in circles around the basketball court. Then added decks of Uno cards.

It was Uno Night.

She filled flasks, pitchers, and bottles with water, quietly blessing each one. She added an eyedropper's amount of an infusion she had made from mint, ginger, and lemon to cover the taste of anti-boo hag curses that Genna had prescribed.

The werewolves filed in. They were herded by prayer warriors. The packs ranged in size, averaging six per table with two prayer warrior chaperons. Each werewolf wore a mustard seed necklace, a face mask, and a name tag. A few still wore dog collars with their names sewn on the side. Imani hated those damn collars but Stacy brainwashed many into believing that they weren't more than animals, not fit to wear jewelry. The werewolves liked the flannel, jeans, and knockoff Timberland boot uniform. The 'werewolf' outfits was required even when it was a hundred degrees outside.

Uno was important because many werewolves were colorblind after the transformation. They had to relearn fine motor skills, remember what numbers were, and how to control their killing instinct if someone added three Draw-2s on top of a Draw-4.

Imani expected to hear gossip about the unexpected arrival of strangers. Instead the large basketball court was quiet with concentration.

She walked around the tables. The faces changed but the name tags stayed the same: Scooby, Snoopy, Balto, Fido, Odie, and other cartoon dog names.

Werewolves had such a short life expectancy that naming them was merely a place holder. A way to stave off the tragedy.

Werewolves were confused by the 6 and 9 cards. They couldn't see green or red. Princess swatted one on the hand for sniffing the cards. "We don't sniff—argh!"

The werewolf ripped her arm off and throat out with a snarl. She turned fast. Magic shimmered like lightning across water as her skin turned to fur. Her human teeth fell out, immediately replaced by sharp incisors which clamped upon the dying prayer warrior's throat.

Most of the flannel and jeans had ripped off during the transformation but the name tag clung to the patchy tri-colored fur. Dominque the werewolf. Usually so quiet. Yet the deep river of rage that ran through her body had nothing to do with size.

The other Gamers and prayer warriors were too busy keeping their own tables under control to come to their sis-in-arm's rescue. Even her partner was preoccupied by suppressing the turns of the other five werewolves who sprouted fur, ears, and tails. The Turn was like a yawn. Some Turned involuntarily. The Church couldn't always suppress it.

No one interrupted the attack that turned into a meal. The wet snap and slurp as Dominque dragged the body to the side of the room where Imani had left a door propped open. It led outside through the Yoruba garden, past the hedges, the lawn jockeys, and into the Taker Trees that lived in the Forsaken Forest.

Imani groomed herself to ease the anxiety. Dominque had made such great progress but she had definitely lived through some things.

Princess was dead too. Another tragedy. The Gamers sniffled

but kept quiet, not wanting to appear weak in front of the congregation.

Tiana and Jasmine hunched at the table with the other beauticians. They exchanged guilty glances but kept slapping colored cards on top of the stack.

Imani followed Dominque at a distance. There would be a lair, maybe even feral werewolves waiting for the kill. She needed to know who wasn't accepting the Church's rehabilitation program.

A soft sound of someone trying to be quiet.

Before Imani could intervene, Amaya ran out of trees and tackled Dominque. She grabbed the werewolf by the scruff of the neck and haunches, whirled her around, and threw her against a Taker Tree. Immediately the roots wrapped around Dominque like amorous tentacles. Dominque fought her confines, scratching and snapping.

Amaya snarled back, otherness crawling over her face. The beautiful brown skin wrinkling like a bedsheet as her mouth made room from her teeth. Her snarl was a deep bone rattling bass, the ancient promise of death in the dark shadows under the trees. The leaves above them rattled like snake tails. The ground shook and swayed.

Dominque tried to rally, foaming around the mouth with frightened aggression. Amaya grabbed her and shook her sharply. Dominque was folded back into her human shape with a wet snap like two sheets of leather being slapped together.

"Come on, dumbass," Amaya shoved her up the path back towards the Church. "I can't believe you killed Princess!"

"Get off me!" Dominque tried to shake her off but couldn't break the hold on the back of her neck.

Amaya frog-marched Dominque back through the trees. "I've had just about enough of your bullshit. You're going to sit. You're going to play Uno. And you're not going to attack anyone. Is that clear?"

"Yeah, yeah, yeah, I'm sorry, okay?" Dominque shook Amaya off. "I didn't mean to do it."

Amaya and Dominque glared at each other. Dominque deflated. She sniffled. "I'm sorry. I can go if you want me to go. I won't say anything."

"I think that you should decide." Amaya planted her hands on her hips. "I don't get it. You've got everything. A mansion. A fancy car. A new phone. You've got a pack that loves you. I thought Princess was your friend. Why are you causing problems? I expected better."

Dominque Turned into a werewolf and ran into the Forsaken Forest. Amaya watched her disappear in the gloom. She angrily wiped a tear away and stomped back across the hedges.

By the time Imani got back to the community center, the tables had changed. The noise level as nearly a din but from laughter. Amaya sat among the werewolves playing Uno. Some of the prayer warriors tried but most were against the walls and in the hallways hunched and muttering ominously while glaring.

The tension shifted when Imani carried a chair over to Amaya and sat down. "Okay, deal me in. I want to play Uno too."

"You saw what happened, didn't you?" Amaya demanded. "You know that she was too wild for the Church. If I've said it once, I've said it a thousand times, only werewolves can teach werewolves how to survive. The wild ones should stay outside in the sunshine."

"Yeah, yeah, yeah," Imani muttered crankily. "But this is the only place they won't get shot. Or skinned."

"I tried to protect her but she's just too skittish." Amaya sounded like she was arguing with herself.

Imani grabbed more cards from the deck. "Let's hope that she survives on her own."

Under the Epidermis

THERE ARE DRIFTS OF HAIR, PRESSING ITSELF DOWN SO the landscape around Dominque was soft brown mountains. The braids, dreadlocks, twists, silk-presses, afros, and free-flowing hair were still attached to the scalps. Others were fragmented in puffs that rolled like tumbleweeds. It looked like the clothing piles in the Boutique.

How did she get here? One moment she was lost in the Forsaken Forest, navigating tar pits. The next moment, she was slipping on hair.

Under the hair were loose teeth and nail clippings. They rattled and crunched under Dominque's sneakers. The ground was spongy with each step. She tried to keep her balance.

Under the teeth and nails were skin. Not smooth but stippled with cellulite, knobby skin tags, keloids, scars, bruises, freckles, old cuts, faded tattoos, hairy moles, pimples, rashes, eczema, and pitted holes.

Slipskins slithered under the skins like anacondas in muddy water. Their back spines momentarily pressed through the skin before sinking back down.

Werewolves crouched on the hair mountains, groping

through the teeth and skins like panhandlers searching for gold. Others feverishly braided the hair, mumbling to themselves.

One werewolf reached down, digging quickly, then pulling free a wiggling wet lump with tendrils questing the air. Dominque recoiled. That was cancer, only it was a living thing. A curse made of flesh. It had weeping sores that oozed tar.

The werewolf put the sentient cancer against his back. The tendrils immediately plunged into his skin, pulling and pushing to cram itself under the epidermis. The werewolf whimpered, forced to lift his arm as the cancer burrowed into his armpit to suckle on his lymph nodes. He went back to digging one handed.

All of the werewolves put the cancers in their bodies. Some were so deformed that they could not stand up straight. It was a Sisyphean compulsion. They could not stop digging up the curses or pull them free of their bodies.

Dominque wanted to run but there was no where to go. Only more hair mountains and rivers of teeth between them.

There wasn't a sky. Just the veiny underside of living flesh. Stacy's many victims were stitched together into a vast quilted tent. They flexed and squirmed. Muffled noise from distant conversations. This magical space was right under the epidermis of every person that the boo hag controlled. She fed on their life force and power like the parasite she was.

A quiet part of Dominque knew that Stacy had never truly let her go. All that running and hiding was a waste of time. This place was a punishment, a purgatory of torturous skin curses. Dominque had earned her place by ratting Stacy out to Genna Bellwether.

She wasn't sorry but she was afraid. She didn't want to die. She didn't want to be riddled with cancer either. It was clearly too late to fake an apology.

She clicked her heels together three times and whimpered a doomed prayer. "Help me, Obi-Wan Kenobi, you're my only hope."

It wasn't original but it was hard to be creative surrounded by a grotesque land of skin. But maybe, just maybe, that pop-culture reference might beat resonate through the skins like stretched drums and reach Genna's ears. Maybe she could come here. Maybe she could kill the witch and then cure everyone's cancer with that medicine bag. It had worked for Aunt Jemima. Why not the lost souls here?

The unsteady ground suddenly dipped, opening like a mouth. Dominque yelped as she tumbled and fell down a slope. Tongues licked her, teeth bit her, and claws cut her as she rolled down an avalanche of discarded skin.

She splashed into a lake at the throat of the hill but it wasn't water or even urine. It was acid. Burning, corrosive, chemical peeling acid like the inside of a stomach.

Desperately Dominque clawed her way up the avalanche, trying to swim upstream to get out as more skin, teeth, and claws piled down. Burying her, drowning her, crushing her under. She was submerged, fighting the onslaught as her organs burned.

Stacy watched, enjoying herself. Usually she tried to salvage something from her prey but she was sick of Dominque. The little nuisance had sold her out to her enemy and needed to be punished accordingly.

Yahtzees

The Yahtzees thought that they were patriotic eagles but to the Youngblood scouts, they strutted and pecked at each other like overweight turkeys, bloated on racism and hate. Stacy and the Old Crow had fed them everything they wanted to hear, stuffing them full of curses. They had more guns than they knew how to shoot. Lots of taxidermied animals pinned on the wall. Bombs, poisons, manifestos, and a strong internet connection. There were women too but most weren't happy. Too busy trying to stay out of the basement.

"Well?" Brother McGruffin demanded as his scouts padded up to his position in the back by the parked cars. "What do you see?"

The Youngblood rubbed his nose to clear the stench. "I thought when you called them jive-ass turkeys that you were just talking. They're actual turkeys!"

Brother McGruffin's gold grill gleamed in the shadows cast by the Yahtzees' floodlights around the perimeter of their stronghold. "You found a way in."

"The cowboy found it," the Youngblood said resentfully.

There were a lot of Texans with guns but only one everyone called the cowboy. Brother McGruffin had been a fan of Spaghetti

Westerns but meeting a genuine gunslinger was a different experience. Genuine killers were never guys you wanted to have a beer with after the hunt was over.

Forty human men and women armored in dark green and black waited in the trees. Their faces covered in black leather masks. Sunglasses with reflective lenses. Helmets. High reinforced collars of their coats to ward off any attacks from teeth or claw. None joked. They waited with patient menace. The Glamazons were another contribution from Genna Bellwether. The woman had her own army. Yet Pacos Bill was a cut above the rest.

"Pacos Bill knows his shit." Brother McGruffin said, "I bet you found a bunch of traps and fake secret tunnels before he showed you the real way in."

"He volunteered to be bait," the Youngblood added. "Why would he do that?"

"Because he knows the Yahtzees."

"I thought he'd feel some kind of way about turning on his people."

"Those ain't his people, Youngblood."

"They all look the same to me."

Brother McGruffin gave the Youngblood a long look. "You need to learn the difference the cowboy and them Yahtzees."

"They're still White." The Youngblood said, focused on the distant silhouette of Pacos Bill, calmly waiting for Brother McGruffin to give the signal.

Troy stood apart from the other werewolves with predatory stillness that had nothing to do with lycanthropy. He had chosen to stay in human form instead of transforming.

Brother McGruffin had real respect for Genna Bellwether. It took quite a woman to wrap a stone-cold killer around her finger like a wedding ring. The cowboy didn't have a problem with who's side he was on. He didn't care what the Youngbloods believed either. He was here because his wife told him to kill everyone on her hunting list.

Brother McGruffin transformed into a wolf and howled. That was the signal to the rest of the pack to charge the Yahtzees.

The werewolves came in through the windows in the kitchen and the dining room. They broke the front door down and the living room windows. Broken glass caught in thick fur like misshapen diamonds.

The Yahtzees scrambled but their guns did more damage to the rest of their militia than the pack rushing down the hallways.

Screams, snarls, and gunfire filled the crowded space. Bullets punched through bodies. Corpses danced as they died.

The werewolves ran on all fours, claws scraping on tile as they rounded corners. Their big teeth closed on legs, ripping out hamstrings and unzipping guts.

Pacos Bill strode calmly ahead the werewolves, shooting anyone who came at Brother McGruffin. He opened doors and disarmed boobytraps.

The second wave of werewolves did the killing. They took their time to rip heads off. The still-twitching bodies were passed outside to the disposal crew.

The third wave stayed outside to run down the Yahtzees who managed to escape the initial attack. They hid in cars, letting the Yahtzees drive them to their safe houses. Then they killed them.

The werewolves got the Yahtzees and their laptops, phones, manifestos, and notes. Nothing especially interesting but they read every page. Just a lot of hate and evil.

The Yahtzees claimed that God was on their side because no one had stopped them from meting out 'justice' to anyone they wanted.

The werewolves killed the Yahtzees. Then picked the bullets out of their skin.

Pacos Bill walked over to Brother McGruffin with two frosty beers. He nodded. "A good hunt." He gestured at open back of his Bronco. "There's coolers for everyone."

The werewolves didn't need telling. Nothing like a cold beer to wash down a fresh kill. The whole hunting party toasted their triumph. This was a good hunt

Brother McGruffin and Pacos Bill drank a beer and watched the Youngbloods.

"There's more on Genna's list," Troy said, showing Brother McGruffin the list that Genna had written.

"Your wife's got some nice handwriting," Brother McGruffin said.

Troy smirked with pride. "She's the best."

The Youngblood watching to them while drinking and eating with the scouts. He envied the mutual respect passed between his pack leader and the cowboy. There had to be a way to get Brother McGruffin to pay him the same attention as he did to the cowboy.

Troy smirked to himself. Genna's plan was working. He no longer felt Stacy's magic pulling him like a current.

Masks

THE MOON WAS AS THIN AND CURVED AS AN EYELASH resting on the cheek of the night. Missy walked behind Professor Onyx and Rainey through through the tinder dry forest. They had stripped down in the Escalade. They were naked except for the masks. The enchanted masks kept the Turn at bay. It was a warm night and far away from civilization. They walked on their tiptoes like coyotes.

While the masks were matching gray and white fur, each had a mane made of curling ribbons attached. The ribbons spilled over their hair and ears and down their back. The ribbons sparkled and bounced as they defied gravity. Professor Onyx's was yellow and purple. Missy's was orange and blue. Rainey's was pink and turquoise.

"We look like Carnival dancers from the neck up," Missy said nervously. The other two ignored her, listening and waiting for something to happen.

Genna had enchanted the wolf masks with a spell that she call *the Spirit of Halloween*. Only their ears, eyes, nose, and the fur on the masks were werewolf. The rest was bare brown human skin.

The masks magically radiated Genna's scent. Wearing the masks helped Missy feel brave.

The breeze wafted her free flowing hair. It felt like someone was breathing on her neck. Her booty and breasts jiggled. She felt self-conscious. She was fitter than she had ever been but she would never be lean like Professor Onyx or muscular like Rainey. She wanted to be okay with nudity but she was suddenly hyper-aware of her size. She was at least twice the width of her pack.

She hadn't thought about her body in negative way since Werewolf 101. But right now, there seemed to be someone pinching her back fat and poking her cellulite and flapping her arms. She rolled her shoulders and tried to shake off that sensation.

The faint pinching turned into a twisting squeeze. Every nerve in her body shrieking as her skin was pulled in different directions.

Missy yelped and spun around, swiping at the air. The pinching stopped. The air shimmered.

Stacy the boo hag was right behind her, hands still up where she had wrenched Missy's flesh hard enough to bruise. An army of werewolves fanned out to the left and right.

"Well, well, well," the boo hag giggled, to hide her annoyance that snatching the Dragonflies' skins hadn't just failed but revealed her presence too. "This is my lucky night. You three are chock full of *her* magic. Did she send you as a gift for little old me?" She smiled with orange teeth. She smelled like putrid magic and meaty honey.

Missy knew that they were in a whole heap of trouble. It was one thing to strategize. It was another to be so vastly outnumbered.

Stacy's minions paced the bushes. They waited with mindless patience.

The several gore crows flew away. They were shadows flapping into the dark sky. The rattle of their wings was loud in the silence.

The Dragonflies paced in a triangular formation, always moving. There was a spell, Missy could see it hanging over the air now. She felt it against her skin like cobwebs. She tested the boo hag's invisible net and yes, they were caged in place.

Some of the wolves in Stacy's pack smelled reluctant but most were Ragers, hungry and slobbering.

Missy wished that they hadn't left the Escalade by the side of the road. She wished that she hadn't been so eager to volunteer to be bait. Genna had made herself a mask just like theirs to show solidarity and form a connection but was it enough? How did it work? She should've asked.

"Are you Stacy the boo hag?" Professor Onyx demanded.

"Stacy is my name and I am a skin witch." The boo hag's many skins fluttered like feathers. Her hair fluffed into a cockatoo's crest before settling down.

"How do we know that you're the real one and not impersonating a witch?" Rainey flicked her hand dismissively. "Stacy's a common name. The Witch Market is full of stolen product."

Missy was amazed at her pack. How could they shit talk when her mouth was so dry that she could barely talk? Still, she had to try. "Yeah, I bet you're just a copycat. Sounds like AI to me!"

"It's not fake news!" The boo hag swelled like a bull frog, the leathery feathers turned to bones and spines. "I am the original Stacy! There can only be one!"

"Isn't that a quote from Highlander?" Missy quipped, giddy with terror. "Now she sounds like a Meme."

"Goddammit, Moon Moon!" Professor Onyx said. Missy was impressed. Even if that was an ancient internet meme, the elder wolf was still trying.

"Yeah, she's just full of shit," Rainey said, keeping the pace. "She kind looks like a chicken to me."

"Come ladies, let's go find the *real* boo hag," Professor Onyx said, "This *jive turkey* is just wasting our time."

Stacy attacked, cawing curses and screaming like a banshee. The tensile strength of the skin net clamped on the three wolves like a bear trap. And snapped apart. Genna's magic shone bright. The enchantment growled. The ribbon afros shook like rattlesnake tails and a deep subsonic growl reverberated through the ground.

The boo hag faltered, thrown from her spell. Lightning spat from the ribbons and pierced the Ragers. For a moment, each werewolf was illuminated in turquoise and purple light. Then burst apart, raining down greasy meat. The other werewolves forgot about Missy, Rainey, and Professor Onyx to focus on snapping up pieces of meat. Each bite freed them from the boo hag's hold. Some werewolves spun around and ran. Other began to vomit and fall over, dead.

It was amazing in a terrifying way. Missy felt the lightning chase through her body, dancing along her skin to raise every hair. She shivered and bit the air. Then was surprised when Stacy recoiled, holding her hand as she wailed.

"You bitches will pay for this!"

"Run!" Professor Onyx howled, hurling herself at the witch. But Missy and Rainey had the same thought. They attacked the boo hag.

The Dragonflies fought the few werewolves who hadn't been distracted by the meat. Then Stacy grabbed Missy by the face and yanked off the mask. She howled in agony as the skin of her face came with it. Her body melting and twisted and warping.

Rainey and Professor Onyx tried to fight but the skin magic wrapped them up and turned them inside out.

Stacy stabbed them. They were turned inside out into oozing balls of meat but didn't die.

The wolves that hadn't gotten caught in the counterattack broke their teeth and turned inside out when they tried to eat the quivering balls of meat.

Stacy cursed the Dragonflies but the spells bounced off and hit the other werewolves. They warped and twisted into squealing agonized corpses, their bones turned the wrong way.

She tried to use the Old Crow's magic and it didn't work. The grand dragon was dead, burned alive and still smoking. Genna's masks had targeted Stacy's backers.

The boo hag shrieked in frustration. She tried to steal Genna's magic from the masks but they disintegrated when she lifted them up. No magic. Nothing but sparkling dust.

Stacy coughed and sneezed, batting at the air, but the glitter clung.

"I see you, bitch," Stacy said but only silence answered. "Come out and fight me!"

She reached out. And got knocked off her feet by the Old Crow's death.

He tried to drag her under. Pull her into the tar and climb over her body to save his miserable life. She had to abandon every skin connected to his feathery ass to stay out of the tar.

Black smoke roiled out of his melting bones. His beak opened wide so the teeth fell out. His eyes glared at Stacy as they rotted into his skull.

Whitney the tooth fairy flitted past, catching those teeth in a little bag as she darted around the tar like a dragonfly. She easily dodged his grasping hands.

"Whitney!" Stacy bellowed. "You're supposed to be dead you toothy bitch!"

Whitney flicked her wand. Bone magic sent Stacy rolling. She landed hard on her face, breaking her nose. It healed immediately but the blood filled her mouth.

Stacy pushed herself back up to her feet, hellfire mad.

She reached out, ready to field an attack but Genna wasn't hiding in the bushes. She wasn't here at all. She was back at the Escalade, looking for the Dragonflies.

Stacy's many skins flushed with rage and embarrassment. She kicked the oozing balls of meat and transported them deeper into her magic.

But it wasn't enough.

Stacy wanted to hurt Genna, not just physically but spiritually. The thing everyone kept repeating about the witch doctor was that she was kind. She had gentle hands. She was a good person. A good witch. Sunshine and buttercups. Nauseatingly genuine.

Stacy *hated* that sanctimonious shit. That was impossible. Genna was a wealthy tyrant just as overbearing as any other rich asshole. She just had better PR.

Who the hell was Genna to tell her what to do and how to be? She wasn't better. She wasn't incorruptible. She was a dragon for crying out loud!

Stacy needed something. No, someone. She had already used up the Dragonflies. She needed someone to leave like a little present that knocked the good witch doctor off her high horse. Have her get so mad that it tore off that mask of goodness. Rage made people sloppy and exploitable.

She searched, reorganizing her meager supply. Furious to see how effectively Genna routed her satellite strongholds. The bitch drained her magic like a vampire without every showing a fang.

Then she found Dominque, walking through the Forsaken Forest. Alone. She went slow, trying to avoid stepping into any tar, not wanting to get her Starry Nights dirty.

Starry Nights. The shoes. Stacy had dumped them with everything else when she tried to throw Genna off the scent. But there was still a spell in the soles of the sneakers. Easy to overlook because it seemed like just a scratch across the Nikie logo.

Dominque had met with Genna. It was the only way those shoes would've ended up back on her feet. This was the leak.

After everything that Stacy had done, Dominque had run away and ratted her out. Stacy had been too busy to chase her down but now Dominque was going to pay for her betrayal.

The Sneeze

Genna cautiously investigated the interior and exterior and the trampled grass around the Escalade. Even though Professor Onyx, Missy, and Rainey had volunteered to be bait, Genna was worried to her boots. She wore her mask, the ribbons whispered over her back like a festive lion's mane.

'Born Under A Bad Sign' sung by Albert King played in the pack's Escalade. The doors were unlocked.

Genna was alone. And realized that she had planned this whole attack poorly. She was used to doing things alone. She should've walked with the Dragonflies, not sent them out into the unlit stretch of highway by Neither World, area between Austin and Buda.

She should've waited to send Troy after the Yahtzees with Brother McGruffin and his pack eagerly providing back up. But the best way to weaken Stacy's power was to divert her attention.

Genna made the masks for the Dragonflies as full of protective magic as she could make but knew in the pit of her stomach that Stacy had already gotten under their skin.

She thought about everything she knew about the boo hag as she crafted. She went to a Spirit of Halloween store for the mask. She needed its silliness. And that was where she got the idea.

How was she going to defeat the skin witch without slaughtering the entire Briarpatch community?

Genna did not want a repeat of what her how town of Sweetwater went through when she and Pipsy fought to the death. A lot of good innocent folks died.

Genna put the scissors in the medical bag. She took out a large baggie of pre-mixed spices and a bottle of rosemary oil. She dumped the oil on herself, rubbing it across her coat, boots, and hat. She combed it intent her long black curls. Then she dumped the spices on herself.

Cayenne pepper, black pepper, garlic, cumin, and salt.

She sneezed.

The boo hag sneezed. The Ragers hiding around the Escalade sneezed. The entire network of werewolves and humans connected to the boo hag's magic sneezed.

Genna laughed like a coyote and ran through the ripple of spells. The medicine bag had turned knives into scalpels. Genna danced and waved through killing curses and booby traps, slicing and healing along the way.

The sneeze had revealed the boo hag's entire operation for only a moment but that was all she needed to locate the real culprit pulling the strings.

Stacy was a White woman. The wife of plantation owners and usually dismissed as a threat. But Genna knew that the boo hag had been pretending to be a Black woman when the witch asked the Klan to save her.

That was an old nasty trick. Usually it worked in the witch's favor. The Lynch mob needed a White woman to save and she loved using their mindless hatred to cover up her misdeeds.

The boo hag attacked Genna with a tide of skins which moaned and bit and screamed. Magic laminated the flesh together with the witch's power sewn in like tiny stitches of leather thread. Heads sewn together screamed at Genna, their eyes rolling and teeth biting.

The cuticle scissors were exactly the right angle to slice

through that enchanted thread. Except the heads launched at Genna and tried to bite her instead of dissolve.

The harder Stacy tried to grab her, the faster Genna spread the spices.

Those spices burned and itched and seeped between skins. Stacy shed that itchy skin again and again. Too focused on Genna to notice who she freed.

Stacy looked like a rotted brown flower shedding brown petals as her skins peeled away from her core.

The werewolves attacked Genna. They were enormous. Teeth thick like tusks. Claws like scythes. Thick fur that shook off bullets even when they burned into their sides. The wolves were not the shaggy canine monsters out of a horror movie but sleek purpose. When they rallied, they moved in deadly choreography. A whirlwind of gravity defying flexibility, teeth and claws. Mountains of muscles and rage. All rabid and fearless. The worst versions of a were-beast with no thought towards self-preservation, driven mad by Stacy's magic. Infected with werewolf rabies.

Genna killed them like the mindless creatures they had become. Dousing only wasted precious spices and oil.

Witch magic was always difficult to fight. That's why one could not simply swing a sword or shoot a bullet. A witch who was good, could reduce that sword to its basic elements at a glance. Then the sword would be air, water, and ashen smoke. Or she would reverse the blood.

Genna had no idea what to do besides plowing forward, deeper into the barbed magic, even as they tore at her skin. Would he be flayed alive by the time she found the witch's core? This was nothing like Miss Bootsie's skin magic. It was foul and bloated with its own self-importance.

She reached into the medicine bag but healing only fed Stacy's magic. She had used the bag's power for a long time. It refused to act against her.

~

GENNA RAN OUT OF SPICES AND ROSEMARY OIL. THERE were just too many skins. Even though the enchantment worked and Stacy left the bodies behind as she chased Genna, the non-violent tactics did not work. Stacy was the kind of bully that never changed their behavior or learned how to be kind.

Cruelty was the only thing that made sense. There was a big death curse looming ahead.

Genna couldn't find a way around it that wouldn't magnify the blast radius. She wanted to kill Happy Meals instead of generally okay people but she couldn't turn the tide.

Stacy had a talent for picking victims. The kinds of monsters and humans who Genna tried to save instead of eat. Healing the Briarpatch had enraged the boo hag into new heights of sadism. Killing Stacy would blow up the Briarpatch. Nothing and no one would survive.

It was a lose-lose situation.

No wonder Imani stayed in her Church. She gathered whoever she could like Noah shoving animals into the Ark to survive the Great Flood.

Despite their encouragement, neither Imani nor Amaya believed that Genna could defuse and destroy Stacy. There was simply too many layers of connection woven together. The medicine bag was no help either. It was Stacy's before it was Genna's.

Genna tripped on a rubbery floor carpeted by armpit hair. Mouths bit her, chewing up her coat. She had to wriggle free.

She stared at the body on top. It was Dominque.

Genna moved slowly, as if against a strong current. Not caring if it were a trap. Knowing that Stacy liked to cause maximum pain just from the curse that Troy had survived.

Dominique lay on the ground. The Starry Nights sneakers were strangely pristine while the rest of her body was blistered and melted from acid burns.

This was worse.

Stacy had made Dominque drink acid. The chemical burns and pockmarked remnants of exposed organs were striated with curses. Slipskins had drained the collagen from Dominque's skin and left exit holes ripped along the torso and back.

Genna slid off the Starry Night sneakers and took the Black Air Forces that Dominque had given her out of the medicine bag. She carefully laced them onto Dominque's feet. She rubbed the soles of Dominque's feet. Slowly the magic healed the wounds but internally and externally. Only for her body to immediately be drained of vitality again by Stacy.

Saliva

MISSY HEARD GENNA'S LAUGHTER. THE SNEEZE HAD started the Turn, unfolding her from the oozing lump of pain that the boo hag had twisted her into.

Missy groaned and stretched. Her hands searched her body to confirm that everything was where it should be. Rainey and Professor Onyx squelched and moaned. They were slower to heal.

Missy searched their cages for something useful but this prison was designed for werewolf ingenuity. She paced around the two pack members instead.

"Come on, hurry up!" Missy muttered.

She Turned into a wolf and began licking their meat. Genna had explained that werewolves produced enzymes in their saliva. It could trigger a quick healing or an infection depending upon their intentions.

Missy had plenty of time to talk with Brother McGruffin's pack but none of them were deep thinkers. They were focused on survival just like Missy.

It was Genna's weird way of thinking that allowed her to see what others did not. Missy hadn't understood most of the witch doctor's longwinded explanations at the time but now she tried to save her pack.

She licked those big oozing piles of screaming flesh and thought positive thoughts. Visualizing Professor Onyx and Rainey. The way they laughed, danced, sang, joked, and made Missy feel welcomed and wanted.

Her saliva shimmered. That shine broke the curse.

Missy stood back as Professor Onyx and Rainey Turned back into themselves.

"What the hell?" Rainey muttered, scratching herself.

"Focus," Professor Onyx said.

"We've got to help the others," Missy said.

The other two listened as Missy explained how she had countered the skin spell.

They healed those still trapped in the Turn. They tried to be patient but most of these werewolves had been mistreated so long that keeping them in dog form was a mercy.

Jive Turkey

THE SKIN TRAP LANDED ON GENNA. THE TAR OOZING from the skin hurt but she didn't move, still focused on Dominque, lifting her up.

Stacy appeared dramatically, swelled in size. "I'm going to skin you alive and eat your eyes!"

Genna looked up at the witch, seeing through the organic bubbling screams. The shifting teeth and twisting hair. The stretching skin of the growing monster changed from a dark brown to a hypothermic white, mottled purple, putrid yellow and gangrenous green along the edges. It grew new limbs like zombie snakes, shards of broken bone bared like teeth and grasping hands. A thousand wailing, wheezing, gasping voices trapped inside the skin, sewn together like a quilt. There was a cadaverously thin woman deep under the stolen skins. Stacy's true self.

The skin pinker and chapped like a mouth at the very top. An opening. A trap.

Genna's eyes glowed as her shape wavered like a heat haze. She pulled out the Kitchen knife that Imani had given her and it hummed, echoing her fury.

The thing about being a fire-breathing dragon was that the rage in her chest never ebbed. Genna learned how to control it but the rage never extinguished. She carried it, fed it her grief, and never forgot. Her fear of losing Troy was still as raw as the day he stepped into Stacy's trap. Finding Dominque cracked Genna's self-control.

Stacy wanted Genna to be a dragon. To make her lose control. To force a Turn. But Genna at her angriest stayed in her human form. Her dragon might was pressurized until the blast was like a fiery punch that pierced through the spells.

Smoke billowed off her hair. Lightning crackled from her eyes. She opened her mouth wider, wider, and wider. The maw full of teeth. The hunger. The rage of a direwolf.

"You jive *turkey!*" Genna snarled.

The phrase *Jive Turkey* reverberated through the Briarpatch and the skins. Every werewolf heard Genna and thought, "Yeah, that boo hag is a jive turkey."

That moment of unified thought turned into something realer than real. A wave of intent, a thousand people leaned the same direction at the same time. They took control of their skins. Just for a moment but it was enough to flip Stacy's curse back upon its creator.

In the Church, Imani slapped down a red Uno Reverse and shouted, "Uno!"

The curse enveloped Stacy in purple flames. It swept over her, filling every lung. The lightning pierced layer upon layer of skin, leaving behind a Lichtenberg trail for Genna to follow.

The curse hit Stacy's core. The boo hag transformed into a giant turkey with a startled squawk.

Stacy cussed and staggered to her clawed feet. She flapped her wings, trying to gather her power but only fluffed her feathers. Curses in the form of billowing dust swept over Genna. The curse failed to land, brushing off the her thick fur.

"You don't scare me!" Stacy gobbled. "I'll kill you!"

"You first." Lightning danced along Genna's big teeth and sparked on the edge of the carving knife.

Stacy reached for her army of werewolves but found them

busy, asking for help, or calling her a jive turkey. She reached for her Yahtzees and found them dead. She reached and reached but the connections had been cut off. She couldn't steal anyone's strength but her own.

Stacy attacked, her beak thrusting out to peck and stab. Her claws out to gouge. She was a turkey the size of a Tyrannosaurus rex. Her wings were brown and her tail fanned wide. Her great claws dug up the ground. Her beak snapped at the air.

Genna leapt, scrambling with one hand, ignoring how her feet sank and skidded into jiggling skin folds as though running on a water bed, not wasting her breath to shout. The feathers tried to cut, blind, and batter as she ran through the gray down. The monster turkey wiggled and flailed, fetid steam rising out of her seeping pores. Her body warping. New mouths opened up, vomiting tar. The stench of bile increased, foaming tar.

Genna dove into the skins, carved down, down, down to Stacy's core. The monstrous turkey bucked and flailed. The body shook, skin twisting to envelope Genna as she kept slicing.

Genna was back in the Kitchen, carving through one body at the joints and muscles. The knife was exactly perfect for carving a turkey. Chef Soledad had taught her exactly where to skin a boo hag.

The braided hair, teeth, and nails from living werewolves were like strings on a puppet. If she cut the right way, she didn't kill them, she freed them from Stacy's magic but it was tricky. She didn't always get it right. She felt werewolves die like snapping wires. And their deaths hurt. She kept cutting.

The Slipskins and other parasitic curses burrowing through the skins shriveled, repelled by the antidotes in her sweat. The inoculations that Genna had created worked. The medicine bag clung to her side, ignoring Stacy's sneaky attempts to steal it.

Stacy shed her skins, torn between fleeing and fighting. Genna burrowed into the seeping epidermis, heaving aside flaps and hunks out of the way.

Stacy panicked. No one had gotten this close to her real self in centuries. This wasn't a single piercing strike. This was death by a thousand cuts. Genna wasn't tired or slowing down. Steadily drilling through the shifting maze of skins to the core.

Stacy shrieked a specific pitch that had werewolves writhing and howling in agony. The banshee shriek hit Genna like a jeweler's hammer striking a tuning form. The terrible penetrating screech was a sonic punch to the soul.

Genna had many skins working in sync. Now they burst apart. Her sense of self fractured. She was a dragon, a human, a wolf, a coyote, and other bodies. Human Genna kept cutting with methodical precision. Her grip on the knife never wavered.

Genna in every form loathed Stacy. She hated her cruelty. She despised Stacy warping the medicine bag's healing power. She grieved for every person whose skin Stacy stole.

The boo hag's other shrieks failed to ward off the twisting tornado of fury that shredded Stacy and all of her feathers apart as every iteration of Genna pounced on Stacy and together they ripped out her spine, her throat, and ate her liver. The monstrous turkey fell under the onslaught, burning with dragon fire.

Meanwhile, deep under the epidermis, human Genna cut through the last protective membrane. The tar failed to burn her skin as she reached in and grabbed Stacy's boney shoulder.

Stacy froze. Staring into Genna's brown eyes. "No, wait!"

Genna plunged the knife under the boo hag's ribcage and carved out her heart. She ripped it free and ate it, chewing fast. Stacy tasted awful but Genna ate her heart then her liver, tar dripping down her chin and burning her throat as she swallowed.

Stacy's death spell detonated like a bomb in her chest. Genna exploded with Stacy's true core but messily. Her skin stretched and tore as it tried to continue the blast. Her magical bodies were hurled into the magical world.

Her human body landed hard in the physical world in a puddle of her own blood. She was on a limestone hill surrounded by cypress trees

Icy weakness kept her flat on her back while her blood turned the dry dirt on the limestone dirt into mud. The pine trees rustled as the breeze explored her injuries.

The tar under the Forsaken Forest receded. Not entirely gone but a path of pale stone rose to the surface.

Stacy's giant turkey corpse roasted next to Genna, cooking in her own juices. The feathers burnt to nubs. Genna squeezed the knife, unwilling to let it go. She coughed, gargling on tarry phlegm. She was dying, poisoned and fragmented. Without magic to heal her wounds, she bled out.

The medical bag scuttled across the stone and began to heal her. Its straps worked like leathery tentacles with thin needles injecting her with potions.

Genna fell into an enchanted drug-induced sleep. The medicine bag dragged her into her shadow. She was transported to the medical tent in the Briarpatch. It wrapped her in a cocoon and sunk her in a van of enchanted honey.

Meanwhile, the smell of deep fried turkey wafted through the Briarpatch. The werewolves sniffed the air. They had to leave their homes, had to run into the darkness rolling fields outside of Austin. They found Stacy's enormous carcass. Their mouths salivated as they stared up at a roasted turkey the size of a tyrannosaurs rex.

Imani, Aunt Jemima, Chef Soledad and the Kitchen staff approached the smoking corpse with their knives out. Other prayer warriors focused on setting foldout tables and unwrapping tinfoil covered trays.

"Happy Thanksgiving everyone," Imani said, blessing the food. "Good meat. Good God. Good food. Let's eat!"

The disoriented werewolves of the Briarpatch hadn't worn their own skins in a long time. But they recognized when the dinner bell was rung. They attacked the turkey.

Missy, Professor Onyx, and Rainey had followed their noses. They feasted. They shoved other wolves to gobble more tender juicy flesh.

"Can you taste the healing?" Missy said. "It's delicious!"

"Don't talk with your mouthful!" Professor Onyx said.

The celebration got louder as more and more werewolves arrived to join the feeding frenzy.

Except for Aunt Jemima. She found Dominque's body tucked against a tree. She carried her away from the feeding frenzy. The sneakers shriveled up as the magic healed her wounds.

Dominque opened her eyes. Aunt Jemima hugged her, rocking back and forth as she sank to the ground. "Thank God!"

TROY COULDN'T FIND THE BRIARPATCH. THE TENT wasn't in the physical world. There was just an empty clearing.

He couldn't get into the Forsaken Forest or the Church either. The trees at the edge of the sunflower field were too closely packed to squeeze through.

He drove the Bronco to their house. It was empty. He tried to call Brother McGruffin. No answer.

The wind whistled a low moan through the empty mansion. Troy walked to his sacred olive trees, got down on his knees, and prayed. Troy tried not to worry. He followed his cleansing ritual. He had to trust his wife. He had to believe and wait.

Scattered Jigsaw

Genna tried not to lose her shit. Maybe this was a dream or a nightmare.

The Briarpatch was blinding neon Candyland-on-an-acid-trip without Stacy's feeding on it. The plants and animals swayed and sang. Genna wished that she had sunglasses.

She couldn't get anyone to speak because the Briarpatch was too busy celebrating. The critters danced and sang. They grinned as they capered, tap-danced, and lindy-hopped. There were unicorns, gryphons, and dragons frolicking with fairies, goblins, and mermaids but most wore animal skins to hide their true nature.

Genna retreated to the medical tent to tend to the wounded. Herself, in every manifestation.

Stacy the boo hag was dead. Genna was not. She had to think positively. This was a magical place not a rainbow-colored hellscape. She had to put herself back together or she'd never get out of the Briarpatch.

The self that was *her* worked as long as she didn't ask how she could walk around without a body of any kind.

"Stay alive," Genna commanded her human body as it lay in a

vat of honey and breathed through air filters that distilled oxygen and nitrogen from magic. She was frightened by her own fragility. Her human body bore the brunt of the damage. Clearly Stacy knew that it was her primary form.

Her coywolf body lay on the ground, absorbing healing energy from the tent and the grass below the carpets.

Her dragon body slept in a factory furnace that pumped out cotton candy clouds.

The chocolate river was not the right place for a mermaid or an aquatic vampire. Genna created a pool of filtered water inside the tent so they would not suffocate.

Some versions of her body were in pieces. They clung to her human body. She had a rattlesnake tail and eight retractable fangs behind her wolf teeth. She had wings. She had horns and back spines. She had lightning sparking in her eyebrows and venom drooling from the corner of her mouth.

She was a volcano spewing molten rainbows.

She was a cyclone twisting and hopping in the volcanic clouds.

She was a forest that had trees growing across the planet. She could taste the different soils where her roots were planted.

She was wildfire that moved like there was no gravity, sliding across the landscape like liquid. The trees danced as they burned. Then regrew. Then burned. A spastic cycle. The tar boiled into water.

Her physical bodies were like a big jigsaw puzzle scattered across the landscape. Her body couldn't figure out what was true and what wasn't. There was just too much wild magic in the Briarpatch.

Genna opened every drawer in the tent. Reread every book in the medicine bag. She lifted up the bottles and concoctions but which to use first? And where? Should it be injected or inhaled or rubbed into the flesh as a salve?

Genna forced herself to breathe, to let go of the panic, and slow down.

She sat next to her human body. She pulled a few levers that lifted it out of the honey. If this was a puzzle then she needed to study every piece.

Genna read her life in the skins like they were tree rings. She spotted the nicks and tears that Stacy exploited. There were similar scars in the coywolf body since it was the second most frequented form. The direwolf body was made of fire and harder to read but still visible. They were the same wounds from the same attack and freshly healed.

Underneath the epidermis were layers of older scars, deep and gnarled from a lifetime of fighting Katie McBride and the Sweetwater vampires. There were hoof prints from getting kicked by a frightened horse. Bullet shards from being shot as a coyote in the wrong place. Scars from traps. Scars from being run over by a car. Scars from doctors with obsidian scalpels.

The oldest stitches were from Miss Bootsie. She had sewn Genna's newborn coyote, wolf, and direwolf bodies into her newborn human body.

Miss Bootsie's craftsmanship compared to Stacy's clinical stitches was hard to see. Stacy focused on quantity not quality. Miss Bootsie was the opposite. All of her power was honed to perfectly sew Genna's many forms together with masterful skill. She contained wild magic and power into a human baby's skin, quite literally bottling lightning in a living jar. Then returned Genna to her parents before they even knew that she was missing.

Here was proof that the witch, who Genna considered as a third grandmother, had stolen her away from her human parents when she was barely a week old. Miss Bootsie carefully cultivated the alignment of the skins so that Genna grew simultaneously in every form. All for the purpose of one day killing her sworn enemy, Pipsy Montgomery. Her death was a masterstroke. Grief had transformed Genna into her masterpiece and weapon of vengeance.

But under that was love. Genna's human parents loved her, her siblings, her family, and her friends did too. Genna's direwolf mother, the Old Night. Miss Bootsie. Sweetwater Forest. Even Katie McBride. She was loved. That love was stronger than hate and sorrow.

Troy.

He waited for her at the olive ranch. Marriage meant something. Their love was beautiful and fun and theirs. No one else had to understand or accept it. She never expected to find a life partner or the peace that came that connection.

She needed to get back to him because he'd be worrying.

Genna picked up a jar of teeth. The teeth rattled. She would rebuilt herself from the marrow. No more scars. No other signatures in her skin but her own.

She sang as she sewed herself back together. The Briarpatch and its denizens sang too.

~

It was Werewolf Wednesday. Genna had been trapped in the Briarpatch for a week.

Troy refused to settle down. He waited, standing outside of Strait-Legged Bacon's establishment. Brother McGruffin joined him. Their black cowboy hats sat low on their foreheads. They drank beer and waited.

Imani passed out name tags to newcomers. She wished that she could bring Genna back. She should have dealt with Stacy on her own instead of outsourcing her problems. No one could figure out what exactly went wrong. How could a boo hag lay a dragon so low?

"He really loves her," Professor Onyx said.

"Is that so hard to imagine?" Imani hissed.

"Yes, it is. Most mixed couples are just in it for the fucking. It's exotic and taboo."

"Maybe when you were young but times have changed. It's normal now."

Professor Onyx shrugged again. Indifferent. "I know. But that cowboy can't go into the Briarpatch because it's exclusively for magic Black folk. And he ain't it. She's in too deep."

"But what's she doing in there?" Imani exclaimed.

"Healing, most likely," Amaya said, walking over while eating a cup of banana pudding. "She ate the death curse. If she can't heal herself then she can't heal anyone."

Professor Onyx and Imani nodded politely and went off to talk to someone else. Amaya followed. "What? What did I say? It's the truth!"

Missy had heard what Amaya said. She clutched the flyer that Genna gave her when they first met. It stank of magic. She showed it to Troy. "Maybe you can find her with this?"

He stroked the flyer and handed it back. "Thanks but no. It's better to let her come back on her own."

Missy liked him and wished that Professor Onyx and Rainey sympathized instead of sneered. He wasn't nearly so scary when he smelled so sad and worried.

"She's been in there a long time," Missy said, probing her worries like a tongue exploring a toothache.

"Time doesn't pass the same in magic worlds. All we can do is wait."

"Isn't there anything I can do?"

Troy watched her for a moment. He glanced at Brother Ruffin, tilting his head. The old werewolf went inside to talk to Professor Onyx. Troy told Missy what little he knew of Genna's hunting cipher. "If you can grab a few Happy Meals that might be like breadcrumbs that she can follow."

"I can do that. You can count on me!" Missy hurried away, determined and excited. She stopped only a brief moment to tell Rainey and Professor Onyx that she'd be back.

"Do you need backup?" Rainey called after her.

"Nah, I'm good!" Missy said, not waiting.

Professor Onyx gripped Rainey's shoulder. "You've got to trust her."

Rainey's gaze settled on Troy's profile. She turned away and drank her beer. She took Brother McGruffin's vacated seat, waiting for Missy to come back.

Cipher

THERE WAS A TERRIBLE KIND OF GENIUS TO GENNA'S hunting cipher. Missy wished that she hadn't learned it.

She found mean little Happy Meals who hated everybody. She made a pop-up app that showed up on a timer in their phones. The AI message used their own prejudices to cement the smell of bait. They all lived in Austin. It took less than fifteen minutes to drive to their locations.

Each Happy Meal promptly followed the instructions. They drove up to the designated location in Cybertrucks. They walked right into the refrigerated truck, focused on their smartphones. They believed so fervently that there was a fortune to make and a deal to win that they put the fabric black bags over their own heads and tied zip-tied their own wrists to the railing.

Not a peep. Not a question. Just a sneer at the other men in the truck. She slammed the door shut and drove to the next pickup.

When the meat truck was full, she ended the pop-up. She did a quick drive-by. And yes, there were a few stubbornly refreshing their phones. She idled nearby and opened the back door. The extra Happy Meals climbed right in.

Missy locked the door, shaking her head. There was no time

to question the effective cipher's ethics. She contacted Possum and Tater's car towing service to make the Cybertrucks disappear.

She drove back to Strait-Legged Bacon. She parked the refrigerated truck down the block from the restaurant in an empty lot of a foreclosed shop.

She pressed the flyer against the Happy Meal's forehead. "I hope you're hungry, Doc."

Invisible vines grew up out of the floor, twinned around him and yanked him into the Briarpatch. He didn't all fit. There was a messy pile of torn fabric.

"You can't do this to me!" The second Happy Meal shouted, still wearing his power suit. His panic set off the others. They tried to escape, plead, threaten, and bribe as the Briarpatch thorns twined up their legs and crushed their bodies.

The truck emptied. Missy squinted, trying to see where the magic had gone and where it came from. The flyer burned up in her hand. She climbed out, rubbing her hands on her hips.

Rainey and Troy stood a safe distance from the truck.

"You've done all you can," Rainey said.

"That's her favorite meal," Troy said. "She loves her Happy Meals."

"I just hope it works," Missy sniffled. "I wish that I could do more."

"You've done plenty," Troy said.

Genna limped in, three hours after Missy fed the Happy Meals to the Briarpatch. The Happy Meals were like breadcrumbs leading her out of the magical forest and into the real world.

She was so hungry that it was hard to think past the menu on the wall behind the counter. It took her a minute and Troy's enveloping hug to realize that the hooping and hollering was for her. Werewolves surrounded her with trays of beef ribs. Genna snatched them from eager hands. She wolfed down the tender smoked meat, her powerful jaws ground bone to mush.

She ignored attempts to congratulate her on defeating Stacy the boo hag and finding her way out of the Briarpatch.

"We thought that you were lost," Professor Onyx said.

"I've been there before," Genna said, while accepting Strait-Legged Bacon's next platter of beef ribs. The hawg allocated all of his inventory to satiating the starving dragon.

She was being polite but Troy was a twitchy menace. Anybody who tried to sneak a chicken wing or hunk of brisket ended up butchered and on the grill. Genna could eat everyone and it would be their fault. For now, she was happy with barbe-cued beef, pork, and chicken.

Imani sat with Amaya, watching Genna eat. Even now, Genna's etiquette and table manners kept the splatter radius to a minimum.

"I knew that she'd pull herself back together," Amaya said tearfully, "She just needed time to heal and rest."

"I knew she'd kill that witch," Imani said, "I'm just glad we didn't get got in the process."

RAINEY PULLED MISSY OUTSIDE OF STILES SWITCH INTO the warm shadows of the parking lot. Missy keep sniffling and wiping her face. Professor Onyx and Brother McGruffin joined them.

"Would you stop crying? She's okay!" Rainey snarled at Missy who pulled up her hoodie to sob in its shadows.

"Doc had us all worried," Brother McGruffin said, "But even she couldn't resist good barbecue."

Silence answered his jovial attempt. Professor Onyx gently guided him back inside so that she could have a private word with her pack. "Listen—"

"You're leaving with him, aren't you?" Rainey said. "Going up North. What about us?"

"You two will be fine," Professor Onyx said, "I need to get back out on the street looking for strays. There's a lot more now that the boo hag is dead."

"You can do that here!" Rainey's plaintive cry was like an anxious child. Missy held her hand. Rainey snatched it away, angry. "Both of you keep leaving me behind!"

"I'm still here," Missy said.

"You went after your new best friend the second that she was in trouble. You couldn't wait to go hunting by yourself!"

"Black Belle needed my help and I promised not to share her hunting cipher." Missy wrinkled her nose, confused and offended.

"You're my pack," Rainey mumbled, refusing to look at either of them. "What about me? Why couldn't I help save Black Belle?"

"I'm sorry, Rainey," Missy said, "I wasn't ignoring you. I didn't involve you because I thought you hated her."

"I did and she still saved my life! I'm a stupid bitch!"

"There will be plenty of opportunities to express your change of heart," Professor Onyx said. "You could do it right now."

"And you!" Rainey snarled. "I can't believe you'd give up everything for a man! Why can't he move here? I hate the snow!"

Professor Onyx could not think of a suitable comeback. Rainey was right and frankly, she hated Northern winters. Snow was better in a photo than under her paws. "I'll talk to McGruffin and see if we can come to an arrangement."

Rainey nodded, mollified by their contrition and mortified by her outburst. Professor Onyx and Missy hugged her tight. Slowly she relaxed.

The Vote

I was the next Werewolf Wednesday and there were four times more kids than adults running around the picnic tables and the playground of Walnut Creek Park.

Imani stopped Professor Onyx as she refilled her sweet tea. "When are you starting up the Girl Scouts again? And what's going on with Brother McGruffin? He wouldn't give me a straight answer about the Youngbloods. Is he moving down here to be with you?"

"I'm not doing the Girl Scouts. Ask them." Professor Onyx pushed her lips towards Missy and Rainey smiling at each other like there was no one else in the world. That smile congealed when Imani asked them the same question. They glared at Professor Onyx who shrugged, unrepentantly.

"She said that you're in charge," Imani said.

"Since when?" Missy snapped indignantly.

"Look at these kids. Somebody's got to teach them how to be werewolves. Hell, someone needs to teach the adults too."

"We don't have a stellar track record. None of our girls made it. I don't think Werewolf 101 taught anything about survival."

"Then do better!" Imani hissed. She stomped off to Eartha and the other exhausted den mothers to spread the good news.

"Well, shit," Missy said, as heads turned with matching hopeful and grateful expressions. "I guess I'll make an itinerary."

Rainey chewed thoughtfully on a forkful of brisket. "I don't think Werewolf 101 was a total failure. We survived."

"No one else did."

"Nothing prepares you for a dogfight, Missy. Nothing."

A complicated silence lasted until Dominque walked over, anxiously holding a beer. "Um, hi. My name is Dominque. I'd like to join your pack. What's the application process?"

"Why? You do you have kids?" Missy said unenthusiastically.

"Hell no!" Dominque's strong response was emphasized by a revolted shudder. "You just seem cool."

"Cool?" Missy chortled. "You're funny."

Rainey sat back and sipped her beer. "You've been watching us, haven't you? Seeing what we're about?"

Dominque swallowed nervously. "You noticed."

"Didn't you run with the boo hag's pack?"

"I didn't have a choice! She was wearing Aunt Jemima!"

Rainey frowned. "Aunt Jemima? The one who works in the Church Kitchen? She's one of the skinned?"

"This was before she joined the Church. I saved her from the boo hag by taking her place." Dominque nodded at Aunt Jemima who sat with other prayer warriors at a table. She nodded back.

"Where are you staying now?" Missy said, pushing against Rainey's recalcitrance. "Do you have any references we'd know?"

"I work in the Clothing Piles behind the Boutique." She looked down at her Starry Nights. "Footwear department."

"She's a boo hag's bitch," Rainey growled. "We can't trust her. She's lying, trying to cozy up and make us drop our guard."

Dominque cringed. "Black Belle saved me. I'll do anything."

"Uh, huh, I bet you will." Rainey sneered, unmoved. "I know you bitches lost a lot of money when Stacy got got."

"We'll talk about it," Missy said.

"She's a boo hag's bitch!" Rainey gestured at the crowd

pretending not to listen. "Did you forget about the Witch Market? Stacy's not the only witch using our hair."

Missy traced the faint Lichtenberg scars on her palms with the tips of her middle fingers. The scars itched. A quiet signal that the magic hadn't faded. It was there, right under the skin. She knew that she was magic. She felt the truth in her bones. She had made a powerful ally in Black Belle. She could teach Missy magic.

She remembered the terror of the Turn; the struggles of being a Youngblood; the pride of being a den mother; and the heartbreak of raising then losing the Girl Scouts. The isolation of trying to be a lone wolf and the successful re-assimilation into the human society. She knew how to be a Black American werewolf.

She thought about Professor Onyx eating Delilah and Black Belle killing Stacy. She considered Rainey's reluctance to lead despite being older and more experienced.

What made a pack leader? It wasn't might or age. It was a willingness to accept responsibility and handle business.

"Black Belle can vouch for me," Dominque said.

"Black Belle is not the pack leader of the Dragonflies." Missy met Dominque's gaze. She did not raise her voice or snarl. "If I accept you into my pack and you betray us then I'll hunt you down and eat you myself."

Dominque sucked on her teeth in surprised horror. Several other werewolves hastily backed away, unnerved by Missy's quiet resolve. Rainey set her beer down with a cackle. "Werewolf 101, trust your gut and don't fuck with Miss Missy."

Across the room, Professor Onyx harrumphed with approval.

BROTHER MCGRUFFIN WALKED OVER TO TROY, standing against a cinderblock wall among the oil drum smokers and quietly drinking a beer. "How're you doing, cowboy?"

Troy's grip on his beer imperceptibly tightened. "She told me to wait and I waited. I thought that she'd be different but she's the same."

Brother McGruffin leaned against the cinderblocks. He lit a cigarette and offered the pack to Troy but he shook his head. Twin streams of cigarette smoke curled out of Brother McGruffin's nostrils. A small gray wisp of smoke traveled through the tight curls of his facial hair. "Missy walking off did more damage to my lady than that old boo hag. She's staying so I'm staying. I needed a break from Freedom Corner anyway. It's time to give the Youngbloods a taste of responsibility."

Troy nodded.

Crickets sang in the distance. Neither spoke. Or went back into the restaurant for a refill.

Strait-Legged Bacon walked out to check on his grills. He didn't bother the two men standing in the shadows. He nodded once then focused on the charcoal and meat.

IMANI SURVEYED THE PRAYER WARRIORS AND PACK leaders assembled in the Church sanctuary. "Okay, let's vote on it. Who here thinks that Genna Bellwether is a witch doctor that we can trust? Her husband is a monster hunter. They're a package deal. I can't deny that Delilah and Stacy went through the same initiation process. So did every beautician and boo hag we let into the community. We don't have any control over what she'll make of us."

"She'll probably make medicine," Amaya said. "She owns the Briarpatch. To her, we're just community service."

The sanctuary rippled with disgruntled mutters. Imani gave Amaya an annoyed look. "Stop helping."

Amaya shrugged, crossing her arms under her breasts. "I'm not making it up. She bought that olive tree farm down the road. According to the survey, that includes the whole Briarpatch. You can see her name right there on the public records. She pays the property taxes, the land rights, and the mineral rights. Which means nobody can come here looking for oil or build a housing redevelopments or anything. She's protecting us for real for real. Google it."

The crowded sanctuary was abuzz with this new information. Genna had utterly failed to mention that she owned the Briarpatch.

"It's not news that the rich stay rich by owning land," Imani said, bored. "We just know the name of our landlord now."

"Wait a minute, she'll still expect us to pay rent?"

"Obviously." Imani grinned like the Cheshire Cat. "She's the good one not the nice one. So do me a favor and pay your taxes."

Amaya seethed in the pews. Her knee jiggled in annoyance. "This isn't about Black Belle. You want to reinstate the Salon, don't you? That's what this is really about isn't it? We can get the oil for our products from Black Belle and everything. We can make it all next door. Stop beating around the bush and ask!"

"Okay, fine. You got me. All in favor of giving hair clippings, nail, and teeth to the good doctor raise your hand."

It wasn't unanimous but Genna became the Briarpatch's new witch doctor. The community missed the Salon more than they feared her power. Like it or not, somebody needed to safely dispose of the hair, teeth, and nails. Braiding at home was fine but beauticians had skills.

Amaya stomped out, satisfied. She was too proud to thank Genna publicly. Imani sucked on her teeth but was secretly pleased that Amaya steered the crowd where she wanted them to go.

IT WAS ANOTHER HOT DAY IN TEXAS. GENNA STOOD IN the shadows of her live oak trees. Her tears gently dried on her cheeks. Troy was inside their house.

Killing Stacy the boo hag and saving the Briarpatch did not

ease her heavy heart. Her skin still felt tender. Saving the were-wolves didn't assuage her guilt about those who died in the process. It was hard to explain the deep dark grief that didn't sound like making excuses.

Amaya hopped out of a clump of weeds. Her fur was the same gray-brown as the grass. The jackalope glared at Genna as she transformed into her human shape. "We voted on it. You're a part of the Briarpatch now."

"That's nice."

"Nice? Nice! You should thank me!"

"Thanks. How's Malcom doing?"

Amaya straightened up, caught off guard. "He's fine."

"That's good. I'm not a trained therapist but I know a few who won't blink about a kid werewolf. And some you might consider meeting with too."

Amaya squinted through her fake eyelashes. Then the aggression melted away, leaving exhaustion behind. "It's like Megan said, I just need to talk to somebody who gets me."

"I like Megan the Stallion too." Genna opened her arms. "Do you want a non-sexual hug?"

Amaya and Genna awkwardly hugged, their breasts bumping against each other. Then quickly let go.

"Thanks for saving the Briarpatch," Amaya said.

"I wish I'd saved more."

"You did what you could."

The wind blew threw the leaves in the trees. The shadows danced around them, revealing Coyote and Anansi sitting on the porch's wrought iron furniture. They watched Genna and Amaya talking and sweating in the High Noon shadows.

Troy carried out a tray of cold Pacifico beers, salsa, and tortilla chips. The Wild West rippled around them as he sat down.

Coyote grinned. Anansi dumped more sugar into her tea, refusing to ingest anything that Troy touched. He wasn't offended. That was why Genna had made sun tea.

Troy loved Genna. It made him brave enough to face the very

real and angry avatars of ancestral rage that never left Texas. His bloodline had been on the wrong side of history. Focused on cursed gold and power. Just sitting here was a test of fortitude. They did not want apologies or postures. Genna was a beloved child, their princess, carrying their gifts into the future. She honored them with every act of kindness as she healed the were-wolves of the Briarpatch. Troy supported her goals.

Anansi and Coyote had also voted.

"Love is love," Coyote said. "And she's better than Stacy."

Anansi harrumphed, annoyed that Troy really was honorable and true to Genna. She had chosen. Anansi decided to allow their union and braided their story together. Coyote laughed. Troy drank his beer, relieved.

Moonlight

GENNA AND MISSY MET UNDER THE MOONLIGHT IN THE shadow of the old live oak tree. It was late at night. The restaurant was closed and the backyard was empty. The moon was visible through the leaves.

"I love this tree," Missy said, "Thanks for inviting me!"

"You're welcome," Genna said, gesturing at the feast that she had brought and artfully arranged on rugs and blankets.

Missy smiled, loving the charcuterie board, the chilled drinks, and perfectly ripe fruit. She sat down on the padded cushions and smoothed her sundress. The struts of her corset creaked. She liked the way Genna kept checking out her cleavage.

Amaya pouted in the Speakeasy, annoyed that Genna preferred Missy. Professor Onyx kept her busy but introducing Rainey. "You could learn a thing or two."

Rainey blushed deeply. "Um, thanks, but I prefer men."

"What about that tall drink of water over there?" Amaya said.

The tall werewolf in a tight black polo shirt and a gold canine walked over. His skin was a dark golden brown and his muscles were sharply pronounced. There was a sun and a moon tattooed on the back of each bicep.

He offered Rainey his hand. She took it, allowing herself to be led onto the dance floor.

Professor Onyx smirked at Amaya. "Sorry, Sister Rabbit."

"It's fine," Amaya scoffed.

Back at the live oak tree, Genna and Missy stiffened as the air shimmered around them. The tree now stood in pure magic of the Briarpatch. The plants and trees pulsed gently with bioluminescence. The medicine bag and the tent were visible, silvery like moonlight reflecting on raindrops on a spiderweb.

"Now that we're here, I can thank you for the Happy Meals," Genna said.

"You're welcome." Missy said, fiddling with her skirts. She squeezed her elbows against her sides, pushing her breasts higher in her dress. She didn't know what to say. Sex had been easy with the Lunas. Maybe because she didn't care. She wanted to have fun. But she did care about Genna. A lot. And she wanted to be submissive. So often she had to be the dominant one simply but now it was okay to be soft and submissive.

Everything was perfect and romantic. They had negotiated. Genna discussed boundaries with Troy. Missy did the same with Rainey and Professor Onyx, even though it was extremely uncomfortable for all three of them. Professor Onyx wanted her to be safe. Rainey needed to work her own ambivalence out before she slept with anyone.

Still, Missy was nervous. She quivered like a rabbit when Genna soundlessly prowled across the blankets. The ignored food and flatware did not even wobble.

Missy leaned back, her thighs spread to accommodate Genna climbing on top of her and caging her with her strength. Missy shivered as Genna's long black curls tickled the crest of her cleavage. "Is this okay?"

"Yes." Missy whispered. Genna hadn't touched her yet and already her whole body throbbed with need. The way she claimed her space. The power made the air vibrate. She lightly traced Missy's cheek. The frisson of heat. Missy gripped her bicep and felt that hard muscle under fine brown skin. Lightning jumped between them. They both shivered as their magic answered their arousal.

Slowly Genna lifted the petticoats one layer at a time. The slide of tule along Missy's sensitized, freshly waxed skin made her shiver. The moonlight catching the silver in her hair. The soft purple glow of her luminous eyes. Her soft mouth and wet tongue. The heat gathering at Missy's core.

"Tell me to stop and I'll stop." Genna said. She laved one breast with her hot tongue and nibbling on a nipple. Then the other.

"Don't stop!"

"I want to fuck you."

Missy moaned lustily, "Yes, oh God, yes!"

"Strap-on or fingers?"

"Fist." Missy had craved it since the Speakeasy.

Genna inched downward to delicately slid her panties off. Was it the callouses in her fingers or the power in her hands? The way she held Missy and stroked her excitement. Gathering her up, building, and building, until the first orgasm rippled through Missy's skin. Genna growled, her teeth bright in the darkness. The deep vibrations pierced Missy and she basked in the sensations, moaning and writhing. Her skin changed colors, like a happy cuttlefish, like a joyful octopus, like an aurora borealis. Genna kept her safe even as the night wrapped around her like powerful thighs.

One orgasm was not enough. Genna wanted more. She demanded Missy give herself over to the pleasure. Called her to howl and scream and claw at the ground. She was relentless, pounding into Missy's wet dripping core. Laving her clitoris until it was so sensitized that even a puff of air made her jump and tremble. The tree cradled their sweaty bodies, absorbing the ambient magic.

Genna cradled Missy in her arms when Missy was spent. She wrapped Missy in a light fleece blanket that was soft and hand-crocheted. She fed her choice cuts of cheese and sliced apple. She coaxed her into drinking cool mint-infused water. Genna told her that she was beautiful and Missy believed it. Missy fell asleep, happy and satiated.

"The aftercare was as good as the sex and the sex was very very good." Missy mumbled.

"I'm glad," Genna said, "You can keep the blanket."

"I get my own Blankie," Missy snuggled against her chest. She almost immediately started snoring.

Magic shimmered over her skin like tossed glitter. The blanket was gone, now a protective shell over Missy's magical body. It would inoculate her from curses and shield her from attacks. It was Genna's way of saying thanks. Paying it forward.

Genna relaxed next to Missy buts stayed awake. She sipped water and watched the night, leaning against the live oak tree. She spotted Imani up in the branches. The cat had watched them without a sound or scent.

Both knew that Missy was like them but different. Missy was a unicorn, a creature of positivity, kindness, and hope. She was still new in her magic. She needed protecting. Just like the Briarpatch.

Genna raised her flask of holy water. Imani blinked, a feline sign of trust.

Higher in the tree, Anansi spun her webs, savoring the wild sexual magic. Coyote yawned in a spun hammock, content.

Epilogue

MISSY SURVEYED THE GIRL SCOUTS AND DEN MOTHERS. She had been the leader of the new Dragonfly Pack for two months. Rainey was out hunting for strays with Professor Onyx. Genna had renovated the old Dragonfly mansion in Wimberley. It was nice to have a powerful friend with deep pockets.

"It's okay to be angry and scared," Missy said, "You have to keep yourself from falling through the cracks. What we do still matters. You are alive for a reason. You are worthy."

Missy passed out loaves of sourdough bread and chocolate croissants. She was proud of each flaky pastry because she finally got the consistency right. "It's okay if you don't like hunting humans. There are other things that you can do to help the pack."

She played *Step By Step* by Whitney Houston as she continued to give the introductory Werewolf 101 pep talk. She tried to focus but could not forget her other Girl Scouts. Her voice wobbled into silence. She ate a croissant to feel a little less overwhelmed. The new pack obediently ate.

"There are really good," a Girl Scout said. "You made them?"

Missy's smile was a little watery but sincere as sunshine. "I'll teach you how to make them."

Author's Note

Dear readers,

I have the Sister's Dilemma. Don't get it twisted, this is a book about werewolves but I think we need a brief detour through **African-American Studies 101, Intro to the Feminine Identity**, and **Basic Lycanthropic Biology.**

Funny how discussing werewolves is easier than thinking about Black women as people.

Are you still here? Good. Now that we're warmed up, let's discuss a few crucial facts that will deepen your reading experience.

Who a werewolf is *before* they are Turned remains just as important as who they become afterwards. So what does it mean to be a Black woman?

1.) African-American Studies 101:

Being Black and American is awesome and complicated. The envy and the ecstasy. The divine and the despair. Black is more than a skin color or an American cultural construct. It's more than dancing or getting a bra that fits or how to properly care for a certain hair texture. It's a way of looking at the world and experiencing it look back.

The race of African-American, called Black in this book, is

collectively four hundred years old (Globally speaking, that is super young for a racial identity.) Blackness is intrinsically linked to the TransAtlantic Slave Trade. What happened in the USA to a whole lot of people for a really long time was a warped extreme of chattel slavery the likes of which no one had ever seen before. It was a game changer. It built America into America, it was awful, and it wasn't made up. We are currently living through the long term consequences right now.

But that's just our origin story in the heroic saga of the Black American. The definition of Blackness is constantly evolving. What seems like the truth now will be woefully outdated in twenty years. That doesn't invalidate the current lived reality or what our parents/grandparents/ancestors dealt with in their time. The point is to see past the vernacular and celebrate the commonalities.

That said, this is still a book about werewolves so let's keep things in perspective.

2.) Intro to the Feminine Identity:

The construct of the feminine identity is shaped by gender roles and cultural expectations like a watermelon growing inside a square box. (Did you feel some kind of way when I used watermelon as an analogy? Good, you're starting to get it.)

Black princess. Black queen. Those words mean different things to different people. So does the word, Bitch and other less savory terms. All aimed at Black women for a lot of stupid and demeaning reasons.

How someone personally defines and expresses their Blackness, sexuality, gender, and femininity is up to them and what they define as right and true.

This is still a book about werewolves. Do your own research and respect other people's definitions.

2b.) Feminine Rage

Black women often have to swallow their rage to survive and

escape the stereotypes that haunt every interaction. To make mental space in their heads and be themselves, not someone else's opinion of what it means to identify as a Black woman. To be poised and beautiful instead of ugly and monstrous (however that is defined).

Rage is real. Feelings are valid. Victim blaming is bullshit but happens anyway. Unleashing rage has consequences. (Righteous, furious vengeance is a beautiful, terrible thing to witness and to experience. Like wildfire and lightning in your veins.)

A Black woman who is also a werewolf has the same problems with self-control. Only the stakes are higher. The cost of rage. Yes, she can eat her enemies but is she overreacting to micro-aggressions? Is someone reaching for her hair to pet her like a dog actually her enemy or just a dumbass? Or are they cruel? Do they want to demean, degrade, and demoralize?

Is that person a vampire? Vampires hate werewolves like hyenas hate lions because they are both apex predators fighting over the same zebra (aka human prey). Sometimes they get along but most times they're fighting over the same resources.

Or is it a just an ordinary human on an ordinary day in an ordinary coffee shop? There is no ulterior motives. They want to touch your hair. Which sometimes is worse.

Is the Black American Werewolf the monster for reacting, for killing, for snuffing out a life instead of expending emotional labor to explain to deaf ears why ***Don't Touch My Hair*** isn't a request?

3.) Basic Lycanthropic Biology:

If werewolves existed, what would they look like?

A werewolf, once they learn how to control their Turn, looks like a human. Right up until they don't.

A fully Turned werewolf can easily be mistaken as just another wolf or a dog.

A half-Turn is the traditional Halloween, torn flannel shirt variety.

No Turn is a human.

Real world comparisons of a werewolf's transformation would be the process of a caterpillar morphing into a butterfly *then going back into the cocoon to turn into a caterpillar again.* It's messy and it's gross.

The hardest transformation is the first Turn. The infectious nature of a werewolf bite can kill nasty and quick like being bitten by a Komodo dragon. Surviving the bite and the initial Turn are one and the same.

The transformation gets easier with practice which is why werewolves join packs to learn how to Turn safely. It is vital to their survival.

The lone werewolf is a danger to themselves, the community, and the world (again, see Hollywood's version of a werewolf, usually alone, insane, prone to biting anyone, and lives about a month after their initial Turn before killing themselves or getting shot).

A werewolf's super-power isn't just hyper-healing or changing their biological morphology from *homo-sapien* (human) to *canius lupus* (wolf), or *canius latrans* (coyote), or *canius familiaris* (domesticated dog). It is the transformation at will.

That transformation is where the magic lives. Involuntarily transformations happen but staying in one shape is a werewolf's primary survival tactic.

There are extenuating circumstances like getting stuck in the Turn, or forgetting that you're a human because you've stayed in beast mode too long, but that's just the reality of being a werewolf.

And yes, they do need to eat humans or other werewolves. That too is part of the magic and the mystery. Cuddly isn't in a werewolf's vocabulary anymore than a tiger is a house cat. They might be affectionate when it suits them but the wildness cannot be tamed.

Direwolves are a mammalian form of dragon. They are apex

predators in the magical world. They eat werewolves, vampires, unicorns, and other magical creatures.

A direwolf, starts life in their animal form and learns how to transform into a human. There are also magic foxes, cats, griffons, etc. Whatever their original form, they were forced to Turn into a human by a witch or some magical incident.

Magical creatures Turn using magic. They don't have the same bone snapping, skin warping transition that werewolves do. They Turn from the unreal to the real. Magical to physical.

Some werewolves and direwolves are wilder than others. Not every werewolf lives in the woods. Especially since the Pandemic, when so many humans with cameras moved out into the countryside. Urban werewolves, like the coyote, can thrive in plain sight.

Werewolf biology is theoretical since anyone who studies a werewolf is either trying to kill them, survive being one, or find a cure.

If you want to know more about these topics then do your own research. Take the extra time to read some books not just websites/social media/whatever the AI says when you google it. Critical thinking is a muscle that must be used so your brain doesn't squeak and strain like a rusty hinge. I usually read at least three books on the same subject to discern what are the commonalities and what's someone's opinion. The responsibility of figuring out 'the truth' is yours.

Ignorance had consequences. And sometimes, ignorance will eat you while you scream.

— K.D. Blade

About the Author

Three years ago, I asked social media if anyone wanted to read a book about Black women who turned into werewolves and ate people. The Internet said yes.

Going viral overnight was a lot like surfing a tsunami, confusing, terrifying, and all your attention is staying balanced and not falling off the board. It was especially challenging since I hadn't yet written a book.

Night Skins was published two months later on Halloween. It was an Amazon bestseller (number #13 on the African American Fiction list) and that was humbling and amazing.

It's been a wild ride since then things changed last year, both physically and emotionally. Losing my dog, Blade, who I got my pen name from, was very difficult.

The book you hold in your hands was created as grief therapy. I think we're all trying to live with rage and grief. A lot has happened but it's important to keep walking forward. In some ways, this book is about surviving grief.

I hope that you enjoy Book 2.

- K.D. Blade

Acknowledgments

There are many people that need to be thanked. To protect their identities I will speak in generalizations.

To my beloved: I don't just lycanthrope you, I love you.

To my family: I descend from giants. Thank you for teaching me how to trace my roots. I love you.

To my friends: Thank you for your support and sharing your lives with me.

To my writing partners and mentors: Thank you for listening instead of rolling your eyes when I change the entire plot line for the billionth time.

To the lonely angry people out there who read because that's the only freedom they have: Be the dream of yourself. Ride your nightmares.

You are all treasured members of my pack.

www.ingramcontent.com/pod-product-compliance
Lightning Source LLC
Chambersburg PA
CBHW061046310726
48969CB00004B/1102